Dear Reader:

The novels you've enjoyed over the past ten years by such authors as Kathleen Woodiwiss, Rosemary Rogers, Johanna Lindsey and Laurie McBain are accountable to one thing above all others: Avon has never tried to force authors into any particular mold. Rather, Avon is a publisher that encourages individual talent and is always on the lookout for writers who will deliver *real* books, not packaged formulas.

In 1982, we started a program to help readers pick out authors of exceptional promise. Called "The Avon Romance," the books were distinguished by a ribbon motif in the upper left-hand corner of the cover. Although every title was by a new author, and the settings could be either historical or contemporary, they were quickly discovered and became known as "the ribbon books."

In 1984, "The Avon Romance" will be a feature on the Avon list. Each month, you will find novels with many different settings, each one by an author who is special. You will not find predictable characters, predictable plots and predictable endings. The only predictable thing about "The Avon Romance" will be the superior quality that Avon has always delivered in the field of romance!

Sincerely,

Walter Meade

WALTER MEADE
President & Publisher

Other Avon Books by
Marsha Canham

CHINA ROSE

Bound by the Heart

Marsha Canham

AVON BOOKS OF CANADA
PUBLISHERS OF BARD, CAMELOT, DISCUS AND FLARE BOOKS

BOUND BY THE HEART is an original publication of Avon Books. This work has never before appeared in book form. This work is a novel. Any similarity to actual persons or events is purely coincidental.

AVON BOOKS OF CANADA
A division of
The Hearst Corporation
2061 McCowan Road, Suite 210
Scarborough, Ontario M1S 3Y6

Published by arrangement with the author
Canadian Library of Congress Catalog Card Number: C84-98975-X
ISBN: 0-380-88732-0

Canadian Cataloguing in Publication Data

Canham, Marsha
Bound by the heart

ISBN 0-380-88732-0

I. Title.

PS8555.A54B6 1984 C813'.54 C84-098975-X
PR9199.3.C352B6 1984

First Avon Printing, October, 1984

Printed in the U. S. A.

WFH 10 9 8 7 6 5 4 3 2 1

For Dianne, with thanks,
especially the last fifty pages.

June 1811

1

THE UTTER and absolute darkness smothered the tiny raft, totally disorienting the two half-conscious passengers.

There was no moon and there were no stars, no visible ceiling to the gray shifting clouds that formed their last recollection before the fog and darkness had moved in to obliterate the world. Summer Cambridge hugged her ten-year-old brother tightly, as much to reassure herself that they would not momentarily drop off the edge of the ocean as to keep him from slipping wearily off the inadequate planking. Every now and then she pinched the numbed flesh of his arm and prayed to hear the sharp little sob—the only sign that he was still alive. Every now and then she hugged him more tightly, trying to forget the events of the past twelve hours.

The storm had struck their vessel, the *Sea Vixen,* quickly and furiously, lashing it with a viciousness unnervingly common to the Caribbean. It was June. It was the beginning of the rainy season, and they had all been warned of the possibility of severe and sudden heavy weather on the route between New Providence in the Bahamas and Bridgetown, Barbados.

The *Sea Vixen* had left Southampton six weeks earlier, trailing ignobly in the wake of two British ships of the line. One had remained in New Providence to fortify the blockade of the American coastline, and the other had left within the week for Bridgetown. Since there was no way of knowing when another escort might become available, the captain of the *Sea Vixen* had prudently taken his place again in the shadow of the immense seventy-four-gun warship the *Caledonia*.

When the storm struck, the *Vixen* had taken the worst of it. It had been tossed about in the raging winds and foam-capped waves as if it were a cork in a whirlpool. Snarls of white water and boiling spray had sucked the battered vessel in dizzying circles, snapping its mainmast into kindling and crushing its sides like papier mâché.

Three men had been dispatched to hold its wheel steady, for as much good as it did them. The *Vixen* leaped out of the sea, almost rising above the water, only to crash back into the next trough with a sickening skidding downward slide. Wave after wave was hurled over the floundering vessel, sweeping away the torn rigging and surging down the open hatchways in cataracts until there was not a patch of dry wood to be found anywhere.

Summer and Michael Cambridge had been huddled together in their cramped cabin, cowering in a high-sided berth, clinging to each other as the sides and floor of their quarters alternately changed places.

"Oh God, Michael, we can't stay here," Summer cried, flinching in horror as the water on their cabin floor sloshed against the side of the berth.

"But S-Summer—!"

"We can't stay here!" She was shouting to be heard over the constant roar under the bow. "Don't you see we'll be trapped! If anything happens, we won't be able to reach the upper deck. For all we know, the captain is already loading the lifeboats!"

"Summer—"

"Do you want to be left behind?"

She hauled Michael out of the bunk and dragged him sobbing and shivering to the cabin door. She was nearly knocked flat as a wave rolled the *Vixen,* but she held on to the brass latch of the door until the ship righted itself again.

The companionway was ankle-deep in rushing water. It washed down the stairwell, shooting past the row of small cabins in its eagerness to fill the decks below. Summer felt the tears streaking her cheeks as she fought hand over hand with the hempen guide ropes to reach the grayish light showing above the hatch.

An even greater horror greeted them at the top.

There was only one sail straining aloft for steerage. Of the acres and acres of canvas and taut rigging the *Vixen* was capable of carrying, only one pitifully small square remained. The rest were fouled in a tangle of twisted rope, broken spars and wildly swinging yards. Lines snaked across the decks and hung over the sides, trailing in the water behind the ship. The sea cascaded over the bulwarks as it would over a dam, sheeting across the open decks unhampered, having already cleared everything from its path.

Summer paled at the sight of the devastation. A fresh torrent of salt water rushed past her down the stairwell, and she felt Michael's grip around her waist falter. Her hands slid along the coarse hempen rope for as long as it took her to regain her balance, and she screamed for Michael to hold on; she screamed for the burning pain in the palms of her hands; she screamed for the sudden wild lurch that brought with it a wall of curling white water.

The rope she was holding snapped under the pressure. She was flung like a rag doll against the carved oak bulkhead, and her arms and legs suddenly lost the ability to respond. She tried to hold fast to the rail leading up to the quarterdeck, but the wrenching, jarring pain was too much, and she slid with the wave, rolling over and over as it carried her to the deck rail.

The roaring water engulfed her, blinding her and tearing the screams from her throat one minute, choking and gagging her with mouthfuls of the ocean the next.

She rolled again, and the deck suddenly vanished. A vast, gray emptiness surged up to meet her, sucking her into its depths with a violence that burst the remaining air from her lungs. She spiraled down, down. . . . She felt the weight of a thousand tons of water hammering her, tearing at her clothes, ripping at her hair, deafening her finally under the liquid silence.

Summer broke clear of the surface, her mouth and nose streaming water. She was tossed giddily upward, and in her panic she began to pump furiously to keep her head above the water, not wanting to believe she was going to die then and there.

A smaller, less-determined wave swamped her, and she swallowed a bitter mouthful of the ocean as it snatched her down again. Her skirt tangled around her ankles, producing another flood of terror when her feet could no longer obey her commands. Her lungs held a burning breath as she began tugging at her clothes. When the weight of her overdress was gone, she tore at the muslin shift, then the single layer of petticoat and the long satin shimmy until her legs were bared and free.

Her head bobbed above the surface again, and she forced herself to concentrate, to *remember.*

Once, when she had been very young, she had fallen into a reflecting pool. It had not been deep, but to a shy and terrified four-year-old, it had represented a bottomless void. Her father had insisted afterward that each member of the family have lessons in swimming and self-preservation in the water—especially since he was due to be posted on an island in the Caribbean.

Swimming lessons in a private pond guarded by servants and watched over by instructors had in no way prepared Summer Cambridge for a maelstrom hundreds of miles from any known land. The ocean floor could be a dozen feet below her or a dozen miles, with countless lurking terrors between. There were sharks in these waters, and barracuda, and . . .

"Michael!"

Summer blinked repeatedly to clear the water out of her eyes. Her hair had lost its combs and fillets and spread around her shoulders like a golden fan.

"Michael!"

What chance was there that he had tumbled after her out the open hatchway? The last she remembered he had been reaching valiantly across the deck in an attempt to pull her back to safety. If he had leaned too far, if he had been swept from the deck after her, what hope was there he could have survived the terrible pounding?

"Summer?"

It was only a weak cry: a gasp, nothing more.

"Michael! *Michael!*"

Summer could not see over the crests of the waves. She had no idea from which direction the sound had come or even if it were a sound at all. It could have been the wind or the pelting of rain on the water.

"Michael?"

Had she imagined it? As far as she could see, there was only green haze and lashing gray foam. The *Sea Vixen* had long since disappeared into the mist to die, leaving a trail of broken timber and trappings in its wake.

"Summer?"

There! A bobbing black shadow on the crest of the heaving water.

"Michael!"

He turned at the sound of her scream. A glimpse of the pale white face and the huge, terrified eyes was all she needed to spur her into kicking toward the small black dot. She clawed into the waves, fighting each handful of water as she pushed it behind her. Time and again she was swamped and sent thrashing in the opposite direction, but she refused to allow the panic to overtake her. It seemed to take a lifetime just to conquer one wave, but she did it, and each one she overcame brought her closer and closer to her goal.

Michael was clinging desperately to a broken beam from the *Sea Vixen*. His hazel eyes were as round as saucers; his normally tanned complexion was as gray as the threatening seas. He did not look at all like the composed, mature young man who had met her on the docks at New Providence. He had been very formal, very proper in his tailored frock coat. He had bowed politely and kissed her hand, reciting the greeting from Father that he had traveled hundreds of miles to deliver as if it were an everyday occurrence. The week was spent convincing her he was no longer the gangling, pesky six-year-old she had left behind.

The facade had shattered over the past few hours, and he was now a very frightened, very discomposed boy. He was sobbing as he flung an arm around her neck, causing them both to flounder momentarily beneath a wave. Summer grasped the beam he was riding, testing its stability. How long could they hang together from a two-foot length of timber? She did not know, but it felt sturdy, and she wept with relief as she rested her cheek on the rough surface.

"Summer, what are we going to do? What is going to h-happen to us? Where is the ship? Why h-haven't they turned back to f-find us?"

Turned back, she thought? Oh, Michael . . .

She should never have left England. She should never have bowed to her father's blackmail. She should have remained with her friends and continued to enjoy the social whirlwind of her life in London. His threat of cutting off her allowance and stranding her penniless had been a trifling one at best. She would not have remained penniless for long. Or unattached. The fact that Sir Lionel Cambridge had also arranged her marriage to a naval officer posted in Bridgetown before she'd had a chance to either approve or disapprove should have added to her stubbornness. She should have followed her first instinct and eloped with the first eligible male she met after receiving her father's final ultimatum.

A mouthful of bitter seawater snapped her to full awareness. The effort it took to lift her head was tremendous. Her arms felt leaden; her legs could not muster a single halfhearted kick. Her eyes had trouble focusing on anything beyond the morass of moving water.

"S-Summer? Are you all right?"

"What?" The croak that came from her lips startled her.

"You f-fainted or something," Michael said tremulously. "I didn't know what to do or how to w-wake you."

"Wake me? How long—?" Summer looked around and gasped. The rain had stopped, and the fury of the storm had abated. The waves continued to churn and toss them about, but they were only petulant now; most of the anger of the storm had been played out.

"Several hours, I th-think," Michael was saying. "I shouted and poked at you, but y-you didn't move. I h-hope I didn't hurt you."

"I cannot feel a thing anywhere on my body anyway," she said, smiling weakly. She recalled Michael's tendency to stutter when he was frightened or upset—something that had supposedly passed with age. She raised a hand from the beam to touch him and reassure him and frowned when she saw the ugly raw redness of her palm. She frowned because she could not recall how the injury had occurred or why it was not hurting. When she replaced her hand on the beam, she noticed that the wood was lower in the water than it had been.

"Several hours," she repeated in a daze.

"D-do you suppose anyone on board the *V-Vixen* has missed us?"

Summer stared at her brother. Fear was bruising the softness of his eyes.

"Of course they have," she said soothingly. "And they're probably searching for us right now. I'm sure if we just hold on long enough . . ."

Her voice faltered. Michael's lower lip was clenched between his teeth, and he was obviously making a supreme effort not to cry. His dark brown hair stuck in sodden clumps to his brow and cheeks; his hands were shriveled and white from the length of time they had been in the water.

"I h-haven't seen anyone else," he cried. "I've f-felt things, though. Th-things that slide past my legs."

Summer glanced involuntarily down at the water, stirred to opaqueness by the storm. "Oh, I don't think . . . it's probably just your imagination."

"I tell you, I f-felt things! Huge sl-slippery things, and I have to k-keep kicking my feet to keep them away!"

Summer could feel herself tensing. Of course there was nothing beneath them. He was just frightened and hysterical. It was only the shock playing tricks with his imagination. . . . wasn't it?

Visibility was nonexistent. The clouds hung so low in the sky they appeared to brush the peaks of the waves. They must have drifted quite a distance, for there was no sign of any other wreckage, no sound other than the slap of water and the hollow moan of the wind. Summer had to blink several times to make sure her eyes were not deceiving her.

"Look, Michael," she whispered, "a raft. At least it looks like a raft from here. See? Over there—those planks floating on the water."

Michael sniffed and craned his neck to follow the direction indicated by her trembling finger.

"If we could paddle over to it, we could climb on top and at least get up where we'd be a little drier. Help me, Michael. Kick as hard as you can."

The thought of clambering onto something solid gave them both strength, and within minutes Summer was steadying the raft while Michael slithered and wriggled himself aboard. After much straining and groaning, she, too, rolled like a wet fish into the center of the strapped planking, too exhausted to do more than utter a brief prayer of thanks.

Michael pressed himself as close to her as was possible.

"Don't cry, Summer. Father says there are d-dozens of ships passing through these waters all the t-time. We just have to w-watch for the right one and hail it."

"The right one?" she gasped. "*Any* ship I see will be the right one, believe me."

"Do . . . do you suppose the *Caledonia* . . . ?"

Michael bit his lip again, and Summer finished the question in her own mind. The *Caledonia* was easily three times the size of the *Sea Vixen*. Surely it could not have met with the same fate?

The desolation closed in around them, and Summer shivered.

How could they have been the only two to have survived? The *Sea Vixen* had carried a crew of seventy-five and a passenger complement of twenty-four. The British warship was manned by three hundred and eighty . . . including Captain Bennett Winfield, the man she was supposed to marry in six weeks' time.

The air was cool, and Summer shivered again as the salt water began to dry and tighten her skin. Her blonde hair hung in a wet mass to her waist, adding yet another chill to her spine. All that remained of her clothing was a brief muslin smock and torn satin pantaloons. She had lost both of her slippers and—her hand flew to her throat—the heavy gold locket and chain that had belonged to her mother.

She lowered her head and closed her thick honey-colored lashes over the tears that were brimming in her eyes. It was not fair that this should happen now. Michael was not ready to die. She was not ready to die, not when everything in her life was beginning to look so perfect!

She thought of Bennett Winfield and the tears came hotter and faster. He was tall and blond as summer wheat, a bronzed sun god beside the pale, vapid men of London. Father had known what he was doing when he sent Bennett Winfield with the ultimatum. He had known the moment she laid eyes on Captain Winfield she would be lost.

"I don't believe you have listened to a word I have said."

He was there. So real she could have reached out and touched him . . . touched the fine line of his jaw, the wide smooth brow, the mouth that was so stern and yet so sensuously intriguing. . . . She reached out and her hand fell limply into the water.

"Of course I have been listening," she replied pertly, allowing the tall, immaculately uniformed officer to lead her deeper into the garden. They located an iron bench along the path, and he gallantly laid down a linen handkerchief before she sat. She folded her hands demurely on her lap, knowing that as he sat beside her and made a great show of straightening his saber, he was also making an unhurried and far from casual appraisal of her.

Her gown was the very latest style from Paris, cut low enough across the bosom that a man's searching eye could swear to a faint hint of pink where the firmness of each breast strained against the silk. Summer's figure was displayed to perfection by the semitransparent gown; her waist was narrow, her hips gently rounded, her legs long and willowy with delicate, trim ankles peeking out below the hem. The actual existence of three layers of clothing separating her flesh from Captain Winfield's gaze did nothing to hamper his imagination or his acute pleasure.

She decided he'd enjoyed enough of the view and opened her fan, gracefully stirring the air against her throat.

"I have heard every word you said," she repeated. "Father is demanding I come home. He is threatening to discontinue my allowance if I refuse, to disinherit me, to disown me. . . . Have I neglected to mention anything?"

Captain Winfield smiled at the flash of mischief in the gray-green eyes. "Only that you would be breaking my heart, madam, if you were to refuse."

He lifted a slender hand to his lips.

"Break your heart? Come now, Captain, you have been in London only a fortnight. Do you mean to tell me you lose your heart so easily?"

"Not easily, I assure you. But completely."

Summer was surprised and a little unsettled by the tingle that rushed up her arm and flushed into her cheeks. She was, after all, no stranger to flirtations, casual or otherwise. Her beauty, her wit, her charm had won over most of the marriageable men in her circle of friends, and she had already refused several offers. No one, least of all herself, could understand why she would even entertain the thought of agreeing to a marriage of convenience.

Not unless they had met Bennett Winfield. Or talked to him. Or felt his magnetism across a crowded room, drawing her as if they were the only two people present.

His lips were on her wrist, then the palm of her hand as he uncurled and kissed each fingertip one by one.

"And I . . . I suppose he gave you instructions to kidnap me in the event all else failed?"

"Would that he had, Miss Cambridge," he murmured. "I can think of nothing that would give me greater pleasure than being alone with you at sea for two months."

"Really? I should think you would soon grow bored with my company. Why, only last evening you were seen to yawn in the parlor."

"Last evening," Winfield's fingers brushed at a stray tendril of blonde hair on her shoulder, "we were in the midst of a roomful of old crones listening to a red-faced contralto trying to warble her way through an aria."

Summer concealed her smile behind her fan. "Mrs. Pithney-Whyatt is very talented."

"I'm sure she is," he agreed quietly. "And I am very anxious to hear your decision."

"I . . . I hardly know you, sir," she stammered, lowering her lashes. "I am very flattered, of course, but I have yet to see Father and speak with him. I mean . . . a letter is so cold and impersonal."

"Whereas you are anything but," he said and leaned forward, pressing his lips to the vein fluttering at Summer's temple. He traced the mist of curls down, down to her ear. Then beneath it. Then along her throat to the soft, smooth curve of her shoulder.

Summer's fan had frozen midstroke. She closed her eyes and reasoned that the night air must be cooler than she thought: She was shivering to the tips of her toes.

"Captain Winfield—"

"Bennett," he murmured, his mouth playing upward along the same lazy path.

"B-Bennett . . . you don't understand. . . ."

His breath was warm on her flesh. She could feel the heat of it rippling through her body, touching off a sweet, heady weakness that did not want stopping.

He raised his head, and his pale blue eyes were gleaming. "I understand you and Sir Lionel are embroiled in a battle of wits at the moment. He wants you home. You want"—he gestured carelessly at the trees, the moon-washed pathway, the glittering lights blazing from the party behind them—"this."

"Is there anything wrong with *this?*" she bristled.

"Certainly not. If there is nothing better."

Summer took a deep breath, and the motion of her fan occupied her for a long moment. "There is nothing in Bridgetown except heat and flies."

Bennett smiled. "There are also long tropical nights, cool breezes and the scent of wildflowers fed by the surf. Who indeed would prefer it over dampness and constant chills, endless plagues and the smell of refuse clogging the streets?"

She glared at him. "There was a plague in Bridgetown the year I left."

"There was an epidemic of measles in the slave population," he corrected her gently. "Not the plague. No whites died."

"Well . . . I have been to court three times! I have been

to see the queen when she was in residence at Hampton Court, and I regularly take tea with duchesses and countesses. What on earth would I find to do in Barbados —sample molasses with the overseer's wife?"

Bennett laughed and shook his head. He lowered his mouth to hers without warning, and before she knew what he was about, she was gathered tightly in an embrace that made her very much aware of the power and strength in the solid wall of muscle that was his chest.

It was not the kiss of a love-struck gallant. It was the kiss of a man, forceful and demanding, one who knew the games well enough but who was contemptuous of all but his own rules. The hot, useless feeling washed through Summer again, and she knew she could not fight it. She shuddered and leaned into him, abandoning propriety to run her hands up around his broad shoulders and to cling to him as the thrills engulfed her whole body. She gasped under the assault of his lips and then again as he stroked the curve of her throat with an impatient hand. The sensation teased her flesh unbearably, and she felt the tremors racing through her arms as she strove to hold him closer, to feel more of this shocking pleasure.

The kiss ended as abruptly as it had begun.

Captain Winfield held her at arm's length; only his eyes continued to devour her.

"Wh-why did you stop?" she gasped uncertainly.

"I stopped, Miss Cambridge," he murmured, "because I am still able to. And because I would sooner cut off my arm as be the cause of bringing a hint of a scandal down around you." He paused, and Summer shivered at the blatant message in his eyes. "And what a scandal there would be, my love, if we were to do half the things my body aches to."

Summer blushed painfully. "You should not speak to me in this way."

"No," he agreed, "I shouldn't. You are correct in saying you have doubts. In your position, I would probably want to know a great deal more about a man I am betrothed to than a mere two weeks could provide."

"That is not why I hesitate," Summer whispered. "I feel

I have come to know you better in two weeks than some men I have known for two years."

"And have you also kissed them as passionately as you have kissed me?"

"Oh, no!" she cried and saw the trace of humor in his eyes. "No, I had no idea a kiss could be something so . . . so . . ."

"It was just a kiss," he said quietly. "And a kiss is just the prelude to something far more rewarding. I want to be the one to share your discovery of it, Summer. I want the air filled with the scent of jessamine and hibiscus, and I want the island breezes to cool our bodies from the heat. You will never regret it, Summer. Never."

Never.

Summer's head stirred from the crook of her elbow where it had fallen. Michael was curled tightly against her, lulled into a fitful sleep by the rocking of the planks on the water. For a moment her eyes refused to open. She knew what she would see: gray water, gray sky, gray nothingness. Bennett Winfield was gone. He had been a mirage, nothing more.

She opened her tear-filled eyes and terror scalded her throat. Michael felt her stiffen, and he sat up, rubbing his swollen eyes with his fists to clear away the crust of salt.

"Wh-what is it, Summer? Did you hear something?"

"No," she said quickly. "No, darling, I didn't. It just surprised me, that's all. I mean . . . the darkness. . . ."

It was pitch black all around them. There was no moon, no stars, nothing to interrupt the void, no way to distinguish between water and raft and body. They could be floating in a foot of water within arm's reach of shore, and she would not know it.

Michael moved closer, and she wrapped her arms around him, sharing what little warmth there was between them.

"Do you think this raft will keep holding us?"

"Of course it will," Summer said, putting more confidence into her voice than she felt. "Why, I imagine if we had something to make a sail out of, it would carry us all the way to Bridgetown."

"If there were stars," he said hesitantly, "we could even determine where we are now. I'm afraid I bothered Captain Burnby into letting me follow the course he'd plotted. As of last night we were off Saint Barthélemy. If we could find out how much we've drifted and in what direction . . ."

Summer let him talk, only partially listening to what he said. She was relieved that for the moment something had taken his mind off the horror around them. Let him dream about being rescued, she thought. Let him fantasize about living an adventure like Robinson Crusoe. She herself would give anything to be washed up on a deserted island about now. Anything at all.

"Summer?"

"Mmm?"

"I'm glad you're here. I'm glad you decided to come home."

"So am I," she whispered and squeezed his narrow shoulders impulsively. She smoothed the dark, tousled hair, sticky from the salt water, and planted a kiss on his brow. "Why don't you try and get some sleep now. We're going to need all of our strength for tomorrow."

Summer knew the fog was dense by the way it clung to her skin, by the droplets that formed together into one large bead, gathering more and more speed as it trickled down her throat and into the cleft between her breasts. Michael was dozing fitfully. She had no idea if she had slept or how many hours had passed or if any time had passed at all. A trite phrase kept spinning through her mind: A watched kettle never boils. Where had she heard it? Did it apply to this smothering blackness? She kept watching for a sign of the dawn streaking across the horizon, but it seemed like it would never come.

Summer closed her eyes. She shifted on the raft to ease the cramps forming along her legs and spine and in doing so evoked a whimper from Michael.

Her eyes opened wide, searching the darkness.

There it was again. A faint, barely perceptible gurgle, as if someone were breathing through a mouthful of water. There was no direction to the sound. It came from everywhere . . . and nowhere. She would almost have sworn that she imagined it except that she felt Michael stiffen. He had heard it, too.

"What do you suppose it is?" he whispered.

"I don't know. Listen and see if you can hear where it's coming from."

"A monster," he breathed, dragging out the word to ten terrible syllables.

Summer swallowed hard. "Don't be silly. There are no such things as monsters."

Michael pulled out of her arms as the gurgle came again, closer this time and followed by a low, plaintive groan.

"Then what *is* it?" he cried.

"I don't know!"

Summer risked swamping the raft as she rose to her knees. The sound was constant now, a curdling moan that seemed to be coming closer on each heartbeat. She felt the terror building in her throat. She turned to reassure Michael—a split second before the fog parted and she saw a looming black shape rearing high above them. It had a single glowing eye that bore down in a yellow fury as jaws yawned toward the tiny raft. Summer pushed her brother into the water and dove clear herself only moments before the flimsy planking was crushed to splinters.

Summer screamed for Michael as she felt herself being dragged by the thing's slow forward motion. She heard an answering scream and flailed desperately for it, but she was too late: The water suddenly thrashed alive, and something cold and solid reached for her, coiling around her throat. Michael screeched a third and fourth time before the sound was choked into silence and she knew he had been caught. For a moment the salt water streamed clear from her eyes and she saw the towering black thing again. The pressure around her throat increased, and she knew she was being hauled toward the glowing yellow light. She struck out at it; she kicked and scratched and fought until she had no more breath to do it, and then she felt the water swirl over her head as a weight pushed her down . . . and then she felt nothing.

2

SUMMER COUGHED and retched a small lungful of salt water over the corner of her mouth. She was draped over something hard and round and was being rolled to and fro slowly to coax the ocean out of her stomach and chest. Her hair dangled in long wet strands, picking up the filth and spittle from the deck. She could hear Michael crying somewhere close by, sobbing and hiccuping intermittently.

"M-Michael?" she gasped and moved her arms in a swimming motion. The roll of the barrel stopped at once, and a pair of hands grasped her under her arms and propped her upright. The world swayed sickeningly for a long moment, but she did not have time to think about it. A frantic burst of sobbing energy flung himself into her arms, burying his face in her shoulder as someone else leaned over and draped a rough wool blanket around her. Some of the nausea lifted, and she was aware of a low murmur of voices.

The *Caledonia!*

She raised a trembling hand to her eyes, brushing aside the yellow web of her hair. Expecting to see the white canvas trousers and short blue pea coats of His Majesty's Royal Navy, she was unnerved by the sight of a score of burly barrel-chested men who needed only cutlasses at their sides and dirks between their teeth to fit the nightmare of a perfect pirate crew. They were hardened, surly men who frowned at Summer and the boy as if deciding whether to keep them or toss them back over the side.

Summer scanned the unfriendly faces until she settled

on one who made the breath catch in her throat and her heart grind to a painful standstill in her chest. He stood a full head taller than the rest, with long black hair curling damply to shoulders easily twice as broad, twice as massive as any on board. His chest was bare, and where the water clung to the swarm of black hair, it glistened like a breastplate, emphasizing boldly sculpted muscles that had been burned to a rich mahogany by the sun. His trousers were wet and hugged his thighs like a second skin. His feet were bare and spread wide apart, his arms were crossed over the incredible span of his chest, and he was staring down at Summer Cambridge with two of the coldest, deepest blue eyes she would ever live to see.

"I suppose I should ask what the hell you two were doing floating around in the middle of the Atlantic Ocean?" His voice was a low rumble of thunder and spoke of unquestioned authority.

Summer opened her mouth to respond, but nothing came out past the dry and puffed lips except a pitiful rasp of air. Michael sat up, still sniffling, still hiccuping, but able to speak.

"W-we were on the *Sea Vixen,* sir. B-bound for B-Bridgetown. The storm this m-morning . . . yesterday morning . . . we were thrown overboard."

"The *Sea Vixen?"* The man's black brows furrowed together.

"Out of S-Southampton, sir."

"Is that where you've come from?"

"N-not exactly, sir. She stopped in the Bahamas first. I b-boarded her in New Providence."

The dark blue eyes narrowed further, and he raised a hand to one of the men standing by. A huge, muscular black man stepped forward, his ebony skin gleaming in the lantern light as if it had been oiled. He moved the light closer to the two sodden figures on the deck.

"You're the whelp of Sir Lionel Cambridge, are you not?" the tall man demanded.

Michael blinked in the harsh light, plainly startled. "H-how did you know that?"

He smiled humorlessly. "I've run the *Chimera* into Bridgetown a time or two. I've also run into Sir Lionel."

The men surrounding them chuckled and sent a quick murmur to update those out of hearing range.

"Th-the *Chimera?*" Michael's hazel eyes widened in terror.

"Aye. You've heard mention of her?"

"S-some," Michael said, choking on the understatement.

The blue eyes shifted back to Summer. "And the silent mermaid here, who might she be?"

Summer felt Michael jolt out of her arms. "She . . . she's my governess, sir. She's been in England. There was a . . . a death in the family, and . . . and she's just newly come back."

"Governess, eh? Well, she scratches like a bloody she-cat. She's damned lucky I didn't just push her under and leave her for food for the sharks." He stopped suddenly and raised his shaggy head, staring intently out into the darkness for a moment. "Mr. Monday, I believe we're tasting a breeze off the bow. I'll want more sail aft to see if we can't catch into it."

"Yas, Cap-tan." The negro grinned, an enormous slash of white, and turned quickly, handing the brass lantern to another sailor. He began shouting orders and dispersing the crowd as another sailor approached the captain.

"Where d'ye want me ter put 'em?" he asked, thumbing his hand toward Summer and Michael.

The captain looked briefly annoyed. "Put the boy in with the crew; he can make do with a hammock."

"An' the wench?"

The blue eyes raked carelessly over Summer's soaked and clinging muslin smock. "We're not a passenger ship, Mr. Thorntree, but you'd best put her in my cabin for now."

"Aye, Cap'n."

"E-excuse me, sir?" Michael called, halting the black-haired giant in his stride.

"Well, what is it?"

"W-we haven't thanked you. For rescuing us. I'm sure Father will r-reward you amply as soon as we r-reach Bridgetown."

The captain grinned at the boy. "I'm sure he will, too. Quite amply."

Michael stared after him as he swung his huge frame up the narrow ladderway leading to the bridge.

Mr. Thorntree cleared his throat to draw attention. He was a scrawny, weathered gnome of a man with short-cropped gray stubble covering his head. His eyes were sunk into folds of leathery crow's-feet, and when he spoke, it was out of the corner of his mouth, past his only two remaining front teeth.

"Ye'll both foller me down now. Ye 'eard the cap'n's orders."

"Captain . . . Wade?" Michael asked tentatively.

"Aye, Morgan Wade. The devil 'imself taken to the 'igh seas, so ye'd best not ply 'im with too many o' yer questions an' argumentations. Ee'd as like t'row ye back where ee found ye as bother ter carry ye ter port."

"Oh, yes, sir," Michael said, scrambling hastily to his feet. "And we are ever so grateful he's willing to fetch us back to Bridgetown."

"Eh? Bridgetown?" The old sailor cackled. "N'owt likely, lad. Barbados is where we're comin' from, not where we be bound."

"But . . . but I told him . . . my father, Sir Lionel—"

"Is a ripe fine barstard," Mr. Thorntree interrupted on a wheeze. "An' will still be there a month from now 'r a year from now, so stow yer 'igh-fangled notions 'bout bein' the guv'ner's son. It don't carry no weight on board the Kameery—as a fact, ye should be t'ankful ee's in a ripe fine mood tonight 'r ye'd be swimmin' from the scuppers on a keel rope."

Summer's cheeks were pink with indignation at the reference to their father. She glanced at Michael and frowned at the hurried, unspoken warning.

The old man crooked a spiky eyebrow appreciatively as Summer wobbled unsteadily to her feet. She swayed against Michael until the dizziness passed, then she drew the blanket protectively around her shoulders.

"Where are we heading, please?" she asked through a shiver.

"Nort'," Mr. Thorntree grunted.

"North!" Michael cried. "But . . . Barbados is south and west of here."

"So ye're a sailor as well as a nob's son, eh? Cap'n'll be ripe glad ter 'ear that. We be a mite short'anded this run. 'Ere, 'ang on ter the lass afore she falls flat on 'er arse. Come on, come on, we'll get 'er below where it's warm, an' then ye can both jaw yer tongues loose."

Summer was grateful for the sailor's surprisingly gentle support as he led them down a stairwell and along a shadowy companionway running beneath the quarter-deck. At the end he opened a heavy oak door, letting it swing wide against the wall. It was a large cabin, furnished in oak and mahogany, with scrubbed and gleaming pine flooring and enough shelves and wire-fronted bookcases to house a small library. Gallery windows ran in a semicircle behind a huge, cluttered desk, and in another corner sat an elegantly carved dining table and four chairs. The berth was at least three times the size of the one Summer had occupied on the *Sea Vixen,* and she cast a covetous eye to the raised mattress and the thick, quilted blankets.

"Up ye get, lass, an' make use o' the bed whilst ye 'ave the chance."

"What about Michael? Where are you taking Michael?"

"Ee'll be bunked in with the crew, never ye mind 'bout 'im. Course, if'n ye'd rather, ye can share a cot there yerself. There be more 'n a 'unnerd-fifty bucks willin' ter keep ye warm."

Summer ignored the cackle of laughter. She reached for the support of the high-sided berth and winced at the pain in her burned hands.

"'Ere," Mr. Thorntree grumbled, inspecting her palms, "best let me get a salve ter put on 'em. Take the burn away. 'Ow'd ye do it, lass?"

"I don't remember exactly. On a guide rope, I think."

"Mmm." He thrust out his jaw. "Bad, were it, on the *Vixen?*"

"Yes." She shivered and pushed the wet hair back off her face.

"Mmm. Back in a nip," he said, and left the cabin.

Summer held her breath until she heard his footsteps fade down the corridor.

"What are you playing at, Michael?" she whispered. "Why did you tell them I was your governess?"

"Because," Michael hissed urgently, "he's *Captain Morgan Wade!*"

"I must still be in shock. . . . What are you talking about, Michael? Who is Captain Wade? He cannot be too sinister if he says he has been to Bridgetown several times and has met Father."

"He's an American privateer! One of the worst thieves and cutthroats in the Caribbean, according to Father. He's a smuggler and a gunrunner and . . . and . . . oh, Father has been trying to catch him up for months now."

"Catch him up?"

"He moves back and forth in the islands buying up legal cargo and making an absolute fortune selling it to the French, who he's not supposed to sell it to. Then he turns around and runs French guns up through the blockade into the colonies, right under the nose of our navy. Can you imagine what manner of ransom he would demand from the governor of Barbados for the return of his family?"

"Ransom?" Summer gasped.

"Of course. Didn't you see the way he smiled when he recognized me? And didn't you hear him laugh when I mentioned a reward?" He lowered his voice even more. "What do you suppose he would do if he thought he had *two* Cambridges on board? He's dangerous, and he's unprincipled, and according to Father, he's killed men with his *bare hands* just for *talking* to him the wrong way! And as for the *Chimera—*"

Michael stopped abruptly and straightened as the footsteps approached the cabin door. It was Mr. Thorntree, followed closely by Captain Morgan Wade.

Summer bit down savagely on her lip. Seeing the rugged features of the privateer in the brighter light of the cabin, she knew Michael's tale was more than the wild imaginings of an adventurous ten-year-old. The captain ignored her and went to a cupboard tucked into a nook behind the berth. From it he took a dry cambric shirt and shrugged into it.

"I sent a lad ter fetch an 'ot cup o' tea fer the two o' ye," Mr. Thorntree said, pulling Summer's gaze away from Morgan Wade. "Told 'im ter put a dram o' rum in it whilst ee were at it. Won't do no 'arm. Give us a look-see at them 'ands now, lass."

Summer held the wool blanket around her shoulders with one hand while the other was treated to some oily brown paste. It stung a moment, then numbed the whole area of her palm, enough that she could flex her fingers without gritting her teeth from the pain. He wrapped it carefully in a strip of linen, then nodded for the other.

The captain walked past them to his desk. Summer was taken aback to see that he had changed from the wet breeches into a fresh dry pair—practically right in front of her! She blushed furiously and dropped the bandaged hand to the mattress to steady herself. The blanket loosened and slipped from her shoulders.

Wade selected a thin black cigar from a humidor on the desk and frowned. "She'd best strip out of those wet clothes and dry herself well before getting into bed. Thorny—fetch her one of my shirts from the locker. We don't need a governess with pneumonia on our hands."

"I'll not get pneumonia, Captain," Summer retorted sharply. "And I assure you Michael and I will do our best to see that we are no burden on your *generosity.*"

"Damn right you won't be, Governess, if you know what's good for you."

Summer's cheeks flamed darker at his rudeness, but he merely grunted at Thorny and strode out of the cabin.

Mr. Thorntree cackled again. "No trouble, eh? Ho! Ye should've been 'ere when all the 'ollerin an' screamin' started. Sparked the cap'n's temper a mite, runnin' into ye unawares the way we did. Could've been another ship, ripe as n'owt. Whoever was on the watch'll prob'ly feel the lick o' the cat tomorry."

"Lick of the cat?" Michael queried.

"Cat o' nines, aye. 'Ere, ain't ye never 'eard 'ow a man learns 'is lessons on ship? Might say as 'ow the cat is our governess."

"Whipping a man for being unable to see in the fog and darkness is barbaric," Summer declared icily.

Thorny curled his upper lip back, debating his reply. "Mayhap so. An' mayhap ee'll be that much sharper next time 'round fer the lesson. Sharks in these 'ere waters 'r mean devils. They take real kindly ter sudden meals. Give a man 'is d'ruthers, I warrant ee'd take a taste o' the cat over bein' fodder fer them big whites anytime. Ye knows it yerself. 'Ow long were ye floatin' 'round afore we picked ye up?"

"Most of the day and all night," Michael supplied in a whisper.

"Aye, an' would ye care ter do it again soon?"

"No, sir." The boy's eyes were round and frightened again. He was remembering the "slippery things" he had felt gliding past his legs.

"Mr. Thorntree," Summer broke in, "Michael has been through quite enough today without you reminding him. And I should prefer it if he stayed in here with me tonight; it would be cruel and inhuman to make him sleep alone in a strange bunk in a hostile atmosphere. Thank you for your assistance, however. If we need anything, we shall address you."

Obediah Thorntree's eyebrows bristled up almost to his hairline. The creases parted, and for a full minute the whites of his eyes were visible.

"Address me?" He looked from one to the other. "Aye. Ye do that, lass. Address me."

He shuffled to the cabin door and was halted by a further question from Summer.

"Is there a lock on that door?"

"Eh?"

"A lock, Mr. Thorntree. Does the door have a lock?"

Thorny scratched his head, screwing up his mouth to a thoughtful pucker. "W-a-ll now, I don't t'ink as 'ow the cap'n would take too kindly ter bein' locked owt'n 'is own cabin. Mayhap ye should wait a day 'r two afore ye try that one on 'im."

Summer was bone-weary and growing more so by the minute. The tempting softness of the bed beckoned her, and she did not see anything to be gained by arguing with an illiterate sailor.

"Very well," she sighed and waved her hand impatiently, "I shall discuss it with him myself in the morning. Good night, Mr. Thorntree."

He gave one last bemused glance over his bony shoulders before pulling the door shut behind him.

Michael released the pent-up breath he had been holding. "Summer! You oughtn't talk to them like that. You're supposed to be my governess, not Lady Muck."

Summer sighed and rubbed her throbbing temples. Her body had no more reserves of strength to call upon, and although she heard Michael's voice, she had no idea what he was saying. She slid sideways onto the berth, curled into a tight ball, and was instantly asleep.

3

SUMMER CAMBRIDGE had never seen a shark, yet she dreamed of them. Sleek, writhing forms circled in the water, razor-sharp teeth gleamed from gaping, white jaws. . . . She spent long hours tossing and turning in the bed, suffering through alternating waves of heat and chills that left her drenched in a clammy sweat. She was dimly aware of someone entering the cabin on several occasions to thrust a cool hand on her brow and adjust the tangle of blankets. She heard background voices and bells and heavy footsteps on the deck overhead, and she could feel the rhythmic dip and sway of the ship thrumming through the currents.

"Summer?" It was a whisper, very close to her ear. "Summer, are you awake?"

A crusted, bleary gray eye opened and sought the source of the disturbance.

"I am now," she said, shutting off the sight of Michael's disgustingly cheerful face.

"Jolly well time, I should think. You've been off in another world for two days now."

"Two days?" The eye opened again and slowly blinked into focus. Summer sat upright, wincing as each movement brought an introduction to muscles she had never met before. Her legs and arms were knotted tight, her stomach ached hollowly, her tongue felt glued to the roof of her mouth . . . and Michael was grinning.

"What do you find so amusing?" she demanded.

"You. You look positively dreadful."

"Thank you very much, Master Cambridge. I feel positively dreadful."

"Not at all the way you looked on the wharf in New Providence," he said pertly. "I thought, 'Oh my gosh, she's come back a real snob. She'll walk about with her nose in the air and not share the time of day with any of us anymore.' That's what I thought."

"Was it indeed." Summer regarded her brother narrowly. "You seem to have changed faces yourself overnight, little brother. What happened to the shy, reserved, young gentleman who was so proper and stuffy he made me cringe?"

"Oh, he's still there, but I rather think you need cheering up at the moment. After all, we have been kidnapped, and we have been forced to join the company of a crew of renegade smugglers."

"You don't know for certain we've been kidnapped," she sighed. "And you don't know that the *Chimera* is smuggling anything."

"Oh, yes, I do. I've had a peek in her cargo hold."

"*What?*"

"It's true. And she's loaded to the gun deck with rum and coffee, English wool and even tea! Those were only the crates I could see. We're in for a jolly good show if the *Chimera* crosses paths with one of our revenuers."

"But tea and coffee . . . there's nothing illegal in that."

"There is if you intend to sell it to the French or run it through a blockade line . . . or if the crates you've got the goods packed in are stamped with the imprint of the *Reliant*."

"Michael—" Summer pressed her fingers to her temples.

"The *Reliant*," he explained patiently, "is a schooner that went missing about two months ago. It was transporting a large cargo of *guns* . . . among other things."

"Guns? But you said tea and coffee."

"Haven't you ever heard of false-bottom crates? Smugglers use them all the time."

Summer was not overly impressed. "And what do you mean by missing?"

"I mean missing. Sunk by pirates. Captured and taken

as prize by American privateers, or French privateers, or Spaniards. I mean missing."

"And you think Captain Wade was involved?"

"Well, I don't think he wasn't, in some way or another."

Summer groaned and leaned back on the bed. "Michael, you are giving me a headache. How can you possibly look at this as some kind of an adventure? We're miles from home and heading in the opposite direction. Goodness only knows when we'll ever be put on the right track again. You heard that miserable little man say it could be a month or a year. As for crossing paths with a British ship—"

She was cut short by an abrupt tapping on the cabin door. It came in advance of a large wooden tray balanced in the hands of Mr. Thorntree.

"Ahh! Glad ter see ye up, lass. Feelin' better?"

"Some," she admitted, craning her neck to see what was creating the delicious aroma on the tray.

"Steamin' 'ot biscuits an' a b'iled capon," Thorny announced proudly. "I told Cook I wanted sum'mit special ter stick good 'n fast ter yer gizzards. Tea's in the crock 'ere, an' a rice duff with a nice bit o' raisins tucked in."

"That's very kind and thoughtful of you, Mr. Thorntree."

"Bah, no bother. The lad 'ere told me 'bout yer fits. Ye never mind n'owt, ole T'orny'll see yer well done by."

"My . . . fits?"

Michael coughed loudly. "Yes, indeed. You were thrashing about something awful in your sleep. Talking all sorts of nonsense as well. Oh, this does look splendid, Thorny. And the pudding looks jolly ripe, not at all like the watery gruel we had on the *Vixen*."

"Aye, Cook 'as a regular fine 'and when it comes ter sweets." He paused, and his lips moved while he counted the faint rings of the ship's bell. "Right. I'll leave ye to it then. Cap'n'll be wantin' me on deck."

"Thank you again," Summer said. "Oh, and Mr. Thorntree—?"

"Aye?"

"Could you arrange to have some hot water sent in? I should like to have a bath if it is at all possible. Michael will be wanting one as well."

"Eh? A wot?"

"A bath, Mr. Thorntree. If you have a large receptacle . . . a cask of some sort, or a barrel . . . it would be that much easier."

"Bleedin' 'ell," Thorny muttered and scratched his head. "Next ye'll be wantin' a fancy ball gown?"

"As a matter of fact," Summer pulled the quilts up to her chin, "I would appreciate some manner of clothing."

"The Cap'n already said ye could 'ave one of 'is shirts," he exclaimed as if astounded a body could want for more.

"Well, I can hardly walk around wearing nothing but that!"

"Ye cain't walk around a-tall!" Thorny snorted. "Cap'n's orders."

"I beg your pardon?"

"Cap'n says ee don't want ye topside. Bad fer the men ter see an 'arf nekkid woman traipsin' up on the decks."

"Let me see if I understand this," Summer began, feeling the anger surge into her cheeks.

"Nuttin' ter understand, lass. Ye're only a wee t'ing. N'owt enough o' ye ter go 'round fer the 'ole crew, so it's best ye don't go wavin' it in their faces."

Summer turned a warm shade of scarlet. She heard a second, warning cough from Michael, but it was too late.

"You can just go and tell your captain that I shall go topside when and if I so choose, and that if he or any of his degenerate crew attempt to dissuade me in any way, they shall have the whole of the British Navy to answer to. It is to be understood that Michael and I are traveling under the protection of Sir Lionel Cambridge. We are British subjects. We are not at war with America—*yet*—and therefore we expect to have every courtesy extended to us until such time as we may leave this ship and return home. Any violation of any kind will be reported and dealt with swiftly and without recourse. Do I make myself quite clear?"

Thorny's jaw was gaping. Michael was staring at Summer in horror, wondering if perhaps she had lost her mind.

"Now," she said archly. "I will have that bath . . . unless you have anything else to say?"

Thorny's mouth snapped shut. He glanced at Michael,

then at Summer once more before hastily retreating from the cabin. Michael continued to gape at her even after the door was safely shut.

"Summer," he said on a rush of air, "are you sure you should have said that to him? He could come back here with a cutlass and slit our throats."

"Oh, good heavens, he wouldn't dare. And it is important not to show weakness. If they are who you think they are and if what they have in mind is indeed kidnapping and ransom, we mustn't let them think they can get away with it without creating an incident in the process."

"You mean a war?" His hazel eyes rounded.

"It would be nothing less than they deserve," she said with conviction. "This Captain Privateer cannot just go around kidnapping His Majesty's subjects without feeling some heat."

Michael grinned suddenly. "Or without being blasted out of the water. Don't forget the *Caledonia* is lurking somewhere about. 'Old Winifred' . . . er, I mean Captain Winfield is not going to just sail away without making a jolly good search of the area to find us."

Summer had moved to the table and was inspecting the contents of the tray. "But it has been two days. We must be several hundred miles from where the storm separated us."

"If we've moved fifty, I'll eat every square of canvas on board this ship," Michael said emphatically. "You may have been tossing about in your sleep, but the *Chimera* has been riding peacefully at anchor. She was damaged in the storm, and I gather Captain Wade wants to be sure she's seaworthy before he takes her out into open water again."

"At anchor?" Summer gasped, licking the crumbs of a buttery biscuit from her fingers. She went to the gallery and unlatched one of the heavy diamond-paned windows. "Where?"

"I don't know," Michael shrugged. "I've asked, but no one will tell me. It's an island friendly to Captain Wade, though. I think."

"An island," she murmured. "If we only knew which one, or if we could somehow get a message ashore—"

The next instant they both whirled to stare at the door as it flung wide open and crashed against the wall. Captain Morgan Wade stood there, his long legs splayed apart, his hands resting squarely on his hips. His jaw was tensed into a hard ridge, and the blue of his eyes flashed almost black.

"I understand you have a message for me," he snarled, taking a step across the threshold.

Summer was sufficiently startled to drop the quilt from around her shoulders. She recovered her composure quickly and met the challenge in the blue eyes with some fire of her own.

"How dare you enter this cabin without knocking! Get out at once. At once, do you hear me!"

Morgan Wade's mouth curved into an ominous smile. He kept his gaze fixed on Summer for several moments before flicking it toward Michael. "Get out, boy," he said evenly. "Now."

Michael looked from the captain to his sister and back to the captain.

"I said now, boy, unless you care to feel the back of my hand."

Michael swallowed hard and edged to the door slowly, pressing as far from the angered captain as he could.

Summer took a step forward. "You have no right ordering him to do anything."

"Shut up!" Wade commanded, "or, by Christ, you'll both be feeling the bite of my hand!"

Summer gasped and retraced her step. Michael exchanged a last apologetic glance with her, then dashed out into the corridor. Wade slammed the door shut and faced Summer.

"Now, just who the hell do you think you are, Governess, and where the hell do you think you are that you can order my men around like servants?"

Summer responded in kind to the insolence in his voice. "Michael and I are British subjects. We travel under the protection of the governor of Barbados."

"On board this ship, madam, I am the governor, the president, the king and any other figurehead you'd care to mention. I decide who does what. I decide who earns special treatment, who earns the lash and who earns the rat watch in the bilges."

"Yes, Mr. Thorntree has already enlightened us on your manner of justice, Captain. I hardly think it worthy of boasting."

He walked a few more paces into the cabin. "I might remind you that you were pulled out of the ocean in the middle of the night—from shark-infested waters—and allowed to stay on board my ship purely out of the goodness of my heart. At least ten of the so-called degenerates on board dove into the water without thinking of the risk to their own necks." He paused and took a deep breath. "For someone so free and easy with her insults, you should learn the basic meaning of the word gratitude."

Summer was not daunted. "For someone so free and easy with his lectures, you should learn the meaning of the word courtesy. Common decency, sir, decrees that you convey us to a British port immediately."

"Not likely, madam."

Summer flushed hotly. "Then if your purpose is to detain us—"

"Yes?" He arched one black brow.

"If that is your intent, be warned, sir: If any harm comes to Michael Cambridge, I will not rest until I see you hung as a pirate and miscreant."

"Assuming you live to see anything at all," he countered dryly.

Summer clenched her hands into two fists by her sides. "How dare you speak to me like this!"

"Have a care I do not dare more, Governess," he snapped angrily, and headed back to the doorway. "As to your bath, unless you have something of interest to barter with other than a sharp tongue, I suggest you do what the rest of us do: Take a dive off the side in calm waters."

"Barter!" she cried. "I have nothing to barter with."

"No?" He stopped with his hand on the jamb and glanced back. He studied her with a maddeningly contemptuous smirk, giving each tear in her pantaloons, each pucker and strain in her wrinkled smock a pointed assessment. "I can think of one or two things offhand that might interest a desperate man."

She gasped and bent over to snatch the fallen quilt up off the floor.

"I should have expected nothing better from you, Captain," she said disdainfully, wrapping the quilt tightly around herself. "I was told you Americans were *all* desperate little men with few values and no moral fortitude. I see now the evaluation was, if anything, charitable."

Wade's eyes narrowed to slits. He expelled the breath from his lungs and closed the partially open door with a bang. She saw him reach up to the bookcase for a brass key. She saw him twist it in the lock and return it to its perch high on the top shelf.

"What do you think you are doing?" she asked in a low voice.

He strode across the cabin to where she was standing, and before she could react, curled one arm around her waist, one beneath her knees, and swept her off her feet. He carried her struggling and shrieking to the bed and dumped her unceremoniously on top.

Summer scrambled to cover herself and pressed as far against the wall as she could go. *"What are you doing?"*

He grinned slowly and in one smooth motion had his shirt lifted up and over his head.

"Showing you just how charitable we Americans can be, Governess."

She stared at the sunbaked expanse of his chest, at the muscles in his arms that flexed as he lowered his hands to the fastening of his breeches.

"You're insane!" she cried. "You wouldn't dare!"

He laughed and caught at her wrists before she could slash her nails across his face. He twisted both arms behind her back and held them effortlessly while his free hand tore at what remained of her clothing.

"No!" she cried and squirmed to break out of his grip. "No, damn you!"

He silenced her by covering her mouth with his. The kiss was long and bruising, smothering her cries before they were fully formed. The hand holding her wrists forced her flat on the bed, and in the next heartbeat he was stretched out alongside her, his leg thrown across the tops of her thighs to control the frantic thrashing.

Summer screamed deep in her throat. She lunged furiously against his hold as she felt his hand skimming purposefully lower on her body. She moaned and tried to free her mouth from his, hoping that to scream, to cry out, to do something—*anything*—would bring help before he could . . .

Wade laughed again when he felt her buck to prevent his hand from intruding between the silky thighs. He took advantage of another reflexive twist to insert a knee firmly into place. His breath came quicker, and his hand rose to caress the fullness of her breast.

Summer moaned again, louder as she felt his body shift. Something iron-hard and determined was nudging into the space violated by his hand, something that pushed forward as he did and split her wide with an incredible thrusting pain.

She gasped and freed her mouth, but there was suddenly no air for screaming. The pain grew until it crested in a wave of red and gold-flecked bursts of fire. She was powerless to do more than sob as he pushed freely, deeply forward. Her mouth went slack. Her eyes opened, and she stared at the dark top of his head, not believing what was happening so coldly, so unfeelingly.

Her hands were released from his grip, but they remained limp in defeat. She prayed only that he would finish what he had set out to do as swiftly and as painlessly as possible. She was vaguely aware of his lips moving along her shoulder, down to her breast, down to coax and pull at the velvety smoothness. She was desperately aware of the steely thickness of him beginning to move within her and of the coarse feel of his flesh moving against hers. The tremendous muscles across his back and shoulders corded as his arms went around her and she was drawn helplessly into his embrace. His mouth was still fastened hungrily to her breast, and she whimpered as an unbidden surge of heat quivered into the nipple.

Summer ground her teeth together to keep from crying out. It would do no earthly good now, except to fuel his arrogance and announce his accomplishment to the rest of the ship. She heard his breath, harsh and ragged against her flesh, and she tried to think of Bennett, of how it should have been, would have been had they both forgotten themselves that night in the garden.

The first wave of pleasure crashed through her without warning, and Summer gasped, arching her head back into the mattress to absorb the shock. It was a sweet and white-hot sensation, shivering through her like an unexpected cool breeze on a stifling afternoon. It left her dazed and breathless and then wide-eyed and frightened as she felt a second, stronger force gathering within her.

Summer shuddered and clawed the broad shoulders, arching to him involuntarily as the tremors began to shatter her body. She heard a groan, guttural and drawn-out, and was stunned to realize it was coming from her own throat. But she could not stop it. Nor could she stop the blinding waves of ecstasy, the whirlpools of pleasure that consumed her, alighting nowhere and everywhere at once.

She felt his breath explode against her flesh, and his chest curved up and away from hers. She saw the shock ripple across his face; she saw it in the bared white teeth and the savage blaze of satisfaction in his eyes.

And then there was only the weight of him collapsing heavily between her thighs. She was reeling from her own shameless behavior, still unable to grasp what had happened. He propped himself on his elbows and studied her, the same maddening little half-smile as before playing on his lips.

Summer refused to meet the mocking blue eyes. Her gaze went instead to where her hands were resting on the darkly tanned shoulders. She jerked them away as if his flesh had suddenly burst into flame, noticing as she did so a trail of fresh blood smearing the hard muscles.

Tears that needed no provocation welled over her lashes when she saw the damage her nails had inflicted on the injured palms of her hands.

Wade frowned and maneuvered himself free. "What have you done to yourself? Let me see."

"Leave me alone," she cried softly. "You've done enough already. Just leave me alone."

He swung his long legs over the side of the bed and walked to the washstand in the corner, scowling anew when he found the pitcher empty. Seeming not to notice or care that he was naked, Wade unlocked the door and left the cabin, returning some moments later with fresh water splashing over the pitcher's brim. He tipped some into the washbasin and came back to the bed.

"Let me have your hands."

"Go to the devil, Captain Wade; to hell, where you surely belong."

He glanced up and she saw the quick flicker of anger give way to amusement. "Pretty language for a governess. And you've more spirit in you than would be safe for any man to show me."

"Any man would not have to lie here and suffer the indignity of rape," she countered bitterly.

"True enough. But then any man who spoke to me as you did would be dead by now."

"A pity you did not offer me the choice, sir."

"For that injustice, madam, you will have to settle accounts with your Maker. I had no hand in turning you out to be such an accommodating creature."

"You expect me to blame Him because you raped me!"

He grinned. "No. You can blame the look in your own eye for that. Give me your hands."

She snatched them out of his reach. "Are you insinuating I invited this travesty?"

"I'm telling you I saw a challenge and accepted it. To a very satisfactory end, I might add. One that was not expected."

"Not expected!"

"No indeed, madam. You have the pout and disposition of a child. A spoiled child at that, and I have never found much pleasure in disciplining children. You have proven to be the exception."

She inhaled sharply. "Your arrogance is not to be believed!"

"Nor is your ignorance. Now give me your hands before I take them."

Summer glared at him a moment longer before slowly uncurling her fists and presenting them. The two partially healed burns now had a row of tiny half-circlets of blood where the points of her nails had assisted her through the ordeal. She took some satisfaction in seeing that most of the blood had been left behind on his shoulders. Still, he dabbed the cuts with the moistened towel, gently enough that she found herself studying him from under the sweep of her lashes.

The first thing she realized was that Morgan Wade was not as tall as she remembered. He was certainly well above average, but not the towering giant that had been burned into her mind from the first sighting on the deck. The strength in his massive chest and arms was real enough though, and it frightened her. He had made her feel crushable. Crushed. And where the crisp black hairs had chafed against her breasts . . .

She felt a blush come and go in her cheeks and forced her eyes to travel up the column of his neck and concentrate on his face. His jaw was square and sharply defined even through the three-or-four-day growth of black stubble. His nose was thin, his mouth wide and expressive—mostly in the ways of scowling. The cold blue eyes were guarded by black lashes; his brow was creased as if subjected to a great deal of frowning. His hair was shiny black and left to fall unfettered to his shoulders; the cut was as indifferent as his manners.

She thought of Bennett Winfield's golden blond hair, how it was neatly gathered and clubbed at the nape of his neck with just the fashionable amount left in flat curls on his brow and cheeks. She doubted if he would ever be seen unshaven or if his uniform would ever be a notch from perfect. His whites would be white; his boots would be polished to a shine; his bicorne would be centered straight and true over his handsome face.

"I take it I am not comparing favorably," Wade murmured, seeing the wry twist to her mouth.

The blush spread down her throat, and she replied tautly, "In all honesty, I cannot think of a single *thing* to compare you to."

He glanced up from her hands. Her eyes did not flinch

when he stared into them. If anything, the color seemed to deepen, to lose much of the softness of the gray and draw attention to the green sparks. They were an odd color, unlike anything he had seen before. The surrounding fringe of lashes was long and thick, several shades darker than what he guessed her hair would be underneath the dull film of salt. Her skin was smooth and creamy white, another oddity in tropical waters and one not likely to last overlong. Her body was as smooth and unblemished as her face. Her breasts were firm and fit snugly to a hand, her waist was trim, her legs slender . . . but it was her eyes that held him, and the more he looked into them, the more he could feel them luring him in, like quicksand, to danger.

"Thank you very much," she snapped and pulled her hands out of his.

"You'll need more of Thorny's salve if you don't want them burning from infection."

"I'll not be doing anything to get them infected," she declared, adjusting the blankets to cover her nakedness.

"No?" He arched a brow. "I'd call working in the bilges pretty risky business."

"In the bilges?"

"Certainly. You don't think you're along for a free ride, do you? The *Chimera* was caught in the same storm you were. We took some damage to the keel. Nothing too serious. We've managed to repair the worst of it, but the pumps will have to be manned, and since I'm shorthanded . . ."

Summer's mouth formed a perfect O. "You would put me to work like a . . . like a galley slave?"

"Come now; let's not get too dramatic. Just say you and the boy will be earning your passage to port."

"Earning—! Michael—!" She jerked upright, gaping at Morgan Wade in horror. "You would dare to put Michael Cambridge to work in a ship's bilge!"

"If I would dare to put you there, I see no reason why His Lordship should be treated otherwise."

"But . . . he is Sir Lionel Cambridge's son! He is the governor's son! You cannot do this."

The mocking smile returned. "Madam, I usually do

whatever I damn well choose to do on board this ship. I am surprised to see you still doubt that."

She ignored the way the dark blue eyes moved slowly and deliberately to the tops of her breasts.

"I don't doubt it for a moment," she said. "But wasn't my humiliation enough for you? Must you add insult to your ransom demands by torturing Michael?"

"Ransom?" Wade lost interest in the plump half-moons peeping over the edge of the quilt. "Now where did that lofty idea come from?"

"Do you deny it, sir? Why else would you not set us ashore immediately?"

"Here?" The black brow arched higher.

"Michael has told me we are at anchor near an island. How long, indeed, how much effort would it take for you to have us rowed ashore? You voiced a dislike for passengers. If holding Sir Lionel to ransom is not your intent, then I demand we be set ashore at once."

"And if ransom is my intent?"

Summer held his gaze until the blue of his eyes seemed to sear right through her. She faltered and lowered her lashes, fighting the sting of tears that signaled another of his triumphs.

The strong, even teeth appeared in a grin. "By God, you are an obstinate creature. And too outspoken for the good of your health. You'd best mend your ways, Governess. Curb that tongue of yours, or I'll be obliged to do it for you."

"Then you are refusing to set us ashore?" she whispered.

"I confess you have intrigued me. I think I shall hold on to you a while longer."

"And . . . and the manner of your holding? Will you truly force us to work for our passage?"

Several moments passed before she heard a deep, rumbling laugh. "Rest at ease, Governess. I hardly think the results would be worth the effort. Besides, this past hour has been payment enough."

He moved away from the side of the bed, and she could hear him dressing, pulling on breeches and shirt, stamping his feet into his tall black boots. She did not raise her head or look at him even though she knew he was watching her.

She heard the deep chuckle again, and his boot steps sounded to the door. When it clicked shut, she waited until there was no more noise from the corridor; then she covered her face with her ice-cold, trembling hands and wept.

4

IT WAS WELL over an hour before Summer was again disturbed, this time by Mr. Thorntree. His arrival was preceeded by much dragging and scraping of wood on wood, and she was relieved to see it was only a sawed-off oak cask he maneuvered through the door. He avoided meeting Summer's eyes, avoided staring too hard at the torn shreds of her clothing that littered the floor.

He was, however, still briny from the confrontation earlier.

"Cap'n says ye earned a bat'," he grumbled under his breath. "An' ee said I was ter tell it to ye jest like that. Ye *earned* it."

Summer shivered and plucked the quilts higher.

"'Ow 'ot d'ye want the water?"

"Scalding."

"Aye."

He shuffled about for a few minutes and stopped when he saw the tray of barely touched food. "Waste o' good victuals, that."

"I'm afraid I lost my appetite."

"Aye."

He pushed and pulled at the cask until he had it near the small potbellied stove in the nook occupied by the cupboard and sea chest. He selected a handful of coals from a metal tin and made a show of building a fire in the stove.

"Cook's b'ilin' the water now. Won't take but a nip."

"Thank you."

He worked his jaw furiously, frowning and scratching his bristly pate until the strain proved too much.

"Cap'n Wade, now, ee's not arf bad, not truly. Ee 'as a temper on 'im, mind, I'd be the first ter admit, but—"

"Please do not insult me further by trying to defend the man," Summer interrupted coldly. "His behavior so far to two shipwrecked survivors has been nothing short of deplorable."

"Aye. Mebbe so, but—"

"There are no buts, Mr. Thorntree. There are only deeds to judge a man by. Your captain falls sadly short of any recognizable codes of conduct known to the human race. And if you intend to report the gist of this conversation to him—again—allow me to simplify the quote: He is an animal. A vulgar, despicable animal who should be roaming the jungles with the rest of the baboons."

Thorny sucked in his cheeks and contemplated his gnarled hands. "Aye. B'ilin' 'ot water ye'll get, lass. 'Ot as I can fetch it."

"And soap," she insisted.

"Eh? Aye . . . aye, I'll see what we 'ave. Seems ter me there were sum'mit smelled suspicious like it down below."

"Mr. Thorntree?"

He stopped at the door and sighed. "Aye?"

Some of the defiance drained from her face. "I'm sorry if anything I said or did this morning caused you unwarranted trouble. I should not be taking my anger out on you."

"Bah, no trouble, lass. Cap'n Wade 'ad a good larf, ee did. Right. Be back in a twitch."

Summer Cambridge stared at the closing door. "A good laugh!" she muttered, and the fury rose in her again. It remained at a healthy simmer until Thorny returned with two buckets, slopping hot, steamy water over the brims. He dumped them into the cask and produced a small wedge of hard soap from his pocket.

"Filched it, I did," he said, winking, "off'n some lad what likes ter smell o' roses."

"Thank you. Will you reach the key down for me?"

"Eh? The key?"

"It is on the top shelf of the bookcase. Of course, I could always push the furniture in front of the door and barricade myself in if you prefer. I do not care as long as I know my bath will go undisturbed . . . by anyone."

Thorny frowned, but he retrieved the brass key from its perch. "Ye'd best not take too long about it."

"Why? Will your captain fail to see the humor of it? Simply tell him that among other things, I earned my right to privacy this afternoon."

"N'owt much o' that on board a ship, lass."

"I am painfully aware of that, Mr. Thorntree. Still, it isn't asking too much if I am to be kept here against my will for God only knows how long. And Michael . . . where is he?"

"Topside, lass. Watchin' the Frenchies take their pound o' flesh."

"The Frenchies?" She turned to the windows again.

"Aye. They be wantin' a couple o' 'undredweight o' Cap'n Wade's cargo ter let us in the 'arbor fer repairs. Smacks o' piracy, if'n ye ask me, but the cap'n didn't 'ave much choice. We was takin' on too much seawater ter make a fair run 'ome."

"Exactly where are we, Mr. Thorntree?"

"Ye knows these 'ere islands?"

"Not well, I'm afraid."

"Mmm. W-a-all, I reckon it wouldn't do no 'arm fer ye ter know. We be off Saint Martin."

"Saint Martin," she repeated in a whisper. She tried to remember her geography, but all she could think of was the immediate area around Barbados. There were so many islands, so many with similar names and so many that changed hands and nationalities so often it was hard to keep track from one year to the next. Saint Martin was obviously north, but how far?

Summer scarcely noticed Thorny leaving. She twisted the brass key in the lock and hung it on a carved notch in the jamb, wondering as she did so why the island's name was ringing bells in the back of her mind. Something about it she should recall . . . but what? The fact that it was in the hands of the French gave her hardly a moment's pause. An American privateer or a French general —she and Michael were prisoners either way. The difference would be the time involved in negotiating a return to Bridgetown. There were always prisoner exchanges taking place throughout the islands. As soon as Father heard they were alive and awaiting rescue, he would move heaven and earth to have them home, regardless of the monetary demands.

Furthermore, the French were gentlemen. The daughter and son of the British governor of Barbados would be treated with every courtesy available. Not like this. Not like . . . this.

Summer dropped the quilt from her shoulders and touched her fingertips to the water in the cask. It was hot but not unbearably so, and she stepped in quickly, sinking to her knees to chase the reflexive shivers out of her body. The rising steam smelled faintly of rum, and she suspected the cask had once been a part of the ship's stores. It was large enough to sit in with a degree of comfort, deep enough for the water to cover all but the rounds of her knees and the tops of her shoulders.

She sighed and ladled several pitchers full of water over her head, letting the heat soothe away the throb in her temples. The soap earned a distasteful wriggle of her delicate nose, but it lathered well and, when rinsed from her hair, left it squeaky clean. Twice she soaped her body, scrubbing with a rough scrap of towel until she was pink and tingling. She found several old and yellowing bruises to explain the aches she felt in her muscles and several new bluish ones to explain the rawness that kept her tears close to the surface.

When she finished scrubbing, she simply sat in the milky water and let it cool around her, paying no mind to the time slipping away tick by tick on the gold watchpiece on the desk.

It was the sound of the ship's bell jangling the end of a watch that finally roused her sufficiently to leave the tub. She dried herself with a blanket she found folded over the sea chest, then sat down to shake her hair dry in front of the stove while she contemplated what to do about clothing. Thorny had not taken her seriously. Her smock and pantaloons, already badly abused from the travail in the ocean, had been torn beyond repair by Morgan Wade.

She bolstered her nerve with a deep breath and opened the teak doors of the cupboard behind her. It held only the bare essentials: three neatly folded cambric shirts, several pairs of black canvas trousers, a leather jerkin, and a second pair of high calfskin boots.

The small square mirror attached to the inside panel of the door gave Summer a shock. Aside from the smudges beneath her eyes caused by the fear and worry, there was an enormous ugly bruise down one side of her jaw. There was a scrape in the center of it where something had struck her or where she had rolled up against something rough in the fall from the *Sea Vixen*. It distorted the lower half of her jaw, seeming to pull the skin taut over her cheekbones. Her lips were dry and cracked, her hair more of a rat's nest than a thing of beauty.

For one irrational moment she was thankful it had not been the *Caledonia* that had found them. She was thankful Bennett did not have to see her like this.

Tears glistened in her eyes, welled over her lashes, and streamed down her cheeks to her chin. She had always been pampered and treated like a rare and exquisite china doll. Her every whim had been catered to; she had never been without servants, never had to lift a finger to do anything menial. She had been the toast of London society. She had been to court *three times!* She had flirted with and won the hearts of some of the wealthiest, most influential men in England! Why on earth had she ever left! Why!

Now she was a prisoner on board a smuggler's ship. She was held captive by a man who had used her carelessly and would no doubt brag of his accomplishment from here to whatever pirate's port they were bound.

"Damn you, Morgan Wade," she hissed. "Damn you for what you have done!"

Feeling better for the profanity, she turned from the mirror and dashed away the wetness on her cheeks. She was convinced now more than ever that Morgan Wade must not discover her true identity. Rumors concerning a despoiled governess would hardly cause a stir of interest. Stories and gossip about Sir Lionel Cambridge's daughter would rock the family to its foundations, not to mention the harm it might do to her relationship with Bennett Winfield. He would have to know, of course, and then he would be bound by honor to avenge her. The thought of what form that vengeance would take raised Summer's spirits and brought back the anger she needed to see her through.

She snatched one of the folded cambric shirts from the shelf and shook out its creases. It was huge and floated almost to her knees. The shoulders were midway to her elbows, and the sleeves hung a foot or more below her hands. The neckline was fastened by a crisscross lacing which ran up the front of the shirt, but even though she tugged the thongs as tight as she could, there were still gaps of flesh showing from her collarbone to her waist. Chewing her lip thoughtfully, Summer took the straight razor she found among Wade's toiletries and solved the problem of the sleeves with two swift slashes. A third shortened the length of the hem and provided her with a belt to cinch the waist. Trousers were next, and she performed the same surgery on a pair until they suited her purpose.

Looking somewhat more decent, Summer took a further liberty and used the privateer's silver-backed brush on her hair until it was free of tangles and hung in a straight wet mass down her back. There were no pins or combs of any kind to keep it from scattering around her shoulders, but she salvaged a length of red silk ribbon from the torn smock and caught the hair together at the nape of her neck. That done, she resolutely unlocked the cabin door, walked the length of the gloomy companionway, and climbed the brief flight of wooden steps to the sunlit main deck.

Her heart suffered a momentary lapse in function when the first thing she saw was a row of black, dully gleaming cannon. They were spaced evenly along both sides of the ship, crouching behind closed gunports like silent lions.

She firmly pushed them out of her mind as she stepped

clear of the hatch and examined the rest of the ship. Above and behind her was the quarterdeck; directly ahead were the forecastle and bridge. Three towering masts rose from the deck of the *Chimera,* strung with a maze of rigging and spars and reefed canvas. Judging by the activity she saw around her, the ship was being prepared to get under way. There were men scrambling up the rigging, men already positioned on the yards, men shouting to other men higher up, across, below—all three masts were a buzz of organized confusion.

Summer heard the rumble of Wade's voice issuing commands. She craned her neck to see around the mainmast and located him easily where he stood on the bridge. The breeze was a smart one, and his black hair was blowing recklessly to and fro as he turned his head to mark the movements of the crew. His shirt was unlaced and billowed open to his waist. The sleeves were full and gathered at the wrist, and as he stood with his hands braced on his hips, the wind puffed out the loose folds, giving an even greater breadth to his arms and shoulders. He paced slowly from one side of the bridge to the other, the dark blue eyes seeming to dart everywhere at once.

Summer saw him nod and saw his lips form a command. The huge negro she recalled vaguely from the first night grinned, cupped his hamlike hands around his mouth and bellowed an order to cut loose the main and steering sails.

Almost immediately there was a sound of lashings being released, of yards creaking to take the strain of canvas unfurling. Nimble sailors shouted exuberantly as they skittered down the guide ropes and moved hand over foot through the maze of rigging. Summer held her breath as she watched the splashes of white canvas blossom open against the blue skies. The sails seemed to tremble hesitantly as they were startled out of their wrinkles; then with an exploding crack of energy, they took up the challenge of the wind and curled against the spars.

The *Chimera*'s response was instantaneous. It rose eagerly in its bows and began gliding through the blue water, carving aside a wash of bubbling white foam as it nosed its way toward the open sea.

Summer walked to the deck rail and braced herself against the gentle roll and sway. Her first glimpse of Saint Martin was one of rapidly shrinking land, and she was surprised to see how far out from shore they had been anchored. She could barely see the town where it nestled in the curve of a shallow bay. The fringe of palm trees was solid green; the beaches were only a trim border of white. A walled garrison which capped a promontory of land was starkly outlined against the sky, and two small vessels were moored sleepily at the single dock.

"I thought you were told to remain belowdecks," came a gruff, all-too-familiar voice over her shoulder.

Summer turned to face him. "And what will you do about it, Captain? Toss me overboard for disobeying? If so, kindly do it now before the distance becomes too tiring to swim."

His eyes glowered for a moment, but in the end he simply laughed.

"And what would you do once you reached shore, Governess? Present yourself to the French commandant and demand an expedient return to the bosom of your employer?"

"I should give myself over to the French, secure in the knowledge of being treated with the utmost courtesy and decorum."

"Oh, you would be treated courteously, all right. From one bed to the next, you would be treated, and when the officers had their fill of you—as unimaginable as that may sound—you would be a treat for the rest of the garrison. It isn't often they find something sweet and fresh like yourself thrown on their doorstep."

She fumed. "The French are not a race of barbarians, Captain."

"Anywhere other than Saint Martin, I might be inclined to agree with you. But here they are a unique breed."

"I don't believe you."

"No? Perhaps you would believe your own eyes then. Have you any knowledge of sea codes?"

"Sea codes? Why on earth would I have any—"

"See up there, on the crest of the hill? The large yellow

square painted on the garrison walls?" He waited until she whirled angrily and followed his finger. "It is a warning, Governess. A caution to all healthy men."

The huge gray eyes reverted to his face.

"Saint Martin is the home of the French leper colony," he said pointedly. "It is, consequently, the only French territory for hundreds of miles in any direction that the British have not troubled themselves to fight over. The soldiers stationed here are the dregs of society, the commandant usually banished here for some stupid crime against the French government. They are usually bitter men, too, having been caught and sentenced to a death-watch. They would have no qualms whatsoever in holding you until your flesh rotted and you no longer were capable of giving them any pleasure."

Summer's chin trembled, and her cheeks lost a degree of their high color.

"On the other hand," he remarked casually, glancing over the side, "if you prefer to take your chances with them, by all means jump ship. Do it before we cross the point though, for the currents beyond the peninsula are strong and treacherous."

He insolently touched a forelock and walked back across the main deck to the ladderway leading up to the bridge. Summer felt her stomach tightening into knots, and she wished feverishly she'd had the foresight to tuck the straight razor into one of her pockets. One slash. One ribbon of blood across that arrogant face would go a long way toward evening the score.

The *Chimera* rounded the point and reared its head into the stiff trades. The order was given to crowd on sail, and Summer left the deck to the sounds of all three masts being fully rigged. She passed Thorny in the companionway but did not acknowledge his mutterings or pause long enough to allow him to manipulate the heavy buckets of cold bathwater safely past a protruding cable. She heard the splat and crash of one bucket against the bulwark, followed by a series of curses and a reference to the dubious origins of all women.

Her response was to slam the door. She stood with her

back pressed against the wood, fighting hard to suppress the urge to scream.

The fire in the stove had gone out. Thorny's efforts to tidy up had included removing the tray of cold chicken and biscuits, folding the quilt across the bed and removing the scraps of shirt and trouser she had merely flung on the floor. Remembering the razor, Summer hurried to the closet and searched through the toiletries. It was gone. She searched the floor in case it had fallen unnoticed, but there was no sign of it. Thorny must have been considering his captain's welfare when he saw the remnants of his clothing.

"Cowards," she spat, and snatched up the hairbrush. She stood in front of the gallery windows, watching Saint Martin fall out of sight. The sound of rushing water and the sight of sunlight glinting off the *Chimera*'s wake helped to cool some of the heat in her cheeks. She removed the red ribbon and made use of the drafts to dry her hair and brush it into a glossy golden cascade of curls. When she turned around to reach for the ribbon again, she saw that she had thrown it on top of a chart on Wade's desk. She traced a finger around the scribbled notations until she found the irregular mass of land marked Saint Martin.

The chart itself was a disgrace; water-spotted and wrinkled, with lines crossing every which way over minute pinholes, bold X's and compass readings that were jotted on the parchment. It was apparently Wade's working copy, for there was a second chart beneath it, identical in every detail save that there were no markings of any kind on it.

Summer sighed and stroked the brush absently through a handful of hair. Since the copy had been used several times already, there was no way of distinguishing which set of penciled lines and navigational plottings he was following this voyage. She had no way of determining where he had been or where he was bound—even if she'd known how to read one of the wretched things.

Her gaze strayed to the desk itself, to the double row of drawers on either pedestal. The brush froze midstroke as she contemplated the inviting lack of locks on each of the drawers.

Michael had said there was never any way to prove Wade's illegal dealings. What if she could return home with the proof Sir Lionel needed to put an end to Morgan Wade? Even a pirate had to keep records of some sort. How much would Wade trust to memory and how much would he confide to his records?

Summer set the brush on the desk top and moistened her lips. Suppose she could find references in Wade's handwriting to the cargo taken from—what was the name of the schooner Michael had mentioned? The *Reliant!* If she could find the proof and hand it to Sir Lionel when they were ransomed free, he could turn around and toss Wade into prison.

Summer glanced at the unlocked door. How long would she be left alone? Thorny had tidied up, Wade was busy with his ship . . . an hour? Two?

She sat in the deeply padded leather chair and noiselessly slid the wide center drawer open.

Papers. Invoices. Bills of lading. She shuffled through them carefully, keeping the neatly bundled sheaves in the order she found them. There were no references to the *Reliant,* nothing that looked remotely suspicious. If anything, the papers looked disturbingly innocent . . . too innocent?

Summer found and opened a leather-bound writing tablet. The top was dated simply "June"; the opening salutation began with a perfunctory "Stephen." She read it hastily, frowning over the brief greetings, the seemingly endless descriptions of weather they had encountered and forecasts he was predicting, all the way to where the bold script broke off two sentences into a paragraph concerning the cane harvest on Saint Christopher.

Weather forecasts? Harvests?

Summer shrugged and replaced the tablet where she had found it. The second drawer she tried was slightly more rewarding. She saw more folded documents, all bearing an official government seal. The first she opened was in Spanish. Her knowledge of the language was poor, but she recognized the official seals and signatures that flowed over the bottom half of the parchment. The other documents were identical, although each was in a different language: One was French, one Dutch and the last in the king's own English.

They were Wade's letters of marque: his formal permission to trade in ports held by the respective nations. He had one for each of the predominant countries claiming colonies in the Caribbean. A ship's captain might understandably have one or two letters of marque in his possession if he conducted regular, legal trade between two sanctioned ports . . . but four? Each letter would have cost a small fortune to purchase, and each would have come with strict embargoes as to where the goods could be transported and sold—embargoes Wade evidently paid little heed to.

Summer was replacing the documents in the drawer when she felt something which obstructed the pages deeper inside. She reached in to the back of the drawer and her fingers brushed against cold metal. It was a small gold case, its lid beautifully embossed with a family crest. The lion's paw hasp opened with a touch of her thumbnail, but her excitement waned as quickly as it had risen. There was nothing dangerous or mysterious about three sticks of indigo sealing wax and an ingot of gold bearing the raised impression of a falcon in full wingspread.

Summer snapped the lion's paw closed and was sliding the case back into the drawer when she paused and angled it toward the bright light. The coat of arms on the lid depicted two rearing griffins on either side of a shield carrying the unmistakable cross of Saint George. Above the shield was the same falcon that had been tooled into the stamp. It was a magnificent crest and an unusual combination of elements that normally signified nobility.

Nobility? She grimaced and guessed that the only noble thing Wade could be accused of was saving the case and seal from a watery grave. She replaced the gold box and the four letters of marque in the drawer and was reaching to try a third drawer when she felt an ominous prickle along her spine.

"I see you've found a way to occupy your time."

Morgan Wade was leaning casually against the doorjamb, his arms folded across his chest. How long he had been standing there, Summer had no idea, but the expression on his face gave every indication he was prepared for blood sport.

"I . . . I was just sitting here and . . . and . . ."

Wade moved and kicked the door shut behind him. "And you thought you might as well see if there was anything worthwhile to steal?"

Summer was shocked. "No! No, I wasn't looking to steal anything!"

"I'm glad to hear it. The penalty for theft on board my ship involves a rather lengthy trial with a filleting knife."

Summer blanched. "I told you, I was not trying to steal anything. I was . . . I was"—she searched for a palatable excuse for being behind his desk—"looking for a chart or a map other than this scribbled thing to give me some idea where we are."

"You already know where we are," he said evenly.

She flushed uncomfortably. "Saint Martin is just a name to me. I have no idea where it *is*."

Wade regarded her for a long moment, plainly not amused by the feeble lie. "So you read charts, do you, Governess? You know all about latitude and longitude?"

"I am not totally ignorant, sir. Although it could be painfully easy to become so, given the company I am forced to keep."

"Clever and sharp-witted," he mused. "I cannot say as I find comfort in my women being either."

"I am not your woman!" she cried indignantly. "And if cleverness and wit sour you, I shall do my utmost to excel at both!"

Wade's grin was slow to come. His eyes flicked to the center drawer and darkened when he saw the corner ajar. "I hope you were not bored with your reading."

"Outraged, perhaps. Not bored."

"And what, pray, has outraged you this time?"

"Your total lack of conscience and scruples, for one thing. You apparently think nothing of dealing with the French and Spanish and Dutch as freely as you would deal with the English."

"It is called free trade, madam."

"It is called treason to deal with an enemy for profit," she countered.

"In case you haven't noticed, I fly the Stars and Stripes. America is not at war with any of the countries you mentioned."

"But her roots lie in England. England's enemies should be your enemies."

"My dear ignorant, if there is any country we should be looking to as our enemy, it is almighty Britannia. We have already had to fight once to prove we no longer want John Bull's rule as our own, and it is beginning to look as if we shall have to do so again."

"You would see your country declare war on England?" she gasped. "You would fight over a few measly pounds of profit?"

"Hardly a few," he said dryly. "And yes, I would fight any country and any ship that tried to dictate who I may and may not conduct my business with."

"Business?" she scoffed. "Is it part of your business to kidnap helpless women and children and hold them against their will?"

He grinned broadly. "I am not holding you, madam. You are free to leave any time you wish."

"And go where?" she demanded.

"Wherever you would care to try swimming for."

Summer's eyes flashed with sparks of angry deep green, and she jumped up out of the chair. "Where is Michael? What have you done with him?"

"I've done nothing with him other than see he is kept occupied and out of my crew's way."

"Are you forcing him to work?"

"I'm not forcing him to do anything," Wade snapped. "He has been watching Thorny repair sails for the past hour."

"Mr. Thorntree's influence is not exactly what Sir Lionel Cambridge has in mind for his son's education."

"I'll tell Thorny you said that. Meanwhile you should be grateful someone is at least taking an interest in the boy—you don't seem to be."

Summer's mouth dropped inelegantly. "Whose fault is

that? Who ordered him out of this cabin? Who threatened to beat him and then proceeded to . . . to . . ."

"To teach you a lesson in manners you don't appear to have retained very well. I am beginning to grow tired of reminding you that neither you nor His Lordship are at all special on this ship. For all anyone knows, the pair of you drowned in the storm and lie at the bottom of the sea."

"A fact which makes you doubly cruel and heartless," she cried. "Sir Lionel is not a well man. How do you think the news will affect his health when he hears that his only son is drowned?"

"Perhaps it will improve his disposition when he hears the boy is alive. Whether he thanks me for returning you or not remains to be seen. I cannot see that your temperament would be of any benefit to his health."

Summer clamped her mouth into a thin, uncompromising line. There was no way to argue with the man. He was baiting her and enjoying it! Michael's bright idea was beginning to fray badly around the edges. As a governess she would have to realize her own expendability and suffer the brigand's remarks in silence. She balled her fists and with a visible effort bit back any further comments.

"Well, now," he murmured. "You may have learned a thing or two after all."

He turned his back for a moment and thereby missed the expression on Summer's face. She was saved from committing a fatal error in judgment by a quick knock on the door.

"Come," Wade barked, shutting the lid on the humidor. Summer's hand fell away from the heavy brass bookend as Thorny poked his head around the door.

"Come ter see 'bout victuals," Thorny said. "An' I brung yer rum."

Wade glanced up over the flame he held to the tip of the thin black cigar. "I'll take my supper in here. Find the lad and send him down; he'll join us for the meal."

"Aye." He set a small earthenware jug on the dining table.

"Tell Mr. Monday I'll be taking the eight o'clock watch."

"Aye. Supper's on its way."

Wade crossed to the dining table and selected two crystal glasses from one of the wire-fronted bookcases on the wall. Summer looked at him with some surprise as he filled both with rum and held one out to her.

"No, thank you."

He grinned past the cigar clamped between his teeth. "Suit yourself, but it might relax you."

"I am quite relaxed," she retorted. "If I were any more so, I fear your attempts at civility would put me to sleep."

He drew deeply on the cigar and exhaled a cloud of bluish smoke as she presented him with her back. The air from the open gallery windows blew the hair back from her shoulders but did nothing to ease the discomfort of feeling his eyes boring into her.

Wade, conversely, was enjoying a sight he had not seen many times in the past dozen years. Her hair had dried into fine strands of spun silk, curling thick and soft over her shoulders to reach well past her waist. The light was behind her, etching the wisps into silvery threads. The oversized clothes did absolutely nothing to conceal the various curves and contours of her body; if anything, they emphasized the more tempting areas and made his hands burn with the recent memory of exploring them.

Wade drained his glass and poured himself another just as Michael Cambridge knocked discreetly on the door.

Summer whirled instantly and ran to his side. She started to hug him, caught herself in time and instead squeezed his shoulders affectionately, hoping he could read beneath her restraint.

He looked changed somehow in the few short hours since she had seen him last. The ever-present smattering of freckles across the bridge of his nose had expanded to cover both cheeks. His eyes were bright, his face tanned and healthy—not at all what one would expect to see on a boy forced to toil unmercifully three decks below the sunlight.

"Good evening, Captain Wade," he said formally. "Thank you for the invitation to dinner."

"No trouble," Wade shrugged. "In fact, you can save me

some trouble by telling your governess here that we haven't whipped you into servitude. She seems to think I've set you slaving belowdecks like a Moorish half-caste."

Michael frowned at Summer. "Oh, no. They're being ever so nice, actually. Thorny . . . er, Mr. Thorntree has taught me how to stitch canvas and tomorrow he says I may even be allowed to work on the sails with him."

Wade crooked an eyebrow at Summer. "Satisfied?"

A voice bellowed, "W'hup ho!" and Thorny pushed his way into the cabin burdened by the heavy tray again.

"I 'ope ye're 'ungry, lad."

"Famished," Michael nodded eagerly.

"Good. We'll fix up some lard on them bones o' yourn afore too long. Sea air, good victuals an' a clean constitution, lad. It'll 'eal up what ever ails ye."

Summer had not realized how hungry she was until the aroma from the two covered crocks launched an assault on her senses. Her mouth flooded and her hands trembled and she found the wait interminable while Wade finished his drink and beckoned them to the dining table.

Michael held her chair and took his own place, then he, too, looked expectantly at Captain Wade, who only waved a hand distractedly.

"Go ahead, Governess, portion it out."

Summer moistened her lips. "Plates, Michael, please."

Biscuits, soft and fluffy, were in the first crock when she lifted the lid. She removed the second lid and felt a wave of dizziness sweep through her as she saw and smelled the rich mutton stew. She ladled a heaping scoopful on the first plate Michael handed her, added two of the biscuits and placed it in front of Morgan Wade. He had not taken his eyes off Summer's face during the serving, but as she leaned forward, they sought the gap in the front of her shirt and settled on the visible white flesh.

He took a deep breath and snuffed out the stub of his cigar, then refilled his glass before reaching for his fork.

Summer tasted a spoonful of the gravy and found it worthy of the aroma. It was thick and heavily spiced; the mutton was tender and the vegetables succulent. She ate every last morsel on her plate and broke a biscuit into the gravy so as not to waste a drop of the juice. Michael's plate was so clean she doubted if anyone would bother to wash it. Neither of them had had food this good since leaving New Providence. The cook on board the *Sea Vixen* had believed firmly in salt beef and potatoes.

Coffee, hot and strong, followed a desert of fresh fruit. Although she suspected the coffee was liberally doctored with spirits, Summer found it so soothing after the strenuous day that she drained two mugfuls and nursed a third. Her mood mellowed considerably, lulled by the gentle motion of the ship and by the sound of friendly conversation.

Michael had broken down early in the meal and between mouthfuls plied the privateer with questions about his ship. How many cannon did it carry? (Thirty-eight.) Were they all the same? (Long guns and carronades, he explained. Different weights, different ranges.) Were they all functional? (Naturally.) Had he used them against any British ships?

This earned a shocked gasp from Summer and a laugh from Wade.

"But what would you do if a British warship chased you?" Michael persisted.

"Now why would any British warship want to chase me?" Wade asked wryly. "Are you suggesting I have something to hide?"

"Oh, no, sir, I just meant . . . well . . ."

Wade leaned back and lit another cigar. "Well, what?"

"One does hear rumors, sir," Michael stammered.

"Rumors, eh? And what do these rumors tell you?"

"That you're not much better than a pirate. That you hide behind your country's flag. That you're responsible for a great many of the ships that are waylaid and have their cargoes stolen."

"All that?" Wade mused.

"Oh, yes. And a great deal more. Father says you cannot get away with it much longer. He says you Yankees will have to choose one way or another and then it will be belly up for the lot of you."

"Michael!" Summer exclaimed, forgetting her weariness.

"Well, that's what he says."

Wade grinned and waved Summer's protest into silence. "And which side does he think we'll choose?"

Michael bit his lip and answered reluctantly, "France. He says you have too many war birds in your congress for you to ever reach a peaceful agreement with Britain."

"I believe the term is war hawks, and he's undoubtably right. But it's not just us, boy. Too many men on both sides of the ocean want to fight."

"Then you agree we shall soon be at war?"

"I can see no other end to it."

Michael frowned. "And will you fight us?"

Wade studied the boy's earnest expression. "Well, lad, I've always taken life one stride at a time. War could be two, three . . . ten years down the wind yet, and I cannot say what my inclinations will be."

"His inclination will be to profit from the conflict," Summer said derisively. She felt Wade's eyes on her, but she kept her own carefully lowered.

Michael broke the silence. "You haven't said what you would do if a British man-of-war intercepted us tomorrow. Would you use your cannon, sir? Would you fire on one of His Majesty's ships?"

"If they fired on me, yes. Without a minute's hesitation. But then I'd also fire on the French or the Spanish or anyone who tried to get in my way and stop me from going on about my business. The *Chimera* is a high-spirited lady with a high-spirited crew. Neither take kindly to a broadside. You might bear that in mind if you are hoping to see a friendly sail on the horizon. We're in open water now. There are no rules out here as far as private merchant ships go; any and all of us are fair game, not just for revenuers."

"You mean the *Chimera* could be attacked by other privateers?"

"There are some who might try," he nodded. "But I rather think it would be the other way around."

"You mean you would attack another ship if you saw one?"

"If the mood was on me, aye."

Michael leaned forward excitedly. "Honestly? A real sea battle? Oh, jolly good!"

"Michael, that will be quite enough," Summer said archly. "You have had a long day and a busy one, and I'm sure you will be having an even busier one tomorrow. I suggest you save some of your energy for then."

"Oh, but—"

"Michael!"

"Yes ma'am," he said, downcast.

Wade tilted his head toward the faint rasp of a curse filtering in through the open portals. He glanced at the timepiece on his desk and was amazed to see how much time had passed. It was almost his watch.

"Never mind, lad, we'll talk more tomorrow. Right now I'm due up on the bridge." He stood up and stretched, regretfully eyeing the soft mattress on the berth. He shut and latched the gallery windows to seal out the dampness and lit the brass lanterns—one on his desk, one hanging from the center beam in the ceiling. Then he stopped beside his desk and removed two cigars from the humidor.

"I'll send someone in to clear away the dishes. Help yourself to the bookcases, Governess"—he glanced at Summer and grinned mockingly—"anything I have is yours."

The flush remained in her cheeks long after the sound of his boots had faded from the corridor. She toyed with her fork quietly for the next few minutes, scarcely remembering that Michael was still in the cabin with her.

"Well, I got the bounder to admit he would open fire on the Royal Navy," he said smugly.

Summer blinked and stared at him. "You got him to admit he would *return* fire . . . something any ship's captain would do. And why on earth were you hounding him about his motives and intentions? He hasn't the most stable temperament I've seen, and he doesn't give much warning between changes. In fact," she added dryly, "he's downright prickly where his patriotism is concerned."

"Yes, but just look at what we'll be able to tell Father! No one has been on the *Chimera* during one of her voyages and lived to describe her activities to the authorities."

"That is certainly encouraging to know."

"We'll be able to tell all about her cannon and her men, what he carries on all three decks . . . his strengths, his weaknesses. I told you, they've given me free run of the ship. Father says the revenuers have tried to follow him to his home port but they always lose him in the islands. Wouldn't it be something if we came home with *that* news?"

Summer was silent another long minute, then shook her head slowly. "Are you certain you are only ten years old?"

Michael grinned and dipped a finger into the empty stewpot. He sucked the traces of gravy off noisily and set about attacking the last crumbs of biscuit.

5

SUMMER SHIFTED uncomfortably on the wooden chair, grumbling as a slender thigh found little relief against the hard round spindles.

Captain Morgan Wade touched a melted wafer of wax to the last of the dispatches he had written and pressed the gold ingot into the seal, leaving behind the impression of a falcon in full wingspread. He tested the hold of the wax and, satisfied, slipped the letter into a bundle with four others and locked them—together with the seal and the leather-bound writing tablet—in a cabinet behind his desk. He made several quick notations in his logbook, retied its narrow rawhide straps, and that too went safely back into its niche.

Summer yawned herself fully awake, startled to see Wade sitting calmly at work behind his desk. His face was trapped in the glow from the lantern, and behind him there was only darkness showing through the panes of the gallery windows. In her lap, forgotten, was the volume of Shakespeare she had started reading.

The timepiece declared it to be a quarter of three.

"Oh. I must have fallen asleep."

Wade glanced up at her but did not comment.

"I . . . I hope I did not disturb you."

"You were quiet enough," he murmured absently, working the points of a compass over his charts. "It was a pleasant change."

She flushed and straightened in the chair. She would have dearly loved to stand and walk the cramps out of her legs, but she did not want to draw any undue attention to herself. She watched the movements of his hands for a few minutes and studied the frowning brow, the growth of stubble beginning to soften the square jaw. Undeniably there would be women who would consider him a handsome man. Perhaps even those who would consider him an extremely handsome man. On the other end of the scale, however, were his arrogance and churlishness, to put a firm damper on anyone's judgment.

She took a deep breath. "Will we be at sea much longer? . . . I mean before we reach wherever it is we are going?"

"A few days. It depends on the weather. Why?"

"I was merely curious to know. Will you be sending a missive with your demands to Sir Lionel as soon as we arrive?"

A brief flash of annoyance glittered in his eyes. "What do you suggest I do?"

"I think you should. I think the sooner you return his son to him, the easier it will be on you in the long run. He is a powerful man."

"So you keep telling me."

"And his authority is far-reaching. He will be livid from the ransom demand, never mind that it should be delayed."

"Suppose I cannot decide what those demands should be?" he said, leaning comfortably back in the chair.

"He is a wealthy man. I'm sure he would be willing to pay handsomely."

Wade pursed his lips. "Suppose I said his money doesn't interest me."

"Suppose I said I didn't like diamonds," she quipped sarcastically.

"I might believe you . . . if you already had more than you wanted."

"You have more money than you want?" she scoffed.

"Let's just say I have more than I could reasonably expect to spend in two lifetimes."

Summer was momentarily taken aback. "Profits from your trade, no doubt?"

He merely smiled.

"Why do you continue at it, then? You told Michael this

evening that your trade was of the utmost importance to you."

"I said my *freedom* to trade was important," he corrected her gently.

"Well, then? What could you possibly prefer over money to make you risk your life and your ship smuggling illegal cargo?"

He shrugged. "I enjoy what I do."

"You enjoy it?" Summer folded her hands tightly on her lap, feeling the resentment flow up into her cheeks. "Does your enjoyment include brutalizing women and children?"

"Come now. You don't look very brutalized sitting there all curled up like a kitten, reading *Midsummer Night's Dream*. If I truly wanted to brutalize you, I'd have you chained in the hold with nothing but the dampness and the rats to keep you company. I certainly wouldn't feed you prime meals and clothe you and give you my own cabin. No"—he took a slow breath and his eyes fell to the rounded swell of her breasts—"I'm beginning to think the arrangement we made earlier suits me just fine."

"The arrangement?" Summer's heart slowed, and she felt a chill sweep down her spine. She could not look away from the blue of his eyes. They seemed to reach out and engulf her, washing the fear through her in a sluggish wave.

"You did ask me what I preferred over money. . . ." He let the sentence hang.

"I . . . I asked you what you would demand from Sir Lionel," she stammered, glancing at the closed door.

"Perhaps you can pay his debts for him in advance. Think how grateful he would be."

"No!" she cried and jumped to her feet, unmindful of the book falling to the floor. "No, that is impossible."

Wade's gaze still held her. He stood up slowly and started to come around the side of the desk.

"Oh, no . . . please, no . . . you can't . . ."

She saw the crooked smile and the darker flicker of intent in his eyes, and she whirled around, dashing wildly for the door. She pulled at the latch, not knowing exactly where she could run to, only knowing that she had to escape. The corridor was dark, and she did not see the enormous black specter blocking her exit until she collided with the gleaming, hairless chest.

She choked off a scream and staggered back, clapping both hands over her mouth.

"Somet'ing wrong, Cap-tan?" Mr. Monday drawled, his teeth glaring whitely through the darkness. With a further jolt of horror, Summer saw that he was totally naked.

"Nothing I cannot handle," Wade said quietly. "But I'll call if I have any further trouble."

"Aye, Cap-tan." He leaned in past a frozen Summer Cambridge and drew the door shut again.

"It's a bad habit I haven't been able to break him of," Wade murmured. "A carryover from his slave days, I imagine . . . sleeping outside the master's door."

Summer spun around to confront him, but the rage and humiliation died in her throat without making a sound. He stood waiting expectantly, his arms folded across the steely breadth of his chest.

"Now come over here," he commanded softly.

"No!" Summer pressed herself against the wall. There was not much free space between the doorjamb and the edge of a bookcase, but she wedged herself into it, fighting to keep the tears from stinging into her eyes.

"You will come to me, Governess. You will render payment for the meal and the hospitality."

"No . . . *no!*" She felt herself slipping. Her body was on fire, scalding her senses as Wade closed the gap between them with firm, promissory footsteps. She saw him reach out and catch her before the faintness took hold. His hand brushed lightly, almost reverently, down the scattered blonde hair before he pushed it aside and his lips claimed the racing pulse beneath her ear.

"Oh God . . ." She writhed against the smooth wood of the panel. His hands were on her breasts, stroking them through the cambric, teasing them into unwitting accomplices. "Oh God, no, please . . ."

His mouth was on hers, crushing the pleading whispers into silence. His tongue shocked her, destroyed her in deep, searching thrusts. His hands were moving beneath her shirt; his flesh was hot upon her flesh. He loosened the scrap of cloth holding her trousers in place, then slid his hands down her bared thighs, pulling her purposefully against him.

Summer's knees lost the ability to hold her upright. Again he caught her. He lifted her, his mouth still fastened to hers, and carried her to the bed. He waited until her eyes fluttered open before he set her down and began releasing the laces of her shirt.

"I hate you," she cried weakly. "I hate you!"

"Yes," he said, and his hands spread the cambric open across her breasts. He lowered his dark head and closed his mouth around one dusky peak, tormenting the sweet flesh until it gathered into taut ridges and sent shivers exploding down her spine. He stroked her thighs and explored every soft curve and valley. He shed his own clothing and joined her on the bed, kissing away her tears as he parted her thighs and moved over her, into her in one smooth motion.

Summer's teeth tore into her lower lip, and her hands pushed feebly against him. He heard the strangled whimpers, and he saw the thick sweep of lashes tremble shut. She twisted her face away, but he twined his fingers into her hair, forcing her to yield to his kisses. Her hands curled into the crisp pelt of hair on his chest, feeling the bands of muscle strain with each unhurried stroke. She could feel the tension building within her again. She could feel the awesome, stretching power of him bringing something to life inside of her, and she knew it was going to happen again . . . soon . . . now . . . !

Her mouth fell open, and her chest heaved for a last breath. Her fingers splayed wide, slipping on the dampness of his skin a moment before they held, and then she was rising against him. She was writhing this way and that; she was wrapping her arms around him, wrapping her long legs around him and surging up to meet him with her entire body.

Pleasure furrowed through her in agonizingly slow waves. Again and again she was inundated, robbed of sight and sound, driven by a need to arch higher, to have him push deeper, to have the shivering ecstasy go on and on and on. . . .

She held him and cried out to him, and when it was

over, she continued to cling to him out of fear—fear now that he would let go. Wade's own violent completion ended on a groan. His grip eased, but he remained locked to her until he felt the shocked exhaustion seep into her limbs. With a gentleness he could not have explained, he brushed the damp wisps of hair back from her temples, touching his lips to the residue of tears that lingered on her lashes.

Her eyes trembled open, condemning him wordlessly as he raised himself from between the soft thighs. Her chin quivered, and she averted her head so that she would not have to see the mockery in the dark blue eyes.

Wade observed the tightness around her mouth—a mouth still pink and invitingly moist from his kisses. His gaze strayed to her breasts, rounded and smooth, to the marble whiteness of her belly and thighs. She was hardly more than a child herself—eighteen? Nineteen? And next to his coarse and weathered body she seemed almost too fragile to handle him. Yet there was nothing childlike or fragile in her responses. It was a woman who clawed and arched to him. A woman who cried out and moved instinctively to heighten her own pleasure . . . and his.

He smiled and felt the instant resistance as he slid one arm beneath her shoulders, one around her waist, and pulled her into the curve of his body.

"What are you doing?" she gasped. "You can't possibly—!"

"I'm going to get some sleep, Governess. And so help me, if you keep me from it, your lovely white backside will be a latticework of switch marks."

Summer held her breath, tensed against the heat of him as he settled into a comfortable position. She was thoroughly pinned within the circle of his arms and could break free only with a major struggle. Her cheek was cradled by his shoulder. She could feel his breath light and feathery on her brow . . . but . . . he was surely not serious in thinking she would sleep with him like this for the rest of the night! Not the entire night!

"Captain Wade, I must insist—"

"Blood red switch marks, madam," he interrupted drowsily. "Dozens upon dozens of them."

6

THE TRIP to Bounty Key took five more days. Summer tried every tactic she knew to avoid Captain Morgan Wade, or at the least to discourage him from seeking her company: silence, anger, insults. The latter tread so near to the edge of his temper she soon considered the risk not worth the brief taste of satisfaction.

In the end he took what he wanted anyway. Regardless of how much she fought him or how hard she pleaded with him, it always ended the same way. Utterly exhausted, she lay curled against his animal warmth and slept the longest, deepest sleeps she ever remembered. Dreamless as well, as if he drained her of even the smallest ability to escape.

She always woke up alone. She never felt him leave the bed, although she always wakened moments after he had done so. Her hand would stray to the warm mattress, and she would shiver herself deeper under the quilt, drifting asleep again instantly yet never quite as soundly.

As she came to anticipate the often-volatile moods of Captain Wade, she also came to know the personality of the *Chimera*. Creaks and sounds and bells became familiar to her. She knew when seas were heavy or calm just by the rhythm of the *Chimera*'s stride. She was by no means an experienced sailor, but even to Summer's untrained sensibilities, Wade's ship was a sleek and powerful beauty.

Where the *Sea Vixen* had balked at heavy seas, the *Chimera* accepted the challenge of them with a toss of its fine head. The *Vixen*'s crew had been silent and morose, always under the watchful, punishing eyes of their officers. Wade's crew, while equally busy, sang ditties and was allowed to gossip and share a pipe while they scrubbed the decks and mended the sails.

They drilled on the cannon every day as well. A particularly urgent clanging of the ship's bell had them mustered and standing at the ready within minutes. On a signal from Morgan Wade, himself stripped to the waist and manning one of the short-snouted carronades, they ran through endless drills of setting, loading, firing, swabbing, practicing with live shot every other time.

Only during those times were Summer and Michael banished from the main and gun decks. Cannon, Wade explained, were like women: temperamental bitches no matter how many precautions were taken. Gunpowder was unstable, the wadding often left the muzzle in a shower of flaming sparks, and occasionally the shot itself exploded moments after being fired.

Summer did not object to the banishment. She cowered in the aftercabin, covering her ears with her hands to block out the roar of gunfire from two decks. She shuddered in sympathy with the *Chimera* after each thunderous volley and began to feel that every muscle and bone in her body creaked with the same degree of relief when it was over.

Other times, such as when the *Chimera* sliced peacefully into the golden glow at sunset, Summer walked the polished decks with reluctant awe. She sensed a freedom of spirit on board, in the ship itself and in the very air she breathed. Her impression of the crew being a surly and misguided lot gave way grudgingly to admiration. They seemed to love the ship and the sea with the same intensity as their captain, and she found herself doubting some of the stories of their ruthlessness and cold-bloodedness with which Michael had frightened her during the first few days.

This was not to say Wade's crew were gentlemanly and conducted themselves with polite deportment at all times. She heard comments filtering down from the rigging whenever she passed beneath. She saw the glances and the open speculation; she saw the eyes move hungrily, lewdly over her body in a way that set her flesh to crawling. It was only Morgan Wade's absolute authority, she knew, that kept her reasonably safe.

As for Michael, he was enthralled. From dawn till dusk he prowled the decks in Thorny's shadow, forever plaguing the crusty old sailor with questions. He was given small tasks to perform. He was shown how to splice and repair rigging, how to properly reef and tie off a sail, then how to climb into the foreyards and set a headsail. His complexion darkened rapidly in the constant sun and fresh air. He lost a great deal of his timorousness and, on the third night out, even dared to ask if he might eat his meal in the crew's mess rather than share the tension of the captain's cabin.

Wade overruled Summer's objection, infuriating her further by sending down a message through a distinctly uncomfortable Mr. Thorntree that he too preferred a change from her stiff-lipped petulance and would be absent until his watch ended at four A.M.

Summer was furious enough to drag a chair to the bookcase, fetch down the key and lock and barricade the cabin door. At four A.M. she was still wide-awake, listening to every sound and footfall. When the right one finally entered the companionway, she held her breath until the door latch abruptly stopped rattling . . . then released it on a cry as the lock splintered and the chair shattered under the tremendous force of a boot.

On the seventh morning at sea, Summer woke, as usual, to the sound of the ship's bell calling the crew to mess. She stretched and yawned, then lay contentedly for a moment watching the play of sunlight reflected on the cabin's beamed ceiling. Her gaze wandered to the desk, to the padded leather chair, to the remains of a cigar tipping out of a tin ash cup . . . to her shirt and trousers lying in a crumple where Wade had tossed them the night before.

The blush prickled up into her cheeks, and she rolled onto her stomach, burying her face in the bunched-up pillow. What he did to her body went beyond mortification. His actions were those of a depraved man. She could only be thankful there would be no scars to show for his vileness, no outward sign that she was changed in any way. She would be even more thankful when and if Bennett Winfield erased all memory of Morgan Wade from her mind and body!

She sat up and swung her legs over the side of the bed. Her hair fell in a tangle over her shoulders, and she pushed it back angrily, casting around for the red silk ribbon that also had been rudely removed. The brigand had actually commanded her to unplait her hair! When she had refused, he had caught her up, had torn the ribbon loose and worked the braid free himself, holding her by two twined fistfuls while his mouth taunted her flesh into submission.

Yes, she would be grateful when it was over. She would be grateful to set foot on solid land again, relieved beyond anything to see the last of Morgan Wade.

The *Chimera* shuddered unexpectedly, throwing Summer off-balance as she was bending down for her clothes. She fell heavily against the side of the bed and gasped as a carved edge of the wood dug into her thigh. The pain was so sudden and so blinding she could do little more than rub frantically at the bruise.

And then she heard it. A grinding, crunching wail of agony coming from somewhere within the bowels of the ship. The hair on the nape of her neck rose in alarm, and the skin along her arms sprang instantly to gooseflesh.

She heard no shots, but her immediate thought was that the *Chimera* was under attack. What else would cause the recurring jolts? What else would produce the continuous rising howl of a beast caught in the steel jaws of a trap?

The ship lurched, and she heard the whining rasp of the anchor cables grinding through the capstan. The forward motion became less pronounced, but raggedly so, ending in a series of shunts as the anchor grabbed for a hold on the bottom.

Summer pulled on her clothes with hands that were ice-cold and fumbled in their haste. She stumbled out the cabin door and ran down the companionway and up the ladder to the deck. She found Michael standing just outside the hatchway, looking pale and fearful as he tried to follow the confusion on the deck.

"What is it?" Summer asked. "What has happened?"

"I don't know. We struck something coming around into the channel. There was an awful crunching noise, and then everything just sort of went berserk."

"Where is Captain Wade?"

Michael shook his head. "Below somewhere. He and Mr. Monday dashed down to see where the trouble was."

"Well, thank God it's nothing serious. You have no idea the things I was imagining. I could have sworn we were under attack." She paused and thought about the absurdity a moment. "You say we hit something?"

"More like we were pushed into it. Thorny said the captain was worried about the currents."

She smiled wryly. "With all of his boasting and bragging about what a fine ship he has and how grown men quake at the very sight of him, he seems to have difficulty just getting from one place to another."

Michael turned and looked at her strangely. "Thorny said the patch we took on at Saint Martin was a poor one. It isn't the captain's fault if it didn't hold."

Summer glared at her brother, shocked to hear him defending the privateer. But he was no longer looking at her. He was staring past her shoulder toward the fore hatchway. Morgan Wade was emerging, his clothes streaming water, his face grim and unreadable. Mr. Monday was a pace behind, and together they thundered along the quarter rail to the bow, barely hesitating long enough to shout a blur of orders before they hurled themselves through the entry port and dove into the sea.

Summer and Michael ran to the rail, joining a handful of jabbering sailors. Both men had already vanished beneath the surface of the water, leaving only a disturbance of spreading rings to mark their entrance. The water was clear for a fathom or more before it gave way to an inky blackness, but the curve of the hull prevented anyone from seeing what was happening. There was no sign of either Wade or his chief mate, and so much time seemed to lapse that Summer's heart began drowning out the sounds of the anxious voices around her. She gripped the rail tightly and curled her lower lip between her teeth, biting down until the flesh was colorless.

She felt Michael clutch her arm, and with a gasp saw

the two strong arms reaching for the surface, followed by the dark head and brawny shoulders. Wade hung in the water for several moments swallowing deep lungfuls of air, then jacknifed under again, passing Mr. Monday.

The pair went up and down several more times before Summer could relax with some degree of certainty that they knew what they were doing. She looked away from the water for the first time and was surprised to see land on either side of the *Chimera*. They were anchored in a channel that divided two small islands similar in shape and appearance and sitting no more than six hundred yards apart. They were jagged cones of rock encircled by dense brush and wide snow white beaches. The descent into the channel was gradual from each shoreline; the water was pale blue for a hundred or so yards of sandbars, then dropped off suddenly to dark bottomless blue.

A burst of water and a roared command drew Summer's attention over the side again. Wade was treading water and shouting at some of the crewmen, who responded at once and threw him a length of thick cable and an iron bar. This time, as he disappeared below, Summer could estimate how deep he went by the amount of rope being pulled after him. Whatever the excitement was about, it was well below the waterline.

She heard more spluttering, but it came from behind her on the deck. Mr. Thorntree was being led coughing and swearing to a seat on one of the gun carriages. Michael forgot Captain Wade at once and ran to Thorny's side, stunned not only by the variety of oaths erupting from the corner of the thin lips but by the quantity of blood spreading across his soaked shirt-sleeve.

"Thorny, what is it? What's happened!"

"Bah! Bluddy patch give way," Thorny said, gulping eagerly from the pannikin of rum thrust into his hands. "Currents 'ere 'r strong, an' them damned Frenchies only 'ad raw timber ter give us—so they said. Like as n'owt the patch tore off comin' 'round the reef. Whatever it is, she's takin' on water like a bluddy sieve."

"Your arm!" Michael cried, watching the mingling blood and water fall in a steady pat—pat—pat on the deck.

"S'nothin, lad," Thorny scowled and peeled back the sleeve. "Cut meself on a splinter, is all."

The wound was jagged and uneven. The hunk of pale oak that had done the damage was still buried in the leathery flesh, raising the skin into a shiny welt from the pressure. Thorny cussed voraciously and grasped the end of the splinter between thumb and forefinger, prying it free. It was three inches long and shaped like a wedge, and the hole it left behind filled instantly with bright red blood, which overflowed and poured down his wrist and hand in a thick stream.

Summer fought the instinct to gag as she pushed Michael out of the way. One of the crew had already stepped in to take charge, tearing off the neckerchief he wore and using it as a tourniquet to tie off the supply of blood to Thorny's arm. A second and third bandanna went around the wound itself, soaking red as they sealed the horrible gaping hole from sight.

Thorny looked paler for the experience. His tongue was thrust into his cheek, and his jaw twitched spastically as more bandages and rum were called for. Summer stared at the blood on the deck, at the blood on the clawed hand, at the splatters staining the clothes of the man bending over to help.

"Come away, Michael," she murmured. "He's all right. He's being looked after."

Michael swallowed hard and nodded. They moved away just as Morgan Wade swung himself up and over the bulwark. He was shedding water like a sheepdog; his hair was smeared over his face, his shirt was transparent where it clung to his chest like a thin, wrinkled layer of skin.

He ran a hand through his hair, pushing it back with an angry impatience. "Thorny? What the bloody hell have you done to yourself?"

"Bah! N'owt but a nick, Cap'n."

"A nick, eh?" He glanced at the hatch. "Have we men on the pumps?"

"Aye. Bailin' lines as well. She's fillin' fast, though."

"I don't wonder. She's got a piece of the reef in her

timbers. Monday and I are trying to get it out, but it may take a while. Are you sure you're all right?"

"Aye, Cap'n, fine. Fine. No call ter stand 'ere gawkin' on me—get on with yer business."

Wade's scowl eased. The blue eyes scanned the crew a moment. "Hawkins . . . Willard . . . we'll need your backs below. Mr. Phillips—"

A youngish-looking man stepped forward. He was of medium height and slight build, and his expression was as earnest as his reply.

"Aye, sir!"

"You'll take the deck watch to make sure we don't bring in more water than we can handle. Put everyone to bailing if you must, but see that she's kept from dropping too low."

"Aye, sir."

"And get some men started on a patch we can shore up from the inside. Tear up a section of decking if you have to, but I want a strong patch."

"Aye, sir!"

"And Mr. Phillips—I'll want two gigs in the water, one at each end of this blasted channel. Tell them to keep a sharp eye out for company. I've no taste to be caught sitting here like a lame duck."

The young man blinked. "Aye, sir."

"And when you've got the pumping under control, I want every able hand down in the cargo hold. We're going to have to off-load the lot of it to keep her nose above the waterline."

Thorny peered up. "Eh? Ye're not aimin' ter chuck it in the drink, are ye, Cap'n? We be only six 'our from the Key, give 'r take. Why n'owt unload 'er on shore an' come back fer it later? Won't take any longer ter do, an' the lads might feel better fer it."

Wade glanced over, quelling his impatience at the sight of Thorny's pale face.

"If'n it's still 'ere, we win. If'n it's gone, we lose, but leastwise we hain't t'rowin it away."

Wade consulted the expressions on the faces of his men. "Aye, you're right. No sense drowning good profits. I'll leave you in charge, then, if you're up to it."

"Up ter it?" Thorny beamed and straightened at once. "Ye'll 'ave 'er weight gone in a twink."

"You just make sure you get that arm tended to first."

"Bah! N'owt but a—"

"Thorny!"

"Aye, Cap'n, aye. Stitch 'er meself if'n I 'ave ter."

Wade's smile had not faded completely when he started back to the side of the ship. He saw Summer and Michael out of the corner of his eye and grunted in passing, "If you're going to stay up top, make sure you are in no one's way."

"Are we going to sink?" Michael asked.

"Not if I can help it, lad."

"But are we in danger?"

Wade halted. "Can you swim?"

"Yes, of course—"

"Then you're not in danger," said Wade, indicating either side of the ship. "You've a choice of two islands to swim for."

He continued to the open gangway, peeling his shirt up and over his shoulders as he walked. He tugged the wide belt from around his waist and unlooped the thong holding his breeches. Summer caught a glimpse of taut buttocks and sinewed thighs before he was arching over the side into the water.

Michael stood at the rail again to watch, but Summer was gazing thoughtfully at the conical island off the port side. It could be done. They were both strong swimmers— the day and night spent in the stormy ocean proved as much. The distance from the ship to the first sandbar was no more than three hundred yards.

"Michael?"

"Mmm?"

"What do you suppose"—she lowered her voice, conscious of the sailors milling past them—"we would find on those islands?"

"Nothing, most probably. They certainly don't look big enough to have people . . . or much of anything."

"What about food and water? Do you think two people could manage to survive until another ship came along?"

Michael frowned up at her. "I think you're potty. It

could take weeks or months for another ship to come along. And even if it did, how could you signal it? How do you know it wouldn't be full of Frenchies? How do you know we wouldn't starve to death long before anyone found us?"

"Are you saying you'd rather stay on board this ship? You *want* to be held for ransom? You *want* to be the cause of holding Father up to ridicule and disgrace?"

"No, of course not," Michael said, flushing beneath his tan. "But at the same time I rather like knowing I'm going to eat and drink and be warm at night. We know Captain Wade has no intention of killing us—how can you know another captain will feel the same?"

"I don't, but at least we would be free."

"Free to do what? Count sea gulls?"

"Michael—"

"Summer," he said and puckered his brow, "we aren't being treated like beggars. We haven't been beaten or flogged or locked in chains. I know you don't like the captain, but he is being rather decent about the whole thing."

"Decent!" Summer had to bite her lip to keep from blurting out exactly how decent Wade was. "You're acting as if you admire that privateer and as if you hope he succeeds in getting his wretched ship safely to port. What happened to the spy who was out to learn everything he could to help Father catch the man?"

"He's still learning," Michael said stubbornly. "But he can't tell anyone anything if he pines away of thirst on a deserted island!"

Summer sighed in exasperation. Possibly—just possibly —he was right. They might be trading in one horror for another. Starvation, thirst, madness: They were all quite possible.

"Right!"

Summer jumped as a strong hand clamped down on her shoulder.

"The two o' ye come an' lend an 'and 'ere," Thorny said. "Ye're both fit ter fetch an' carry. We've an 'old full o' cargo what needs shiftin'. Lad, ye get on the ropes 'ere an' steady the crates as they come up over the side o' the bay.

Lass—ye can start with a couple o' lanterns an' move 'em where the boys needs light ter see. Let's move sharp now. Quicker we lighten 'er belly, quicker we 'elp the cap'n."

Summer had a lantern and a coil of rope thrust into her hands. She was hustled forward through the cargo hatch, down two steep flights of ladders, until she reached the lower deck. She was told by a series of grunts what to do, where to stand, and where to throw more light. All around her were the sweating, straining bodies of the crewmen, most of them half-naked in the moist, stale heat of the hold. Boxes and crates were handed up as fast as hands could stack them into nets and haul them topside. Everyone had to shout to be heard, and the hold reverberated with the sounds, increasing in volume until they were an unbroken din.

Some of the remarks were directed at Summer and had nothing to do with her duties. Several times she was jostled and various parts of her body were brushed against by design. She had to grind her teeth together and endure the grinning faces; to do anything less would have been a victory for them and a dismal loss of dignity for her. She guessed that they knew what went on in the captain's cabin nightly. No doubt it had happened countless times before and would happen countless times again with other women. She would show them, though. She would prove to them she was different. She was not broken or dispirited, and she was certainly not about to wither under a handful of bullying louts if she could help it.

By late afternoon her determination to work just as hard and just as long won grudging smiles of approval. The jeers stopped, the accidental brushings stopped, and she was even referred to as ma'am and miss instead of just you. Their work had produced results also. A vast area of the cargo bay was cleared, and most of the men were shifted to the upper deck to help load and row the longboats to shore. Summer began to hope for a reprieve, but there was no sign of Thorny's grizzled head poking into the hatchway to call her. Her arms ached from holding the lantern, her feet were cold and waterlogged from the dampness, and her stomach was beginning to rebel from hunger.

At last there were only the huge rum casks left to roll onto the nets and hoist above. Summer was only half-heartedly watching the two men whose job it was to maneuver the casks into position, when she felt an arm snake around her waist and a hand cover her muffled cry of surprise. She was lifted off her feet and dragged backward to a dark section of the deck, well out of sight and earshot of the hold.

She twisted and fought against the grip at her waist, striking out with her arms and legs to try to kick and scratch her way free. The hand covering her mouth was choking her. She heard several grunts as she was repositioned and a healthy curse as her nails raked deeply into the soft flesh of a cheek.

A scream managed to break through the smothering fingers, but it was cut off before the echo had a chance to bounce off the walls. She was dumped flat onto a pile of empty sacks and rolled onto her back while her captor positioned himself above her.

"Captain's supposed to share all the profits," a voice rasped. "He's supposed to share the prizes equal. I hear tell you been givin' it to the old man every night . . . the nigra too. Don't matter none to me, long as I get what's comin'."

Summer moaned as the pressure on her mouth increased. She lunged to one side as a hand was thrust roughly between her thighs and began kneading her through the coarse fabric. She could not see the face of her attacker. He was nothing but a series of hot pantings and clumsy fumblings.

He slapped away her hands when she attempted to gouge for his eyes. He slapped at her legs when she kicked him, and she felt the nails of one of his hands dig cruelly into her flesh as he groped beneath her shirt.

"Ain't this sweet," he murmured. "Ain't this just the sweetest . . ."

He laughed huskily and groped to unfasten her trousers.

"Open up, ya bitch. Open up, I'm tellin' you, or it's gonna come worse for you . . . *Ahhhh!*"

Summer felt the crushing satisfaction as her knee

landed squarely against his groin. The pressure on her mouth was released instantly as the sailor clutched himself and rolled to one side. Summer scrambled to her feet and ran sobbing from the storeroom, practically bowling Michael over as he sauntered down the companionway.

"There you are. Thorny sent me to fetch you . . . Summer?" His jaw dropped and his eyes widened.

"I'm getting off this ship!" she cried. "I'm getting off it here and now, and if you don't want to come with me, that's fine, but I won't stay on board another minute."

"What happened! There's blood all over your cheek!"

"Just a friendly attempt," Summer hissed, "by your fine captain's crewmate to become a little friendlier."

Michael gasped. "Did he hurt you? Who was it? I shall tell the captain, and he—"

"No!" Summer cried, and tears filled her eyes. "No, Michael. The captain won't do a blessed thing. Do you honestly think he'd take the side of one of us against one of his own men?"

"But he would have to believe you."

"Michael," Summer grasped his shoulders, "are you coming with me or not?"

His face twisted with indecision. "Yes," he whispered, "yes, of course I'm coming with you. But we have to hurry. The cargo is all transferred, and they're getting ready to try to sail out of this beastly channel."

"Quickly then," she urged and took his hand. "Is there a gangway off one of the lower decks somewhere?"

"Off the gun deck," he murmured, frightened almost as much by the unnatural brightness in her eyes as by the prospect of stepping into the ocean again.

"Do you think you can make the swim?" she asked, knowing the reason for his fear. "The water is calm, and it's only a couple of hundred yards. I'll be right there to help you."

"I can make it," he said determinedly. He led the way along the narrow passage and up the ladder to the gun deck. They both paused at the top of the hatch, staring at the double row of long guns that made up the *Chimera*'s main battery. Each monster was eight feet long and was capable of hurling twenty-four pounds of solid iron more than a thousand yards with deadly precision, further if the gunners counted on luck. Here the planking in the outer hull was four feet thick, the air reeked of iron and old gunpowder, and the deck underfoot, although scrubbed regularly with soapstones and varnished often, bore the dark stains of past battles.

"There," Michael whispered, pointing to a wooden hatch. It was raised by means of a pulley and opened onto a railed platform that jutted out from the *Chimera*'s side. Beneath it, running all the way to the waterline, were wood slats which formed the rungs of the gangway ladder.

The water directly below them was dark blue and slapped gently against the hull of the ship. Further out it became silvery as the last glare from the sun reflected off its surface. With any luck at all, anyone glancing off the side would not be able to distinguish two extra bobbing dots from the dark caps of the waves.

"Let's go," she murmured and stepped out onto the platform. It would have been an easy dive of fifteen feet, but the noise would have drawn attention. Summer used the rungs, pausing to guide Michael's feet after her, and in a few moments felt the cold water of the channel swallow her feet, her knees, her thighs, her shoulders.

She waited for Michael to adjust to the shock and kicked off strongly from the side. They were dwarfed beside the huge frigate, and for the first time Summer felt a pang of doubt as to the wisdom of what she was doing. She pushed it resolutely to the back of her mind, needing only to think of the sailor in the storeroom to bolster her courage.

Fifty yards out they were in a direct line with the blazing glare of the sun as it dipped toward the horizon. Summer dared not look back. She forced herself to stroke slowly and cleanly, to listen to Michael and gauge her speed to his. She stopped now and then to tread water, waiting for her brother to catch up. He seemed to be struggling after only a third of the way, and she realized he must have been working hard on the deck all day long to prove his manliness to Wade's crew. He was gasping as he churned the water laboriously beside her, obviously straining to keep abreast.

"Are you all right?" she asked. "Are you feeling any cramps?"

"No," he gasped and coughed out a mouthful of seawater. "No, I can make it."

"We'll go slower. We'll stop every ten strokes, okay?"

"Yes," he coughed, "ten."

She reached out again, watching Michael closely as he desperately kicked after her. She had not gone even five strokes when she heard him gag and shrill her name . . . and at the same time she heard a loud, continuous clanging of the *Chimera*'s alarm bell mustering the crew to gun stations.

7

CAPTAIN MORGAN WADE was disgusted. At himself, at the leak in the hull, at the sun for dropping faster in the sky than it normally did. He would have liked another twelve hours to complete the temporary repair on his ship, but he could not risk it. Not when the only warning of danger would be seeing the sails of an enemy ship slide around the tip of one of the islands. He had recalled the men in the dinghies. The last of the cargo was ashore and camouflaged; the winch was manned and ready to haul the anchor aboard.

He would have to limp as best he could to Bounty Key and pray not to meet with any hostile vessels in the next six hours. He had the darkness, and that was good. The *Chimera* would respond. Sluggishly to be sure, but she would respond. The leaking was under control, and the pumps were keeping a steady level of water. All he needed was six unmolested hours.

He glared down at his scratched and bleeding hands. He and Mr. Monday had pried and torn at the ravaged copper sheathing to bare the timbers and find what was causing the leak. A large chunk of coral had slashed into the *Chimera*'s hull when they had been blown up against a reef during the storm. The Frenchmen who had assisted them at Saint Martin had supplied them with inferior materials—deliberately, he wondered?—and it had given with the strong currents leading to the mouth of the channel.

Wade's frown smoothed suddenly when he saw Thorny emerge from the shadows of the crew's quarters. The arm must have been a brand of fire all day, judging by the way it was cradled against the old sailor's ribs, but it would be a cold day in hell indeed before he would complain.

"Well?"

"Cain't find 'em. Lad wanted ter show yer 'ow good ee is at setting the fore's, but I cain't find 'im nowhere. Looked fore. Looked aft. Even looked down the 'oles in the beak'eads case they fell in, but there ain't no sign o' them. N'owt less'n ye count this."

He held out a long, thin length of red silk ribbon. Wade stared at it, and his hands tensed on the deck rail. "Where did you find it?"

"One o' the men give it ter me. Ee found it in a storeroom for'ard o' the 'old where she was 'elpin out."

"Who else was down there?" Wade asked, his eyes narrowing to blue slits.

"Tim-boy, Pow'll . . . the new man, Beavis. First two seen 'er by the step one minute, gone the next."

"And Beavis?"

Thorny thrust out his jaw. "Sent two o' the lads ter fetch 'im. Aye, 'ere they come . . . jaysus."

Morgan Wade's face blackened like a gathering storm cloud. The man, Beavis, was struggling as he was led by two of his mates up the quarterdeck toward the bridge. He had signed on a month ago in Aruba and was not one of the regular crew. He saw the captain and his jaw sagged; a jaw covered with spidery runnels of fresh scratch marks. Wade noted them, noted the shifty, darting eyes, and his voice came out low and ominous.

"Where is she?"

The man licked his lips. "I dunno what you're talkin' about. Where's who?"

Wade advanced on him, flexing his hands into fists. "I am not a patient man, Beavis, and I rarely ask the same question twice."

The two men holding Beavis tightened their grips as he snarled and jerked back.

"I ain't done nothin' wrong! Ain't done nothin' nobody else ain't wanted to do since she come on board. The bitch was askin' for it, I tell you. She was waggin' it all around the hold, and—"

Wade's fist smashed into the undefended jaw, snapping the burly head backward. He felt and heard the crunch as several teeth broke.

"Where is she?"

"I didn't do nothin'! I swear I didn't do nothin'!" Blood and bits of teeth spluttered onto the man's chin. "She wanted me to, begged me to, but I know'd you wouldn't like it so—"

Wade swung again, this time burying his fist in the man's belly. Beavis doubled in two, meeting Wade's knee squarely as it crushed his nose into bleeding pulp. He screamed and tried to wrench away, but Wade's next blow—a cutting right to the man's jaw—knocked him nearly senseless.

"Mr. Thorntree!"

"Aye, Cap'n?"

"Put this man in the shrouds. Spread-eagled and stripped the way Mr. Monday likes them. We'll start him off with fifty lashes to see if it loosens his tongue."

"Aye, Cap'n," Thorny nodded grimly and signaled to the men holding Beavis. The order was interrupted, however, by an urgent shout from high up on the mizzenmast.

"Sails, Captain!"

Wade's dark head jerked up. The lookout was thrusting a knotted fist to the eastern exit of the channel. There, seen only as a ghost of an outline in the eerie light, were the sails of an approaching ship.

Thorny was by Wade's side in a flash. "Who the 'ell might that be, d'ye suppose?"

Wade called for a spyglass and mounted the bridge.

"D'ye t'ink she's seen us?"

"She's seen us," Wade snarled, holding the glass to his eye. "We're standing on the horizon like a bloody silhouette."

"Colors?"

"None yet."

"How far?" Mr. Monday asked, joining Wade on the bridge.

"An hour. Less if she has the wind." The blue eyes glittered, and he sucked in a deep breath. "And by God she does. She's running up more sail! Sound the alarm. I want the decks cleared and the crew standing by. I don't know who she is, but I have no intention of inviting her aboard."

"Aye, Cap-tan. Shot?"

"Double and round, but wait until we see how she blows before you give the order to load."

"Aye."

"Mr. Phillips!"

The second mate stepped forward eagerly. "Sir?"

"I want every scrap of canvas on that she'll hold. And get that deck cleared . . . *now!*"

"Aye, sir!"

"Oh, me bluddy sweet jaysus," Thorny muttered.

"What is it?" Wade demanded, his voice rising over the sound of the insistent, clanging bell.

Thorny lowered the spyglass. "In the drink, Cap'n. Over yon. Two o' them—the lass an' the lad."

"What!" Wade followed Thorny's outstretched finger and did not need the spyglass to see the two bobbing heads, one surrounded by a halo of yellow hair. "By all that's holy—"

He raised the glass and swung to mark the progress of the approaching ship.

"A boat, Cap'n?"

"There's no time!"

Thorny's eyes bulged from their sockets. "Ye ain't just goin' ter leave 'em in there, are ye, Cap'n? The currents—"

"Mr. Phillips!" Wade shouted furiously. "Get this ship under way!"

He flung the glass into Thorny's hands and vaulted over the bulwark, landing catlike on the deck below. He ran for the rail, cleared it, and plunged into the channel water, breaking into a powerful front crawl before he was fully afloat. Ahead of him he saw the girl struggling to keep Michael's head above the rippling water. Another two, three yards and they would be in the rip current, an incredibly strong undertow that divided the two sandbars. She was in trouble even now. The boy was panicking and thrashing his arms and legs in all directions. The water was swirling over her head, and she was being blinded and choked by her own hair.

Wade reached the two of them just as Summer's arm slipped from Michael's shoulders. Her mouth filled with water, and she was sucked under by the current, her head reeling from a blow from Michael's fists. Wade had to dive to catch her. He hooked an arm around her waist and hauled her back to the surface against the tremendous pull of the water. He draped her ice-cold hands and arms over his shoulders and tilted her head upward so that she could cough the water out of her mouth.

"Hold on to me! Do you hear me, dammit? Hold on to me or I'll have to leave you here!"

The gray eyes fluttered open and focused on Wade's face.

"You're going to have to hold on to me," he repeated urgently. "Can you do it? Can you tighten your arms around me?"

She coughed and nodded, and her arms quivered feebly as she leaned on his shoulder. He started kicking back for the *Chimera*, with Michael supported by one arm and Summer clinging to his back. He had covered only a few yards when the gleaming black head of Mr. Monday appeared by his side, and the chief mate took hold of Michael.

Half-a-dozen helpful hands were waiting to take Michael and Summer up on deck. Wade came up the rope ladder a pace behind them, his great body shaking off the water as he shouted orders to the crew. The *Chimera* was beginning to glide forward as the first of her sails filled in the erratic breeze.

"Steerage, Mr. Phillips! Hold that rudder fast! Get those bloody sails rigged or we'll be up to our throats in coral! Thorny—take these two down below and lock them in a forward storeroom. See they stay put if you have to tie them hand and foot!"

"Aye, Cap'n!"

Mr. Phillips lowered the spyglass as Wade mounted the bridge. "She's a second rating, sir. Fifty-two guns if she's a one. Full-rigged for speed and coming on us fast."

"Colors?"

"She's showing the Union Jack, sir."

"The *Northgate?*" Wade blinked the salt water out of his eyes and swept the horizon with the spyglass. "It would have to be. She's the only fifty-two-gun in the area."

"But the *Northgate* is a warship, Captain. Her commander has no grounds to attack us."

"Care to tell him that, Mr. Phillips?" Wade murmured dryly.

The young second mate looked out past the channel again. "He won't have the light much longer, sir. What do you suppose he is after?"

Wade lowered the glass. "He's coming straight on, so he's not shy."

"He's going to come through the reef?" Phillips's eyes widened. "At night?"

"The British Navy is plagued with fools, Mr. Phillips. They don't consider a chase sporting unless they fly it by the skin of their backsides."

"Yes, sir. Shall we take evasive action, sir?"

Morgan was studying the warship. It was coming on with amazing speed while the *Chimera* was barely moving. "There is nothing we can do until we clear this blasted channel. On the other hand, he has a choice: He can try for the strait and use his speed to catch us, or he can—*by Christ!*" The spyglass shot up again. "He's tacking for position! The bastard is going to lay a broadside on us and hope to take us where we stand. *Monday!*"

He did not wait for a response. He leaped down the ladderway and headed for the stern, noting as he went that his men were standing anxiously silent by the cannon. Thorny darted out from the afterhatch in his crablike step and followed a few paces behind the captain.

"He'll aim high," Wade shouted for the benefit of his men. "He'll be going for the sails and rigging. Monday—how do we stand?"

"Crew is ready, Cap-tan, but we doan' have position. We got t'ree, maybe four gun we can use."

"Damn," Wade muttered and stood at the rail. His hands grasped the polished oak, and his eyes blazed furiously as he watched the British frigate pull sharply to port. There was nothing he could do. The islands sliced the wind currents to pieces, and even with every sail furled, the *Chimera* was laboring to maintain a slow drag. There was not enough leeway to maneuver. The four swivel guns he had mounted on the stern rails were six-pounders and not worth a bucket of spit at this distance. He had no option but to hold steady and pray the techniques of the British Navy had not changed over the past dozen years.

"Here it comes, lads," he said quietly, seeing that the frigate had completed her turn. A score of tiny white puffs of smoke blossomed from her gunports, followed seconds later by a staccato of deep bellowing booms. Wade barely flinched as the shots whistled by. He heard one tear through the upper royals, but for the most part they fell harmlessly into the water, sending up fountains of spray.

"The bluddy fool done it," Thorny gasped. "Ee opened fire!"

"Aye, and he has a feel for the range now," Wade reasoned. "This next round will be hotter. He'll have to make it count before he swings too far astern . . . *damn!*"

Another eruption of smoke poured through the gunports, and this time the *Northgate* fired from both decks. Wade braced himself instinctively as the spouts of water shot up all around the hull of the *Chimera,* dumping spray onto her decks. He heard a terrible screech and cracking of timbers and several more hot whistles as the iron shot tore through the sails.

Wade glanced to either side of the *Chimera*. There were fifty yards or more to go before he could order a reply. They were through the channel, but there was still the outlying reef to juggle past . . . just a little more speed . . . a little more wind . . .

"Mr. Monday, have every gun on the starboard side ready when we take the turn. Double shot them. You'll have ten seconds, no more, to let loose a clear volley."

"Ten is good, Cap-tan." His chief mate grinned. "Damn good."

The thunder of the *Northgate*'s third volley ripped across the *Chimera*'s stern, setting the masts, the rails, the decks underfoot to quaking. There were screams now and a call to tend the fires that were starting from the burning shreds of canvas that floated down over the deck. A crewman lost his footing on the mainsail yard as the lower spar was shot out from under him. For one sickening moment he appeared bound for a crushing blow up against the spiked mast, but he fumbled free and managed to fling his arms around a taut line.

Wade's face remained impassive.

Then the *Chimera* was free of the reef. Mr. Phillips tore at the wheel, spinning it to bring the rudder sharp about. She seemed to skid sideways for an eternity before the sails filled to their limit and sent her leaping forward. The eternity was no more than the ten promised seconds, however, and on a signal from Captain Wade, the *Chimera*'s cannon roared a murderous retort to the *Northgate*. The nineteen starboard guns blasted almost simultaneously before Wade's arm had completed the arc. The frigate rocked with the recoil, and the air filled with hot, boiling clouds of acrid smoke and sparks.

As soon as the shots cleared the muzzles, the cannon were pulled in, swabbed and reloaded, but the island winds had boosted the *Chimera*'s speed, and the land mass moved swiftly to block off their target. The last glimpse of the *Northgate* was relayed by a man high on the mizzenmast and brought a resounding cheer from the rest of the crew. He reported crushed sail and a blown mast with at least five direct hits on the deck of the British ship.

Wade heard his men cheering, yet his face remained grim. His ship was damaged, and he now had wounded men on board. The crew would no doubt plead with him to swing about and chase the *Northgate* to continue the fight, but he knew another hour would put them in total darkness. His men had heart, and his ship had heart, but by God, they hadn't come this far to throw everything away on a fool's ploy.

"Crowd on everything we have, Mr. Phillips," he ordered. "Get us out of here."

"Aye, sir."

"Thorny—damage?"

It was not nearly as devastating as it could have been. The sails could be repaired, so, too, the length of rail that had been blown away. The torn rigging and damaged spars would hold until they made Bounty Key. Seven men were badly injured, and many more had suffered minor burns from the fires. The main wounds were to the men's pride. The faces of the crew all bore the same expression:

They were raw and chafed by the humiliation of being caught so easily. The British warship had wasted no time in pressing its advantage, and the outrage left a bitter taste in every man's mouth.

"Mite too close fer comfort, wouldn't ye say, Cap'n?"

"Just a mite, Thorny. Just a mite."

"T'ink ee'll be blamed fool enough ter foller us?"

If the British commander is suicidal, Wade thought, yes. It would take several hours to turn the heavy ship and be in position for the run at the channel. There was no moon, and unless the captain knew these waters, he was asking for an obliterated keel.

"I doubt it, Thorny. Not this far into darkness."

"Bah! Prigs, the lot o' them. 'Ere, ye'd best let me 'ave a look-see at that cut, sar, afore ye bleed all over the deck."

"What?" Wade glanced down. He had not felt anything, but there was a quantity of blood on his shirt below his ribs. He lifted the wet cambric and saw a shallow graze where a flying splinter or piece of iron had found him. "I'll be damned."

Thorny chuckled. "Aye, that ye will, Cap'n. An' ye'll 'ave the lot o' us along fer comp'ny."

Wade grinned briefly, then turned his thoughts to the *Chimera*.

8

STUART ROARKE jammed his hands deeper into the pockets of his thin jacket and started pacing the crest of the hill for the hundredth time. This made the sixth night in a row he had paced, the tenth night of constant twenty-four-hour watches, the thirteenth night since he had begun to consider Morgan Wade overdue. It was not the first such vigil and by no means the longest. It certainly provided fodder for the imagination, though. Whole scenarios played themselves out in Roarke's mind, from simple mutinies to full-scale tricountry wars—with Morgan blasting and roaring away in the middle of everything.

He stopped at the highest observation point and adjusted his round wire-rimmed spectacles.

He should have gone with Morgan this trip. It was the first he'd missed in over two years, and during the past six nights of pacing, he repeatedly vowed he would never do it again. The wound in his thigh would have healed as quickly at sea as it had on land—more quickly, he was sure, for he would have had other things to occupy his mind.

Roarke's soft brown eyes moved slowly over the oyster-colored sea, and he cursed the poor visibility. The moonless night had cloaked Bounty Key under fine clouds and shifting mists. The breeze was steady but light, making any approach to the key a tedious one. Dawn was striving to push over the horizon, and the chill of the long night had seeped right through Roarke's clothes and dampened his skin as well as his spirits.

He saw an arc of lantern light lift and settle on the

opposite crest of the crater. A second arc appeared on his side, a third from the point completing the triangular watch. Every direction was covered. On a signal there could be thirty men in boats ready to tow the *Chimera* into the cove. On a signal he could have the huts emptied and a hundred men manning the island's hidden defenses. On a signal he could put the *Vigilant* out to sea and scour the direction Wade would be coming from—but he knew many more days would have to pass before he could justify that. For now he could only wait.

He debated lighting the pipe he carried in his pocket to help him relax, to help him while away a few more minutes. But his tongue was already coated with a bitter fuzz from the countless times he had done so to no effect. The palms of his hands were clammy. His stomach churned like a small volcano, and if something did not happen soon, he feared he would explode.

All he had been doing for the past month was waiting. Morgan had insisted he miss this trip, had insisted he take it easy until the last of the infection worked its way out of the saber cut on his thigh. Roarke's hand dropped to it now, and he scratched at the numb weal of scar tissue, cursing Wade's assurances that it was to be only a quick run to Antigua and back for the shipment of French guns. British revenue patrols were lighter than usual, the Spanish privateers were asleep, and the Portuguese were off chasing a Dutchman near Barranquilla. It was to have been a quick trip with little risk and no chance of a confrontation along the way.

So why was he thirteen days overdue?

Roarke's wife, Bettina, had been overdue as well. A full three weeks by her reckoning, and that was another reason Morgan had ordered Roarke to remain behind. Not that he had been much help to his wife when the time came. He had suffered every pain with Bett, every choked scream had had an echo in his own throat . . . but he and his wife had a son; a healthy, bright-eyed son born on the eve Morgan should have sailed into port.

Roarke looked up suddenly as the low, trembling echo of a conch shell quivered across the hollow silence. It was coming from the first-position watch, from the leeward side of the key. Roarke was running before the sound had completely died, back along the pathway, tearing the scrub and brush aside as he skidded and scrabbled down the quarter-mile descent to the cove.

He hit the beach, and his arms and legs pumped in a blur. He swerved past the iron bell and gave the pulley three hard jerks, then was off again, circling around the seemingly endless curve of the lagoon and up into the gap in the bordering palms where the path was. The grade was as steep as the one he had just descended, and his injured leg began to cramp on him less than half way up. He was too exhilarated to care. The *Chimera* was sighted. Wade was back, and . . .

He heard pounding footsteps ahead of him in the gloom. The watches stood in pairs, and one of the men was on the way down on a collision course with Stuart Roarke.

"Hold up there, man; what is it?" Roarke gasped and grabbed the man's arm. "Isn't it the *Chimera?*"

"It's the *Chimera,* sir, but she's in trouble. She's listing to port and carrying damage in her yards. The flags are up for a tow."

"Damage—" Roarke repeated the word to himself. He shook away the images that crowded into his brain and released the man's arm. "Right then, off you go. Muster all the longboats and . . . and make ready for any casualties they might be bringing in. Have them seen to first. I'll want a full crew standing by to relieve Captain Wade's men."

"Aye, sir."

Roarke spurred himself up the steep path. At the top he shouted for the watch and sprinted toward the answering hail.

"There she is, sir," the watch said, pointing straight out.

Roarke removed his spectacles and lifted the telescoping spyglass, bringing it to bear on the gently swaying shadow that moved toward them through the mists. It was the *Chimera,* all right, and she was coming in under half sail. He could see signs of activity on her decks; canvas was being reefed, the mooring cables were being hoisted from below and being secured for the coming tow. He followed the lights milling about on deck—men with lanterns meant wounded were being brought topside.

Roarke blinked the chill out of his eyes and trained the glass higher up, examining each of the three masts to their peaks. He could see charred, hanging bits of canvas and at least two gaps where spars and rigging should have been. He traced her hull from bowsprit to stern, hesitating over a missing length of deck rail and one large pockmark where a shot had glanced off her timbers. There were lights coming from the stern gallery, and he hoped—he uttered a silent prayer—that he would find Wade on deck and not prostrate in the berth of the aftercabin.

Roarke handed the glass to the silent watch. He replaced his spectacles on the bridge of his nose, his movements precise and calculated to buy a few moments of thought as he tucked each wire arm just so behind his ears.

"I'll be below, Loftus," he said. "Signal when she's within range."

"Aye, sir."

Roarke turned and swiftly retraced the route to the beach. Men were scurrying about carrying torches and setting up lanterns along the jetty. The six biggest longboats were dragged down off the sand and launched by men who wore bleak, reflective expressions. Oars were loaded and slotted into their locks. Ropes, cables, bitts were fitted in beside the men in anticipation of any difficulties the *Chimera* might have.

Roarke hailed the longboat closest to him and climbed aboard. He heard the conch moan from the peak of the crater, and he took a steadying breath before he nodded for the oarsmen to go.

Summer's first glimpse of Bounty Key was a distorted one. It was a dark blot against a dawn sky seen through the fractured surface of the diamond-paned gallery windows. She guessed it to be their destination by the way the *Chimera* was riding in the water: slow and easy, sidling up to the island as she would to an old friend.

Summer had not seen or heard from Morgan Wade since

he had ordered them locked in a stuffy, airless storeroom deep down in the ship's belly. When the terrible barrage of cannon fire had abated, she and Michael had been taken back to the captain's cabin, but there again they had been locked inside with no word of explanation. Summer had tried the door and found it blocked and guarded from the outside. The man would not answer any of her questions, would not tell her what had happened. He simply glared at her as if she had personally invited the British warship to attack.

Wade had every right to be angry with her, she conceded. He probably could have made it through the channel and eluded the other ship without exchanging a single shot had he not taken the time to swim out to save Michael and herself. She had been selfish and unthinking to risk Michael's life in a reckless attempt to escape. She should have been able to foresee his panic. He was so determined at times to present himself as a young adult, she kept forgetting he was only a boy. A child. Thorny's vivid explanation of what the rip currents would have done to them had left her shaken and badly frightened. If not for Morgan Wade, both she and Michael would have been torn apart.

She looked at her brother now, huddled beneath the quilts on the captain's bed, and her heart missed a beat. His eyes were squeezed shut as if he did not want to wake up. His body was curled into a ball; his hands were clasped into fists. She knew she would not fight any longer. She would stop fighting everything and everyone. She would scrub Wade's decks on her hands and knees if he ordered it; she would polish his boots and take his insults; she would hold the sheets on his bed aside if that was what he wanted, if that was what it took to get Michael safely home again.

"Oh God," she whispered and pressed her fingers to her temples. "Oh, Michael, I'm so sorry."

The bump and slide of something brushing along the *Chimera*'s hull made Summer raise her head and turn her tear-filled eyes to the gallery windows. She saw the increasing lightness in the sky and knew the stars would have winked out of sight one by one.

She tucked the quilt higher under Michael's chin and went to the windows, unlatched one of the panels and pushed it wide. She knelt on the leather chair and propped her chin on her hands as she watched the land move slowly by. There was a mist hugging the base of the island. It clung to the rocky shoreline and swirled out behind the *Chimera* in thinning whorls. There was no beach that she could see, no bay to anchor in, no sign of a nestled village or of any life at all on the high, formidable slopes.

The land began to close in behind them, and she wondered if the *Chimera* were being turned around. But then a second wall of greenery and rock appeared on the starboard side to block the view of the open sea.

Summer straightened abruptly and lifted her chin off her hands. She thought perhaps she was imagining the walls of land coming together, but no—they had entered a narrow passage of some sort and were being guided and towed around a sharp elbow. No wonder the revenue cutters had never been able to follow Wade. His hideaway port was sealed off completely from the outside. If the mouth of the passage were invisible from the sea—and she suspected it was—he would seem to simply vanish once around the protective screen of the island.

She was startled out of her contemplation by the sound of laughter out in the companionway. She closed the window hastily and went back to the bed, with only seconds to spare before the latch tripped and the cabin door opened. It was Morgan Wade and a man she had never seen before.

The newcomer was tall and lean with short sand-colored hair and dark brown eyes that were magnified slightly behind wire-rimmed spectacles. Her surprise at seeing him in the cabin was matched by his surprise in seeing her perched on the side of the bed, and the sentence he had been in the middle of trailed away in a mumble.

Wade did not glance at the berth, did not acknowledge there was anyone else in the cabin.

"I've made up a list of supplies we'll need to make repairs. Where the hell did you say Bull went?"

"What? Oh, ah, he's off sounding out those four new guns you brought back for him."

"Sounding them where?" Wade demanded, knowing full well Captain John "Bull" Treloggan would not test a gun unless he had a specific target in mind.

Roarke smiled wryly. "There was a rumor of some Jamaican rum on it's way up through the straits making for Barcelona."

"Rum? What in blazes do we need with more rum?"

"Lafitte has offered us a fair price on every puncheon we can lay our hands on. Rum and gunpowder are running about even pricewise on the black market."

"Why doesn't the bastard just go out and get it himself? I've never known Jean Lafitte to sit back and be content to take deliveries."

"Frankly he's, ah, been entertaining a pretty stiff British blockade around New Orleans. He's been drawing heavy fire since opening the route to us through Cat Island. He figures a little rum in exchange for cooperation is the least we can do."

"He does, does he?" Wade unlocked the cabinet behind his desk and withdrew his documents and dispatches. "And what else have the two of you been cooking up in my absence?"

"Well, ah—" Roarke glanced uncomfortably at the bed where Michael was beginning to stir awake.

Wade looked up. "Oh. The boy is Michael Cambridge, the girl is his governess. We fished them out of the drink off Saint Bart's."

"Cambridge?" Roarke's expression altered at once.

"Aye. Sir Lionel's cub. They were on board the *Sea Vixen* bound for Barbados."

"The *Sea Vixen,*" Roarke murmured, and a look came into his eyes as if he were mentally leafing through a sheaf of manifests. "She's British registry . . . a passenger ship, for Christ's sakes—what happened?"

"It was none of my doing," Wade said defensively, arching a brow. "She was caught in the same storm that threw us up on the reef. We just happened to cross paths afterward and found these two floating on some debris."

"Did the *Vixen* go down?"

"I saw no wreckage apart from these two, but—" He shrugged.

"And you brought them here?" Roarke's eyes widened incredulously. "Morgan—"

"I had every intention of letting them off on the Virgins when we passed—" Wade cut in sharply, "but the governess there went through my desk like a plague of locusts. I couldn't be sure of what she saw and wasn't about to ask."

Stuart Roarke looked at Summer, causing her to redden self-consciously.

"I see," he murmured at length and glanced away again. "What now?"

"Now we haul the *Chimera* onto the blocks and see if we can't repair her properly. As soon as Bull gets back, we'll retrieve the cargo from the Sisters and deliver it, along with these"—he tossed the packet of dispatches on the desk—"to Norfolk. From what you've been telling me, we can't afford to lose a single crate or barrel. I'll see to it myself."

"What about the *Northgate?* She'll still be in the area, won't she?"

"I sincerely hope so," Wade said, and his blue eyes were like chips of flint. "I sincerely and truly hope so. I owe her captain a few lessons in gunlaying."

"Morgan—"

"He took us at anchor, Roarke. He saw that we were crippled and unable to return fire, and he raked us without even offering the option to stand to."

"Would you have taken it?" Roarke asked dryly. "Would you have allowed the Royal Navy to board you?"

"Not bloody likely."

"Well, don't you think the captain knew that? You've used about every other trick in the books to catch the revenuers unaware. It may just have crossed the Englishman's mind you were only feigning your predicament."

"Nevertheless, it is a debt I won't be forgetting too soon."

"You seem to have chalked up a lot of debts for a trip that was to be so unremarkable."

"That French bastard must have known the patch he gave us would buckle in any kind of a current. Hopefully the *Northgate* took her frustrations out on whatever ship the Frenchman alerted to follow us."

"You don't know that he did. He may have intended just to see you sink gracefully to the bottom."

Wade shook his head. "He knew what we were carrying. There is enough powder in those barrels to—" He stopped, catching the warning frown on Roarke's face. He had forgotten the listeners on the bunk. "I must be more exhausted than I thought," he muttered. "What I wouldn't give for a hot bath, a hearty meal, and a full bottle of rum."

"All arranged," Roarke grinned.

Michael whispered a question in Summer's ear, freezing as Wade's eyes flicked instantly in his direction.

"So you've decided to join us again, have you, lad? I trust you feel better than you did when you were brought down here. Though if it were by my choice, you'd feel a good deal worse." He looked at Roarke and explained, "They tried to swim for it off the Sisters."

Roarke's eyes widened again.

Summer draped a protective arm about Michael. "Please don't take your anger out on Michael. If the fault was anyone's, it was mine."

Wade crossed his arms over his massive chest. "Are my ears deceiving me, madam, or was that just an admission of stupidity?"

She flushed. "It was no such thing. Under normal circumstances, Michael and I could have swum the distance easily."

"You must give me your definition of normal one day," Wade mused, "for surely nothing on this voyage has come remotely close to it."

"You have my complete agreement there, Captain," she said coolly. "And since this so-called voyage has come to an end, may I ask what you have planned for us now?"

Wade smiled briefly at Roarke. "Among her other lovely qualities, the governess seems to think she knows our business better than we do ourselves. She thinks we should send a ransom demand to the boy's father without delay. She has found my company objectionable and barbaric and wants a speedy end to our association."

Roarke adjusted his spectacles and dropped his hand to clasp the other behind his back. "Only the two complaints? You must be mellowing."

"My very thought." Wade's grin broadened. He gathered up his logbook and papers. "Come along then, Governess, and bring the boy. We'll see what manner of hospitality I can frighten you with on shore."

"Are we still to be treated as prisoners?" she asked haltingly.

"Prisoners?" The dark blue eyes locked onto hers and held for several moments before his gust of laughter heightened the flush in her cheeks. "There are no locks on any doors, madam, if that is what you are asking. And since we are on an island, I fear you can only run in circles. Unless, of course, you prefer to swim for it again . . . how far would you say it was to Crab Key, Roarke? Ten miles?"

Stuart looked pensive. "More like twelve. Fifteen if the currents are against you."

"She obviously doesn't think too much about currents," Wade remarked, "and she has a streak of stubbornness in her wide enough to handle any undertow."

Summer turned her back on the two of them as she helped Michael down from the bed. Wade's laughter carried out into the companionway, and she held Michael's hand, arching a stiff chin past Roarke's mockingly gallant bow.

The *Chimera,* she was astonished to see, was tied up to a jetty that ran half the length of the deepwater inlet. The lagoon was enormous, capable of sheltering three or four ships the size of Wade's frigate. A neat row of longboats were drawn up onto the sandy beach, and men were moving back and forth on shore greeting the crew of the *Chimera*. The cove was completely enclosed by trees and a high, rocky crest of land. Summer's earlier surmise that Wade's port would be invisible from the sea was reinforced when it took her several minutes of searching to locate the exit.

"Coming?" asked Wade, holding a hand to her from the gangway. First Michael, then Summer was assisted down the narrow boarding plank to the jetty. She inspired varying degrees of interest and curiosity in the new men, curiosity that was quickly satisfied by the *Chimera*'s crew.

She held Michael's hand as they followed Wade and Stuart Roarke along the dock to the beach. The sand was soft and cool underfoot and she suppressed a shiver as the dampness rustled down through the ring of stooping palm trees. As soon as Wade finished giving last-minute instructions to the men, he headed toward a space between the trees leading over a sandy knoll.

"Where do you suppose they all live?" Michael whispered.

"I have a feeling we are about to find out," Summer replied, not waiting to be called again. She set off up the knoll after Wade, followed in turn by the weary members of the *Chimera*'s crew.

Bounty Key was shaped like a concave wishbone whose ends overlapped to form the hidden cove. The neck of the wishbone created a second natural harbor on which Wade had apparently spent a great deal of time and money to make it appear harmless. Small stone and thatch huts were clustered in the scoop of the bay, and there was a second long jetty anchored to the rocks to which small fishing boats were moored, complete with the nets and tools of the trade. Further out in the bay, riding easily at anchor, was a slim, graceful two-masted schooner, half the size of the *Chimera* and, again, suited to its innocent surroundings.

The bulbous swelling at the head of the wishbone earned a gasp from Summer Cambridge and a "gosh" from Michael.

"You act surprised, Governess," Wade said wryly. "What were you expecting? A pirate's den? Stone fortifications and a castle keep?"

Summer flushed again, for his accusation was not far wrong. She did not expect to see lush trees and manicured gardens covering the slope to the sea. She certainly did not expect to see—sitting like a whitewashed jewel against a backdrop of blue sky and crisp green lawns—a house of such elegance and beauty it could have taken its place alongside any one of a dozen manors in the English countryside. It was two stories and sat sprawled atop a level saddle of land midway up the slope. The upper story was balconied and fenestrated, its railings and posts ornately carved and shaded from the sun by clinging vines of corallila and ivy. The main floor was surrounded by a wide veranda. The windows, arched and stretching floor to ceiling, were louvered and reinforced by intricately designed hurricane shutters. The main house was joined by a covered flagstone breezeway to a second smaller building that contained the kitchens and servants' quarters.

"Captain Wade!"

The happy shriek cracked the air and brought an instant grin to Morgan Wade's bearded face. The source of the jubilant cry was running toward him from the beach, her black face beaming, her hands waving and her feet churning the sand out in small puffs behind her.

"Captain Wade!"

"Reeny!" he roared and caught the woman as she hurled herself into his arms. He swung her around twice, setting her to fits of laughter as he growled good-naturedly and scraped the curve of her throat and shoulder with his furry chin.

"Where you been, Captain?" she demanded, pushing breathlessly out of his grasp. "You had us all plum frettin' out of our minds."

Wade laughed and slapped her playfully on the rump. She wore a brightly patterned wrap skirt and nothing else. "Have you managed to keep these pirates under control?"

She grinned, and her mouth turned down slyly. "Much as I hankered to, Captain."

She was still smiling as her jet black eyes darted past Wade and settled on the phalanx of crewmen coming over the knoll. The laugh became a throaty growl, and she took a deep breath, making her breasts jut out like two ripe fruits.

"Where you been, black man?" she scowled. "Why you always gotta be the last man off that blamed ship?"

Mr. Monday stopped dead in his tracks. She moved forward, hissing like a panther stalking its prey.

"Maybe one day I ain't gonna wait. Maybe one day I'll just take me the first man I see comin' off that hill. Maybe I got me better things to do than standin' around waitin' on some dumb nigger boy who don't know he got a good thing when he sees it. Well? Ain't you got nothin' to say?"

Mr. Monday's eyes narrowed during the ensuing laughter from the rest of the crew. His teeth appeared in a formidable snarl, and his head bent forward to take one of the woman's thrusting brown nipples into his mouth. His arms went around her waist, and he lifted her, tearing off the red sarong in the same eager move as he brought her grinding against him.

Morgan Wade reached over and took a gaping Summer Cambridge by the arm, leading her away past a wave of shrieking half-naked women running to greet their men.

"I believe in keeping my crews happy," he said easily.

"Yes, I can see that," she stammered, feeling her cheeks throb dully with embarrassment.

"I also have my own ways of disciplining them when they get out of hand. You could have saved yourself a swim yesterday if you'd come to me first."

Wade waited for the huge gray-green eyes to lift to his before he released her arm and joined Roarke on the path skirting above and behind the cluster of huts. Summer stared at his broad shoulders, at the profile of his face as he conversed with his companion before she slowly started walking after him. She felt Michael's cool hand slip into hers and squeeze it for reassurance.

They arrived at the wide front steps of the main house and climbed noisily to the vine-draped veranda. A servant appeared as if by magic, his livery picture-perfect, his woolly black head bobbing as he grinned a greeting to Captain Wade.

"Captain, sah. Good to see you home safe."

"Jonas. You old fox, I hear you've been worrying Reeny while we've been away. It's taking ten men to hold Mr. Monday down."

The black eyes popped enough to threaten the safety of

the sockets, then he saw Wade's grin and seemed to shrivel where he stood.

"Mastah Wade, Captain, sah, you got no call to go foolin' wid an ol' man's heart."

Wade's laughter rumbled from his chest. "It keeps you young, Jonas. Have you my rum poured and my cigar waiting?"

"Yas, Captain, sah. Everythin's ready and waitin' on you and Mastah Roa'ke in the study."

"Bless you, Jonas—oh, we'll be having two extra guests staying with us. I want you to take them upstairs and see that they have everything they want . . . hot baths, fresh clothes, whatever."

"Yas, Captain, sah."

"That's it then, Governess," said Wade, turning to Summer and Michael. "I trust you can find a way to make good use of the day. Mr. Roarke and I have a great deal to do, but perhaps you will join us for supper this evening. Nine o'clock?"

He did not wait for an answer. He nodded curtly and disappeared into the cool interior of the house, leaving Summer and Michael to the servant's care. He smiled and requested politely that they accompany him around the side of the veranda, as if nothing were out of the ordinary, as if the captain always returned home with a woman and a young boy in tow.

Summer and her brother exchanged a glance but said nothing as they warily fell into step behind Jonas. When they walked around the corner of the porch, Summer saw a staircase at the end of the wing which led to the balcony above. The bedrooms they were shown to were light and airy, with dazzling white walls and polished mahogany floors. The furnishings were simple but made from the finest fruitwoods and richest fabrics. There were separate bathing and dressing rooms off each bedroom, bellpulls on the walls for summoning the servants and broad-leaved palmetto fans suspended from the ceilings and operated by a series of ropes and pulleys that led out into the hallway. There were no partitions on the balcony to divide one room from another, only doors opening onto the breezy walkway from each suite.

Convenient, Summer thought, noting that and the absence of locks on any of the doors.

The brass bathtub in her room was filled and waiting for her by the time she returned from seeing Michael settled in his suite. She was shown where the soap, towels and bath salts were and given a thick white bathrobe to wear until Jonas could find suitable clothing.

The bath was heavenly. The tub was enormous—deep enough for the water to reach her chin, long enough to stretch her legs flat. Jonas had been generous with the perfumed salts, and she luxuriated in the jessamine-scented bubbles until the skin of her hands and feet was wrinkled white. She wrapped herself in the thirsty bathrobe and stretched out on the cool sheets of the four-poster bed, intending only to ease the ache behind her eyes and steal a few quiet moments to sort out the thoughts colliding about in her brain.

When she awoke, the louvers had been partially shut, and a bright orange-and-red sunset showed behind the flimsy veiled curtains. The room was steeped in soft shadows and deliciously scented by the riot of blossoms growing outside her window.

Neatly laid out on a wicker chair was a set of woman's clothing, complete to the flesh-toned satin shimmy and pantalets.

She held the white muslin dress up to her shoulders and stood in front of the full-length mirror in the dressing room. The size was almost perfect. She would have had little choice in any event since the shirt and trousers she had arrived in had vanished.

Summer dressed slowly, as excited about feeling satins and silk next to her skin again as she had been the first time she had dressed for a ball. The muslin gown had a tiny fitted bodice and a straight skirt, gathered under the breasts and belted with a sash of embroidered blue satin. The sleeves were long and divided into several sheer puffs by matching thin bands of blue. There were no stockings and no dainty slippers, but as she tucked her feet into the leather sandals and examined herself critically, she decided a person would be hard-pressed to find much fault with her appearance.

She brushed her hair vigorously and twisted it into a glossy golden coil, holding it in place with the ivory combs she found on the dressing table. She teased and licked and wound just the right number of wisps to form a shimmery haze against her cheeks and throat. She pinched her cheeks and bit her lips and corrected a final tendril of hair before pronouncing herself fit.

There was no timepiece in the room, no way of knowing what the hour was. Judging by the progress of the sunset, she guessed it to be near enough to nine o'clock to collect Michael and face the ordeal of a dinner hour. If Wade had indeed consumed a full bottle of rum, he would be drunk and surly. And if his henchman's display of humor this morning was any indication of character, there was another source of irritation she would have to contend with.

She refused to worry about it. She refused to worry about anything other than keeping a cool and level head. Summer walked the length of the balcony to Michael's room, reaffirming inwardly her resolve not to create any more ripples on the surface of Wade's little pond. She could do it. She could show these barbarians a thing or two about perseverance.

Michael's room was empty.

Summer retraced the route Jonas had taken, mildly disconcerted but certainly not daunted. She descended to the veranda by the steep back staircase, making very little noise on the wooden slats as she paused in front of several brightly lit windows to peek inside. The dining room was prepared and waiting, lit by multitiered silver candelabras centered on a table set with immaculate white linen and gold-edged china.

Probably stolen, she thought. Looted from one of his hapless victims like the seal and crest.

The room beside the dining room appeared to be a library. A single lamp glowed from a side wall sconce, but she saw enough to know it was probably one of Wade's personal, private sanctuaries. No frills, nothing stood in the way of wood and leather and practicality. There was nothing to distract him from plotting his raids and counting the profits from his smuggling ventures.

Summer arrived at the end of the veranda and stood for

a moment at the railing, gazing out at the last fading glimpse of pink washed across the horizon. The water was faintly brushed with silver, the surf glittered where it crept onto the white sand. Tiny cocoons of lamplight marked the windows of the huts, and farther out along the beach, she could see where a bonfire had been lit in anticipation of an evening of celebration.

Summer held her breath and turned.

Morgan Wade was standing on the veranda less than a dozen paces away. A cigar smoldered between his long fingers, forgotten for the moment as the dark eyes savored the soft white outline of Summer against the failing sunset.

He had shed the familiar cambric shirt and salt-stained trousers and had scraped the ten-day's growth of black fur from his face. His ebony hair was trimmed neatly to his collar; the starched points of the collar touched against the square jaw, and the black silk cravat he wore was tied to within an inch of fashionable fullness. His coat was deep blue velvet, cut away over a richly embroidered silk waistcoat and pearl gray breeches. No amount of tailoring, however, could conceal the broad shoulders, and no amount of mellow evening dusk could take away the rakish effects of sea and sun from his complexion. The combination of elegance and savagery left Summer almost as speechless as she had been the first time she had seen Wade aboard the *Chimera*.

9

"My god," Wade murmured, moving in and out of a shadow as he walked over to Summer. "What a truly lovely woman you are. Sackcloth did not do you justice, madam."

"Thank you, Captain Wade," she said haltingly, feeling suddenly awkward and tongue-tied. "And thank you for the hospitality you have shown thus far. The dress . . . everything is wonderful."

"I can see that. And it is my pleasure, I assure you." He stopped within arm's reach, and she had no choice but to look up into his face. Her lips parted slightly, and her eyes remained locked to his as if by a physical bond. The hollow fluttering spread from her stomach to her knees to the ice-cold tips of her fingers.

The line of Wade's jaw softened into a smile, the first she'd seen that totally removed the threatening, guarded expression that had seemed permanently etched around his mouth and eyes.

"I believe I would have planned this evening differently had I had my full wits about me," he said quietly. "And I doubt if I would have insisted that Mr. Roarke take you back to Bridgetown tomorrow."

"Tomorrow?" she whispered.

"Aye. You did express a wish for haste, did you not? Besides, I have a cargo to retrieve and a delivery to make. And then I've a mind to see just how thick the blockades are becoming along our coastline. I'm afraid I wouldn't be very good company for the next month or so."

Summer was as yet unable to break out of his visual embrace. "Tomorrow will be quite satisfactory. Thank you."

"Stuart is a good man. He'll see you home safely within the week."

With an effort Summer turned and stared out across the beach again. A week, she thought, and closed her eyes gratefully.

"What of the ransom?" she whispered. "Do you trust Mr. Roarke to collect that as well?"

At the sound of a brief laugh, Summer faced him.

"There will be no ransom, Governess."

"No ransom?"

"There was never any intention on my part to collect one."

She frowned. "But you said—"

"*You* said, madam. I merely listened. It was your assumption that all men who sail under a particular flag are barbarians and pirates. I, however, never once mentioned kidnapping or ransom demands."

"That first day . . . when you recognized Michael . . ."

"What exactly did I do?" He arched a brow.

"You . . . you . . ."

"I put you in a cabin—my own, to be precise—and endeavored to make you both as comfortable as possible under the circumstances. It was no fault of mine your imaginations carried you off in twenty separate directions at once."

"I did not imagine being raped," she said coldly, feeling her face and throat flush a deep angry red.

"No." He paused and a tic pulled at a muscle high on his cheek. "No, and for what it is worth, I regretted losing my temper at the time."

"So much so you repeated it that same night? And each night afterward, demanding my cooperation in return for the privilege of being allowed to eat and sleep aboard your ship? Really, Captain! Your remorse is touching."

"I said I regretted my methods, madam, not the deed itself. My only complaint would be that you wasted so much time and energy fighting me."

Summer was shocked. A retort as scornful and cruel as the situation demanded refused to come to mind, and she could only gape up at him in disbelief.

He extended his arm and bowed. "Shall we? The others are waiting."

"I am not hungry," she said icily. "Please make my excuses; I prefer to return to my room."

Wade smiled easily and caught her elbow as she whirled to leave. "Whereas I prefer your company at the dinner table."

Summer winced as his grip tightened. For a moment she debated fighting him—slapping the arrogant smile from his face, kicking out and wrenching free—but she knew it would only amuse him and make her look like more of a fool than she felt already.

She allowed him to guide her along the veranda and through a set of sparkling French doors into a brightly lit room. It was a formal receiving room, furnished in rich brocades and striped velvets. The walls glittered with silver sconces, and in the corner a marble fireplace commanded a seating arrangement of three low divans. Michael was there, scrubbed and combed, looking quite gentlemanly in a plain white shirt and navy breeches.

He jumped to his feet as soon as he saw Summer. "There you are. I was just about to run up and fetch you. We've all been sitting here and smelling dinner for absolutely *hours!* Gosh . . . you look wonderful."

Wade seated her at one of the divans. "Dinner will be in a few minutes. You know everyone here, I believe."

Summer refrained from rubbing the tender flesh of her arm as she glanced around the room. Stuart Roarke was standing beside the hearth, dressed as elegantly as Morgan Wade and just as unable to conceal his pleasure in her transformation. It was a reaction shared by Mr. Thorntree—himself looking starched and polished in a tight-fitting dinner suit—and Mr. Phillips, the *Chimera*'s young second mate. The only face that remained stonily indifferent was Mr. Monday's.

"Traditionally," Wade said, drawing her attention away from the company, "I enjoy the first dinner ashore with my officers. I hope you do not mind being included, especially since they have all promised to be on their best behavior."

A few smiles appeared, and the men took their seats again.

"It shouldn't be too hard," Wade continued, "since the main source of ribaldry happens to be absent for a few days. Which reminds me, Roarke—how did your son's arrival affect Bull's disposition?"

Stuart Roarke reddened slightly beneath his tan and adjusted his spectacles. Before he could formulate an answer, Michael had straightened bolt upright on his chair.

"Bull Treloggan!" he exclaimed. "Captain Bull Treloggan . . . the *pirate!*"

"You know of him, too, I suppose?" Wade asked, amused.

"Everyone knows about Bull Treloggan," Michael said in awe. "He's an honest-to-goodness pirate, isn't he, sir? I mean, he and Jean Lafitte . . . why, they practically *own* New Orleans, don't they? My gosh . . . I've heard he wrestles with lions and bears and even has his teeth filed into points so that he can chew his enemies to pieces. Do you know him? Do you honestly know him?"

"We've shared the odd meal together," Morgan said dryly.

"Gosh." Michael breathed. "And are all the stories true?"

"In all honesty, lad, I'd have to say his tongue is sharper than his teeth. Mind you, I'll admit he did rather a gruesome job on a Dutch slaver last year. Tore him to shreds, didn't he, Roarke?"

"Without batting an eye," Roarke agreed, staring intently at the drink in his hands.

"And Stuart's the man to know, lad," Wade said. "He's had a run-in with Bull once or twice himself."

Michael gaped at Stuart Roarke. "Have you, sir? Have you actually fought with Bull Treloggan?"

Stuart's finely shaped mouth twitched at the corners. "Well, ah, verbally, yes. We have had several warm discussions."

Thorny spluttered over a mouthful of rum, and Mr. Monday's teeth appeared in a grin.

"Oh." Michael's face fell. "That isn't the same thing, though, is it?"

"Depends on 'ow ye look on it, boy," Thorny snorted. "Bull's growl is ripe enough ter put a man under at the best o' times. An' rare's the man who walks away with dry britches. Roarke 'ere not only walked away, but ee walked away with the man's only daughter. Eloped, they did, an' both still alive ter enjoy it."

Michael regarded Mr. Roarke with a new respect. "Bull Treloggan is your father-in-law, sir?"

"That he is," Roarke sighed. "Much to his everlasting regret, I might add. Bett and I can only hope he'll mellow in the coming years."

"He can hardly help it now that you've made him a grandfather," Wade laughed and lifted his glass. "To that end, I propose the first toast of the evening: To Alexander Roarke. May he grow to be as fine a man as his father."

The men rose and murmured a hearty "To Alexander" and downed their drinks.

"Your wife is not here?" Summer ventured to ask.

Roarke smiled. "She gave birth only two weeks ago. Alexander is a strong babe, and the birthing was difficult. Bett sends her apologies and her regrets. She would have liked to hear all the news from England."

Jonas appeared in the doorway then and announced dinner.

Summer saw Morgan Wade moving toward her, and she reached for Roarke's arm before the captain had covered half the distance. She saw him hesitate and frown, and she saw Roarke's complexion darken, but she smiled steadfastly and chatted about some trivial nonsense as she walked beside Roarke down the hallway toward the dining room.

Summer's appetite completely deserted her. She felt uncomfortable in the all-male company, though she could not find fault with their manners or behavior. The flow of small talk was steady and bland, and after the tiny coup in the receiving room, Wade seemed content to ignore her. That plus the fact that Jonas hovered nearby to tip the wine bottle each time the level in her glass fell helped to ease her through the two-hour meal.

Summer declined the offer of brandy and conversation in the drawing room, pleading a slight headache and a wish to retire early to her room. The men seemed relieved, and she could imagine the cravats being loosened, the language becoming freer, and the cigars being lit as soon as she departed the room.

The doors to the library happened to be open onto the veranda as she strolled past. With a curious detachment that came with the full glass of wine she was taking to bed, Summer walked inside.

Her first thought was that for a renegade privateer, Wade's collection of novels and manuscripts was impressive. She perused the titles and authors along one row of shelves, and when she arrived at the end, she stopped—not knowing how she knew he was there, only knowing that he was.

"Have you read all of these, Captain?" she inquired without turning.

"Sad to say, no. I have always had the honorable intention of doing so, however."

"Honorable?" She arched a brow delicately and glanced at him. "You must define the word for me someday, Captain, for surely nothing in your nature so far indicates you know the meaning of the word."

His mouth betrayed a smile as he watched the glass rise to her lips and come away again somewhat lighter.

"Tell me something, Governess. You seem overly anxious to get back to Bridgetown. I take it the sole reason is not your undying loyalty to Sir Lionel. Have you . . . other commitments you are returning to?"

"If I have? What possible interest would they be to you?"

He laughed and moved away from the door. "None. Although I suppose if I thought I was sending you home to the arms of some stableboy, I might be tempted to keep you here until you came to your senses."

"Keep me here? But you said—"

"I said you were leaving for home tomorrow, and I meant it," he assured her. "Unless of course you would prefer to remain here as my guest for a few days."

Summer found herself looking into the unreadable dark eyes, wondering why the casual question suddenly did not seem so casual.

"Are you asking me to stay?"

Wade saw the greenish tint flare into her eyes and neatly parried the sarcasm. "No. I already told you I wouldn't be here. I merely thought you might want to take a day or so to enjoy the feel of solid land beneath your feet."

"I will enjoy the solid feel of Bridgetown beneath my feet, sir. Between then and now I wish only speed."

"Will noon tomorrow suit your purposes?"

"Adequately. But will the *Chimera* be ready?"

"The *Chimera?* Good God, no. She'll be a month or more on the blocks. You'll be going back on Mr. Roarke's schooner, *Vigilant.*"

"Oh. I see."

The smile was back. "She isn't as large as the *Chimera,* and there are not nearly as many corners to snoop into, but she's light and fast. You'll be in the arms of your stableboy soon enough."

Summer flushed under his steady gaze. Her discomfiture was divided equally between the word *snoop* and the deliberate reuse of the term *stableboy.* She turned and started walking back alongside the bookshelves, her fingers tapping lightly on the wineglass.

"This stableboy of yours," Wade grinned, "is he a tolerant lout?"

"Tolerant?" she snapped, her flush deepening as she halted. "By tolerant I assume you are asking if he is a gentleman? The answer is yes. A very fine, *respectable* gentleman. One who puts your own tawdry behavior to shame."

"Meaning he will forgive and forget?"

She stiffened. "There is nothing to forgive. *I* have done nothing to be ashamed of."

"No, indeed," he murmured, "and it pleases me to hear you say that. I would hate to think of you pining away for an innocence you neither had nor wanted."

"Not wanted!" she gasped. "How can you possibly say such a thing!"

"Madam, you may have been virginal in body, but your spirit was plainly impatient to be set free."

Summer had come to the end of the row. The only thing between her and Morgan Wade was a small square table. Her head swam suddenly, and she raised a trembling hand to her temple.

It must be the wine, she thought dizzily. Why else would I be listening to such effrontery without scratching his eyes out? How can he dare to stand there so calmly and accuse me of . . . of *wanting* his attentions!

She went to set the glass on the table, not wanting to have anything more to do with the wine or the man, intending to storm past him, to show him precisely what she thought of his assumptions, but the goblet missed the edge of the table and tilted, splashing some of the deep red Burgundy down the front of the white muslin skirt.

"Oh, no!" she gasped and stepped quickly back as wine and crystal shattered onto the floor. "Oh! Oh, I'm . . . I'm sorry . . . I—"

"It doesn't matter," said Wade quickly, grasping her shoulders to prevent her from bending over to pick up the shards of crystal.

She met the dark blue gaze, and for a full minute she could not move. Her chin trembled and her eyes grew inordinately bright and she was aware of a spreading heat where his hands burned her flesh through the thin muslin gown . . . but she could not move.

"The goblet . . ." she stammered weakly.

"I'll have Jonas clean it up."

"But the dress . . . perhaps if I rinse it out at once—"

His grip became more forceful. "I said it doesn't matter."

Summer's heart refused to leave her throat. The room began to sway alarmingly, and the sound of his breathing drowned out all else, even the rush of palm trees and surf.

"It was inexcusably clumsy of me, Captain," she whispered. "If you tell me the cost of replacing the goblet and the dress, I shall see to it that you are reimbursed."

His expression was curiously restrained as his hand moved up to cradle her chin. "I told you once before, money means nothing to me."

"But the goblet . . ."

"If you insist on reimbursing me, you already know the cost."

"The . . . cost?" His mouth was only inches from hers. Summer watched it move, watched it form words that were wrong . . . all wrong.

"Then again, I would not want it said that I forced payment from you for something so trivial."

"No . . ." His fingers seemed to be tilting her head higher. Something was doing it, because she was only a breath away from touching him. "This isn't fair," she said softly.

"What isn't fair?"

His lips curved into a smile, and she thought of how they felt, warm and searching, on her flesh.

"The wine . . ."

"I did not force you to drink it. Although I'll admit I did not stop you, either. Wine often makes a person see things . . . and do things . . . without the distraction of a conscience. And I confess I wanted you without a conscience tonight."

"But . . . why? What more could you possibly take from me that you haven't already?"

"My lovely innocent," he murmured. "I don't want to *take* anything from you."

His mouth began to brush hers, lightly, teasingly, and even though her lips were parted, his did hardly more than graze them. Summer's hands inched slowly up the hard surface of his chest and followed the lapels of his jacket up and around his neck. Then she wrapped her arms around him and pressed her body forward into his. Her brazenness shocked her, as did her mouth by reaching greedily for his with a need that drove every other thought from her mind. She heard him laugh softly, but it did not matter. Nothing mattered other than the promise in his hands and the hunger in his strong, powerful body.

He picked her up into his arms and went out the French doors and along the veranda to the rear flight of stairs. She raised her head from his shoulder when she saw him stop at the door to her suite. She only sighed and lowered it again when he carried her inside and kicked the door shut behind them.

July 1811

10

SIR LIONEL CAMBRIDGE was a gruff burly man in his early sixties. He possessed a head of snow white hair that led down onto his fleshy jowls in a froth of sprightly mutton-chops. His moustache was waxed into two swooping hooks. He had heavy-lidded hazel eyes and a mischevous twinkle in them that had not been tamed at all in the years Summer had been away. The dispatch Stuart Roarke had sent on ahead of them after docking in Speightstown, ten miles up the coast from Bridgetown, must have preceded their arrival by only minutes, for there was a crowd of servants gathered on the steps of Government House as the coach drew up to the front entrance and, behind them, emerging with his cravat only partially tied, a nervous and red-faced Governor Cambridge.

He clutched Summer and Michael to his bosom, weeping openly. First one, then the other, then both were crumpled like rag dolls, held away to arm's length, then crumpled again. There was a grand introduction to the servants as if the Cambridge offspring were strangers to their own house. Some of the staff shouted the joyous news to strolling passersby, who in turn spread the news like a bushfire through the streets of Bridgetown.

The *Sea Vixen* had gone down with a loss of all hands. The island was draped in mourning, sharing the grief of their governor over the loss of his two children. The memorial service had filled Saint Michael's Cathedral with dignitaries from neighboring islands, representatives from the Admiralty and from the merchant community. Sir Lionel himself had opened the services to include the friends and relatives of the other twenty-two passengers who had gone down with the ship, a gesture which had endeared him further to his stout supporters and somewhat less to those beginning to show signs of dissension.

He had no thoughts of politics now. Summer and Michael were home. They were hugged and petted and praised for their courage. They were swept along in the excitement and taken to their rooms, there to be lavished with baths and perfumes, fussed over and treated like baby chicks fallen from the roost. Summer was not permitted to lift a finger on her own behalf. Three maids saw to her bathing needs. Her hair was washed and scented and shaped into a slippery mass of golden curls; her face was powdered and rouged; her whole body was rubbed with oils, then clothed in silks so fragile a rough thumb would pierce them. She relaxed with a hot, spiced pitcher of sangaree, and then when she felt she was up to it, she descended the spiral oak staircase to the main drawing room where her father was anxiously waiting.

Michael was already there, bristling under the rosy effects of a hot bath and scouring. He looked plainly uncomfortable in clothes that were stiff and confining, and he grew more impatient by the minute, wishing he could be off to regale his peers with tales of his adventures. The stories would have put him in good stead for months to come.

One of the few discussions between the Cambridges and Stuart Roarke during the week on board the *Vigilant* had ended with them reluctantly agreeing that for the time being, there was no reason to mention Morgan Wade's part in the rescue. The suggestion had originated with Wade himself, Roarke said, and it made sense. Sir Lionel's position would not be compromised, and Summer—being thought of still as Michael's governess—would not be subjected to the curiosity or abuse of gossips. Roarke had been deliberately vague in the dispatch he had sent from Speightstown, signing it simply "S. Roarke."

"Thank God is all I can say," Sir Lionel beamed. "Thank God you have come home to us safely. We'll have no more need of mourning clothes and black sashes on the windows —by Jove, I must remember to cancel the stone from the masons. Michael, my boy"— he thumped his son affectionately between the shoulders—"I can see now I sent the right man to New Providence to meet your sister. A man who kept a level head and did not allow her to drown, no, sir."

Michael blushed self-consciously. "Actually, sir, we sort of saved each other."

"I fainted for several hours through the worst of it," Summer said quietly. "If not for Michael holding me, I very likely would have drowned without ever waking up again."

Sir Lionel looked at his son, and his face glowed with pride.

"But if Summer hadn't gotten us out of the cabin in time," Michael insisted, "I should jolly well think we'd be crushed to splinters at this very moment."

Sir Lionel sighed heartily and trumpeted into a square of linen. "I say—this calls for a toast. Several toasts."

He signaled to a hovering servant, who immediately stepped forward with a tray of glasses and a decanter of port. Sir Lionel handed one to Summer, one to Michael, and took a third for himself.

"To the Cambridge family," he announced and downed the glassful in a single swallow.

Summer and Michael exchanged a smile and sipped.

The butler appeared in the doorway. "Excuse me, sah. A gentleman is heah requesting an audience with Miss Summah. He says it is a mattah of some urgency."

Sir Lionel frowned. "Well? Who is it, man?"

Bennett Winfield, as sunbleached and golden as Summer remembered, brushed past the startled butler without waiting to hear the introduction delivered. He tossed his bicorne onto one of the nearby chairs and went straight to Summer, gathering her into his arms before she had time to react to his arrival.

"Summer! Summer, it is you. When I heard you'd been brought home, I didn't believe it. I thought it had to be a cruel joke or a case of gossip gone awry . . . but my God, it is you." He held her out to arm's length, letting his eyes devour her. "We searched and searched. We crossed back and forth over that damned stretch of ocean so many times the crew was threatening mutiny. And then when we found the wreckage—" His voice trailed away, and he squeezed her hands in his, raising each in turn to his lips.

"Well, ah—hem. I, ah . . ." Sir Lionel crooked a brow and turned to Michael, winking. "I'd say perhaps this calls for another round, what?"

Bennett stood away from Summer and bowed stiffly to Sir Lionel. "Excuse my impertinence, sir. I came straightaway when I heard, and I guess I have not quite had enough time to absorb the shock."

"Nonsense, m'boy," Sir Lionel exclaimed. "Quite all right. Wilkins—pour the commodore a drink. We'll let our first toast be to impertinence . . . to the sorry lack of it in my family's absence."

Summer was genuinely surprised. "Commodore?"

"Why, yes." Bennett smiled. "One of the reasons I was sent to England, as it turned out, was to acquaint myself with the *Caledonia* before I assumed command of her."

Sir Lionel chuckled. "You could say it was a wedding gift from your godfather, Admiral Stonekipper. Neither he nor I could see the use of having a mere captain for a son-in-law."

The glasses were filled and tipped, and Summer recovered sufficiently to take a seat on the divan. The sight of Bennett brought back the memory of those hours spent drifting on the raft. She had clung to the hope of seeing him again, and now here he was before her, making the past two weeks feel as though they had happened in a dream or a nightmare. She and Michael might both have been sitting refreshed and rested after having just disembarked from the *Sea Vixen*.

She observed her father and Bennett as they smiled and touched glasses. Sir Lionel seemed to have lost ten years in the past four hours, and Bennett . . . in his crisp naval uniform of dark blue coat and white breeches, his high gleaming black knee boots, his gold braid, his neatly clubbed blond hair . . . he was the man she had traveled halfway around the world to be with. Hope of seeing him again, of becoming his wife, had kept her alive. He had been with her in her dreams through the hours she had floated in the gray mists; he had been in her thoughts during the hurt and humiliations she had suffered at Morgan Wade's hands. Bennett was here, and she was still the same Summer Cambridge who had left England wanting a fine home, fine parties, elegant clothes and a handsome, dashing husband . . . wasn't she?

"Are you all right, my dear?"

"What? Oh. Oh, yes, Father. I'm fine."

"Just happy to be home, are you?"

"Yes." She smiled. "Just happy to be home."

Two days after their triumphant return, Summer and Michael were summoned to the library. Sir Lionel looked somewhat disturbed as he ushered them into seats and waited for the tea to be poured and served. Summer glanced askance at Commodore Bennett Winfield, but his face gave no hint as to why the meeting had been called. Twice her father had broached the subject of their marriage, and twice she had neatly avoided giving any direct answers. This time she suspected there would be no more corners for her to hide in.

"Is this important, Father?" she inquired sweetly. "I promised to go shopping with Clarissa Wallace this afternoon."

Sir Lionel harrumphed to clear his throat. "Well, quite frankly, I don't know. It concerns the note we received prior to your arrival the other day."

A cool prickle touched the back of Summer's neck. "The note?"

"The one Mr. Roarke sent on ahead of you from Speightstown."

"Yes." Summer moistened her lips. "He thought it was better to ease the shock of our return rather than to have us simply appear on the doorstep. Was it wrong?"

"No, no. I am not questioning the man's conduct . . . er, not entirely, that is."

"Then what are you questioning, Father?"

Sir Lionel frowned. He paced the length of the oval carpet, stopping to meet Bennett's eye before proceeding.

"Frankly, I'm questioning just who the deuce this Mr. S. Roarke is and where he comes from. I inquired at the Colonial Office to ascertain where I might forward a case of fine Madeira by way of thanks, only to learn that no one there had ever heard of him. You say his ship *Vigilant* picked you up off Saint Barthélemy, yet he is not listed as one of the island's residents. When I searched the ship's title, I found she was not even on the official registry. How do you explain that?"

Out of the corner of her eye, Summer saw Michael squirm lower into the cushions of the couch as if he could make himself invisible.

"Possibly because she wouldn't be on the British lists, Father," she answered quietly. "She might be on the American one, though."

Sir Lionel coughed over a mouthful of tea, spluttering most of it back into the delicate china cup. "American! Did you say American?"

"Yes, Father. Mr. Roarke is an American. I'm sorry, I thought I mentioned it before."

"You most certainly did not," he said indignantly, clearly undecided as to what his reaction should be. Britain's relationship with America these past few months had been deteriorating at an alarming rate. The Yankees were becoming adamant about their rights to trade freely with whomever they chose—and lately they had been choosing France. Sir Lionel looked to Bennett for guidance, but the commodore's expression had become suddenly thoughtful as he studied the subtle changes on Summer's face.

Sir Lionel harrumphed loudly again and glared through his bushy eyebrows at his son and daughter. "Two weeks in the hands of one of those American scoundrels . . . I suppose he plagued you with all manner of questions about our government and our policies?"

"Oh, no, sir," Michael said hastily. "Mr. Roarke wasn't like that at all. He wasn't the least bit curious."

"No? Then I suppose he tried to instill his own philosophies into you? All of this drivel about free trade and sailor's rights?"

"N-no sir. The only thing Mr. Roarke tried to teach me

was how to properly read the wind and clouds and how to judge the water currents by the changing colors and . . ."

"Yes, yes, all very interesting, I'm sure."

"Well, it is, sir," Michael said defensively. "Mr. Roarke says it is all important to know if a man wants to go to sea."

"You want to go to sea, do you, Michael?" his father asked gruffly. "Even after what you and your sister went through?"

"Oh, yes, sir. Mr. Roarke says you have to . . . to grab your fear by the throat and choke the life out of it, otherwise it could rule your life forever. He says he learned that lesson long ago from Captain Bull Treloggan, and if anyone should know about—"

"Bull Treloggan!" Sir Lionel gasped. "The man is associated with Bull Treloggan!"

Michael reddened. He saw the stricken look on Summer's face and knew he had made a mistake. "Well, I . . . y-yes, sir. He is."

"In what capacity?" Sir Lionel demanded.

"S. Roarke," Bennett murmured. His pale eyes flicked from Michael's face to Summer's and widened as if two disjointed thoughts had suddenly become connected within his mind. He stood up so abruptly that Michael flinched instinctively, pressing closer to Summer on the divan. "*S. Roarke!* The *S* wouldn't happen to stand for *Stuart,* would it?"

"Good God, man," Sir Lionel frowned. "What is it? You look as if you've seen a ghost."

The color in Bennett's face had all but drained away beneath his tan.

"Not a ghost, Sir Lionel. Believe me, he is very real."

"Who? Who the blazes are you talking about? Who is this Stuart Roarke? *Will someone kindly tell me what is going on?"*

"I hardly think kindness and Morgan Wade belong together in the same sentence."

Sir Lionel's eyes bulged out of their creases. "Morgan Wade! What has any of this to do with Morgan Wade?"

Summer set her cup and saucer on the table and folded her hands on her lap. "It is really quite simple, Father. It was not Mr. Roarke who picked us up after the *Sea Vixen* floundered. He brought us home, true enough, but it was Captain Wade who found us."

"I don't know how I failed to make the connection as soon as I read the note," Bennett said harshly. "How many S. Roarkes can there be in the islands?"

The governor huffed. "Why in heaven's name was I not told of this immediately?"

"We thought we could spare you some of the anxiety you are experiencing this very moment," said Summer. "For a few days, at any rate, until the shock of our homecoming passed. We had every intention of telling you . . . of telling you everything. . . . we just thought we should wait for a better time."

"There is no better time," her father declared. "No worse time either, for that matter. My God . . . *Morgan Wade!* Of all the pirates in all the seas, you had to be rescued by him!"

Michael regained some of his courage and straightened from Summer's side. "His ship had been damaged against a reef in the same storm, and we both sort of bumped into each other. He wasn't exactly thrilled to see us, but Captain Wade saved us from certain death. There were sharks and all sorts of—"

"His ship!" Sir Lionel gasped. "You were taken on board the *Chimera?* On board an armed gunrunner? Bennett—" He held out his cup. "Rum. To the brim, if you please . . . and forgo the nicety of diluting it with tea."

"We did not choose our rescuer," Summer said. "At the time we would have been grateful to see Blackbeard himself if it meant being warm and dry again."

"Yes, yes, daughter, but . . . Morgan Wade!"

"Was he anywhere near the *Sea Vixen?"* Bennett asked in a low voice. "Either before or after the storm?"

"No, sir," Michael said firmly. "We drifted a day and a night before he found us, and afterward he went straightaway to a port on Saint Martin to try to repair his ship."

Sir Lionel clutched the side of a table. "He took you to a leper colony?"

"Oh, no, sir! No, we didn't actually go right in to the port. He simply anchored there long enough to make a temporary repair. No one was allowed to leave the ship, and no one from Saint Martin was allowed on board the *Chimera.*"

Sir Lionel swabbed the beading moisture from his brow. "Yes, and then what. Go on, boy. Saint Martin . . . and then what?"

"Sir?"

"Where did he take you from there?" Bennett asked levelly.

Michael lifted his gaze to the commodore. "N-north, sir."

"North?"

"Yes, sir. He never did tell us where we were going. Or where we were when we got there."

"I'll wager he didn't," Bennett agreed dryly. He continued to gaze speculatively at Michael for a moment, then turned away.

"And how did the bounder treat you?" Sir Lionel demanded.

Summer was amazed at how calm she sounded. "Quite well, actually. He recognized Michael at once. We assumed he meant to hold us to ransom, but as it turned out, that was not the case. He was preoccupied with his ship most of the time and . . . and in a hurry to reach his home port to see to his damages. We were almost there when—"

Bennett had turned to face her again. *"He took you to Bounty Key?"*

It was asked with such ferocity, Summer stared up at him. "If that is the name of his island, yes. You already know where it is?"

"We have a name only." Summer saw a sudden hard light come into the pale blue eyes as he paced back toward the divan. "It does not appear on any maps we have. . . . We do not even know which chain of islands it is a part of."

Summer shook her head slowly. "All I can tell you is that it was a five-day sail from Saint Martin."

"Direction?" Bennett snapped. "You must have had some idea of direction."

"North," Michael said when the pale eyes drilled into him. "N-north, sir."

"In daylight hours and for how long? Was he under full

sail or half? Eight knots? Ten? Did he trim his speed at night, or did he take advantage of the darkness to confuse you? I need to know more than just *north*, boy."

Michael was stung by the rebuke, and it was Summer who came to his defense.

"He doesn't know any more than that, Commodore Winfield. He had just survived a very frightening ordeal. Neither of us was too concerned about speed or direction; we were more concerned with being warm and dry and safe."

Bennett drew himself up. "You had cause to be concerned for your safety, madam?"

Summer heard another choking sound come from her father but ignored it as she gazed unwaveringly at Bennett. "Are you asking me a question, sir?"

"Five days and nights on board the *Chimera* bear questioning, yes. Wade's reputation as an officer and a gentleman is somewhat clouded."

"As is yours at this moment," she replied evenly, the green in her eyes flaring dangerously bright. "And it was *seven* days and nights on board his ship, plus a further night ashore . . . where we were treated with . . . with the utmost respect and courtesy."

The pale eyes narrowed. He took in the flush to her cheeks and the tightly clasped hands folded on her lap. "Forgive me," he said quietly, "but I am only voicing a concern as to what the mere mention of the man's name in conjunction with yours will bring down upon your fine reputation. I'm sure you can imagine how the gossips will delight in exaggerating this incident beyond all proportion."

"Good Lord, he's right," said Sir Lionel. "People will assume the worst, especially if the scoundrel brags about having my son and daughter at his mercy for two weeks. He had no need to hold either of you to ransom—he can make a laughingstock out of us without ever demanding a copper."

Summer could not keep her seat any longer. She stood up and faced the two men squarely. "Not two days ago you believed Michael and I to be dead and rotting somewhere at the bottom of the sea. We stand before you today—alive and remarkably healthy—and your foremost concern does not appear to be how we managed to survive, rather if our survival has now cast a shadow on the good Cambridge name."

The governor was instantly contrite. "Now, daughter, we are only concerned for your welfare."

"*Mine,* Father?"

Sir Lionel reddened. "Well, naturally you can see how being obligated to the man places me in a deuced awkward position."

"I can see why you might have preferred a ransom demand," she agreed angrily. "At least then you could have refused to pay if the goods were damaged in any way."

"Now, daughter—"

"Don't 'now, daughter' me. I had truly forgotten what small minds these island people have. But if my reputation is your main source of concern, you may calm yourself. The world will not hear a thing from the lips of Captain Wade. He had no idea I was your daughter."

"What? What's that you say?"

"For that you may thank Michael. He reasoned that if blackmail was indeed among the captain's motives, it would be far less ruinous to admit to only one of us being a Cambridge."

"Well, who the blazes did he think you were?"

"I told Captain Wade Summer was my governess," Michael said hesitantly. "He hardly paid her a second thought."

"Is this true?" Bennett asked.

Sir Lionel guffawed. "He had no idea who you were?"

"He never even asked my name," Summer said tautly.

"Good grief. And this man Roarke, daughter, he knew nothing either?"

Summer swallowed the resentment building in her throat. "No, Father, he knew nothing. He brought his ship into port at Speightstown and for all I know is halfway home again by now. I hardly saw him during the time we were on the *Vigilant.*"

"Why didn't Wade bring you back himself? Or drop you at a friendly port along the way?"

Summer had known the question would arise, and she had rehearsed her answer a dozen times, a dozen different ways. Well, you see, Father, he had guns on board, and . . . He was in a hurry, Father, because he was smuggling guns, and . . .

"Michael already told you," she said quietly. "The *Chimera* was damaged in the storm. He could not afford to stop. But he did send us on our way the day after we arrived at Bounty Key. I gather he wanted to personally supervise the repair of his ship, and so he sent us with Mr. Roarke."

"And his connection to Wade?" Bennett asked.

"I don't know exactly. He seemed more interested in the ship and the cargo than he did in us."

"Cargo?" Sir Lionel looked up from his glass. The room again became ominously silent.

"Tea, sir," Michael said promptly, "and rum. Or so he said. We . . . we weren't allowed to wander about very much. We had to stay in our cabins most of the time." His voice trailed away, and he absolutely refused to look in Summer's direction.

"What about the other fellow, Roarke?" Bennett inquired. "Was he carrying anything on the schooner, or were his bays empty?"

Summer realized at once the basis for his question. "I'm sorry to disappoint you again, Bennett, but Mr. Roarke showed far more caution than you give him credit for. The course we traveled was not a direct one. He took the same number of days to bring us home as the captain did to carry us away, even though the *Vigilant* was definitely lighter and faster."

The commodore acknowledged Roarke's astuteness with a slight nod of his head. "He seems to have been very thorough. However, it can be equally to our benefit if his presence raised no comment in Speightstown. It means his association with Morgan Wade is not generally known."

"You had no difficulty in relating the two," Sir Lionel said bleakly.

"Only because Wade is a subject of personal interest to

me. I don't imagine there are five people on the island who even know Stuart Roarke exists."

"Then how the blazes did you know?"

Bennett waved away the question. "It isn't important. What *is* important is keeping his anonymity. If we handle this correctly, it becomes entirely possible for the less-pleasant aspects of this whole incident to go undiscovered."

"Explain yourself, sir," the governor chafed. "What's done is done and cannot be undone."

"What exactly has been done?" Bennett arched a brow. "Your son and my fiancée have been returned safely home by a gentleman identified only as S. Roarke. Since both the name and his less-palatable connections are somewhat vague, we can be fairly safe in assuming that Morgan Wade's part in this might never come to light."

"You want us to lie about who rescued us?" Michael cried, his visions of glory fading before his eyes. "You mean we can't *ever* tell anyone we were on the *Chimera?* Or that Morgan Wade himself jumped into the sea to rescue us? Or that we were on board when—"

"Not unless you want your sister to suffer the consequences," Bennett interrupted irritably. "Not unless you want your father to bear the ridicule of his political enemies."

"Speaking for myself," Summer argued, "I am not the frail soul you are painting me to be. I would not perish on the mere speculations of a handful of frustrated rumormongers."

"Nevertheless, daughter, you have more to think about here than your own reputation. Or have you forgotten that your fiancé has a career in the navy? D'you think he should be saddled with a scandal as promising as the likes of this one if it can be at all avoided?"

"I think perhaps," Summer slowly turned to Bennett, "if there is any doubt as to his priorities, the commodore should know that I would not hold him to any commitments he may have made. I would understand completely if he wished to have the engagement postponed or terminated altogether."

"Terminated? Good Lord, I had forgotten. . . . it already

has been." Her father reddened. "Because of those blasted memorial services. It wouldn't take more than a greased palm here and there to get the wheels spinning again, though. And the chapel is still reserved for the last Saturday in July."

"That is only three weeks away, Father," Summer pointed out, shivering with a sudden chill that swept through the room. "Perhaps Bennett and I should both take more time to consider the consequences."

"There needn't be any consequences," Sir Lionel retorted. "And I believe appearances are of the utmost importance here. If everything proceeds according to plan, there need never be an eyebrow raised in speculation; if they're altered, the tongues will surely wag."

Summer disregarded her father and looked up at Bennett. "You are not bound by honor to go through with the marriage, sir. I repeat, I gladly release you from any and all commitments."

Commodore Winfield hesitated a fraction longer than was comfortable in the heavy silence. In the end he raised one of Summer's hands to his lips.

"But I am bound, dear Summer. Bound by far more than words and conventions. I am bound by my heart and my soul to take you as my wife. If you harbor doubts, if you wish to take a week or a month or a year to make your final decision, so be it . . . but it will not change mine."

Summer felt a second chill sweep along her spine. The pale blue eyes held the same degree of sincerity as they had the night in London when he introduced her to responses she had not known she was capable of feeling. Yet something was different. There was no innocent flush of eagerness in her cheeks, no spidery thrills of anticipation racing through her limbs at his touch. She knew the reason. It would be the same reason that a week or a month or a year would do nothing to alter. But what choice did she have? What choice did any woman have who had been pampered and spoiled into helplessness? She was trapped by convention, just as surely as Bennett was trapped by his strict code of honor.

Her lips moved, and she heard herself accepting Bennett's proposal. She saw her father dab the linen across his brow in relief, and she heard the joyous call for the finest champagne the cellars had to offer. She felt Bennett's lips brush against her hand, and in the split second that their eyes met and held, she knew there would be no further mention of her nights on board the *Chimera.*

11

THE MARRIAGE of Summer Cambridge to Commodore Bennett Winfield took place as scheduled, on a hot sultry day three weeks after the miraculous return from the sea. Guests were drawn from the island's elite. Lawyers, bankers, businessmen and merchants mingled with cane growers and rum exporters, who in turn toasted the newlyweds with every high-ranking member of the Admiralty and government present in Barbados and the neighboring colonies. It was not the elaborate social event of the season originally conceived, for the shadow of the *Sea Vixen* still loomed in the background, but it was impressive, and the bride and groom were duly wined and dined both before and after in the usual rounds of luncheons and teas in their honor.

The Winfields, on Sir Lionel's urging, took up residence in the south wing of Government House. Bennett's naval duties would be taking him away for long stretches of time and, her father declared, Summer would appreciate the company as well as the excellent experience to be gained acting as hostess at the government functions held daily under the vast tiled roof.

A marriage was what was sorely needed in the family, Sir Lionel decided. New blood. A firm hand. Summer was far more reserved than her heated letters of the past year had indicated, but she could lapse at any time, and she was still inclined to speak her mind without pausing to weigh the outcome. A strong hand and a healthy dose of childbearing would straighten her out in no time.

No one questioned or doubted the story of the rescue by

S. Roarke. It was left to speculate that he was a wealthy cane grower from the Windward Islands who had luckily happened by after the storm had ravaged the *Sea Vixen*. As Bennett predicted, no one associated Roarke with Morgan Wade, and in that respect, the gossips of the town had a poor July.

Not so the cane growers, who harvested a record crop that year, or the merchants, who were selling goods as fast as they could import them—from whatever source—because of a growing fear of total embargo if war was officially declared between America and Britain. The increased traffic in ships going both ways naturally bred an increase in the numbers of ships and cargoes waylaid by privateers of all nationalities. Many were caught and summarily punished by the British revenue cutters that patrolled the area. Many more made good their escape, growing both wealthy and notorious by capturing the ships and their valuable cargoes. Summer was mildly disconcerted to learn that the West Indies had become a veritable hotbed of intrigue in her four-year absence. Every drawing room conversation centered on politics and the growing problems of piracy. Worse still, rarely an evening went by that there was not some mention of the most successful privateer of them all. . . .

"Morgan Wade! Bah! We've been trying to pin down that bastard for three years now—begging your pardon, Mrs. Winfield—but he's like a ghost. He comes and goes as if he's sprouted wings, and you never know when he's going to light down next. Or where." The speaker was the senior naval officer in charge of the port authorities on Barbados. Old and crusty, Admiral Sir Reginald Stonekipper was a longtime friend of Sir Lionel's and often shared a meal and exchanged opinions with him under the roof of Government House.

"Why, only two months ago," the admiral continued, "we had a report of a sighting—from a fairly reliable source, I might add—*seven hundred miles* due south of where he was raking the bejesus out of a pair of Portuguese traders. We know it for a fact because when he finished with them, he had the cheek to offer us the hulls at what *he* considered to be a fair price."

"And did you take them?" Sir Lionel asked.

"'Course we took them," the admiral snorted. "Then we sold them back to the Portuguee for twice what we paid. But that's not the point here. The point is, it's high time something was done to put an end to his philandering. A definite and permanent end."

"You have to catch him first," Sir Lionel said. "And you have to catch him raking a British ship. I don't mind saying I give a hearty cheer every time word reaches us that he's downed another foreigner. I also have to say he's pretty clean whenever he sails into my jurisdiction. Never fails to send over a case of prime rum or brandy."

"Hmph. Twice he's been impounded in the harbor, and twice, by God, he's had his ship searched to the timbers."

"More's the time, Reg, that he's sailed away laughing out of the side of his mouth. We cannot touch him if he's holding legal, and he knows it."

"Rubbish, I say. We know he just bought a huge shipment of gunpowder and muskets from the French. Where is the legality in that?"

"Show me on his manifests where it states guns and powder—better yet, show me where it doesn't state guns and powder . . . then show me the guns and powder—and I'll have him tossed in a jail cell before the ink dries on the warrant." Sir Lionel leaned back in his chair, puffing furiously on a cigar. "You cannot do it, because when you board him and give search, you find not a whiff of it."

"Because we've only been able to search him in port. If you could catch him and stop him on open water, my guess is we'd have a treasure chest, gentlemen. A veritable treasure chest."

Commodore Winfield was present, and his adjutant, Harvey Aslop. Seated next to him was a lesser naval attaché, and on the far side of the room, Summer Winfield.

"So how does he do it?" Sir Lionel asked. "How does he go from a legal cargo—complete with bills of lading and official sanctions—to damned contraband?"

"He obviously stops somewhere along the way and switches cargoes," Bennett drawled. "It is the where of it that appears to be stumping the revenuers."

Admiral Stonekipper clamped down on the soggy end of

his cigar. "It isn't for lack of trying that they've failed to stop him. For six months now they've sent one ship after another out to give him chase. And that's precisely what he gives them . . . a merry chase."

"You have the *Northgate,*" came a thin, nasally voice from the settee. "She's rated at fifty-two guns, if I am not mistaken. And as of six weeks ago you took delivery in Barbados of the *Caledonia*—seventy-four guns. I hardly think Wade should be laughing."

Sir Lionel squinted past his bushy white eyebrows at the attaché seated opposite his son-in-law. Farley Glasse had been in Bridgetown less than two months and had arrived on the doorstep tonight in the company of Admiral Stonekipper. He was an oily little man and had not said much all evening; now he needed to be put in his place.

"The *Northgate* and the *Caledonia* are both warships, sir. They have enough to do worrying about controlling the blasted French, let alone starting an incident with some damned Yankee renegade."

Glasse sighed. "This same damned Yankee renegade, as you call him, is smuggling guns and armaments through the blockade lines to the American mainland. You are not dealing with a simple smuggler carrying embargoed tea to old Virginia ladies."

"What are you suggesting we do about it, sir?" Admiral Stonekipper snorted.

"It seems to me that one well-placed broadside—"

"Would give us another incident like the *Chesapeake,* or the *Little Belt,*" Bennett stated flatly. "We would be at war with the Americans before the smoke cleared."

"The instances you refer to, Commodore, were both justifiable. The *Chesapeake* carried British deserters; we merely removed them. As to the other," Glasse shrugged, "I was not the only one amazed by Parliament's reluctance to throw down the gauntlet."

In early May a British frigate had stopped an American brig and had seized a crewman suspected of being a British deserter. In the ensuing uproar, the Americans had dispatched one of their warships, the *President,* to search out the *Guerrière* and return the sailor. Midmonth it had caught up to a British ship and opened fire, only to discover it was not the *Guerrière,* but a smaller, inoffensive vessel, the *Little Belt.* The British public was outraged at the effrontery of the Americans, who had simply apologized and sent the brig on its way. The Americans touted their own as heroes and stirred the patriotic spirit to fever pitch.

"Are you suggesting we take the initiative?" Sir Lionel scratched savagely beneath his periwig. "When we are already fighting both the French and the Spanish?"

"I suggest we cease to label piracy as anything but. I suggest we stop sending inadequate cutters and naval sloops after Wade when they haven't a hope of doing anything but increasing his reputation. He has attacked and raided British merchantmen, has he not?"

"Only sporting, if you think of it," Admiral Stonekipper grunted, "since our privateers have taken American ships. To make a case hold against Wade himself, we would have to have proof."

"We would have to catch him in the midst of a fracas," Sir Lionel remarked. "Or, as Reg has said, take him with the illegal goods on board. Neither of which seems too likely."

Glasse pursed his lips. "Have you thought of using a decoy?"

The admiral almost swallowed his cigar butt as he rammed it into his mouth. "We've tried two, by God!"

"And?"

"Both ended up being sailed under a prize crew of Wade's men, past the revenue ships that were sent to catch him, past the whole goddamn fleet blockading the Yankee coastline, right into a goddamn American harbor where they've been stripped and refitted and turned out again flying the goddamn Stars and Stripes!" He agitated the cigar to the far corner of his mouth and glared at Summer. "Begging your pardon again for the profanity, my dear."

"That's quite all right, Admiral." She smiled. "Would you care for more coffee or curaçao?"

"Don't mind if I do to both," he said, and glared at Farley Glasse with the expression of a caged lion wishing his bars were loose.

Summer smiled at her husband. "Bennett?"

"No. Thank you." His eyes flicked away from her face without returning the smile.

"You know this man Wade, don't you?" Glasse asked abruptly.

Summer was startled by the question, and the coffeepot rattled the spoons on the tray as she set it down too heavily.

"Insomuch as anyone else who has followed his escapades knows him," Bennett replied smoothly. "Although I must say I have no deep admiration for the man."

"Have you taken the *Caledonia* out yet?"

"Not as yet, no. I have been having a few minor alterations done to her while I have the chance."

"Really? I would be intrigued to see how one goes about altering a supreme work of art."

"This work of art wallows, Mr. Glasse," Bennett said easily. "She was dragging at least ten wagonloads of barnacles on her sheathing that had to be scraped before she could hope to muster anywhere near the speed she was designed for. I have also taken the liberty of moving some of her guns and substituting more thirty-two pounders for the less-effective twenty-fours."

"You sound as if you know your business, Commodore."

"I had a good teacher in Admiral Nelson," Bennett said as if it was the only explanation necessary.

Glasse nodded and gave what for him passed for a smile. "Indeed. But when I asked you if you knew Wade, I was naturally referring to earlier on in your respective careers. You were with Admiral Nelson off the Barbary Coast back in '02, were you not? About the same time Morgan Wade was serving in the American Navy."

Bennett saw Summer's expression of surprise out of the corner of his eye and kept his voice level. "That was nine years ago. We were both junior officers; he a lieutenant and I only a midshipman. Our paths never actually crossed other than that the ships we served on happened to be in the same general vicinity. The Americans, if you recall, initiated the most action."

"My point precisely, Commodore. You were in an excellent position to observe Morgan Wade—observe his blooding ground, if you will. He led several high-risk forays against the Tripolitans and scored several brilliant coups."

"He has no lack of nerve or initiative, if that's what you mean. As to the brilliance of his tactics, I can only say that had he been serving under my command, he would have been court-martialed many times over."

"So he should have been," Glasse agreed silkily. "And yet I doubt if the Americans would have risked drawing attention to the fact that they had a titled Englishman in their ranks."

"What's this you say?" Sir Lionel paused midscratch, leaving his wig at a precarious angle. "A titled Englishman? Who the blazes are you talking about?"

"Morgan Wade," Glasse responded blithely. "We have every reason to believe he was born Edmund Granville—Sir Edmund Granville upon inheriting his father's barony. Unfortunately"—and here Glasse's voice sharpened—"there was some rather unsavory business involving an unsolved murder which spurred him into leaving England in a hurry. In any event, Lord Granville disappeared from London twelve years ago—just about the same time Morgan Wade's name appeared on the Yankee naval registry."

"What makes you think they are one and the same man?" Sir Lionel asked, looking skeptical.

"Timing, for one thing. Morgan Wade does not exist prior to twelve years ago. For another, we have this—" Glasse paused and reached into an inner pocket of his coat. A small indigo disc was unwrapped carefully from a layer of linen and was transferred onto the tabletop for inspection. It was a round of wax. Sealing wax.

Summer did not have to lean forward as the others did to know it would bear a stamp of a falcon in full wingspread. She remained seated stiffly in her chair and stared fixedly at a speck of dirt on the woven carpet as Glasse continued speaking.

"Several documents surfaced a few months ago carrying the Granville seal—the one you see here. It naturally roused some curiosity when it was identified as a family stamp that had—in effect—ceased to be in use some twelve years ago."

"Documents? What kind of documents?" Admiral Stonekipper asked brusquely. "And where were they found?"

"They were in amongst some ship's papers. A ship that had been intercepted trying to run the blockade into Philadelphia—a privateering vessel, one whose captain was willing to exchange some information in return for the release of his ship and crew. He claimed to know nothing about the documents themselves, but he did tell us they originated from Morgan Wade." Glasse's black ferret eyes shifted around the circle of interested faces. "The papers looked innocent enough on the surface—polite, informal letters chatting about weather and local customs. One particularly intuitive young man, however, was bothered by the trivial details and investigated further. He discovered that storms were reported where no storm had occurred. Harvests of sugarcane were praised where there were only barren rocks and windswept beaches."

Summer's eyes rounded as she stared at the speck of dust. She was remembering the letters she had found in Wade's desk. Weather forecasts . . . harvests . . . she had thought it peculiar at the time.

"Imagine our surprise when the storms were interpreted nicely as naval maneuvers. The harvest he mentioned on the island of Grenada was, in fact, the new garrison stationed there. All of this and more was being relayed to the American War Office through a Captain Stephen Decatur—"

Summer closed her eyes and saw the salutation plainly . . . "Dear Stephen. . . ."

"—another veteran of the Tripolitan wars and one of Morgan Wade's close personal friends."

"Espionage is a way of life in the West Indies, Mr. Glasse," Bennett said derisively. "Spies are thicker than mosquitoes in some instances."

"Ah, yes, but if I can prove that Morgan Wade and Sir Edmund Granville are one and the same man, he can be apprehended without any fear of repercussions from the

Americans. He can be brought to trial not only for privateering and smuggling, but as a bona fide traitor to the Crown."

"And you base your suspicions on the evidence of a seal and the word of a fellow privateer?" Sir Lionel scoffed. "Flimsy at best, sir. Flimsy at best."

"Granted, the link is flimsy, but it bears investigation. Wade's exploits are becoming too widespread, too heroic in proportion to ignore the man much longer. All the Yankees need is one hero—one rebel who succeeds in making fools of us all—and they'll have the incentive to flood the Caribbean in droves."

"They're already here in droves," Admiral Stonekipper muttered. "You would have my compliments, Glasse, if you could remove Wade and his kind and have to answer to no one for the action."

"That is, essentially, why I am here, Sir Reginald. I represent certain factions of our government . . . men who anticipate the war between America and Britain becoming a reality within the year. It is no secret that the Americans are presently ill equipped to engage in any lengthy naval warfare. Their navy consists of three heavy frigates and a laughable fifteen mismatched sloops and schooners. Their crews are young and inexperienced. Their land militia is untrained and disorganized."

"They repelled us once with similar odds as I recall," the admiral said dryly.

"Hardly similar, Admiral. We have one hundred ships in the blockade line alone. We have another eight hundred at our disposal, of which fewer than half are occupied in the war with Europe. No, sir, their only strength lies in their leadership. Men like Decatur and the secretary of the navy Paul Hamilton, men who can recruit the private forces and thus gain the loyalty—and incredible firepower—of men like Morgan Wade."

"And you think you can change all of that by arresting and removing one privateer?" Bennett Winfield looked amused.

"It is my job to discourage the private forces. How better to do it than cutting down one of their most prominent members?"

"You still have to prove your case against Wade," Bennett reminded him. "If what you say is true and if he is in the employ of Captain Decatur, they will accept nothing less than cold, hard evidence for the arrest. That will mean getting damned close to him, something no one has been able to do so far."

"Indeed. His intelligence network appears to be astonishing . . . and almost as reliable as my own. However, I was hoping your wife might be able to shed some light on the matter."

Glasse was smiling as he made the statement, a smile which seemed to freeze the air in the room. One by one the shock of his words registered on the men's faces, and they turned to stare at Summer Winfield.

"My wife, sir?" Bennett's voice was dangerously low. "In what way were you hoping she could help?"

"She was on board the *Chimera,* was she not?" Glasse looked to Summer for confirmation. "Both you and your brother were picked up by Wade off Saint Barthélemy after the *Sea Vixen*'s unfortunate demise."

Sir Lionel's brows knitted together. "You are going to have to explain yourself, sir. I'll not have anyone coming into my house making wild accusations and upsetting my daughter."

Glasse was still regarding Summer with a cadaverous smile. "I assure you it is not my intention to upset Mrs. Winfield. I merely hoped to learn more than what was in the official report of your rescue."

Bennett surged to his feet. "Now see here, Glasse—"

"Sit down, Commodore Winfield. There is no need for a display of chivalry. For my part, I can promise you that nothing your wife says will leave this room. I can also promise you that my sources are impeccable. I happen to *know* Mrs. Winfield and her brother were rescued by the *Chimera,* not the *Vigilant.* I also know Captain Morgan Wade was at the helm, not Stuart Roarke, although I can fully appreciate why the distinction was not made at the time."

"You are coming very close to abusing your welcome, sir," Bennett said coolly. "I urge you to caution."

"How the blazes did you deduce it was Wade?" Sir Lionel

demanded. "Oh, do sit down, Bennett. Obviously there were more than five men on this island who were familiar with the name Roarke. At least let us hear what the bounder has to say before we run him through."

Glasse cleared his throat and straightened his waistcoat. "My deductions were not all that difficult, not to someone who has studied Wade's background as closely as I have. Stuart Roarke's name has been mentioned several times as an associate, although in what capacity it is not generally known. Here, too, Mrs. Winfield may be able to help us. . . . Does he or does he not work for Morgan Wade?"

Summer met the black eyes unwaveringly. "He does."

"Ahh," Glasse leaned forward, "and were you taken to Wade's island? To Bounty Key?"

"We were."

"And . . . ?"

"And we spent one day there before we were brought back by Mr. Roarke. If you were hoping I could tell you where the island is, I'm sorry to have to disappoint you. As I have already explained to my husband, I have no idea. Michael could tell you it lay in a northerly direction; I can only tell you it had white beaches and a quaint fishing village. There were no castles, no dungeons, and no walled garrisons."

"A deep-water harbor? Surely you would know that."

Summer's eyes took on a slight greenish cast. "The *Vigilant* had no trouble with anchorage."

"And the *Chimera?*"

She hesitated a heartbeat's length. "I did not see the *Chimera* after we were put ashore. She was not anchored with the *Vigilant*."

Glasse digested this scrap of information. "You mentioned a fishing village. Did you happen to hear a name?"

"If it had one, I wasn't told."

"I can attest to the fact that Summer did not even know the name of the island until she heard it from me," Bennett said.

"Very well, but did the island have any special features? Any landmarks that might be visible from the sea? Any volcanoes? or reefs?"

Summer moistened her lips. "Volcanoes? No, nothing like that. Nothing visible at all. A beach, a village . . ."

"Yes, yes." Glasse frowned. "What of land masses nearby . . . other islands perhaps?"

"Unfortunately we arrived before dawn—in darkness—and when we left, both Michael and I were told to remain belowdecks until we were well away from the island. Mr. Roarke took several changes in course, though; of that I am fairly certain."

"Why do you say that?"

"Unless I am mistaken, sir, the sun still rises in the east and sets in the west."

Sir Lionel guffawed loud enough to earn a glance from Farley Glasse. He adjusted his periwig and signaled for the brandy decanter to be passed his way. Glasse reverted his attention to Summer. The undercurrent of hostility was not lost on him. Her thick lashes could not totally conceal the sparks in the depths of her eyes. Her cheeks were warmly flushed, her lovely mouth was firm and unyielding. He sensed she knew more than she was imparting.

"You did not see the *Chimera* again?"

"No."

"Have you any idea where it was taken?"

"Probably away to be repaired. As I recall, the captain was furious when he found out it would take a month or more to make her seaworthy again."

If Glasse had had longer ears, she was sure they would have perked up.

"The *Chimera* was damaged?"

Summer did not answer at once; she smoothed a wrinkle on her skirt. The dress was one of her favorites among her new purchases—peach moiré with a soft rose velvet overdress. She doubted if she would wear it again in the near future.

"Forgive me for saying so, Mr. Glasse, but you seem to have tried and convicted Captain Wade without actually having any proof of his guilt. What is to stop ten other privateers from taking his place even if you manage to try him for treason?" She arched a brow delicately. "What grounds will you invent for dealing with the others?"

"Wade is as guilty as sin, Mrs. Winfield. Discounting the charges of treason and espionage, as Sir Edmund Granville he is still sought for the brutal slaying of a young woman in London. Murder, Mrs. Winfield. Indefensible. Your apparent sympathy for the man is highly irregular under those circumstances."

The color in Summer's cheeks deepened. "I have sympathy for any man who is convicted without a chance to properly defend himself," she said slowly, "regardless of the charges."

"He will have ample opportunity to do so, Mrs. Winfield."

"With men like you as his judge and jury? I would be surprised if he reached the courtroom alive."

Glasse was mildly taken aback. His eyes glittered maliciously at the defiance in her manner, and he wondered just how far he should test the commodore's patience.

"You have a point to make, madam?"

"A point, sir? I believe the *Northgate* made it when she opened fire on Captain Wade while his ship was at anchor, crippled and visibly unable to defend itself."

The silence in the room could have been sliced through with a knife. Only Farley Glasse gave no indication of surprise.

"It is a common enough practice, madam, for a ship to fire a warning shot across another's bow to signal it to stand to."

"This warning shot—would it be twenty cannon firing at once?"

When no one answered immediately, Summer searched out Harvey Aslop, Bennett's adjutant. He was dreadfully shy in the presence of women, especially those with whom he was smitten. He saw the wide gray eyes on him now and shifted awkwardly on his seat. "Well, ma'am, not exactly. Twenty guns would be more like a full broadside."

"And if it was followed almost instantly by a second and third volley?"

Lieutenant Aslop's gaze flicked past Summer and caught the slight shake of Bennett's head. He turned painfully red and lowered his eyes.

"At anchor, you say?" Sir Lionel queried.

"Indeed, Father. Not a sail rigged."

"You mean to say the *Chimera* was attacked—at anchor —with you and Michael on board!"

"Actually, we were in the water . . . swimming. We barely made it back on board in time to enable the captain to elude the *Northgate* without taking any serious damage."

"Come now, Mrs. Winfield," Glasse said sardonically. "You press your credibility. You don't expect us to believe a British ship of the line could fire a series of broadsides at a stationary target and leave it unscathed enough to sail away?"

Summer countered the sneer easily. "As I heard it told, the *Northgate* took the worst of it on a single volley from Captain Wade. Not only that, but she missed the channel completely and had to veer sharply to avoid running aground on one of the islands."

"Why haven't you mentioned this before now?" Bennett asked quietly.

"To be quite honest, I don't know. Outrage perhaps. Or embarrassment that an officer of the British Navy would fire on a helpless ship and crew."

"Who is the captain of the *Northgate?*" Sir Lionel demanded of Admiral Stonekipper.

"Chap by the name of Forbes, I believe. If what Summer says is true, he won't be much longer."

"You should have someone at the helm who knows his business," said Glasse.

"His business?" Summer shook her head in disbelief. "And if Michael and I had been killed, would you have the excuses at hand to explain it away?"

"I have no need of excuses to explain my behavior, madam," he said coldly. "Whereas you, dear lady, will find it downright uncomfortable if it is discovered you are withholding information that would see Morgan Wade into our possession. I caution you against any such treasonable actions, regardless of whether you feel you owe the man a debt of gratitude."

Bennett was on his feet a split second before Harvey Aslop. "That remark was uncalled for. My wife has been through a great deal as it is without having to suffer your insolence. You will apologize at once and remove yourself from this house."

Glasse's lips twisted down. "Naturally, I meant no offense. Forgive me, Mrs. Winfield. I must confess to a certain degree of zealousness where my pursuits are concerned." He stood and bowed formally to her, then to Sir Lionel before walking to the door.

"And not a moment too soon," the governor grumbled. "Another minute and I'd have called him out myself. Bennett, Aslop—have a drink, lads, and calm yourselves down. He isn't worth the sweat."

Admiral Stonekipper frowned at the soggy end of his cigar. "He'll be trouble, though, mark my words. And not the best enemy to be had, either. I've seen dozens of them in my day: troublemakers, warmongers. They don't care who they fight as long as they find the jugular and are in for the kill." He glanced up from beneath his brows. "If there is anything at all in the bilges for Glasse to sniff out, my guess is he'll sniff it. Likewise, if there is anything more you can tell us, Summer, you'd best have it out now."

"I don't believe this," she cried indignantly. "Are you doubting my loyalty now, too?"

"Good God, no," the admiral chortled. "These two young whips'd have me flat out and gelded in no time . . . er, pardon me."

"You did neglect to say anything about the attack," Sir Lionel chided. "I'm all for admiring a fox who's cunning enough to outwit the hounds all morning long—but it doesn't mean he shouldn't be run to ground. And treason, by God! If the man's an Englishman—"

"Believe me, Father," she said bitterly, "Morgan Wade is no more an Englishman than is his President Madison."

"Summer—"

"There is absolutely nothing more I can add to what I have told you already. We were on the *Chimera* for seven days—two of them anchored off Saint Martin. We sailed five days and five nights and were attacked on the last day by a British frigate before we made it safely to an island which I would not know again if I sailed directly past it! If this concludes the interrogation, *gentlemen,* you will please excuse me. I seem to have developed a sudden headache."

She stood up and swept past Bennett to the door. She did not acknowledge the hasty murmurs or the call to "hold up there" from her father.

"By Jove, she takes after her mother," he grumbled, spreading his coattails to sit again. "Never once ended an argument face-to-face with that woman, either."

"Well, she did tell us something we didn't know," Lieutenant Aslop ventured to say when they were settled with cigars and more brandy.

Bennett glared at him. "You'd best explain that, sir."

"Oh, I meant no disrespect, Commodore. It's just that, well, Mrs. Winfield did say five days and five nights, with the attack occurring on the fifth day. As soon as the *Northgate* returns from patrol, her log should tell us precisely where the . . . er, mishap took place. It narrows the area for Bounty Key considerably."

"Do you know how many deep-water channels there are in the Northern Crescent?" the admiral snorted.

"No, wait," Bennett said, narrowing his eyes. "Aslop has a valid point. Summer said the *Northgate* had to veer sharply to avoid running into an island. If one assumes she meant there was not a wide enough berth for two ships to pass, she has given us more than a slim clue. Sir Lionel, perhaps we could look at one of your charts of the West Indies?"

"Certainly m'boy." He led the way across the hall into a paneled library. Every free foot of space on the walls was taken up by charts, mounted and framed as if they were expensive works of art. Hung on one wall was a large scale representation of the Caribbean with the islands marked in as accurately as they were known. "Will this one do?"

"Splendidly. All right, Aslop." The commodore stood in front of the chart. "Five days. You and I have patrolled these islands as many times as any men. . . . where would a five-day sail from Saint Barthélemy put us? We know the *Chimera* is a light frigate, third or fourth rating comparably, smaller across the beam than the *Northgate* and much faster. She carries three masts, and at full rigging can reportedly reach speeds in excess of fifteen knots."

Admiral Stonekipper whistled appreciatively.

Bennett nodded grimly. "She's a beautiful design to begin with, and I understand Wade has made several innovations over the years, including armaments. He carries thirty-eight guns in his main battery—twenty-four long guns and fourteen heavy carronades—plus an assortment of lighter swivel guns and bow chasers. It is unusually fine equipment for a privateer."

He turned back to the map. "As you say, there are a thousand channels in these islands, but what we are looking for is a narrow deep-water straight approximately four days' sail from Saint Bart's."

"She was taking on water," Aslop reminded him. "That would slow Wade. And if it were me and my ship, I'd be inclined to hang the risk and plot a course as direct as I dared."

Bennett nodded. "A steady nor' by nor'west, according to Michael. Not at full sail . . . say eight, ten knots at the most. He could have made it as far as the Cats, but I don't think so. He could have veered during the night, back-tracked, threaded his way down through the Mona Passage and ended up somewhere around Jamaica, but again, I don't think so. His home port is somewhere in this area, gentlemen"—he circled an area of the map with a finger—"I'd be willing to stake my gold braid on it."

"The Twin Sirens, sir," Aslop gasped excitedly. "Almost dead center."

Bennett studied the map closely. "By God, you're right. If that's the channel Summer was speaking of, we're damned lucky we didn't lose the *Northgate* altogether."

Sir Lionel was craning his neck to see and holding his wig in place at the same time. "What the blazes are you talking about? Why should we lose a frigate up there?"

"Well, sir, Summer implied that the *Northgate* had a near miss with one of the islands. The question was on my lips, just as I could see it on Glasse's, but he let his pomposity get in the way." Bennett used his hands to act out the motion of ship and land. "Why didn't the ship just tack around the island and come at Wade from behind? One plausible reason could be the Twin Sirens."

"They're part of a reef, sir," Aslop explained further. "Bloody treacherous if you haven't been forewarned. The Sirens look innocent enough, two cone-shaped islands in the middle of apparently clear seas. But they are, in reality, only two visible tips of a vast ridge of coral, most of it lying less than a fathom underwater. It stretches at least ten miles in either direction, and the only way through it—"

"Is through the Sirens," Sir Lionel guessed.

"Or the Sisters, as they have been dubbed," Bennett said. "The channel dividing them is a natural rift in the coral, but you have to approach it just so or you risk tearing the keel off your ship. As I understand it, the Sisters were a favorite killing ground for pirates. They could either give chase to a ship and watch it trap itself on the reef, or they could lure it into the channel and have the currents do most of the work for them. For Wade to have anchored there means he knows those waters damn well. He'd have to know the winds and the currents like the back of his hand to risk it."

"Well, I'll be damned." Sir Lionel drained his glass loudly. "You're a credit to your uniform, Bennett, m'boy. Both of you young men are."

Commodore Winfield smiled blandly. "Now all we have to do is isolate the islands within a day's sail or be lucky enough to stumble across the one Wade calls Bounty Key. It is a shame we don't know ahead of time when he plans to cut through the Sirens. It would be a fairly simple maneuver to lie somewhere on the other side of the reef—there are dozens of little islands to give cover—and simply follow him home."

Admiral Stonekipper nodded thoughtfully. "How long do you estimate your work on the *Caledonia* will take?"

"Two weeks," Bennett replied. "Then another ten days or so for sea trials."

"Hmmm. These sea trials . . . where were you proposing to conduct them? And are you certain ten days is a fair enough test?"

Bennett returned the admiral's steady gaze. "Why,

naturally it would be better to run her completely through her paces."

"On a patrol, for instance? I imagine the revenuers would be appreciative of extra support. I understand the French are becoming a nuisance through the Mona Straits . . . and points north."

"North, sir?"

"Mmmm. Wouldn't hurt to go up and have a closer look at those dozens of little islands you mentioned . . . discreetly, of course."

"Of course," Bennett smiled.

"When is the *Northgate* due in from her patrol?"

"Within the week, I'm sure."

"This Captain Forbes . . . I don't know the man all that well. It won't do to have a hothead at the wheel, though, not when the climate is beginning to warm up. What about Ashton-Smythe? I heard he was up for a command of his own."

"I believe he is, sir. Emory is a good man; his officers speak highly of him."

"I believe I'll give it some serious thought. In the meantime, Winfield, I trust I can leave the details of your sea trials to you. A lot of nonsense, this business about not using our warships to go out and hunt the blighters down. Never mind. That'll change any day now, mark my words. As soon as the king's mistress finds herself short of spices and sugar for her sweets, we'll be given our hunting orders. For the moment"—the admiral indicated the door—"I might suggest a little sweetening closer to home. I have a feeling we were all to blame for Summer's headache. You will extend our apologies to her?"

"Of course, sir."

Sir Lionel chuckled and thumped his son-in-law heartily on the shoulder. "Hold her hand and tell her she's very clever. That'll warm her soon enough. Tell a woman she's foolish and pea-brained, and they lord it over you for weeks on end. Now, gentlemen, if we have concluded our business . . . I have some rare Jamaican rum that wants tasting."

Harvey Aslop declined politely, citing a midnight duty watch on the *Caledonia*.

Bennett lingered in the library, listening as the rumble of voices crossed the hallway and faded behind the closed doors of the drawing room. He stared thoughtfully up at the map and finished the two swallows of brandy remaining in his glass.

The Twin Sirens.

"I'm looking forward to meeting you there, Captain Wade," he murmured. "More than you can know."

12

SUMMER TRAILED her hand down the iron grillwork that covered the lower half of the window. She was in the sitting room that comprised part of their suite of rooms in the south wing of Government House. The lamps were not lit, and she was curled into the cushions of the window seat, bathed in the glow of moonlight streaming through the open shutters. Her hair was brushed loose and gleamed silver in the light. Her skin was faintly luminescent. The vines growing through the grillwork had sprinkled the cushions with fallen jessamine petals, which she collected and set free on the currents of night air. Directly in her line of vision were the formal gardens, the rows of palm trees and flagstone pathways, the arbors, the huge central fountain that trapped the moonlight and turned the water into a cascade of spilling diamonds.

She sighed and snapped off a fresh blossom.

Tonight's display in the drawing room had not been an isolated incident. For some inexplicable reason the tension and confusion she had felt since disembarking from the *Vigilant* had not lessened a degree. There were a number of causes, she supposed. Unavoidable mention of Morgan Wade, for one thing, kept the memories alive and thriving. Her feelings of guilt seemed to grow every day, guilt for what had happened, guilt over her inability to just come right out and tell Bennett what had taken place in the aftercabin of the *Chimera*, guilt that she could not forget what happened that night on Bounty Key.

Why? Why couldn't she forget? The wedding had been a

complete success. She had looked and felt her radiant best. Bennett had been breathtakingly handsome. He was proving to be a kind and considerate husband, a gentle, patient lover. Smooth—that was how she thought of Bennett. His skin was smooth, his voice was smooth, his motions were smooth and cool and precise. She might never have known there was anything missing from their marriage if not for the seven tumultuous days and nights spent with Morgan Wade.

Summer squeezed her eyes shut, forcing away the sudden image of a dark smiling face. She could hear him laughing as if he were in the room with her—the deep, resonant lash of sound that had her temper instantly on guard and her flesh tingling in anticipation.

Bennett's laugh was smooth and calculated, like everything he did. He was stern and cool and efficient. He was the perfect gentleman in every way, the perfect husband, the perfect lover. She knew there were women on the island bitterly envious of her, of what she had with Bennett Winfield. She knew that most arranged marriages were dismal stilted affairs where both partners ground their teeth, held their chins high and endured as best they could. So why was she miserable? Miserable and . . . and restless.

She had startled him—startled them all tonight—with the story of the *Northgate*'s attack on the *Chimera*. She had seen the anger flush into Bennett's cheeks with the embarrassment of having to question her like any other stranger. She should have told Father and Bennett everything right from the beginning. She should have let the words tumble out without stopping to think, without stopping to reason if it felt right or wrong to say them. Wade deserved to be caught and brought to trial for his crimes. My God . . . a traitor, a spy, a murderer, a smuggler, a rapist . . .

She crushed the blossom in her fingers and threw it out the window.

Why should she feel as if she were betraying him? She was the one who had been betrayed—physically and emotionally. Glasse had sensed she was lying tonight, hiding something; she could see it in the ferret eyes. Bennett had known it, too, just as he knew there was more to the story of her time spent on the *Chimera*.

Summer looked up suddenly and felt the two warm spots rise in her cheeks.

"Bennett. You startled me. I did not hear the door open."

He was just standing there in the shadows, his white breeches and starched collar catching the dim light from the window.

"I'm sorry. I thought you would have heard my boots. Why on earth are you sitting here in the dark?"

"I prefer it when . . . when I need to think. Darkness and quiet—" She saw him walk over to the table. "Has everyone left?"

"Aslop had the watch. Your father and the admiral are introducing themselves to a bottle of rum."

She smiled dourly. "Meaning they will be tippled by the early hours, and poor Wilkins will have to slide them both into bed."

Bennett lifted the glass chimney from a lamp, fetched a taper from the fireplace and touched it to the wick. It flared and smoked greasily for a moment, then settled to an even flame. He waved the match out slowly and replaced the chimney.

"I'm afraid I have some bad news," he said, studying her face in the glow. "The admiral wants me to take the *Caledonia* out for her sea trials. He is anxious to see the results of my changes."

"So soon? I mean . . ."

He smiled briefly. "Not much of a honeymoon, was it? And he does want us to leave as soon as possible."

"Of course. I understand." She reached for another blossom. "When will you be sailing?"

He watched the movement of her arm, the slight swell where her breasts pushed on the shimmery satin dressing gown. "If I truly drove the men hard we could be ready within the week"—his eyes rose to her face—"but I told him we couldn't possibly leave before the end of two."

"How long will you be away?"

He took a deep breath. "Several weeks. A month perhaps."

"Oh."

"I'm glad you sound disappointed; it makes me feel a little better."

"Of course I'm disappointed," she said and quickly lowered her lashes. "I'm only just getting used to being called Mrs. Winfield after a week. . . . I should have liked a year or two before I had to start explaining where my husband has gone."

"Your father will see that you are kept busy." His face was out of the lamplight, and Summer could not clearly see his expression. "You looked troubled when I came in. Has Farley Glasse upset you that much?"

"No." She sighed, after a moment. "Not really. I suppose I have been expecting something like that to happen. It just caught me by surprise, that's all."

"You stood your ground well enough. And while I might not admit it in front of the admiral or Sir Lionel, you were justified in defying the man. His type are graced with too much power and not enough sense of how to use it. Mind you, I'd also have to concur with the admiral: Glasse will make a formidable enemy."

"I am not a threat to him."

"Not personally, but your politics are."

"Politics? I have no politics."

"You defended Morgan Wade. He is an American privateer, one who causes us all unnecessary aggravation. By defending him, you as much as openly denounce our own policies."

She rounded on him. "I was merely defending the right for any man to have justice and a fair trial. Glasse has condemned him without any pretense of offering either."

"Wade hardly deserves applause or sympathy. He is a spy and a murderer."

"There is no proof of either charge, only speculation. Glasse's speculation."

"How much proof do you need?" Bennett asked coldly. "He sells guns and information to our enemies and hides behind an American flag. He is a man without any loyalties at all. To any*one* or any*thing*. And furthermore" —he pulled his coattails forward and sat on the vacant half of the window seat—"I do not intend to sit here and argue with you about the merits of a Yankee privateer . . . not with the moonlight doing such wonderful things to your eyes and your hair. . . ." He leaned forward and pressed his lips to her temple.

"Then you are not angry with me?" she whispered. "You are not going to tell me I behaved childishly or unthinkingly?"

"Testily, perhaps. Not childishly." His hand traced a line down her cheek and toyed with a silvery ringlet.

"I'm sorry if I embarrassed you."

"No harm done." He paused and added on a quieter note, "However, I do wish you had told me about the *Northgate* sooner. It could have saved us both an awkward moment or two."

"Yes, I suppose so. I thought perhaps Michael would have mentioned it to you; you seem to spend so much time together."

"He never speaks of anything that happened," Bennett murmured, and his hand brushed aside the hair trailing over her shoulder. "In fact, I don't think your brother approves of me overmuch."

"Michael? How can you say that? He is forever badgering you with questions."

Her husband smiled. "About ships and armaments and naval strategies, he is indeed full of questions—and amazing theories. But when it comes time for answers, he becomes remarkably shy. Not unlike his sister, whom he dotes upon."

Summer straightened slightly, trying not to tense against the feel of Bennett's fingers where they traced lower along her neck. "I'm sure you will win him over. He has only had Father to keep him company for the past four years, and"—she closed her eyes. Bennett's lips had replaced his fingers, moving leisurely along the curve of her throat—"and he really has . . . no one. . . ."

She could feel his breath warming the expanse of her throat, spreading the tingle down her arms and into her chest. She knew he felt it as well, and his hand came up and tucked beneath her chin, tilting her lips up to meet his. Her mouth was soft and moist and willing, and he explored it thoroughly. The breath halted in her throat, and she swayed against him; her hands moved up to his shoulders, and she gave herself into the circle of his arms, returning his kiss with a sigh.

Bennett abandoned her mouth and lowered his head, following the deep plunge of her dressing gown down to the invitingly fragrant cleft between her breasts. She ran her fingers into the wheat-colored hair, forcing herself to relax as he worked the ribbons of the bodice loose and sent his hand and mouth searching beneath the satin.

Summer watched the nuzzling blond head, the greedy suckling lips and tongue, and she smiled as the heat began to wash into her like waves of golden honey. Everything was going to be all right; she knew it was. She was married to a man who loved her; she was married to a man she had true affection for. She tightened her hands and pressed into him, feeling her skin constrict with pleasure.

Bennett carried her into the adjoining bedroom and set her on the deep feather bed. He stepped back to loosen and discard his own clothes—slowly, methodically draping his tunic and shirt, breeches, stockings and drawers over the arms of a chair. His body was pale and cool to the touch; his chest was hairless and sculpted into bands of lean, smooth muscle.

He covered her with tiny nibbling kisses and murmured her name once before settling himself between her thighs. Summer sighed, and her arms went around him.

This was the way it was meant to be. A place for quiet loving tenderness, not a battleground of clashing wills. Bennett was here, he was her husband, and she wanted to love him.

She trembled as his hands circled her waist. She whimpered softly and rose against the stabs of pleasure using her hands, her hips to urge him closer, deeper. She gasped and strained upward . . . but the slow stretching promise of release was simply not there. There was no growing wave of passion, no sweet ache of his body joining to hers. A response was barely being touched on when he grunted and pushed a final time, his entire body stiffening against the violent surge of ecstasy. He groaned and heaved the air from his lungs, collapsing heavily on top of Summer as she choked back a cry of disappointment.

She bit down on her lips, shutting her eyes against the memory of jet black hair and massive rippling shoulders. She felt Bennett stir, and she relaxed her arms and legs from around his body, enough that he could prop himself on his elbows and gaze down at her.

The pale blue eyes were glittering strangely; the jaw was squared and taut.

"How dare you," he hissed.

Summer's mouth went slack, and she blinked her eyes clear. "Wh-what?"

"How dare you call out to another man in my bed," he snarled.

Summer was unprepared for the sharp quick slash of his hand across her cheek. "It was bad enough I had to take his leavings, but by God, I'll not take this."

"Bennett, I—"

The hand came down twice more, shocking her into silence. He pushed himself free in disgust and sat at the side of the bed, needing several deep breaths to calm himself. When he had regained control, he stood up and began to draw on his clothes, taking the same methodical care as he had in removing them. He did not look at Summer again, did not heed her weeping or the sight of her cringed into a small ball. He dressed and strode from the room, slamming the door hard behind him.

September 1811

13

"OH, THERE IS no mistake, Mrs. Brown, I assure you." Doctor Von Zernak wiped his hands on a square of white towel and came around the side of the curtain just as Summer was fastening the ribboned belt of her frock. He was a short, wiry man with a huge split-veined nose that gave him the appearance of a parrot.

Summer's gaze was fixed out the window, watching the crowds mill about on the street. She had come to a doctor in Speightstown to avoid any undue attention; now she was glad.

"Mrs. Brown? Mrs. Brown, are you all right?"

She started at the touch on her arm. "What—?"

"I know, my dear, sometimes these things come as a shock. Still, you did say your bodily functions have been awry?"

"Well, yes, but I thought . . ." Summer ran out of words. She had thought it was the shock. The ordeal of the shipwreck. The tension . . . her two months of marriage had produced a great deal of that.

Doctor Von Zernak frowned. The young woman's reaction was hardly one of pleasure. He shrugged and scribbled the name of an alchemist's shop and a blend of herbs that would ease the internal discomforts.

"You must try to take better care of yourself in the future months, Mrs. Brown," he chided gently, handing her the slip of paper. "The cramps and sickness you have been experiencing are quite normal, but we must try to build up your strength. You'll have to find your appetite again if you want to bring a strong, healthy child into the world."

Summer only smiled halfheartedly.

"Well, no matter. Babies are remarkably determined at times. Once they conquer the first three months, they often become downright tenacious. I would say you are well out of the danger period, and since you appear to be reasonably healthy—"

"What did you say?"

"I beg your pardon? Oh, about the danger—?"

"No . . . no, you said . . . three months?"

"Why, yes. Judging from the size and position . . . of course, you can appreciate the difficulty in being precise, but together with your own corroboration"—he nodded and pursed his lips—"I would say three months at the very least."

Summer's gray eyes enlarged until they seemed to overwhelm the pale face. She took a firmer grip on the edge of the table.

Three months!

Three months ago she had not even been in Bridgetown. Three months ago she had been . . . on board the *Chimera!* She had been with Morgan Wade!

"Mrs. Brown?" Doctor Von Zernak was openly concerned. Her face was turning ashen before his eyes. Her hands were trembling and ice-cold; her lips were all but bloodless. "Mrs. Brown, you mustn't upset yourself."

"No, no . . . I—" her hand reached out suddenly, grasping his arm. "Are you absolutely certain? Is there any way you could be mistaken? Forgive me; I don't mean to question your ability, but you did say there was no way to be precise."

He sighed and took both of her hands in his. Too many times he had been asked the same question for the same indiscreet reasons: a husband away, or a husband too inattentive to his wife's needs . . . or simply no husband at all. This one was so young and so vulnerable, and he saw the desperation in her eyes. He wished he could tell her anything she wanted to hear.

"My dear Mrs. Brown. It is my opinion that barring any unforeseen difficulties, in less than six months' time you will give birth to the child you are now carrying. You may wish a second opinion, and if that is the case, I can recommend several good physicians on the island."

"No," she whispered, and her hands slipped from his. "No, that will not be necessary. I believe you; it's just that . . . I wasn't prepared. I mean . . ."

"There now." He smiled and tried to sound cheerful. "Nothing extraspecial in life is ever expected. That is why we refer to them as surprises. And this little surprise you are carrying will bring you more happiness than you think possible now; you just wait and see."

Summer took a deep breath and reached for her gloves.

"Now I want you to promise me you will take this herbal mix. We want to deliver you of a strong child, and in these tropical climates the tendency leans to early, sickly arrivals."

"Early!" She gasped the word without thinking.

The doctor glanced over the rims of his pince-nez and sighed. He took back the slip of paper, jotted down the names of two more herbs and inked a small star beside both.

"Have a separate sachet of these made up. Brew a strong tea out of them and drink it twice a day, once in the morning and once late in the evening. There are no guarantees, of course, but . . ."

"Thank you. You've been very kind."

"Mmmm. You just see that you take care of yourself. You'll have to fatten yourself up some, or all the herbs in the world won't help. I take it you have your own family doctor?"

Summer flushed slightly. "Yes, in Bri—" and her jaw snapped shut.

"Bridgetown, eh? Well, there is no need to see him at once if you'd rather not, but I would be inclined to tell him about the herbs should any complications arise."

"Complications?"

"Bleeding near the end of term. Excessive swelling of the joints—ankles in particular. And of course if you should go too far past the nine months."

"I promise I shall tell him."

He assisted her to the office door. When she was out on

the stoop and down the stairs, he shook his head and clucked inwardly over his own foolishness. She must have known what she was doing at the time. He was just a soft touch for big eyes and small miseries.

Summer walked the two blocks of storefronts to where the carriage was waiting and signaled for the driver to take her back home. The trip would take an hour, perhaps long enough to settle the churning in her stomach.

Three months.

Morgan Wade's child.

Why? Why did it have to happen to her, and why now of all times? Her relationship with Bennett Winfield was not the best, especially since he had returned from his first patrol with the *Caledonia*. He had been surly and short-tempered, and it had been only through bits and pieces of conversations she had learned the reason for it. He had scoured the islands north of somewhere called the Sirens for a month, waiting for the *Chimera* to make an appearance. When he returned to Bridgetown, he was met with the news that Morgan Wade had somehow slipped past him and had been seen several days ago lying off Saint Lucia.

Summer closed her eyes and leaned back wearily in the seat. The carriage rolled and swayed in the ruts of the roadway, and she noted absently that the crest they were on skirted the same bay where Stuart Roarke had docked the *Vigilant*.

It was foolish and childish and naive, but in all of these weeks she had not considered the possibility that she had left Bounty Key carrying Wade's child. There had to be some semblance of love present to produce a child, surely there had to be. She may have been swept up in the turmoil, the excitement, the intrigue, despite all of her protests to the contrary . . . but it certainly was not love. Love was tenderness and affection and easy laughter. It was a look or a word or something to make the world grind to a breathless standstill without even having to touch. That was love, and she had no such feelings for Morgan Wade.

Only that once—in the study—but it had been the wine. The amount of wine she had consumed and the accident with the crystal goblet had made the world stand still for an eternity. *But it had just been the wine!*

Summer felt a splash of wetness on her hand and brushed her fingertips across her cheeks, dashing away the warm spill of tears. It was too late for any of this. She was carrying the consequences of that one night when she had allowed her body to overrule her conscience, and it was too late for recriminations. There was far worse to come: She still had to face Bennett and suffer the cold accusations in the pale blue eyes.

He had left Bridgetown on the *Caledonia* two nights after the terrible scene in the bedroom. In those two days he had barely spoken to her and on his departure had kissed her perfunctorily on the cheek, but only because Sir Lionel had been present. Summer's anxiety and guilt had festered during the six weeks of his absence. She had lost weight and lost most of the sparkle from her eyes.

When Bennett arrived home, she had been as nervous as on her wedding night. She'd changed her dress three times before being satisfied; she'd scolded two maids and worried a third into tears when her hair refused to respond to the curling tongs. Bennett had walked into the front hall, and for all of five seconds she had felt that her efforts had not been in vain, that he had forgiven, that he was determined to forget. His eyes had quickly lost their glint of approval, and the smile had been caught and forced into submission. That evening he had remained in the study with Sir Lionel until she began to wonder if he would retire to the bedroom at all. But he did. And he had taken her with such careless brutality she was still numb from the shock of it the next morning. Each night since had been a repetition. Her body ached; her flesh was marred with scores of bruises. And now she had this to face him with.

The carriage seemed to make remarkable time, and it drew to a halt on the cobbled drive of Government House long before Summer had collected her thoughts. She murmured her thanks to the coachman and entered the house as if she were walking through a dream. She heard voices coming from the receiving room and veered away from the door, knowing the last thing she needed or wanted was to have to pretend to be charming and gracious for her father's boorish associates. Thankfully the doors were closed but for an inch or so, and she could move stealthily past without being seen or heard.

"The last sighting we had of the *Chimera* placed her just off Ragged Point," a male voice said sharply. "She should make port within the next day or so if our information is correct."

"Bloody cheek," Sir Lionel snorted. "You'd think he'd stay well away from this island."

"It wouldn't be sporting," Bennett said dryly. "And it is more or less what I expected of him. The sheer arrogance of the man would prompt him to touch in on Barbados."

Summer held her breath, frozen in front of the doors.

"You say he does business with the Marlowe Brothers here?"

"Yes, sir. They appear to act as the middleman between Wade and the Spaniards."

"Have we enough men watching the warehouses?"

"More than enough. If Wade makes arrangements to purchase those guns through Marlowe, we'll know it within the hour."

"And you've managed it all without rousing any suspicions?"

"The guns have changed hands so many times, gentlemen," came a thin, nasally voice, "I find it difficult to recall myself exactly where they originated."

Summer pressed herself flatter against the wall, her heart leaping up into her throat. Farley Glasse.

"Fine. When we take him, I want every crate and barrel smashed to splinters. I want that entire ship torn apart stem to stern if need be. I want to be able to show the difference in black and white—what he purported to load and what he was found to be holding. Commodore Winfield—you still think your best chance is to take him off the Sirens?"

"I do, Admiral Stonekipper. When he picks up those guns from Port-of-Spain, he's not going to want to dally too long getting them back to Bounty Key. He'll have heard by now that the navy has stepped up their patrols, that we have begun stopping all ships suspected of dealing with the enemy. He'll assume, as we've planned, that the Sirens offer him his only safe option. To that end, I propose we send the *Northgate* on ahead—immediately if possible—to reach the Sirens and block his escape on the far side of the reef."

"And the *Caledonia*?"

"I intend to take her out of port and lie far enough offshore to avoid detection. When the *Chimera* has loaded her cargo, we'll follow in her wake and hopefully catch her between us at the Sirens."

"Rather extraordinary measures, wouldn't you say, Commodore?" was the hesitant reply. "Two heavy frigates? Two warships on an open hunt? The Americans won't like it if they get wind of it."

Summer could almost hear Bennett grinding his teeth. "That is precisely why we cannot take him too close to a British port, sir. Nor can we bottle him up in the harbor in Trinidad; the Spanish would be on us in no time. And he has speed as well as neutrality on his side. Trying to take him in open water has already failed more times than the navy would care to admit. One warship trying to chase him through the Sirens, as Captain Forbes would have told you, is inadequate. If he makes it through the reef, we lose him in the islands. This is the only viable way, sir. The *Northgate* facing his bow and the *Caledonia* on his stern. Hopefully he will realize the futility of even trying to break past us, and we will take him without firing a single shot."

"If you do have to fire, though . . ."

"If I have to fire, sir, I promise you, you'll have his obituary in my report."

"If you have to open fire," Glasse said coldly, "there will be no report. The French will be taking the blame for the kill."

"Just how do you expect to accomplish that?"

"Quite simply. A word here and there, a rumor that Wade tried to win out against a warship . . . all neatly supported by debris from the French vessel the *Étoile*."

"The *Étoile*?"

"A fourty-four gun frigate the *Northgate* stumbled across in the same general area as the Sirens a short while ago. It was hulled rather badly, I'm afraid. Beyond salvage. But Captain Forbes did manage to keep a few mementos, including her masthead."

"I see. Very neatly done. But how do you propose to keep Wade in sight without being seen yourself?"

"With this, gentlemen," Bennett said.

Summer heard a shuffle of feet and was poised to run for the stairs, but none of the footsteps approached the door.

"Good Lord!"

"Indeed," Glasse chuckled. "Several of them were delivered to me just this past week. They are incredible spyglasses, gentlemen. To anyone watching—or searching—the *Caledonia* will appear as nothing more than a peak on a wave on the horizon. To Commodore Winfield and to Captain Ashton-Smythe—whom we now welcome eagerly to the ranks—the *Chimera* will be plain enough to count the rings on her masts."

"By Jove!"

Bennett laughed. "My father-in-law has just discovered how exceptional the view is. . . . May I draw your attention to the upper windows of Madame LaRose's fine establishment."

There were more eager laughs and ribald remarks, then the sound of crystal kissing crystal, and Glasse's voice rose above the noise.

"I toast our success, both on land and at sea."

Summer released her pent-up breath and moved away from the doorway. She hurried up the winding staircase to the south wing and did not slow her pace until she was safely in her sitting room with the door firmly shut behind her. She pulled off her gloves and untied her bonnet, flinging both on a nearby chair. She draped her shawl over the armrest and walked wearily to the cushioned window seat.

Her husband was laying a trap to follow and capture Morgan Wade. She knew the *Caledonia*'s sea trials had been impressive. Her firepower was awesome, her speed and handling at peak efficiency. Bennett was making no attempt to disguise the fact that he wanted to be the one who brought Morgan Wade to justice. From the tone of his voice, she knew this was his plan. His and Glasse's.

Justice? What kind of justice was there in setting a trap? If they planned to let the French take the blame, it meant they expected to leave no witnesses behind to testify otherwise. No witnesses meant no prisoners, despite Bennett's earlier claim that he would see a fair trial for them all.

Thorny, Stuart Roarke, Mr. Phillips . . . they had all shown her kindness in one way or another. Even Mr. Monday had followed Wade into the currents off the channel when she and Michael had foolishly attempted to swim ashore.

And Morgan Wade.

Summer closed her eyes and leaned her brow on the cool wall. Try as she might, she could not hate him. She could not forget him either, and now, if anything, the memory would grow stronger each day. He could have left her to drown. He could have abandoned her on Saint Martin. He could have let the currents deal with her and perhaps saved his ship in the minutes it took to swim out to her and Michael. But he didn't. Did that now mean she owed him more than what she was already paying?

Summer's eyes widened, and she gazed slowly down at the soft outline of her belly. She felt it again: a startled, struggling flicker, like a butterfly beating its wings against a pane of glass.

"What can I do? There is nothing I can do to help! There is nothing I *should* do to help!"

The flutter became stronger, angrier.

"Damn you, Morgan Wade," she whispered. "Damn you!"

She whirled at the sound of footsteps approaching her room. Bennett came through the door a moment later and hesitated on the threshold. He glanced at the bonnet and gloves on the chair, then at the window.

"Back so early? Did you leave anything in the shops?"

"I . . . I was at the dressmaker's."

"And?"

She turned away. "And she said the gowns I ordered would take another week or so."

"A week? Then it's a shame I won't be here to see them. I'm taking the *Caledonia* out on patrol again. Something has come up, and I'll be leaving at dawn."

He closed the door and stood watching her expectantly.

"I heard voices when I came in," she said coolly. "Was that the 'something that came up'?"

Bennett folded his arms across his chest. "You did not care to join us?"

"Not especially. I heard that awful man's voice and walked straight past."

"Farley Glasse?"

"I am surprised Father continues to allow him in the house."

"He was here by my invitation," Bennett pointed out quietly.

"You don't find him offensive?"

"To tell you the truth"—he snapped the gold buttons fastening his collar and thrust a finger down to loosen it—"he is more of a bore than anything else. But he knows what he wants—and what I want—and he wastes no time on pretensions, as you noted once before."

Summer averted her eyes.

"You said you overheard us talking," he continued easily. "Exactly what did you hear?"

"Not much," she said and then faced him. "Only that you are going out after Morgan Wade again."

Bennett's mouth curved down. "And the thought distresses you?"

"Bennett, please . . ." She sighed.

"Does it disturb you to talk about him? You seem able enough to defend him in front of others; why not me?"

"I don't defend him," she argued.

"You don't go out of your way to condemn the man either . . . considering."

"Considering what?" she snapped. "Say it, Bennett. For God's sake, just say it! Don't keep tormenting me with your horrid little smiles and bits of sarcasm. I did not invite his attentions—he raped me! Why can't you believe that?"

"Oh, I believe it. I would have found it impossible to believe if he hadn't. You are a beautiful woman, Summer.

Beautiful and highly desirable. Any man with half an appetite would have had you beneath him before the seawater dried. I myself was sorely tempted to deliver you of your innocence back in London . . . and perhaps I should have, garden party or no. At least I would have had the satisfaction of knowing I cheated Wade out of something."

Summer clasped her hands tightly together. "Please—"

"Instead I have this," Bennett carried on, noting the white lips and the downcast eyes. "I have something I cannot see and cannot fight cropping up in my bed at night. Well, I will not tolerate it, madam. If it takes a killing to purge his shadow, then so be it."

"Why did you marry me?" she asked with a shiver. "If you knew what happened on the *Chimera* . . . why did you insist on going ahead with the marriage? I offered you the choice. I offered to release you from your promise."

Bennett leaned casually against the wall. "I suffered under the misguided notion that you might thank me for it one day. You did not appreciate the gesture?"

"Gesture?" she whispered. "Was that all it was to you?"

"Good heavens, no," he said and smiled. "Your father added fifty thousand pounds and clear title to the Dover cane plantation."

Summer's gray eyes registered shock. Dover was one of the richest plantations on the island. It produced almost a quarter of the total sugarcane crop for Barbados . . . and it had supposedly been designated as part of Michael's inheritance.

"Don't look so horrified, my dear. You should know by now that your father does not stand on ceremony. Ambition and greed go hand in hand in life. I have a great deal of the one, and your father has the profits to show for the other."

"What are you trying to say?"

He moved away from the wall. "Marrying the governor's daughter and acquiring one of the more profitable tracts of land in Barbados has assured me of a comfortable future. Having a naval officer—hopefully an admiral, in short order—as a son-in-law all but ensures your father's position here in the islands. His fortunes have not all been amassed by, shall we say, *ethical* means." He stopped, and the smile became slightly mocking. "That isn't to say I do not feel any attraction to you, my dear. I do. You seep into one's blood and make a man almost forget his priorities in life."

Summer stared at Bennett, astounded that he could be making such admissions so calmly, so totally without reserve, when it was partially because he continued to act the role of injured party that she was still plagued by guilt.

"You were the one who wanted the truth," he murmured. "And I might remind you I was not the only one who was offered the opportunity to refuse the arrangements."

"No," she said, finally finding her voice. "No, you were not. But you should have told me about your ambitions from the start. It might have made us both feel less like fools."

"I doubt it. I still would have had this husbandly need to see Wade out of my bed and stretching by his neck at a yardarm."

Summer was prepared to cast a scathing retort his way but faltered when she saw his hands begin to free the buttons down the front of his tunic. Her mouth went dry and her heartbeat thudded to a standstill.

"What do you think you are doing?"

His smile broadened. "Bidding farewell to my wife, of course. I shall be absent from the warmth of your bed for some time. . . . I would be remiss in my duties if I were to depart without leaving you with fond memories. And now that we have cleared the air, so to speak, there will be no more need to carry on this little sham of righteousness you have been striving to uphold. If there is something extra you need by way of . . . inspiration . . . I would be happy to oblige. My own pleasures have been somewhat hampered of late by your refusal to . . . relax."

"You are contemptible," she said, rising from the seat and starting to walk past him. His hand slashed out and wrapped cruelly around her arm.

"And you, madam? You find nothing slightly contemptible in a wife who cries out for another man in her husband's bed?"

"It happened once," she said from between clenched teeth. "Only once. And I believe I have paid for it a hundred times over."

"Maybe so. Then again, maybe it will take a thousand times for me to forget." He pulled her toward him, and his mouth crushed down on hers.

"Bennett, please—" She struggled against him, but his grip held firm, and she could feel him tugging at the cloth of her bodice. "Please, be reasonable."

"Reasonable?" His blond head came up, and there was an ominous gleam behind his eyes. "I am the most reasonable man you could have hoped for, my love. I have taken your spoiled nature and your petulance with some humor. I have tolerated your moods and your grand silences—not to mention the frigid martyrdom you oblige me with in your bed."

"You have never given me cause to offer anything but," she cried angrily, pushing free of his embrace. "You strut into the room and say nothing. You make no attempt at tenderness or understanding—you simply take what you want, however you want, and expect me to feel grateful for the service. Well, sir, the only gratitude I feel is when you leave my bed in the morning."

She whirled around and walked to the door. The latch, when she rattled it, did nothing, and she turned to find Bennett standing in the same place, holding up a hand to show the key looped around one finger.

"Is this what you are looking for?"

"Unlock this door at once," she ordered calmly.

"I don't believe I will," he said quietly. "Not until you and I reach an understanding."

"What kind of an understanding?"

He advanced a step, and she saw the fine sheen of moisture on his brow. The pale eyes were frightening in their intensity, and she took an involuntary step back.

"The understanding that you belong to me body and soul, Mrs. Winfield. When I tell you to come, you will come. When I tell you to get down on your knees, you will get down on your knees. If you try to deny me anything, in any way, I might be forced to seek further redress at the cost of your father's peace of mind."

"You would tell him?"

"About the so-called rape? I would indeed. And about how I, as the injured party, have striven to please you to no avail. An annulment at this stage of our relationship would hurt you, madam, far more than it would hurt me."

"You wouldn't dare," she whispered, shaking her head.

He held out the key. "Try me. Unlock the door, and we shall see which of us has the most to lose."

Summer thought of the child growing in her womb, and her face lost it's color. Annulment was out of reach. Divorce was unthinkable; the scandal would draw even the king's attention, and the child, when it came, would be regarded with nothing but scorn and ridicule. And yet . . . perhaps the very thing that locked her into the marriage could save her.

"I'm pregnant, Bennett," she announced coldly. "I was at the doctor's this afternoon, not the dressmaker's. He informed me I was two months with child. Two months, Bennett. What do you estimate your chances would be for an admiralty were you to discard a wife and unborn child?"

Bennett stiffened, and his face lost the edge of triumph. His eyes narrowed and fell in spite of himself to the smooth plane of her belly.

"Would you still care to go and see Father now?" she asked, matching the scorn she had heard in his voice. "You might find it harder to convince him of what a shrew I am, of how cold and unloving I have been."

Bennett's gaze bored into her. The muscles in his jaw tensed, and his fingers curled around the key until the knuckles were white.

"Two months, you say? Meaning that in seven months' time we should have a blond, blue-eyed infant to show for our loving efforts? Wade's hair is black, as I recall, as black as his eyes—and his soul."

Summer did not flinch from the veiled insinuation. "I would appreciate it if you would unlock the door now. I thought I might go down and tell Father the happy news."

He stared at her another full minute before walking slowly past her and slotting the key into the lock. Before he allowed her to leave the room, he blocked her path one last time.

"If, in seven months' time, madam, I have any cause to doubt the parentage of the brat you are carrying, these last few days will seem like a blissful fantasy to you."

14

THE NIGHT was moonless. The chill had driven people off the streets and into the warmth of the crowded taverns. The interior of the coach was damp from the sea air that reached through the open windows and pressed Summer into a shivering bundle in the corner. The colder she became, the closer she came to the limit of her patience. It had been a foolhardy idea from the beginning. She had no way of knowing if her note had been delivered to the correct tavern or if anyone would respond to the name of the merchant she had overheard Admiral Stonekipper mention in the study.

She was on the verge of signaling the driver when the sound of a slow footstep on the cobbled street brought her sharply forward on the seat.

The shadow was tall and lean. He walked with a wary eye on the street as well as on the darkened, recessed doorways.

"Mr. Roarke?"

The man halted abruptly. He was trapped in a splash of light from one of the windows, and the brightness slanted off the round spectacles as he sought the source of the whisper.

"Mr. Stuart Roarke?"

"Aye," he said slowly, squinting to see through the darkness, "my name might be Roarke."

"Please—" She unlatched the carriage door and nudged it open. "I mustn't be seen talking to you, but please believe me; it is very important that I do."

Roarke glanced over his shoulder. It was well after

midnight. There was no one else on this side of the street, no one within a hundred paces.

"I have an aversion to entering dark coaches, madam. Especially when I do not know whose it is."

"I am alone, Mr. Roarke," Summer said, leaning further out of the window. She pushed the hood of her cloak back so that her face was silhouetted in the soft glow. "And I am already absent far too long from my home."

Roarke recognized the muted blonde features at once. He crossed over to the coach and stepped inside, taking the seat opposite her in the darkness.

"Mrs. Winfield. I confess you have managed to startle me. Doubly so, since you obviously knew the right name to use in order to arrange this meeting."

"I apologize for the deception. I used the name Marlowe because I did not think my own would succeed in bringing you here . . . but you knew who I was?"

She could not see his face, but the light jumped off the surface of his spectacles as he nodded. "I knew you were Sir Lionel's daughter as soon as I read the list of passengers presumed lost with the *Sea Vixen*. As to your marriage, I only heard of it this afternoon."

"Does . . . does Captain Wade know?"

"No," Roarke said bluntly. "He doesn't. And I am too well acquainted with his temper to want to be the one to enlighten him unless it is absolutely necessary. He and Commodore Winfield share little affection for one another."

"I would prefer if he never found out. About Bennett or about our meeting here tonight."

He said nothing, but the spectacles winked again as he glanced out the window.

"I should also like to apologize to you for my behavior on board the *Vigilant*. It was unpardonable, and I had no right to vent my anger and hostility on you."

"Mrs. Winfield, there is no need to apologize. My own mood was less than companionable as I recall. But I'm sure that isn't why you asked to meet me here tonight."

"No, no it isn't."

"You implied you had important information for me."

Summer moistened her lips. She was beginning to see

his face through the shadows and wondered briefly if she had made a wise choice after all. "Yes, Mr. Roarke. Not so much to tell you something as to warn you."

"Warn me?"

"Yes, my . . . my husband is setting a trap for the *Chimera*. He and several others have worked out what they consider a perfect plan to capture Mor . . . Captain Wade and arrest him for transporting an illegal cargo."

The silence stretched taut between them.

"What kind of a trap do they have in mind, Mrs. Winfield?" he asked quietly, and Summer could detect the instant suspicion.

"My husband took the *Caledonia* out of Bridgetown two days ago, but he is staying well within range to see you when you leave the harbor. He plans to follow you to Port-of-Spain, to wait until you have the guns you have purchased on board, and then he will follow you again as far as the Sirens. He has already dispatched the *Northgate* to wait on the far side of the reef."

Stuart Roarke's face gave absolutely no indication of any reaction, but inwardly he was stunned.

"How do you know all of this?" he asked finally.

"Does it matter, Mr. Roarke? The fact that my husband and half the navy know Captain Wade's plans for the next few weeks should be of more concern to you."

"It is," he admitted grimly.

"The guns," she said and chewed savagely on her lip. "I'm not positive, but I think they were part of the arrangements. I think my husband arranged for the men you deal with to have access to them so that they would innocently be a part of the trap."

"I see."

"Then you believe me?"

"To a point I would have to say you leave me no choice but to believe you."

"To a point?"

"How does your husband plan to follow us around the Caribbean undetected? The *Caledonia* is a first rating, unless our information is wrong. Not altogether invisible against the horizon."

Summer forced a calmness into her voice that she was

far from feeling. "He has a new spyglass . . . a telescope of some kind. I gather it allows him to stay well down on the horizon while it presents you quite clearly."

Roarke was silent another minute.

"Mr. Roarke, I know you find it hard to believe me, but I am telling you the truth. I can even tell you that should the captain not surrender at once at the Sirens, they plan to sink the *Chimera* and leave no witnesses behind. They intend to blame it on a French warship . . . the *Étoile*, I believe . . . so that there will be no repercussions from your government."

"Tell me, Mrs. Winfield, why are you here? Why are you warning us? Forgive me for being blunt, but you are obviously going against the wishes of your father and your husband, not to mention your country. It is more than mildly treasonous for you to be here at all."

"I am well aware of that, Mr. Roarke. I have asked myself the same questions a hundred times in the past several hours. I should be doing everything in my power to help my husband, not Morgan Wade. And please do not think that under any circumstances I would be inclined to do it again. No, perhaps the answer is simply that I owe him this one favor. By warning him of the trap at the Sirens, I clear the debt I owe him for saving my brother's life."

Roarke noted the glaring omission but let it pass. He was watching her hands tearing and worrying to death a corner of a lace handkerchief.

"I . . . please, Mr. Roarke . . . will you act on the information I have given you?"

"I will consider it, yes, Mrs. Winfield."

Her hands stopped trembling as if by magic, and she sank back against the seat cushion. "Thank you," she whispered. "And about our meeting—?"

"You have my word, madam, that Morgan will not hear of it from me. And now I had better let you be on your way."

The coach rocked as Stuart Roarke opened the door and stepped down onto the street. He made sure the latch was fast and was about to back away when he felt Summer's hand rest lightly on his.

"Yes? Was there something else?"

He waited, but the words swimming in her eyes would not come to her lips.

"Good night, Mrs. Winfield," he said gently.

"Godspeed, Mr. Roarke."

She melted away from the carriage window, and he heard a faint tap on the driver's box. A few moments later he was alone on the cobbled street, listening to the sound of the hoofbeats clopping away. He turned and hurried down a series of winding streets, his brow furrowed in concentration, his mind a whirl of questions. As he approached the front of one particularly noisy tavern, the door swung open to an uproarious bellow of laughter.

"There you are, you bastard!" Morgan Wade grinned drunkenly and swaggered out onto the boardwalk. His arm was draped around the shoulders of a buxom red-haired beauty, and she was giggling as his hand fondled lustily beneath the bodice of her blouse.

"Stuart, me buck-o, Lettice and I had all but given up on you. Where the hell have you been?"

"Some last-minute business," Roarke said uneasily.

"Business, eh?" Wade belched and leered down at the whore. His leather jerkin was unlaced; his shirt was spread wide over the black curling hairs on his chest. The woman had her arms around his waist and was running her hands greedily over his hard flesh. "What do you think of a man who thinks of nothing but business on a fine night like this?"

She giggled again and sidled closer, whispering something in Wade's ear. His brow shot up, and he regarded her in some amazement.

"A damn fine idea," he murmured. "But are you sure you can handle the two of us?"

Stuart grimaced and glanced down the street. "I could use a few drinks," he muttered. "Would you care to join me?"

"Join you?" Wade squinted at Roarke, then moved his hand so that the cotton blouse was scooped beneath the woman's bounteous breast. "And leave all this warm woman-flesh to grow cold?"

"We have to talk," Roarke insisted quietly.

"Talk?" Wade grumbled and blinked slowly. "No wonder Bettina loses patience with you if all you want to do is talk."

Roarke sighed and reached into his pocket, producing a gold coin. He held it up in plain view and beckoned to the whore to remove herself from Wade's embrace. Her eyes shone greedily and she weighed the coin against the promise of the drunk swaying heavily against her shoulders. She snatched at the coin and twirled out of Morgan's grasp and was gone in a wink back into the noisy interior of the tavern.

Morgan straightened with a relieved sigh. "A true savior, Roarke. She was becoming downright persistent."

"Did you find out anything?"

"Aye. The *Caledonia* left on Wednesday's tides. That white-assed bastard Winfield was at the helm."

"So that much of our information was correct. . . . He's going to try to catch us with the guns."

"So it would seem."

"Any ideas as to how he found out about them?" Stuart asked casually.

"None," Morgan grunted. "But I don't like it. Perhaps I should have been the one to meet with Marlowe."

"I don't think it came from him. He has more to lose than we do."

"His fine reputation?"

Roarke shrugged. "If he loses that, he loses his livelihood. Besides, I found out some interesting things tonight."

"Come along then, we can talk on the way."

"On the way?"

Morgan grinned. "We've another meeting tonight that might require your fine touch."

Roarke knew better than to ask any further questions and fell into step beside the captain. Morgan tucked his shirttails into his breeches and retied the laces of his vest as he walked.

"That wench's hands were faster than a hummingbird's wings," he muttered absently.

"She obviously pleases Admiral Stonekipper."

"Unfortunately the same cannot be said for the intrepid

admiral. According to Lettice, he's all sweat and no results."

"Perhaps you should have taken the night with her," Roarke suggested. "Given her something more than a coin to remember you by."

"Aye, maybe." Wade glanced away. "Tell me what Marlowe had to say that was so interesting. I'm beginning to grow weary of all these games, Stuart. Just once I'd like to have it out with them . . . all of them."

"The time is coming, Morgan. War is so thick in the air you can smell it. But we aren't ready yet. You know that as well as I do and as well as Stephen does."

"Aye, but it leaves a man wanting just the same. What have you found out about the *Caledonia?*"

"Winfield had her stripped and refitted with lighter guns. She's carrying eighty-two, all told, not a threat to be easily dismissed."

Wade snorted. "She's a bloody razee to begin with. Whoever lopped off her top deck couldn't save her from wallowing like a sow in heat so it's not likely Winfield can do much better. He won't get close enough to count our sails."

"He may not have to."

"Meaning?"

Roarke hesitated. Despite his promise, he had a nagging feeling he should tell Morgan about Summer Winfield.

"Meaning I'm told the Royal Navy has a new toy. A glass ten times as powerful as anything we could lay a hand to at the moment. It came to me from two different sources, so I'm inclined to believe it exists. He'll be able to hug the horizon without giving us a hint as to where we pick her up."

"And your guess to that?"

"It's not a guess. Winfield's out there now waiting for us. He's already sent the *Northgate* on ahead to the Sirens to wait for our arrival."

Wade glanced sidelong through the shadows. "The *Northgate?*"

"Aye. She has a new captain at the helm, promoted

several weeks ago out of Saint Christopher. Ashton-Smythe. Have you ever heard of him?"

Wade was thoughtful a moment. "I've heard of him. Spit and polish, like the rest of them, but he has a brain to go along with it. What happened to Forbes?"

"I understand he's on a ship bound for home. He'll be bucking heads with the French by Christmas."

"Winfield must not have liked another showman in the same arena."

"Obviously not."

Wade sighed. "So. They're planning to sandwich us at the Sirens, are they?"

"So the rumor goes," Roarke said quietly.

Wade shook his head. "The bastards will never learn, will they? No doubt this is a bid for those admiral's bars Winfield is so hungry for. By God, you know I think he'll make it, too. He kisses the right appendages and warms to the right wives. I'll eat the *Chimera* from the skysails down if it isn't in his plans to woo the queen within five years." He paused and chuckled. "Unfortunately he won't get there on my wind. For now he'll have to content himself with the heat and flies."

"You're going to pass on the guns?"

"I'm going to give it serious thought. I'm also going to give serious thought to going home for Christmas. What say you to that, Roarke? Virginia in December is cool and crisp—it puts a man's thinking back into perspective."

"Are you saying you've lost yours?"

"It feels sadly mauled of late, aye."

"You wouldn't also be toying with the notion of a visit to Norfolk while you're sailing by, would you?"

"I might be. It's high time Stephen Decatur and I had a long talk face-to-face."

"Horn to horn is more like it," Roarke said dryly. "And he will only tell you what he's been telling you all along. His hands are tied. We have to wait, Morgan. We cannot be the ones to start an incident now."

"What do you call sending two warships after us—a friendly sparring contest?"

"Winfield has the excuse that we are smuggling guns to

come after us, whereas we have no reason for an attack against him. If you want to see him fume to the point of melting his buttons, just stay put in the harbor for the next few months where he can't touch us."

"Aye, my ship would be safe in port, but that's not what she was built for. And it isn't my aim to make him simply angry. I want him making mistakes. Bad mistakes."

"And he will. But don't let him be the cause of you making any."

Wade scowled. "Between you and Decatur I feel as potent as a schoolboy pelting stones at the windows."

"Well, you shouldn't. You and Bull have had a freer hand than any dozen other privateers combined."

"Only because we do what we do so well," Wade grinned humorlessly. "And don't you mean because we've been used more freely? Maybe that is what tires me the most—letting everyone else's judgment rule my life instead of following my own."

"When has anyone ever told you what to do and lived to brag about it?" Roarke saw a shadow pass briefly across the brooding eyes and cursed his tongue. They were nearing the end of a grimy laneway, and he had to slow his step to match Morgan's.

"You didn't happen to hear anything"— there was a slight pause, and the black brows came together—"about the lad, did you?"

"Michael Cambridge? Not a word. Was I supposed to?"

"No." Wade's frown deepened uncomfortably. "It was only out of curiosity I asked."

Like hell, Roarke thought. "Then would it ease your curiosity to know he no longer has a governess?"

Wade halted in his tracks. "Where has she gone?"

"She's married, Morgan. As to where she's gone, I didn't ask. I didn't think it was that important to you."

Wade's face remained impassive. "It isn't," he said curtly and started walking again.

It would do him no earthly good to know, Roarke reasoned, and yet . . . "It wouldn't be too difficult to find out if you wanted to see her."

"No." Wade's pace quickened. They reached the end of the alleyway, and at the rear door to a tavern Wade

paused and turned to Roarke. "She was right about one thing. We do lead desperate little lives, don't we?"

"Morgan—"

"Come along, Roarke, I've a sudden yearning to see the bottom of that bottle you mentioned."

Wade's blue eyes raked the smoky interior of the tavern, noting the faces that shouldn't be there and acknowledging the nods from his men who were already strategically placed. Two more of Winfield's spies were going to find it difficult to wake up in the morning.

"Ah—there he is." Wade grinned and slapped Roarke on the shoulder. "Put a happier look on your face, Stuart, lad. That's your father-in-law you're frowning at."

15

Captain Emory Ashton-Smythe maneuvered the fifty-two-gun frigate *Northgate* through the channel dividing the Twin Sirens and anchored well out of sight off one of the small, mosquito-infested islands west of the reef. He had two of the new brass spyglasses on board, and because he knew it would be several days before the alert would go out to be on the watch for the *Chimera,* he prowled the windward side of the coral banks by day, hoping to root out an unsuspecting smuggler or two to prove his worthiness as commander of the *Northgate.* He laid on a double watch and had his gun crews run through stiff drills. Had he needed any evidence that Wade was a formidable adversary, he had only to stand on the bridge of his ship and look down over the newly patched sections of deck planking and rail.

Commodore Bennett Winfield remained in position off Barbados for three days and three nights, keeping a close watch on the *Chimera*, anchored in Bridgetown's harbor. He moved in closer by night and marked each hour's passage by the blinked codes dispatched from high on the crest of a hill. The signals also assured him that Wade was not using the cover of darkness to slip out of port. By day he drilled his crews. He regarded their sweating, well-honed ministrations with a dispassionate confidence. Wade was about to pay for his past errors . . . and Summer was about to learn a harsh lesson in reality.

Winfield was roused at dawn of the fourth day with the news that the *Chimera* was weighing anchor and the first of its sails were appearing up her masts. He kept a tight rein on his emotion as he issued the order to alert all crews and prepared to follow the privateer's ship.

"His heading, Aslop?"

"South by southwest, sir, as you anticipated."

"Trinidad," Winfield nodded. "How long would you estimate it will take us in this weather?"

"If it holds? No later than four bells tomorrow, sir."

"My prediction is that it will hold, Lieutenant. Call the officers to breakfast now, if you please. I find myself with a strong appetite this morning."

"Aye, sir."

"And keep that damned ship well in sight."

"There should be no problem there, sir. She's presenting us with a clear, sharp target. A shame our guns are not as powerful as the telescope."

"In due time I have no doubt they will be. For now, keep me informed of the *Chimera*'s movements. And lay us low enough on the horizon not to give rise to the least suspicion."

Lieutenant Harvey Aslop did as he was ordered, an easy task since the *Chimera* maintained an unhurried six knots throughout most of the day. He had to order the *Caledonia* trimmed for it cut through the water like an impatient mare held to a tight rein. So intent was he on following the commodore's orders that he was too low to see a second set of sails skimming across the horizon—sails that were, conversely, in plain view of the *Chimera*.

"There she is," Roarke said quietly, handing the glass to Morgan Wade. "Right on time."

"Trim us down," Wade grunted, swinging the spyglass to their stern after making his own visual confirmation. "Not too obviously, though. Bull knows he is to keep ahead of us, but I'd as soon not take any chances on the *Caledonia* spotting him. Damn—are you sure Winfield's out there?"

"He's there, all right," Roarke said.

"Like a fly buzzing you at night," Wade muttered. "You know it's in the room with you; you just can't see it."

Roarke passed the order to Mr. Phillips to take in sail. Almost immediately two of the flying jibs were reefed, along with one of the small foresails.

"Winfield's bound to move up on us with the light failing."

"Aye. We'd best give them something to look at." Wade lowered the spyglass. "Light up the deck lanterns and have the stern cabins bright enough to see a dozen miles away. Another hour and we can signal the *Gyrfalcon;* then we'll pull up even more to give Bull a clear run."

"You don't think Winfield will suspect something?"

"Not when he knows we don't have the guns on board yet."

"I still say we should pass on the shipment altogether."

"Winfield has arranged to provide us with five thousand prime English muskets. How can I, in all conscience, disappoint the fellow? No, we'll accept his guns and give Commodore Righteous Winfield a lesson in humility he won't soon forget. Or forgive." Wade chuckled dryly. "He never could take a loss of face in his stride. As temperamental a son of a bitch as any the Royal Navy has spawned. He was known to have a penchant for taking his frustrations out with his fists. I pity his wife and family, if he has one."

He raised the spyglass to his eye again, thereby missing the look on Stuart Roarke's face.

Commodore Bennett Winfield lowered his glass, smugly contemptuous as he saw the lights glowing to life on the *Chimera.*

"He always was a cocksure bastard. Look at him, Aslop. Sitting there like he owns the whole damned ocean."

"I've ordered a total blackout for the *Caledonia*, sir. No lights, not even for cooking."

"Good. Give the men an extra ration of grog for their trouble."

Bennett watched the progress of the *Chimera* for several minutes longer, then handed the telescope to Aslop as he observed the rapidly shrouding dusk. "Carry on, Lieutenant. I shall be in my quarters."

"Yes, sir . . . sir?"

"What is it, Aslop?"

"Sir, does something . . . well . . . does something feel wrong to you?"

"Wrong? In what way?"

"I'm not sure. As I say, it's just a feeling—"

Bennett Winfield relaxed. "If Morgan Wade was the least bit suspicious of our presence, he would be crowding on sail and cutting north to lose us. He wouldn't lead us straight to the guns. And he certainly wouldn't slow down, not with the wind changing as it is."

"I suppose you are right, sir."

Winfield's eyes narrowed. "I am right, Lieutenant. Now carry on about your duties."

"Aye, sir." Aslop watched his commander leave the bridge, then released the pressure from his lungs. Winfield's temper had a very fine thread holding it together, and he knew the commodore enjoyed playing God when he had the deck beneath his feet. But the feeling that something was amiss would not leave, and the lieutenant did a complete sweep of the horizon with the powerful telescope. He gave an order for the man sitting fifty feet aloft in the crow's nest to do likewise, and even though the report came back "all clear," he refused his relief at the end of his watch and continued to pace the bridge uneasily.

When dawn arrived, pink and hazy, Aslop had still not managed to shake off the prickle scratching his spine. The *Chimera* was there. The *Caledonia* was keeping an even pace with it, and there was only the faintest rime of cloud curling over the seascape to mar an otherwise perfect sky. Yet he refused relief for the fourth time and only knuckled his eyes harder to drive away the burn of salt and fatigue.

The wind was building. Aslop's prickle grew in proportion when the privateer failed to take advantage and instead dropped the speed of the *Chimera* to less than four knots and flew barely a quarter of its sails.

The lieutenant had just finished giving an order to have the watch in the nest changed every hour, when Bennett Winfield emerged from the forehatchway, his fully rested and laughing complement of ship's officers strutting behind him, picking the breakfast out of their teeth.

Winfield mounted the ladder to the bridge, not a blond hair out of place, not a visible wrinkle to his uniform, not an embossed anchor on his buttons angled the wrong way. The pale blue eyes flicked critically over the loosened neckcloth and the trace of stubble on his adjutant's jaw. He arched a brow and gazed out across the water, noting the stiff breeze and the growing crust of cloud.

"Aslop, you look like the devil. Didn't you sleep last night?"

"No, sir."

"Any particular reason?"

"No, sir."

"Just your . . . feeling?"

"Sir." Lieutenant Aslop approached Winfield haltingly. "At this pace we're still a full day out of Port-of-Spain. The wind is strong off his starboard side, and if he cared to run up half as much sail again as he has, he could be in safe anchorage before noon. Instead he keeps slowing down."

"Your conclusion?"

"He knows we're here. He's playing with us. Somehow, Wade knows we know about the guns, and I'll be willing to wager that within the hour he cuts loose and heads directly into that—" Aslop raised an arm stiffly and pointed to the clouds. A squall was building, darkening the surface of the water as it approached.

"Your recommendations?" Bennett asked quietly.

"Close up on him now, sir, or we'll lose him."

"And if he sees us?"

"We can gain raking distance within two hours."

"What makes you think he would allow us to get that close? Conversely, what makes you think he is not tempting us to do precisely that?" Bennett glanced toward the squall. "Even if he does run for the heavy weather, where can he go? He may be only guessing that we're here; he cannot know for certain. He may be tempting us to do what you are suggesting for that very reason: to find out. If he runs for the weather, we'll still be on him. Believe me, Aslop, I have no intention of losing Captain Morgan Wade. None whatsoever."

"But, sir—"

"Go below, Lieutenant. That's an order. Have a hearty meal and clean yourself up; you'll feel better for it."

"Aye, sir."

Bennett presented his back to the lieutenant, dismissing the young man summarily. Aslop handed the spyglass reluctantly to one of the other smirking officers and left the bridge, but he could not help pausing at the entrance to the forecastle quarters and staring out across the dark patch on the horizon. His grip on the oak tightened, and then he shook his head in resignation and ducked inside.

An hour later the *Chimera* disappeared.

Bennett Winfield watched, unperturbed, as Aslop's prediction bore fruit. The *Chimera* tacked suddenly on a course straight south, straight into the curtain of the squall. Wade was fully rigged within minutes of the turn and running in excess of eighteen knots, when he was swallowed into the sheeting rain. Winfield was still not overly concerned. He called for more sail and closed the gap quickly, surmising correctly that the disturbance was only a brief trick of the weather. But when the winds and rain played out and the *Caledonia* shook off the last of the squall, the frigate was gone.

Winfield ordered the heavy sail maintained and scoured west and south of the *Chimera*'s last sighting. When nothing more spectacular than a British sloop crossed their path, he barked an immediate, hasty course change —north to Trinidad and the town of Port-of-Spain.

By then the wind was against him. It took nearly twenty hours to cover the distance, and when he arrived, the *Chimera* was gone. So were the guns, Winfield discovered, after a second, lengthy delay and an exorbitant bribe. He was told that the *Chimera* had spent less than two hours in port and now had an impressive head start due north.

Commodore Winfield drove his ship and his men to the breaking point in an effort to reach the Sirens in time to salvage his plan. Days later he stood rigidly silent on the deck of the *Caledonia*, listening to a red-faced and stammering Captain Emory Ashton-Smythe swear that he had not seen a sail in the past three days. His captured prizes of two French merchantmen did nothing to assuage the commodore's fury, and Ashton-Smythe retreated to the *Northgate* with a harsh reprimand ringing in his ears.

Thereafter by day both warships searched the length of the coral reef. Nights found them anchored in humid, windless coves slapping at innumerable mosquitoes and plucking multilegged beasts from their skin and food. A month of short tempers and frayed nerves resulted in Winfield using the pair of French ships as targets for his gun crews, hulling them in under ten minutes apiece and taking one hundred and twenty outraged Frenchmen as prisoners.

With his rage still boiling at peak level, he ordered the British ships home to Bridgetown, stopping off first at the naval base on Saint Christopher to deliver his prisoners. There he learned that the *Chimera* had not only eluded the *Northgate* and outfoxed the *Caledonia*, it had broken through the blockade line patrolling Norfolk, Virginia, and was last reported anchored alongside Stephen Decatur's frigate, the *United States*.

Bennett's rage deepened to a cold fury. He lashed out at the two most readily available victims: Harvey Aslop was stripped of his rank and left on Saint Christopher to ponder his future. Captain Emory Ashton-Smythe was cited for dereliction of duty and ordered to pay a heavy fine. He retained command of the *Northgate* despite Bennett's efforts to the contrary but lost the right to claim the two French ships as his kill. Neither man said a word publicly in his own defense, but privately the rumors were set afloat that the commodore's credibility had taken a sharp dive downward, as with so many others before him who had pitted themselves against Morgan Wade.

June 1812

16

SUMMER'S CHILD was born during a torrential downpour, on a dark and foreboding night the first week of April. She was a delicate pink mewling bundle with vivid blue eyes and a froth of auburn hair that Sir Lionel Cambridge declared was the exact shade of his own dear departed wife's. The birthing was a slow and torturous affair, watched over by a physician and an alchemist, both of whom shook their heads over the excessive bleeding, but who continued to reassure the mother-to-be that it was perfectly normal to feel as if her insides were being torn apart and that seventeen hours of drenched, writhing agony was not unheard of.

Commodore Bennett Winfield, when advised the trauma was at last ended, climbed the stairs from the library where he had been drinking heavily and strode into his wife's room unannounced. He took one look at the wrinkled, exhausted child and left again without a word or glance at Summer. The nurse was shocked. The maids wept in sympathy for their poor, weakened mistress. Only Summer was unaffected. She closed her eyes and savored the total absence of pain for the first time in forty-eight hours.

Sir Lionel was euphoric. Champagne flowed like water, and no praise was too grand for his brilliant son-in-law. Visitors and well-wishers streamed through the doors, and the piles of beribboned, multicolored gifts and parcels grew by the score. Summer opened some, showed no interest in others and rarely left her room to greet guests. Her only constant visitor was Michael, who was intrigued by the tiny hands and tiny feet and tiny toothless expressions of his new niece.

The child was christened Sarah Hogarth Winfield, Sarah for Summer's mother, Hogarth for Bennett's mother's maiden name. Sir Lionel was jovially insistent that the next child would be a boy, named Lionel Humphrey after the respective grandfathers. His gift to the new parents and Bennett in particular was an additional two-thousand-acre parcel of land which, when combined with the acreage of Dover plantation, ensured Bennett's wealth and prosperity.

Sarah Winfield plumped rapidly into a beautiful child. She rarely cried and seemed almost as content to while away the hours of each day in the loving arms of her mother as Summer was simply to hold her. The baby blatantly refused the services of a wet nurse, to the nanny's consternation and Summer's acute pleasure, and stubbornly wailed her annoyance when anyone other than her mother or her adoring new uncle tried to pick her up.

Michael was thrilled and decided Old Winifred was a prude and definitely a bit "grotty" for thinking a son could have been any kind of improvement over Sarah. He sang to her and told her stories. He became Summer's steadfast companion and loyal supporter, taking Bennett's place by her side for long walks in the public gardens.

Aside from the formal ceremony of the christening, Bennett did not show any interest in his daughter. His public reticence became undisguised hostility when he and his wife were alone, and Summer would often find him staring at her or at Sarah, drink in hand, his cold pale eyes as flat and lifeless as a stranger's.

Her dread of a confrontation with Bennett was not eased by the almost constant talk of war. Dinner conversations were dominated by politics; luncheons and teas were apt to erupt into shouting matches; even the gardens and streets were crowded daily with uniforms, as the parade grounds of the Savannah Garrison became a training camp for recruits to the home guard. Talk of an invasion was on everyone's lips—not of the Caribbean but of America. The British fully expected to reclaim their territory from the churlish Yankee upstarts and teach them once and for all who ruled the seas.

To that end Commodore Winfield's patrols increased. His prize record grew impressively, and he stopped more ships and seized more illegal cargo than a score of revenue cutters combined. His main target continued to elude him, but his coups were so profitable to the government and so inspiring to his fellow officers that his embarrassment at the Sirens was readily forgotten. In its stead grew a speculation that when and if Morgan Wade ever dared to return to the islands, the sleek black panther—as the *Caledonia* was fondly referred to—would run him to ground within the month.

The Governor's Ball had been an institution in Barbados since the first appointed governor had declared the morals too lax and the climate too fertile, eroding the good honest structure of English society. Only the rich and the very rich were presented with the small gold invitations, and this year, like every other, the ball was held on the eve of June twenty-fifth. The coaches and carriages of diplomats and wealthy plantation owners lined both sides of the boulevards in front of Government House for a mile in either direction, each with liveried manservants proudly displaying the house and family colors.

Inside, the buffet tables sagged under mountains of food and drink. Crystal glasses were filled with champagne from a three-tiered fountain, and pastry chefs beamed from behind platters of their finest concoctions, intoxicated by the praise of sticky-fingered guests.

The enormous ballroom swelled with colorful, beautiful people, who swayed to the music of a twenty-piece orchestra. The gowns of greens, peaches, and yellows swirled in amid a sea of proper dress uniforms. The lights were dazzling. The sparkle from dozens of candelabra glistened overhead like a wreath of silver stardust, falling here and there to highlight a flash of jewels or a gleam of buckles, buttons and swords.

Sir Lionel Cambridge headed the reception line, resplendent in the snow white breeches and scarlet coat of office. His moustache was waxed to needle-sharp points, his cheeks were rosy, and his eyes were an eruption of tiny red veins from sampling and approving wines all day. Michael stood by his side wearing a replica of his father's uniform. He was very stiff, very formal and extremely proud to be participating in the festivities for the first time.

Summer and Bennett Winfield were next in line. He was the man she remembered from her first heartrending introduction in London—poised, charming, exceedingly handsome with the flush of sea air still on his cheeks. His mood had improved remarkably over the past few weeks, although Summer could not have explained why. He had been exceptionally good-humored and attentive since returning from an escort duty four days earlier. As a result, Summer was lulled by a sense of well-being she had not felt in a longer time than she cared to think about.

Her gown was partly responsible. Bennett had selected it for her at an extravagant cost, and its simple, flawless design drew the eyes and admiration of every man and woman present. It was of cream-colored satin, so slippery and sensuous it seemed to mold to every curve of her body. Cut astoundingly low across the bosom, it dipped into a wide vee before meeting the high waist of the skirt. There, nestled enviably in the center of the generous expanse of rounded flesh was the second cause of Summer's lightheadedness: Bennett's belated gift for the birth of their daughter: an emerald-and-diamond necklace that lay against her skin like a ring of green fire.

Summer laughed and smiled and radiated happiness. She greeted each guest as if they were warm, personal friends, accepting compliments and flattery under the approving eye of her husband.

"Well, Commodore Winfield, I see I must commend you again on your capture of such an exquisite bride. She grows lovelier each time we meet."

Summer smiled tightly and lowered her lashes as Farley Glasse bowed over her hand. His black eyes were boring through her gown, causing her flesh to crawl and a shiver to race along her spine.

"May I be so bold as to steal her away, just for this

one dance?" Glasse asked. "I fear once the receiving is officially ended, I may not have a chance to compete with the scores of her admirers."

"I don't mind at all," Bennett said. "And I'm sure Summer will appreciate the interruption."

She looked up into the pale blue eyes, and saw nothing but the warmth of his smile. She murmured her acceptance to Glasse and daintily took up the train of her gown. Glasse was clumsy and wooden in his movements, unable to follow the flow of the music, and seemed unable to concentrate on anything above the level of her bosom.

"Your husband is a lucky man indeed, Mrs. Winfield," he mused. "He will go far in this man's navy, due in no small part to a supportive family life."

"Thank you, Mr. Glasse."

"Your daughter is how old now?"

"Nearly three months," Summer answered, tensing perceptibly.

Glasse felt it, and his mouth curved down at the sides. "As lovely as her mother, I'm informed . . . although to hear Sir Lionel tell it, she is the exact image of his wife."

"I'm afraid I have only fleeting memories of my mother. She died when Michael was born."

"Ah, yes, one of the tragedies of this climate. So hot and sultry babies are often brought into the world at a terrible price."

Summer glanced around, hoping for a reprieve.

"Isn't that so, Mrs. Winfield?"

She turned quickly. "I beg your pardon?"

"I said . . . unlike the slave population. It appears to double almost daily despite the heat and inconveniences. Then again, they do represent a profitable industry for the islands. Those born and raised here command top prices in America."

"I find the slave trade rather repulsive, myself," Summer said and flinched as his boot scuffed against her ankle.

"You and many others," he agreed. "Why, only last week a shipful was waylaid by a corsair and the cargo set free on one of the islands. You know of whom I speak, of course. Morgan Wade."

Summer held her breath. She had not heard that Wade was back. In fact, she had not heard much about his activities at all of late.

"I'm told he sets the blackbirds free whenever he takes a ship and finds them on board. Not very enterprising for a man in the business of making profits, is it?" Glasse misstepped an intricate movement in the dance and laughed. "But I had forgotten, you bear some admiration for Captain Wade."

When Summer did not respond, he clucked his tongue. "He was becoming quite a hero in these waters, wasn't he? Hopefully all that will change now that your husband has acquired his sea legs, so to speak. If I were a gambling man, I might even be persuaded to place a sizable wager on which of the two will triumph: the *Caledonia* or the *Chimera*."

"Are you so certain they will come together?" Summer asked. "The captain has managed to disappoint you before."

"You refer of course to the incident last September? We certainly did have prime fools made of us then—or more particularly, your husband. One cannot help but wonder how Wade knew he was being followed or how he knew to avoid the area of the Twin Sirens."

"Perhaps he does not travel the same routes twice," she suggested blandly.

"Or perhaps his plans were altered at the last minute?"

She gazed unwaveringly into the glittering eyes. "I suppose that is the difficulty with setting traps: The intended victim does not always cooperate."

"Trap, Mrs. Winfield? . . . may I call you Summer?"

"I prefer Mrs. Winfield. And what else would you call it, sir? Lying in wait for his ship, plotting in advance where he would be the most vulnerable—the word *trap* seems to come to mind so easily."

"Your husband discusses his plans with you, does he?"

"Rarely," she said evenly.

Glasse laughed, and his eyes reverted to the rise and fall of her breasts as the music and the dance came to an end. "How fortunate for us all that we learn from our mistakes. This time your Captain Wade will not find us so easy to dupe . . . no matter how many spies he has set out to warn him."

"This time?"

"Why, naturally, Mrs. Winfield. We cannot allow him to simply take up where he left off after all these months. You speak of traps and strategems with such authority, it might interest you to know that your husband has personally offered the perfect bait this time."

Summer felt the chill of apprehension ripple through her even as Glasse began guiding her back toward the receiving line. She saw Bennett's suntanned features angled in her direction, and she had time to wonder briefly at the knowing smile he gave Farley Glasse . . . and then her gaze froze on the main entrance hall.

Captain Morgan Wade was standing in the open doorway, as cool and indifferent as if he belonged. His black wavy hair was as unruly as ever, standing out in the sea of white rolled periwigs that surrounded him. His handsome face wore the familiar half-mocking smile. His broad shoulders were encased in an elegant maroon cutaway jacket set off by a silvered brocade waistcoat and white breeches. He exuded an air of power and insolence that slowly drew every eye in the room his way. And every eye that was not on Morgan Wade was fastened on the woman standing by his side: as cool and seductive a beauty as Summer had ever seen.

"Well, imagine that," Glasse murmured. "He actually had the gall to accept the invitation."

"Invitation!" Summer gasped. "You invited him here tonight!"

"Only as a matter of formality, my dear. We heard he was in the area, and as it happens, he owns a sizable sugarcane plantation outside of Marchfield. We could hardly invite every other planter on the islands and not him. Besides, there is an unwritten amnesty during the entire week of the Governor's Ball. He knows he's as safe as a virgin while he's anchored in Bridgetown."

Summer whirled and stared at Morgan Wade. He was not looking out over the dance floor and so had not seen her yet. Bennett was watching her closely, observing her shock and dismay, and she knew, suddenly, the reason for his cloying good humor of the past few days. The bodice of her gown cut into her flesh as she tried to calm her breathing, and she realized that there, too, she had fallen into his plans. He had clothed her like a prime courtesan, proclaiming his absolute possession for everyone to see.

. . . He even offered the perfect bait. . . .

Summer's eyes rested on the woman accompanying Wade, and her heart took a further sickening plunge. She was nothing less than what Summer expected to see with a man like Morgan Wade—and what a fool she was to think he would remain alone for any length of time.

"Mrs. Winfield, you seem a little pale," Glasse breathed in her ear. "Perhaps you should be by your husband's side at a time like this."

"Oh, no! No, I—"

"Come along, Mrs. Winfield." His voice was grating and his grip decisive on her arm. "We mustn't keep you from your duties as hostess."

Summer's head swam in a mist of confusion as she was led to the entrance of the ballroom. She could hear Michael's enthusiastic greeting and Morgan Wade's deep, throaty laugh.

"Is Mr. Thorntree with you, sir? Is he in Bridgetown?"

"He is indeed, lad. I'll tell him you asked after him; that should raise a spark or two."

"Oh, yes, please do, sir. And the same for Mr. Roarke and Mr.—"

"Now, now, Michael," Sir Lionel interrupted. "You mustn't pester Captain Wade. I'm sure you will have ample time later to chat with him."

Wade's smile altered subtly. "I must say your invitation came as a surprise, Sir Lionel. I am honored."

"Well, ah . . ." Sir Lionel cleared his throat. "Nonsense, m'good man. It was the least I could do. We were mighty grateful to you last summer, mighty grateful."

Wade nodded curtly. "Allow me to present Mrs. Teague . . . Sir Lionel Cambridge."

The beauty held out a hand to Sir Lionel, who had already warmed several shades darker at the proximity to her cleavage. Her gown was rose-colored and consisted of two sheer layers of tulle, the top one seeded liberally with spangles of silver beading around the hem. She was nearly as tall as Wade and had deep chestnut brown hair and the green eyes of a tigress. Sir Lionel continued to hold her hand as he proceeded with the introductions.

"You, er, know my son-in-law, Captain . . . Commodore Bennett Winfield?"

"By reputation only," Wade said easily, bowing. "I understand our paths have just missed crossing one another on several occasions."

Bennett's gaze was locked to Wade's, and for a moment he could not speak. Had he needed any further proof, it was there in the depths of the dark, slightly violet blue eyes. Sarah Hogarth Winfield's eyes were the same dark, slightly violet blue.

"Your reputation, Captain Wade," he said tersely, "leaves my own somewhat lacking, I'm afraid."

"Not at all. My associates tell me the *Caledonia* has become a formidable sight on the horizon."

"My duty is to keep the sea lanes clear for British ships going about their lawful trade. If your 'associates' feel threatened in some way, perhaps they should look elsewhere for business."

The two men sized up one another silently.

"Perhaps they should," Wade murmured. "Is there any small corner of the ocean you monarchists deem to be unclaimed territory?"

Bennett's smile was equally sardonic. "I'm not sure. I could look into it for you if you are toying with the idea of a permanent change of climate. But forgive me, I am being remiss. . . . you have, of course, met my wife?"

The dark blue eyes were on Summer without warning. She was braced to see almost anything—from horror to complete surprise. Anything but polite nonchalance.

"Mrs. Winfield. It is indeed a pleasure to see you again. You will have to accept my belated congratulations. I was only recently informed of your marriage."

"Thank you, Captain. And how is Mr. Roarke?"

"As well as can be expected." He smiled. An introduction was made to Mrs. Teague to which Summer murmured something hopelessly inadequate, and then he moved on.

". . . Mr. Farley Glasse—" she heard Bennett say. She looked up in time to see the blue eyes flick away from her face, and she remembered, with a jolt of panic, what she had neglected to tell Stuart Roarke that night in the carriage—"He is attached to the Admiralty in an advisory capacity."

"Captain." Glasse savored a deep breath, like a cobra preparing to strike. "I have long been looking forward to meeting you. We too seem to have had paths that have crossed but never quite touched."

Wade arched a brow. "Glasse? The name is not familiar to me."

"There is no reason why it should be," Glasse shrugged. "My dealings were more with your father . . . when he was the king's exchequer."

Something shadowed Wade's eyes a moment. It passed quickly, so quickly Summer wondered if the others had seen it at all.

"You must have me confused with someone else, sir," Wade said, keeping his voice level. "My family were Virginia farmers whose only dealings with the king involved chasing his soldiers off their land thirty-odd years ago. Now, if you will excuse us, I see we are holding up the guests. Gentlemen"—he raised one of Summer's ice-cold hands and pressed it to his lips—"Mrs. Winfield."

Summer watched them descend the four shallow steps into the ballroom. Mrs. Teague moved as if on a cushion of air, impervious to the stares and whispers that followed in their wake. She held attentively to Wade's arm as he smiled broadly and tilted his dark head to exchange some remark with her.

"Well, my dear, that was a fair performance," Bennett said. "Not perfect, but passable."

Summer rounded on her husband. "You truly surprise me, Bennett. Each time I think you have stooped as low as you possibly can, you prove me wrong."

"Whereas you are as predictable as the trade winds, my pet. Always stormy, always going against the tide." He glanced at Wade and his companion. "You seemed distressed at the captain's choice of a partner."

"Why should that distress me?" she snapped.

"No reason. It was merely an observation." He smiled and turned to Farley Glasse. "Have the arrangements all been taken care of?"

"Adequately." Glasse bowed stiffly to Summer and Sir Lionel. "And now I shall beg my apologies. Urgent business calls me away."

"Business?" Sir Lionel frowned. "Ah . . . ahem, yes. Yes, nice of you to come, Glasse."

The attaché smiled cryptically one last time at Summer and strode toward the exit.

"What business?" Summer demanded. "What other treachery have you planned for this evening?"

"Treachery?" Bennett looked amused. "At the Governor's Ball? Come now, Summer, you're allowing your imagination to run rampant again. What possible treachery could we concoct? The man is a neutral, his ship is anchored peacefully in the harbor."

"In Bridgetown?"

"As safe as anywhere else, I should think."

"That is exactly what your Mr. Glasse told me, and it sounded just as phony and insincere coming from him."

He took her arm and led her down onto the dance floor. "What possible concern is it to you how sincere I am about my dealings with Morgan Wade?"

"Absolutely none," she said, sensing his pleasure at her discomfort.

The pale eyes raked down over the hard swell of her breasts, down to linger on the lithe, satin-sheathed body. "I am relieved to hear you say that. I should hate to think what effect a lot of unfounded gossip would have on you or your daughter."

"Sarah? What does Sarah have to do with any of this?"

"Nothing at all . . . if you behave yourself. On the other hand, a word here, a word there . . . she could grow up to be the most talked-about bastard in town."

Summer's heart ground to a halt. He saw the gray eyes widen, and his hand circled her waist to keep her from stumbling out of their stride. He danced smoothly for a sequence of intricate turns before looking down at her.

"Did you really think you could get away with it?"

"Bennett, I—"

"Uh-uh," he cautioned, and his hand squeezed hers. "It won't do you any good to lie at this stage, and frankly, I'm beyond giving a damn. If it becomes common knowledge, it only makes you the whore and me the injured, lovesick husband willing to forgive the errant wife, et cetera, et cetera.

"We are, after all, civilized adults," he continued. "You need something from me, and I need something from you. Surely we can arrive at an amicable arrangement to suit us both?"

"Arrangement?"

He laughed and drew several knowing glances: They were the perfect couple, dancing and enjoying each other's presence.

"You needn't look so horrified, my pet. Your body has long since ceased to interest me. I have found, over the past months, that there are an astonishing number of willing participants in the world, greedy, eager little bitches who have nothing more important on their minds than finding new ways to please me."

Summer averted her eyes, feeling the revulsion wash through her in cold shudders.

"No, my dear, what I want from you is precisely what you are giving me here tonight. I want a beautiful, gracious wife on my arm, a charming hostess at my dinner table. In exchange I will be the perfectly charming, gracious husband. I will accept the responsibility of being the father of your child, and I will give her anything and everything you might want for her. Oh, yes—and in the matter of your past association with Morgan Wade, it should be forgotten and unmentioned. There will be no communication, no accidental meetings on the street, no contact present or future in any way, shape or form. Although"—he glanced past her shoulder to where Morgan and Mrs. Teague were parting the crowds with their dancing—"he hardly appears to want it himself. Arianna Teague. It seems I have heard the name mentioned with fond reverence"—he laughed briefly—"however, my dear, should you unwisely venture to see your ex-lover, I shall declare the child a bastard to anyone who will listen. I will disown her publicly, divorce you and do my damnedest to bring ruin down upon your entire family."

He smoothed a golden curl off the curve of her shoulder. "Does that sound agreeable, my dear?"

Summer could only stare up at him with loathing, knowing he had won. He would do as he threatened and take pleasure in seeing her and her family humiliated beyond salvation. She had no recourse but to accept the fact that he would and could use Sarah's future to hold her where he wanted her. She stared into the pale blue eyes and felt the jaws of the steely trap snap shut.

17

Summer danced and feigned gaiety through the rest of the evening somehow, conscious of Bennett following her every move. She purposefully went out of her way to avoid all contact, visual or otherwise, with Morgan Wade.

He did not lack for attention. He proved to be an accomplished dancer and, when he was not with Arianna Teague, selected only the most beautiful women to partner him. Rumors and speculations were rife, and hardly anyone passed a word in conversation without lowering lashes and voices and speaking about him from behind raised hands. He was thought to be by far the handsomest man present . . . the broadest across the shoulder . . . the finest tailored . . . the most outrageous . . . the most charming. . . . The list of his attributes grew until Summer's head swam and her temples pounded with the tension. The men in the room glowered at him unceasingly, affronted by the attention he received. Remarks were made deliberately to be overheard, which for the most part earned only an icy stare and a smile in return.

Wade and Mrs. Teague left shortly after midnight, to the acute disappointment of many hopefuls.

Summer was relieved and managed to carry on for two more hours until the baccarat and backgammon tables were set up in the gaming rooms. It was the time for lovers to steal away unnoticed, for chaperones to usher the younger charges home and for the serious gamblers in the crowd to settle down to business. No one paid any heed to Summer as she headed wearily up the stairs, feeling the aches and bruises in her feet at each step. The party would go on until dawn, and the noise followed her, drifting hollowly up and along the empty corridors.

She stopped first in Sarah's room, holding up a hand to the nurse as she tiptoed over to the cradle. The baby was sleeping soundly; her thumb was jammed determinedly into the pink mouth and was being fretted with tiny, quivering suckles.

Summer smiled and touched her lips to the down-covered head.

Nothing will ever hurt you, she declared inwardly. Nothing and no one, regardless of what happens to me or what I must endure.

She walked slowly to her own bedroom and stood at the window for some time, watching the stray couples strolling along the pathways and around the fountain. The night air was cool where it brushed her cheeks, helping to ease some of the burning fatigue. Her fingers were clumsy and leaden as she began pulling the long hairpins out of her curls, letting them fall on the window cushions like discarded petals. She unfastened the clasp of the emerald necklace and let it trickle through her fingers; she removed the gold earrings she wore and the delicate filigreed bracelets. She walked through the bedroom into her dressing room, where she began shedding her clothes.

All of her motions were trancelike and wooden. She did not want to think about anything; she wanted only to look at the water, the towel, the hairbrush and not have to think about anything or anyone. The loose-fitting nightgown sighed against her skin as she turned down the lamp in the dressing room and walked back out to the bedroom.

She halted halfway across the slash of moonlight that was streaming in through the open window. Her hand was poised on a brushstroke, and her skin tickled lightly with the knowledge that she was not alone.

"Bennett . . . ?"

She gasped, and the brush fell to the floor.

Morgan Wade was lounging in the brocade wing chair, his coat unbuttoned, his silk cravat loosened and the ends trailing down over the ruffles of his shirt. He looked as if he had been waiting comfortably for some time.

"You!" she gasped. "How did you get in?"

"The door was unlocked."

"But . . . what are you doing here?"

"I thought perhaps you could tell me." He saw the confusion on her face and reached to an inside pocket of his coat. He was only partially silhouetted by the moonlight, but she recognized at once the folded sheet of personalized writing paper he produced. It was pale blue with a delicate scroll of silver around the edges and the monogrammed initials S W in the upper right-hand corner.

She lifted her eyes to his. "I don't understand."

Wade arched a brow and unfolded the note. "Morgan," he quoted, "I must see you as soon as possible. Urgent. Please come. Summer."

"I . . . I didn't write it," she said lamely. "I didn't send you any note."

"I realized you didn't as soon as I saw the look on your face downstairs." He returned the note to his pocket. "Which leaves very few alternatives."

Summer glanced nervously at the door. "You mustn't be found here. My husband—"

"Your husband is thoroughly entrenched at the backgammon tables. He is a devout gambler, so I'm told, and with the amount of gold at stake down there, I doubt very much whether he'll leave without trying for his share. Besides"—the dark blue eyes dropped lower, lingering on the moonlit curves of her body—"he saw me leave several hours ago and would assume I was being entertained elsewhere."

Summer's cheeks flushed a violent red. "How dare you force your way into my bedchamber. This is not your ship, Captain Wade. You cannot come and go as you please."

"You obviously did not want to be seen talking to me downstairs."

"Nor do I want to talk to you here. Will you please leave at once! Go to your . . . your Mrs. Teague. I'm sure you would find a warmer reception there."

"Is that what has you worried?" he grinned. "Mrs. Teague?"

Summer flushed again. "Nothing about you or your Mrs. Teague worries me, Captain."

"I'm glad to hear it. Arianna is lovely to look at, but she finds it difficult to string too many words together at one time."

"No doubt she has other attractive qualities to compensate."

"No doubt she has. Unfortunately I haven't had the time or the inclination to discover them. Roarke merely thought it prudent for me to have a suitable companion tonight."

"Roarke thought?" she whispered.

"Aye. He thought I might need a distraction to keep both my temper and my manners in check. As usual, he was right."

"But you cannot stay here," she said through clenched teeth. "I did not speak to you downstairs because I have nothing to say to you. And contrary to what you may think, Bennett will not remain at the party much after my departure."

"The loving husband, is he?"

Her mouth compressed into a thin line. "I fail to see what business it is of yours."

"I noticed how loving and attentive he was all evening. You would be astonished to know how many good people made it a point to tell me how happy you and your husband are together. What a loving couple the pair of you are. What a wonderfully dedicated husband and doting father he is. It warmed me all over."

Summer's breath backed up in her throat. She opened her mouth to answer his sarcasm, to defend Bennett and to order Wade out of her life once and for all . . . but nothing came out.

He smiled as if he could hear the pounding of her heart within her chest. He stood up and moved closer into the moonlight.

"Summer. The name suits you. I often wondered—but then I suppose it was my own fault; I never asked. Names have a way of interfering at times." He laughed softly and the sound quivered along Summer's spine. "I had the devil of a time figuring out why someone would date the note instead of signing it—until Roarke enlightened me, that is."

"Please . . . please will you leave? I have already told you I have nothing to say to you. And so far you have said nothing I wish to hear."

"Then what are you afraid of?"

"I'm not afraid."

"No?"

"No," she whispered. "I have stopped being afraid of a great many things lately."

"Then it must be that pride of yours making you tremble the way you are."

"Or anger," she countered neatly.

"Or anger," he agreed with a smile. "Very well, Mrs. Winfield, you win. I'll leave . . . as soon as I have the answers to a few questions. Surely, under the circumstances"—he patted the pocket where he had replaced the note—"you cannot deny me that much."

Summer exhaled sharply. "I don't know why you were invited here tonight. I don't know whose idea it was. I did not know a thing about it until the moment you walked through the door."

"That was painfully obvious," he mused, moving a step closer.

"As for the note—"

"The note did what it was supposed to: It made certain I would come tonight. It also earned Roarke a dressing-down he won't soon forget."

Summer moistened her lips. "Was that all you wanted to know?"

"Not quite. What can you tell me about Farley Glasse?"

"Not much. I avoid him whenever I can. He seems to have some idea of proving you to be a titled Englishman"—she saw his eyes narrow—"and to have you arrested on a charge of treason. He probably has men watching you, and if they see you leaving my room—"

"No one will see me. His watchdogs have already been led off on a merry chase."

"You knew about them?"

Wade chuckled dryly. "The harbor is so thick with spies a man has difficulty pushing through the crowds. Your Mr. Glasse has the bay blocked and the ship under constant surveillance. He even managed to discover which tavern my men frequent and replaced the barmaid with a sloe-eyed minx who is equally as energetic but nowhere near as comforting."

"And none of it worries you?"

"There is no reason to fear something you already know is there. It is the unknown that takes a man by surprise. For instance—who is Sarah's father?"

Summer's hand flew to her throat. "Wh-what? Her father?"

"I told you, your guests were extremely talkative. You were married three weeks after Stuart returned you. The child was born less than the allotted time after . . . a case of being several weeks early or several weeks late."

"Bennett Winfield is my husband," she said haltingly. "He was here at Sarah's birth. H-he named her after his mother—"

"I'm told she has big blue eyes."

"Bennett's eyes are blue."

"And that she has dark hair."

"No," she said and backed up. "No . . . she is nothing to you. *I* was nothing to you, nothing but an idle way to pass the time."

"You were hardly that," he murmured and took a step after her. "And had you admitted to being Sir Lionel's daughter at the outset, you might even have arrived home with your virginity intact. Although"—he paused and shook his head slightly—"I think not. We were like spark and tinder from the very first moment."

"Don't come any closer. . . ." She stumbled back. "You sent me away. You didn't care what happened to me then. . . . Why should you care now?"

He smiled briefly. "But I did care. More than I should have, and that was why I had to send you away. I'm also admitting I made a damned stupid mistake. It isn't the first one I've made in my life, but possibly it was one of the worst."

"Oh, no, please . . ." She came up against the solid wall and could do nothing as his hands reached for her.

"If you tell me it's too late, I'll go. If you tell me the child is not mine and tell me that you love your husband, you'll never have to see me again."

"I mustn't see you again," she gasped, feeling his hands slide up her arms to her shoulders, up to cradle her chin and force her to meet his eyes. "I mustn't ever—"

His lips covered hers and she moaned. She shuddered, and her vision blurred with tears.

"Who is the father of your child?"

"No . . . no, I—"

He kissed her again, longer this time, and his body crowded hers against the wall, pressing his heat against hers through the thin nightdress.

"Who?"

All she could see was the incredible drowning blue of his eyes. All she could feel was the surety of his hands, and all she could think of was their ability to set her body and soul on fire. But it had been so long . . . so long. . . .

"Summer—"

"You," she gasped. "You are Sarah's father."

"And do you love him? Do you love Winfield?"

"Oh, please, Morgan, you have to go—"

Wade swore under his breath and kissed her again. Deeply, purposefully, demanding a response. He loosened the ribbons of her gown, and his hands searched beneath the fabric, caressing her bare flesh until Summer's knees buckled and she had to reach up and hold him. His mouth was on her lips, on her temples, her eyes, her throat . . . he pushed aside the edges of her nightdress and started tracing a hot path downward. Summer sagged against him, sobbing under the bittersweet torment.

"Do . . . you . . . love . . . him?" he hissed.

"No," she cried. "No, no . . ."

He laughed softly and swept her up into his arms. He carried her to the bed and tore off the offending nightdress in one smooth stroke. The glow from the moonlight bathed her flesh in silver, turning her hair into a web of shimmering silk. Wade's hands shook slightly as he stood back to shed his clothes. In moments he was naked beside her, burning with impatience yet forcing himself to move slowly, to reacquaint his mouth and hands with every curve and valley that eagerly awaited him.

He kissed away the tears on her lashes; he kissed her lips and murmured her name. He stroked his hands gently along her thighs and swallowed her cries as his heat invaded her, expanded within her, became a part of her.

"Morgan," she gasped, "oh, Morgan . . ."

Her arms, her long legs wrapped around his powerful body. He twined his hands into the tousle of blonde hair and held her in a kiss, smothering her screams as she shuddered beneath him again and again. Her nails scored the flesh of his shoulders and she half laughed, half cried with the joy of it.

Harder and deeper his body pushed into hers. He sucked in a mighty lungful of air and bent his head to her shoulder, feeling himself slipping, slipping. . . . His hands dropped to her waist, then to her hips, and a groan spilled the ecstasy from his body.

He continued to hold her, continued to press his lips to her throat and shoulder long after his arms had trembled with the last of his strength. Her eyes were closed, and he kissed them tenderly before he lifted his head and gazed down at her.

"I am truly sorry, madam," he murmured. "I did not want it to happen that way. I fully intended to keep you beneath me for hours until I had you begging for mercy."

Her answer was a sigh, a soft breath that caressed his skin and changed the gentle smile into a gentler frown.

"Something tells me you were sorely in need of that, Governess. Has your husband been that much of a fool?"

She searched the dark eyes for a hint of sarcasm, but saw no trace of it. Only concern. She ran her fingers lightly across his wide brow, brushing aside the unruly black waves. Her hand dropped, and she turned her head to one side.

"Bennett has not touched me since . . ."

Wade tilted her chin, forcing her to look back up at him.

". . . since hearing I was with child," she said in a whisper.

"He knew it was not his?"

"He had his suspicions. He had his accusations and his jealousy." She paused again. "And they were well-founded. He was not wholly to blame for the way he reacted. I was bitter and . . . and not totally compliant all of the time."

Wade observed her for a full minute before he lowered his mouth to hers, then to her cheek, her temple. . . . "I have already apologized twice to you, madam. Twice in one night. It would do irreparable damage to my character were I forced to do it again."

Summer shivered as his lips circled and pulled at one straining breast. She felt the quick, stinging response, then heard the husky laugh as he raised his head again.

"I am glad to see you are a good mother to my child, not a fashionable one."

"Morgan, you have to leave. This was a terrible risk and a foolish thing to do, and . . . and it mustn't ever happen again."

"Never?"

"No, ne—" She stared as she felt him moving again. Slowly. Easily. And his hands were on her thighs guiding her firmly against him.

"Forgive me again, madam, but as you see, I have a great need to make up for lost time."

She caught her lower lip between her teeth and reached up to wrap her hands around the column of his neck. The black curling hairs on his chest brushed lightly over her breasts, teasing them, making her arms tighten and a cry come softly to her lips.

"Morgan . . ."

His strong white teeth flashed in a grin. "Still stubborn, are you, Governess? Still determined to argue with me even though you know you must lose."

"Lose! Oh . . . you're doing it again," she whispered.

"I'm flattered you noticed."

"I don't mean that," she said on a gasp. "I mean you're not playing fair."

There was a slight hesitation before he answered. Long enough for him to feel her supple body begin to move with his.

"I never play fair, madam. Not when the stakes are this high."

Summer lost track of time. She lay curled against Wade's body, her head resting on his shoulder, her arm draped limply across his chest. The scent of his skin, the feel of him, the sound of his deep, even breathing was being carefully locked into her memory; each touch, each caress, each moment of blinding, soaring ecstasy would be brought out and relived again and again when he was gone.

She saw the first creeping fingers of dawn light stretch in through the window and the breeze pluck tentatively at the lace curtains. Quietly, carefully so as not to disturb him, Summer slipped out of bed, drawing on a pale green silk robe to cover her nakedness as she walked to the window. High on the surrounding hills splashes of yellow indicated the city was beginning to come to life. The baby chicks in the garden were calling petulantly for breakfast, the ever-present rush of palm trees grew in volume as the wind swept up from the harbor. The dairymaids would be in song soon. The fish hawkers would be chanting. The farmers would be rolling their vegetable carts into the streets. It was time for Morgan to leave.

She closed her eyes and concentrated on the buttery contentment she felt throughout her body. Could any woman feel as satisfied, as complete as she did now? The months of bitterness and emptiness had fallen away as if they had never existed, and yet she had forgotten so much. She had forgotten how he liked to fill his hands with her hair and feel it against his own dark skin. She had forgotten how he could find and tease the secret places until she was begging shamelessly for him. And she had forgotten how he could be rough and careless in his lovemaking one moment, then exquisitely tender the next, almost without warning. He had been so right that night on Bounty Key when he'd said she had wasted so much energy fighting him. She had been so foolish, so blind. . . .

Summer sighed as she felt Wade's hands curl around her waist and draw her against the heat of his body.

"I thought you were asleep," she murmured.

"Is that what feather beds are for?" he asked, nuzzling the nape of her neck.

She smiled and watched the first brilliant streamers of sunlight splitting through the trees.

"We haven't any more time," she whispered.

He turned her around and his mouth covered hers. His lips were incredibly warm, incredibly greedy and only raised her feeling of panic closer to the surface. She had to be strong now. She had to be . . . for Sarah.

"Morgan—"

"Come back to bed."

"There are already servants moving about. The gardeners will be out soon to tidy up after the party. If someone sees you—"

He straightened and his mouth curved down. "I warn you, you'll suffer for your obstinacy later. I've an unforgiving nature when it comes to being ejected from a warm bed—I'm surprised you have forgotten."

"I haven't forgotten." The smile faded as she watched him draw on his shirt and breeches. "Morgan . . . there mustn't be a later. You mustn't come here again, or try to see me again. You do know that, don't you?"

He looked up at her from the edge of the bed as he pulled his boots on. "I know nothing of the sort."

"You know as well as I do this should never have happened."

"It isn't what your body has been telling me all night."

Summer flushed hotly. "Morgan, please, you are not making this any easier."

"It was not my intention to make it easy," he said bluntly. "It was my intention to leave you no choice but to come with us."

Summer's eyes widened. "Come with you?"

"Aye. To Bounty Key, temporarily anyway, until I can get you and the child safely onto the mainland. I have a home in Virginia—"

"Sarah and I cannot go anywhere with you," she cried. "Not to Bounty Key, not to Virginia . . . not anywhere! You know we can't."

"You say that as if it is written on holy tablets. Believe me, a bolt of lightning will not strike you down for going against convention. If that were the case, I should be nothing more than a charred heap by now."

"I am a married woman," she said slowly. "I am also the governor's daughter. . . . It goes beyond mere convention."

"Why? Does being the governor's daughter make you immune to happiness? Does it mean you have to live out the rest of your life trapped in a marriage to a bastard like Winfield? Over my dead body, madam. The *Chimera* is leaving Barbados tonight. I want you and Sarah both to be on it."

He announced it so calmly, so simply that Summer was speechless for the time it took him to finish dressing.

"You are insane," she said at length. "We are not going anywhere with you, least of all on board a ship that probably will not even make it out of the harbor—or have you forgotten Farley Glasse so soon?"

"I haven't forgotten," Wade said grimly. "But it will take a better man than Glasse to put irons on me. And the man I leave you with would have to be a damn sight better than Winfield. He'll make an old woman out of you twenty years before your time. Sarah will turn out to be a weak-kneed simpering brat who has nothing more rewarding to do with her time than to see whose trousers she can explore under the table linen."

Summer gaped at him in astonishment. "And what are you offering her? An island crawling with misfits and drunkards? Lessons in smuggling and slaving and murder? Will you have Thorny teach her the ways of the world and Mr. Monday demonstrate his prowess to her on the beach? Dear God, spare me your arrogant moral judgments of my family and homelife. Bennett may not be perfect, but our life with him will at least be respectable. Sarah will grow up with a name and a certain degree of protection as Bennett Winfield's daughter—what will she have as Morgan Wade's baseborn child?"

"She'll be free."

"Free to do what? She'll be trapped, Morgan, trapped and branded. Oh please, don't you see . . . if it was just me—" Her voice faltered and she had to dig her nails into the palms of her hands. "She's all I have. She's all I have of you and all I can ever have of you."

"Not if you come with me, it isn't."

Summer fought the searing ache of tears building behind her eyes. "As what, Morgan? Governor Cambridge's disowned daughter? Bennett Winfield's runaway wife? Shall I be known as your mistress or your whore for as long as it takes you to become tired of me?"

The blue eyes were cold and hard. She saw the tic shiver high on his cheek, and she knew she had struck a terrible blow.

"You call *me* arrogant, madam?" He snatched at his jacket and crossed to the narrow balcony leading off the bedroom. He searched the grounds below for some signs of movement before he swung a leg over the rail.

He glanced back one last time. "The *Chimera* sails out of Six Man Bay at midnight. You have until then to change your mind."

18

Summer Winfield balled her hands into fists and tried to quell the instinct to scream. The nerves in her entire body were stretched to the breaking point, and the tension created such a humming in her brain that it all but drowned out the sounds of Michael laughing in the anteroom with Sarah's nanny.

She stared down at the empty cradle in disbelief. Her breasts ached suddenly, violently, stinging in a reaction to what her eyes refused to accept. She spun on her heel and ran to the nursery door, halting before any word of alarm left her lips.

What could she say? What could she do? The nurse would panic and protect herself by running to either Bennett or Sir Lionel. They would come upstairs, ask questions, badger her and . . . and dear God, Bennett would know. He would know by looking at her, and then it would be finished.

Michael laughed again, and Summer pressed her brow against the wood of the doorjamb, needing a few precious seconds to think. Think!

She had spent most of the day supervising and directing the small army of servants who had scrubbed and polished and restored the rooms to order after the party. She had welcomed the hard work, and it had almost succeeded in taking her mind off Morgan Wade, off the very real sense of loss that burned inside her, off the memory of his face as he had glared back at her from the balcony.

Arrogance? No, she was not being arrogant, not intentionally. She was only being rational. How could she,

Summer Cambridge, leave a way of life that had been all she had known for twenty years? She had experienced more fear in that one week on board the *Chimera* than she had in her entire life. Even if she could overcome her fears, she had to think of Sarah. She had to choose what was best and safest for their child. Just because she had destroyed her own chances for happiness, there was nothing on earth that would make her destroy Sarah's.

She straightened and squared her shoulders.

"Michael?" She opened the door a crack. "Michael, could you come in here a moment please? No, it's all right, Lottie, you may go to bed now. I'll see to the baby."

"Yas'm." The big black nanny ambled out of the playroom, still chuckling over something Michael had said. He was grinning as well when he came into the nursery.

"I suppose Sarah won't go to sleep without a story from her uncle Em?"

"Come in here quickly," Summer said, grabbing at his sleeve.

"What is it? What's all the—" He was looking at the cradle, at the absence of blankets and hanging rattles and baby. "Where is Sarah?"

"Michael, listen to me. This is very important, and there is no one else I can trust but you. Will you help me?"

"Of course, you know I will, but where is Sarah?"

Summer bit down on her lip. "Gone."

"Gone!"

"Yes, I—"

"You mean *kidnapped!"*

"For God's sake, Michael, keep your voice down!" she hissed.

"But someone ought to know! We ought to get help if she's been stolen away!"

"No. No! She hasn't been stolen. I mean, she has, but . . . but I know who did it. At least, I think I know who did it."

"Who?"

"There isn't time to explain!"

"Who did it!"

"For heaven's sake." She pinched his arm and shut the door tightly. "Will you keep your voice down if I tell you?"

"Who took Sarah?" he demanded in a whisper, nodding.

"Captain Wade did—now you promised!"

Michael's eyes were the size of silver coins. "Why would Captain Wade steal Sarah?"

"Oh, Michael"—Summer's shoulders drooped, and the tears trembled on her lashes—"because . . . because it's too long and too complicated to explain."

"Is he Sarah's father?"

Summer blinked up through her tears. "Wh-what?"

"I knew it!" he cried excitedly. "I knew she was far too pretty to belong to stuffy Old Winifred. Oh, Summer, this is jolly fine news! Does it mean we're all related? Does it make Captain Wade my . . . my something or other?"

She swallowed her amazement. "It makes him underhanded and conniving. He's stolen her, Michael. He's broken into our house and stolen my baby!"

"Well, she's his baby, too. And I don't think he had to break into the house to take her; there were so many maids and workmen milling about all day—"

"Michael!" Summer ground her teeth together as the urge to scream became paramount again. "It doesn't matter *how* she was taken. I've got to go and get her back without anyone finding out she was ever missing in the first place."

"Oh. Yes, I see. Winifred would have fits, wouldn't he? But how do you know where she is? How do you know where Captain Wade has taken her?"

"He told me he was leaving Six Man Bay on the midnight tides. If I hurry I can reach the *Chimera* before he sails and . . . and . . ."

"And steal her back! We'll take the ship by storm and steal her back!"

"*We* won't be doing any such thing. You have to stay here."

"What?"

"Someone has to stay here," she insisted, "to make sure no one comes into the nursery until I get back."

"Oh, gosh," he said and was genuinely crushed.

"You won't be missing any fun, believe me. Now, do you know where Father keeps the keys to his gun chest?"

The hazel eyes popped wider than before. "You're going to shoot Captain Wade?"

"No, of course not—not unless I have to. But I might need a pistol to get on board."

"Well, yes, I know where the keys are."

"Can you get them?"

"I could. But why don't I just get you a gun from my room?"

Summer was taken aback. "What on earth are you doing with a gun in your room?"

"Two of them actually. Father's old dueling pistols. He gave them to me years ago."

"Do they work?"

"Well enough to shoot squirrels from my window. I never actually hit any, though—ouch!" He jerked his arm back as she pinched him again. "All right, I said I would get them for you. Do *you* know how to shoot?"

"No," she admitted.

He was silent a moment. "There's really nothing to it. I suppose I could show you what to do and have them all loaded. All you have to remember is not to shoot your foot off. Come on, we'll do it in my room."

An hour later Summer was seated in the back of the small carriage, cloaked and hooded beyond recognition. The two fully loaded dueling pistols nestled in their velvet-lined case were clutched with trembling earnest on her lap. She left the curtains open, needing the wind against her face to help keep her thoughts cool and rational.

The road to Speightstown was full of jarring memories. How long ago had she ridden it to find a doctor unfamiliar with her face and position? Before that, the *Vigilant* had docked to put Michael and her ashore. Would the *Chimera* be there now? Would the *Caledonia* have prevented Wade from leaving Bridgetown, and if so, had Bennett boarded the *Chimera?* Had he already found Sarah and arrested Morgan for kidnapping . . . ?

"Hurry," she urged the driver silently, "hurry, hurry, hurry. The *Chimera* has to be where he promised, it has to be."

The main harbor of Speightstown was behind them, and

she could see the dark shimmer of Six Man Bay where it started to curve out from the land. But there were no ships at anchor! She could not see anything larger than a fishing ketch!

No! There she was! Just as Morgan had promised. The *Chimera* was moored to the dock, her sails reefed, her gangway lowered and waiting patiently.

Summer reached forward and slid open the trap to the driver's box. "Stop here. I don't want to go too close."

The coachman grunted a reply and pulled up on the reins. He thought the mistress's request an odd one, but he knew better than to ask questions.

"Wait here," Summer ordered crisply, stepping down from the coach. She had removed one of the pistols from the case and held it tucked beneath the folds of her cape. Two were not necessary. If she missed with the first shot, she would not have the nerve to fire again.

She hurried along the side of the road, covering the last few hundred yards in the shadows. Luck was with her, and she passed no one on the way although she could hear a rowdy cheer coming from a tavern set further back on the road. She veered off the lane and ran down to the docks, pausing behind a large stack of crates to catch her breath.

There was a guard standing at the gangway, casually leaning on the *Chimera*'s bulwark. He was hunched over, studying something intently in his hands. . . . no . . . he was whittling! It was Thorny!

Summer nearly called out to him in her relief. Then she remembered that he was probably stationed there on Wade's command. Were there others? Was Morgan expecting trouble?

She searched the length of the dock but could see no other shadows. Everything was quiet. It did not look as if he expected to sail within the hour. And there was no one else with Thorny on the deck.

Summer took a deep breath and walked boldly out onto the wharf, walking straight to the gangway, straight up to the deck level. Thorny's gristled head jerked up, and his eyes screwed to slits when he saw who it was.

"W-a-all now, if'n it ain't the governess. What brings ye owt ter the Kameery this late of a night?"

"I want to see Captain Wade."

"Eh? Cap'n don't take ter visitors, n'owt even when they's—"

Summer raised the gun out of the folds of her cloak. "You will stand aside, Mr. Thorntree, or I swear I shall blow a hole in your belly large enough for a parade of visitors to march through."

Thorny's jaw sagged open. He gaped at the brass and cherrywood dueling pistol, then at the pale, determined face. "I 'opes ye knows 'ow ter use that."

"Where is he?"

"Who?"

"Where is he?" she demanded and cocked the pistol the way Michael had shown her.

"In 'is cabin, in 'is cabin! Goin' over the charts."

"Will you stand aside please?"

"Aye, aye . . . movin' . . ." He crabbed backward and pressed himself against the rail.

Summer followed the quarterdeck to the stern and entered the gloomy hatchway leading down to Morgan Wade's cabin. Behind her she heard a shout and a mutter of voices.

Let them be concerned, she thought savagely. I will indeed shoot if I have to. He has my baby. He has my baby!

The cabin door was shut. The corridor was dank and musty, flooding her senses with memories, but she pushed them all aside and walked purposefully toward the sliver of lamplight. She did not stop to knock. She wrenched the latch and shoved the door wide, aiming the pistol where she saw him leaning over his desk. Wade looked up as the door slammed open. He reached instinctively for his own pistol lying on top of his charts.

"Don't do it," she cautioned. "This gun is primed and loaded, and at this range I doubt very much if even I would miss."

Morgan's hand froze. He straightened slowly to his full height, and the expression on his face darkened.

"This is a hell of a way to come aboard my ship," he said quietly.

"Where is she? Where is my daughter?"

The blue eyes flicked to the gun. Summer inched it higher until it was pointing dead center of the massive chest.

"I will pull this trigger, Captain Wade," she promised. "I do not want to do it, and I am frightened to death to do it, but I will . . . and if you refuse to answer me, I shall aim to kill you. I will only ask one more time: Where is my Sarah?"

"Safe."

"Take me to her."

"I'm afraid I can't do that."

The hand holding the gun shook noticeably. "What did you say?"

Wade's eyes flicked again, this time past her shoulder. "Not until you put the gun down and calm yourself. Right at the moment you're in no condition to see anyone, much less my daughter."

"I want my baby," she cried, and the tears welled in her eyes.

"Then put the gun down," he commanded gently. "Or use it. Whichever you decide, you'd best do it quickly before Mr. Roarke takes it in his mind to decide for you. He's standing right behind you, if you'd care to look."

The breath left her lungs on a sob. She began to lower the heavy weapon, to turn to face this new threat, when her finger trembled too hard against the trigger. The sound of the gunshot roared in her ears, followed instantly by a crash and splintering of wood. Her hand was numb after the excruciating jolt, but she felt the gun being wrenched from her fingers. She covered her mouth and began screaming, keeping her eyes tightly shut against the horror she anticipated seeing. She was pulled forward by rough hands and shaken so hard her head snapped to and fro. It was Morgan holding her. He was alive, and there was as much alarm in his eyes as there was anger.

"You damned fool," he cursed and drew her against his chest. "You damned hotheaded little fool! You could have killed yourself or been killed coming on board my ship waving a gun around."

"My baby!" she sobbed. "My Sarah!"

"All right, all right, she's fine." Wade smoothed the hood back off her hair, nodding to Stuart Roarke as he did so. "Have the child brought here."

Stuart adjusted his spectacles and looked down at the smoking pistol in his hand. He said nothing, though, and left the cabin.

"Hush now," Wade said, brushing his lips over Summer's temple. "Hush. You will have your baby in a minute. Are you hurt? Did you hurt yourself?"

Summer had covered her mouth again and was gaping in horror at the blood spreading wetly down Morgan's arm.

"I shot you!" she gasped. "Oh, Morgan . . . I shot you!"

He cursed again and released her. "By God," he muttered, "so you have."

"Oh, Morgan"—fresh tears spilled over her cheeks—"I'm so sorry!"

He frowned and rolled up the sleeve of his shirt. The ball had grazed the surface of the muscle of his upper arm, but there appeared to be more blood than damage. The worst of the punishment, he noted with yet another flow of curses, was divided between the corner of the wire-fronted bookcase and the sill of the gallery.

"Oh, Morgan—"

"Damnation!" He shook his arm as the pain began to wear through the numbing effects of the gunpowder. The blood had trickled down as far as his wrist, and as he shook it, some spattered on the floor.

"Oh, Morgan—"

"Say that once more," he growled, "and I'm liable to forget why I brought you here."

He shook his arm out again and reached for the bottle of rum on his desk. He unstoppered it with his teeth and spat out the cork, then took several deep swallows before he held his breath and liberally doused the wound.

"You'll be the death of me yet, woman," he grimaced. "First sharks, then rip currents, now loaded pistols—"

Summer was neither watching nor listening. She was reaching for the squalling pink bundle in Thorny's hands.

"Sarah! My beautiful Sarah, you're all right!"

"Of course she's all right," Wade snapped. "Did you think I would have her slung up in the rigging?"

"I didn't know what to think!" she countered furiously, whirling to confront him. "Any man who would deliberately steal a child away from her mother would be capable of anything!"

The *Chimera* swayed unexpectedly, catching Summer off balance.

"Here," Wade said gruffly, "sit down before you fall down. And you'll watch your tongue with me if you value keeping it. She wasn't stolen, and neither one of you is suffering for the experience—yet."

Summer allowed herself to be helped into the leather chair. She cradled Sarah and kissed the coppery curls, whispering reassurances until her daughter's crying slowed to a dull fret.

"She's starved half to death," she said, casting a scathing eye at Morgan Wade. "How were you planning to meet that contingency, Captain?"

He merely glowered at her as Thorny cackled under his breath and tied a strip of linen around the wounded arm. Sarah began to wail bitterly at the layers of clothing that refused to obey her gropings and Summer's temper flared anew.

"I hope you are satisfied with your night's work. I have never seen her cry so hard. I trust you will not force me to fight my way off your wretched ship now."

She started to rise, but another slight lurch set her down heavily. Sarah wailed all the harder for the sudden jolt and needed to be soothed and petted until she found the comfort of her thumb.

"Well, sir?" Summer demanded.

"Well, madam? You said the child was hungry. . . . Feed her."

"Here?" she cried. "On this . . . this . . ." The word did not immediately come to mind, and she released a sharp breath in exasperation. "Am I free to leave?"

"You are free to go anywhere you like," Wade said brusquely. "If it's ashore, however, you'll have to swim for it."

"What? What did you say?"

Wade indicated the gallery windows. "It seems you've just made it aboard in time. Mr. Roarke was able to catch the tide after all."

"The tide—" Summer's mouth dropped open. Too late, she realized that the cabin was swaying rhythmically—far too rhythmically for a vessel moored to a stationary dock. "Oh, my God! You didn't! You wouldn't! *My God—we're moving!"*

"I told you I was leaving on the tide," he said easily.

"But not with me on board!" she cried and jumped to her feet. "You have to turn back! You have to put me ashore!"

"I'm afraid I can't do that. If we stop now, we'll be caught in port until high tide tomorrow."

"Then you can just lower a boat and have me rowed ashore when we clear your blasted port."

"I can't do that either," he said on a sigh. "We've a fair wind by the feel of it. Enough to carry us out to open water. I couldn't risk losing such a clean start, not when there would be so many eyes searching for us in the morning."

Summer stared out the gallery windows in dismay, watching the shore lights wink by at an alarming rate. She gasped as the full import of his words struck her.

"You were waiting for me! You gambled I would come after Sarah alone—that was why you took her!"

"Not such a gamble, in truth," he admitted. "I fear I am almost coming to understand the way your mind works. Thanks, Thorny. See if you can find the governess something hot to drink."

"Aye, Cap'n. B'ilin' 'ot, I warrant."

"If you had guessed wrong," Summer persisted, ignoring Thorny's cackle as he left, "what then? What would you have done then? What if I hadn't checked her crib until tomorrow morning?"

"You would have been a poor mother and not deserving of her."

Summer was astounded by his audacity. He had kidnapped Sarah and now kidnapped her. . . .

"Do you know what you've done?" she asked in a horrified whisper.

"I have a fairly good idea."

The ship tilted as it maneuvered into the wind, nudging Summer into the shattered bookcase. Wade steadied her, then selected a thin black cigar from the humidor.

"You will forgive me if I leave you for a while. Mr. Roarke may need me on deck."

"You can go straight to hell, Captain Wade, for all I care."

"Now where have I heard that before?" he grinned, pausing at the cabin door. "Make yourself comfortable. I'm sure you know where everything is."

Summer clenched her teeth in fury and grabbed the closest object she could lay a hand to. It was a heavy brass bookend, and it crashed against the closing door, leaving an ugly dent in the blond wood before it rebounded to the floor. She stared at the dent with a sense of helpless outrage and slumped into the leather chair, refusing by sheer force of will to cry. Sarah's crying startled her out of her stupor, and she immediately unfastened her cloak and parted the bodice of her dress. She winced as the gums clamped vehemently around the jutting nipple, but her anger soon welled to the surface again.

What would Bennett's reaction be when he discovered them gone? It would look as if she had run away to be with Morgan. Michael was the only one who knew the reason she had come to the harbor tonight, but when he found out the *Chimera* had sailed with both of them still aboard, he would probably assume, like everyone else, that she had made the choice of her own free will.

Bennett Winfield had never needed much provocation to chase Morgan Wade. Now he would come after the *Chimera* with blood in his eye and the full sanction of the navy behind him.

Summer was worried, despite her anger at Wade's deception. He must know Bennett would come after them. As would Sir Lionel and the entire British Navy if it came to light that she and Sarah were the victims of a kidnapping. Morgan would be a wanted man. His letters of marque would be useless in British ports; there would probably be an open warrant for his arrest, if not an outright bounty placed on his head by the government.

Summer sat her daughter upright on her knee and coaxed the bubble of air from her stomach. Sarah grinned and batted a fist against Summer's chin, happy to have some attention at last.

"Why is he doing it?" Summer whispered. "Goodness, how successful can he be as a privateer if he spends his time kidnapping women and children!"

And then she saw it.

The bright red of it caught her eye over the top of Sarah's head, and she opened the drawer in Wade's desk to see all the way inside. It was lying there coiled neatly on top of his logbook where he could not help but see it and touch it and remember every time he made an entry. It was the red silk ribbon she had worn in her hair every day for the week she was on board the *Chimera*.

She knew it was the same one. It still had some of the frayed threads poking through where she had torn it from the trim on her smock. It had been all she had salvaged from her clothes. She could not even remember when or where she had lost it. She lifted it gingerly out of the drawer and held it closer as she thought back over the long months.

He had kept a trifling thing like this . . . why?

The only answer she could think of brought a flush into her cheeks because she knew it couldn't possibly be true.

Summer looked down at Sarah and heard the sob escape her throat as she saw the tiny fist clutch at the dangling end of the ribbon.

Captain Morgan Wade barked out a sharp correction to their course and ran a hand through the waves of his black hair. His arm had passed the painful, stinging stage and was throbbing in direct proportion to the anger pounding in his temples.

Women! He'd spent half a lifetime avoiding them. They were nice to look at and nice to keep a bed warm at night; he'd enjoyed more than he could recount over the years, and none of them—not a one—had talked to him the way this one did and got away with it. Certainly none had taken a shot and lived to tell. So what did he need with her? And a child . . . what was he thinking of?

Probably the same thing that had plagued his every waking moment and even intruded in his dreams through this past year: a pair of gray-green eyes that had the ability to set his blood boiling one minute and reduce him to shreds the next. A body so welcoming and so perfect the memory of it had left all others drab by comparison.

Morgan turned away from the deck rail and signaled to Mr. Phillips to run up the royals.

"Why don't you go below, Morgan," Roarke said quietly. "You aren't really needed here; everything's under control."

"What makes you think I'm needed below?" he snarled. "She's already expressed her opinion of my night's work."

Roarke looked at the bandaged arm and smiled. "She couldn't have been that angry, or she would have aimed for something else."

Wade glared at him and muttered an oath. But he left the bridge and ducked into the hatchway leading down to his cabin. He paused at the door and caught himself about to knock—knock on his own door, for Christ's sake—then set his mouth in a grim line and wrenched the latch open. She was still sitting in his chair, although now her cloak was off and she held the babe suckling at her breast. Her hand fluttered up to shield her nakedness, falling again when she identified the intruder.

"There is a draft from the door, Captain. Please close it."

Morgan shut the door but remained where he was, frowning at the woman and child.

"You may come all the way in," she said, mildly amused at his sudden awkwardness. "Unless you intend to shout and stamp about, that is. Your daughter has been upset quite enough for one night."

"I only came to fetch a clean shirt," he grumbled. "It can wait. I can come back later . . . when you've finished."

"Haven't you ever watched a child nursing?"

"Of course I have," he lied.

"But not one of your own?"

The dark blue eyes narrowed. "What kind of a question is that, woman?"

"A logical one. It has occurred to me as I sit here on your ship being spirited away in the dead of night—for the second time—that I know precious little about you. I do not think it is at all inappropriate of me to want to know if there are any more little Wades running around."

"And if I say scores?"

She paused a beat before she answered. "I would have to say you lacked character."

"That, madam, should be the least of my faults." He walked over to the cupboard and yanked out a clean shirt. He shrugged out of the torn, bloodstained one and discarded it in a heap on the floor. He moved close to the desk as he rebuckled his belt, his gaze fixed on Sarah's face.

As the baby sensed the new disturbance, her mouth stopped and loosened its hold as she looked around. Dark blue eyes met dark blue eyes and held for the span of several breaths before she squirmed and returned to more important matters.

A grin broke through the stern expression on Morgan's face, and he sat on the corner of his desk. "Does that mean she approves?"

"She has a fair temper. You will know it immediately if something is not to her liking."

"Just like her mother," he murmured wryly.

"I was thinking: just like her father."

The blue eyes lifted to hers and held.

"How is your arm?" she asked finally.

"It will mend. How is your disposition?"

"Improving."

His eyes wandered over her hair, down to the curve of her cheek, where there were still traces of tearstains, to the ivory whiteness of her breasts and the darker, prominent nipple. Without warning he leaned forward and laid his fingertips a scant inch from Sarah's busy mouth, feeling the pull and suck as the child fed. A tiny fist uncurled and batted hesitantly at this new impertinence, grasping one of the strong fingers when she found it warm and willing.

Summer had to lean her head against the backrest of the chair. The combined sensation of Sarah's mouth and Morgan's hand on her breast sent a rush of heat flooding through her body.

"She seems to enjoy that as much as I do," Morgan said,

noting the flush that came into Summer's cheeks. When there was no response other than a slight heightening of color, he bent his dark head to her bared breast, circling it with his tongue and leaving behind a teasing, moist kiss. He heard the stifled gasp and raised his mouth to hers, kissing her as thoroughly as he dared.

Her eyes were shining and her breath stilted when he finally straightened.

"Morgan, what are we going to do? Bennett will come after us, and Father—"

"You let me worry about them."

"But you don't understand. Bennett will not stop now until he kills you. He went into a terrible rage when he found out how you tricked him at the Sirens. I know he has something planned this time, and now, with Sarah and me on board—"

"He'll never catch the *Chimera,*" Wade assured her calmly, seeing the quick shadow of terror come into her eyes. "Not unless I want him to. He won't catch me, and he won't touch you—not ever again; you have my word on it."

"I wish I could believe you," she cried desperately. "But you don't know him; you don't know his . . . rages. He's changed so much over the past year—" Her eyes filled with tears. "I want so much to believe you."

He cradled her face in his strong hands. "Then do it. Believe me. Because I do not intend to ever lose you again. And in case I still haven't said it right"—his voice lowered to a whisper—"I love you, Governess. More than life and breath, more than anything else on this earth."

Summer could do little more than stare up at him.

He wiped tenderly at the tears flowing over her lashes, but they continued, and in the end he gave up and laughed gently, kissing her, smiling against her mouth when he felt a grasping hand reach up between them and tear at a fistful of hair on his chest.

"Exactly like her mother," he murmured.

19

Stuart Roarke was standing on the bridge, taking a reading from the sextant, when he saw Summer stroll by on the quarterdeck. He set the instrument aside and smiled as she looked up.

"Good morning, Mrs. Winfield. I hope you slept well."

"Shamelessly well, Mr. Roarke. And please, call me Summer."

He swung his lean frame down the ladderway and joined her at the rail. The sea was a deep aquamarine blue, the sky a blaze of azure. The sails overhead were a startling white and were so motionless in the steady breeze they might have been carved from marble. There was not a ripple on the surface of the canvas, not a sound other than a low humming to betray the strain. Roarke had them trimmed to a steady ten knots, and the *Chimera*'s passage through the smooth water was as light and graceful as a nymph's.

"Then I shall settle for nothing less than Stuart," he said shyly, smiling as he presented a wiggling finger to Sarah.

"I would like that. As much as I would like to have an honest friend . . . one who would tell me if there were any sign of a ship following us."

Roarke smiled again. "Not a one."

"Not even a dot on the horizon?"

"Not even a speck of dust. There hasn't been time. Even if your husband's ship was rigged for sailing, he would be hours behind us. Morgan is a careful man, though it often appears the opposite. He likes to give me credit for taking most of the precautions, but he went to the Governor's Ball knowing full well a trap was inevitable again. A great deal of money went to the right hands to make it seem as if he had nothing more important on his mind than an enjoyable evening of partying."

Sarah chortled and leaned abruptly forward, attracted by the play of sunlight on Stuart's spectacles. He laughed and steered mother and daughter toward a thick coil of cable so that they might sit down.

"The ruse will not last long once the authorities realize the *Chimera* has left port," said Summer, adding bleakly, "and who he has on board."

"Well, ah, as far as they are concerned, the *Chimera* has not left yet."

"How could they miss seeing her go?" Summer frowned. "Morgan said himself the harbor was blocked and the wharfs were crawling with spies. There would have been an alarm sent up as soon as her anchor was pulled in."

"Yes, there would have been. I'm sure the whole island would have been alerted to it—if anyone saw her move."

"I'm afraid you've confused me completely," she sighed. "My father spoke at length just yesterday about the embarrassment of having the *Chimera* moored in Bridgetown."

Roarke laughed. "They have all been seething over the *Chimera*'s presence for two days now, watching her, plotting every move she makes. They clearly saw Morgan leave her in a longboat to attend the Ball, and fully a half-dozen carriages followed a discreet distance behind him. Just as many followed and reported him being rowed back out later that evening."

"Later that . . . but he was . . ."

"Elsewhere," Roarke said delicately. "Yes, I know. And I would not have fooled anyone on a close inspection or in daylight. But at night, at a distance"—he shrugged and smiled modestly—"I passed as easily as the *Gyrfalcon* does."

"The *Gyrfalcon?*"

"Another of Morgan's whims, but a rather clever one.

The *Chimera,* you see, was never even near Bridgetown. The *Gyrfalcon* is an exact duplicate—a twin, if you like—right down to her markings and trim. She's come in handy on more than one occasion like this, not to mention the fact that we confuse the hell out of the British Navy on a regular basis."

"The reports," Summer gasped, "the conflicting sightings! The accounts of seeing the *Chimera* in two places at once!"

Roarke grinned. "A clever bit of chicanery, aye."

Summer's hand flew to her throat. "And the guns last September?"

"The *Gyrfalcon* collected the guns at Port-of-Spain while Morgan detained your husband. The plan was a hasty one, concocted after a warning had been whispered in our ear about a trap in the works"—he glanced sidelong at Summer and saw her blush deepen—"but it saved us both ships, since the *Gyrfalcon* was originally supposed to sail straight back to Bounty Key . . . straight into the guns of the *Northgate.*"

"What will happen now? What will you do if the *Gyrfalcon* is blockaded—or sunk at her moorings?"

"Well, yes, that is an unpleasant possibility. Also one that we had to risk. Her captain is a . . . bullheaded . . . man. I somehow think he'll come out of it in one piece."

"Bullheaded? You mean the *Gyrfalcon*'s captain is Bull Treloggan?"

"My illustrious father-in-law," Roarke nodded. "Rather a cozy arrangement to say the least."

"But if he's been in port for two days, why has no one discovered the ruse? Surely the customs men would have searched the *Gyrfalcon* as a matter of routine."

"You would think that, wouldn't you? And normally they would have."

"The amnesty?" she guessed.

"Aye, and the fact that Morgan was invited into port. They also arranged to have the *Caledonia* anchored off her stern . . . a ploy that suited Morgan's fine sense of humor perfectly."

"I wasn't aware he had one," Summer commented dryly.

"Oh, he has one, believe me. I've been the brunt of it long enough to know."

Summer glanced at him over the top of Sarah's head. It was all so absurd. So foolishly, brilliantly, masterfully absurd! A child should not have been duped so easily for so long. No wonder Morgan scoffed openly at men like Farley Glasse and Bennett Winfield.

"I hope you will not take offense in this, Stuart, but you and Morgan—you seem an odd combination to be friends."

"We are more than just friends. We're brothers. Half brothers, to be more precise. Same father, different mother."

For the second time in as many minutes, Summer's mouth popped open in surprise. "Morgan never mentioned it."

"He rarely does—by my request, not his."

"But why?"

Stuart took a thoughtful breath and adjusted his spectacles. "Well, obvious differences aside, I just don't think I compare favorably with Morgan. As Stuart Roarke, I'm good at what I do. I command a certain degree of respect, something that might be harder to come by if I was thought to be moving in Morgan's shadow."

"What exactly do you do?"

He smiled and toyed with Sarah's finger. "For one thing, I designed and built the *Chimera* . . . and the *Gyrfalcon*. Everything from topsail to keel is by my own specifications, according to my own designs, which, by the way, the British shipbuilders scorned years ago as being impractical. Even the cannon we carry are cast out of specially alloyed iron to make them stronger and more accurate. You won't find a faster pair of ships on the water, nor safer ones. Part of me is built into every beam and spar, and I'm damned proud of them."

"So you should be," she said, in awe. "But why are you here in the middle of the Caribbean smuggling illegal cargoes and playing cat and mouse with naval warships? Why not build your own shipyards? You could become a very wealthy man on the reputation of the *Chimera* alone."

He regarded Summer with the same strange gleam in his eye she had once seen in Morgan's. "I suppose I could."

She sighed. "And I suppose you are going to tell me you have all the money you need, just as Morgan says he has more than he could possibly spend in two lifetimes."

"What is the difference, when you come right down to it, between being rich and being very rich? It's just that much more to keep track of."

She was being gently mocked, and she knew it. "It doesn't explain why either of you risk your necks to prove you can outsail and outthink the British Navy."

"Someone has to do it. America will never go back to being just another British colony, but so far all they've done is shout slogans and wave their fists around. We have no navy to speak of, no army either if it comes right down to it. We have brashness on our side, though, and a careless type of courage that comes with the arrogance Britain herself forced on us forty years ago. It is ludicrous to think we could enter into a war with England and win—but I'd be willing to wager my last shirt that we will. Morgan is just showing them how to do it."

"Then what Farley Glasse said is true—America will have to rely heavily on her private forces to survive the first months if war comes?"

"First months? We'll be blockaded tighter than a drum within days. Our supplies will be cut off; the half-dozen heavy warships we do have will be bottled up in their ports and useless."

"Then all of this—the smuggling and the gunrunning and the cat and mouse . . . it is all a big rehearsal. You expect to be playing these games for real in the near future."

"Morgan did say you were clever."

"I am also a British subject," she said quietly. "And if Mr. Glasse was not mistaken, so is Morgan."

Roarke's eyes narrowed. "Morgan?"

"Isn't he Sir Edmund Granville? A titled Englishman who fled to America years ago to avoid a charge of murder? And doesn't he now spy for Captain Stephen Decatur, who, I assume, knows all about the *Chimera* and the *Gyrfalcon?*"

Roarke studiously avoided her gaze as he wriggled his fingers again for Sarah.

"He does. And your Mr. Glasse seems to be remarkably well-informed. Except for one small detail—Morgan is not Sir Edmund Granville. . . . I am."

"It isn't an uncommon story," Roarke began. "I'm surprised it even interests anyone after all these years. My father was a titled and prominent member of the King's Council. My mother was soft and frail and seemed fated to suffer at the hands of the foolish men in her family. Like the true English gentleman Sir Hugh was, he married wealth but gave his heart to a raven-haired, dark-eyed beauty he'd met on a voyage to America. A year after he returned home to England, the woman's family wrote to him that she had died shortly after giving birth to his son.

"He sent for the child and, like the truly genteel woman she was, my mother took the boy into our home and raised him as if he was her own flesh and blood. It took four years and three daughters before Lady Madelaine produced a legitimate heir for the baron, but by then her health was showing the strain, and I arrived early, sickly, and without an encouraging word from any of the attending physicians. I remained pale and sickly throughout my youth, while Morgan"—he stopped and laughed—"Morgan was much like he is today. He cowed the servants into obeying him. He terrified his tutors and called them fools when they tried to teach him things he considered useless—then turned around and astonished them by the amount of knowledge he could absorb if he set his mind to it. Which was rarely. He spent hours walking along the cliffs staring out to sea and hours at the wharfs learning more by listening to the old sailors than he could from a hundred geography lessons. He laughed off the punishments he was given and constantly challenged anyone who tried to discipline him or make him adhere to any rules other than his own. And as I recall, he had most of the female servants stumbling about the house in a daze by the ripe old age of fourteen.

"Mother finally reached the end of her good humor and generosity when she found him, ah, in a delicate state with her favorite niece. She didn't bother to ask who had instigated it or to consider that her niece was five years his senior—she simply ordered Father to have him removed.

"I remember the day he came to tell me he was leaving. The door to my room blew open, and he stood in the entrance like a storm cloud, a cape three sizes too big whipped over his shoulders and a crazy grin on his face, as if it had all gone according to some master plan of his. Home to America, he said. That was where he was bound. And if I ever took it in my head to shake off the lunacies of my birthright, I was welcome to join him."

Roarke paused and smiled ruefully as he stared out over the ocean. "To a ten-year-old boy with the croup it was not the most appealing offer he could have made. At any rate, he left and signed on as a cabin boy aboard a Yankee merchantman in port, and that was the last we heard from him. I recovered from the croup and the flux and the yellow fever, and in due time, when Father died, I strutted about London like the ripe young peacock I was certain I had become.

"Father had arranged my marriage years earlier to a wealthy young heiress, but in true Granville tradition, I fell blissfully in love with an actress. I assumed she returned my fervor, but as it turned out, she was merely using me to assist her real lover out of a sticky situation. He was married, you see, and the wife was refusing to let him go. I was led by the nose to a hotel room one night, where I assumed I would be guided through heaven's gate and back again. Instead my drinks were doctored, and when I woke up the next morning, I had a head on me three feet wide and a dead woman on the floor by my bed."

"The wife?" Summer guessed.

"Yes, but I didn't know it at the time. I didn't know anything except that I was in the room with a dead woman and had no way to prove that I hadn't bashed her head in with a candlestick. I couldn't remember anything beyond having my clothes rather pleasantly stripped from my body. Naturally I did what any sensible young man of almost eighteen would do in a situation like that and escaped aboard the first ship leaving England."

"But didn't you try to find the other woman, the actress?"

"I may have been blind, but I wasn't stupid. Besides finding the dead woman, I also discovered that my clothes, my money, my watch and rings . . . everything was gone. I was meant to be found, and I was meant to take the blame for the murder. I had a feeling that if I went to the theater, my loving little Floretta would have denied being anywhere near the hotel."

"So you left England, you left your family without any kind of explanation?"

"Only one sister was alive for my fifteenth birthday, and that same summer the two of us and Mother took the yellow fever. As ironic as it sounds, I was the only one to survive. There was no one to do any explaining to."

"It seems your Floretta made a careful choice."

Roarke snorted derisively. "I must say it soured me toward women for some time. I landed in Boston with a new name and an invented past and a firm resolution to have nothing more to do with the softer sex."

Summer hid her smile. "And so you found Morgan?"

"Actually, no. He found me. I spent a few years working my way down the major coastal ports, figuring that sooner or later I'd either hear about Morgan or find him. I was in Virginia tracking down one of many rumors that he'd changed his name, when the first night in town, the door to my room burst open and there he was. Larger than life, looking just the way I'd pictured he should—except for the brace of pistols he held pointed straight at my heart. He said he'd heard of a Stuart Roarke asking too damned many questions about him and thought it high time to see for himself if he could provide the answers. That was nine years ago, and speaking for myself, I have never looked back. I scarcely remember who Edmund Granville was, and at times I find it hard to believe he ever existed at all."

"But he did exist," Summer said quietly. "And Farley Glasse has the evidence to prove it."

She saw the frown crease his brow and explained Glasse's disclosure of the seals and the family crest almost a year ago.

"So that is why he assumes Morgan is Edmund Granville. It was another calculated risk, I suppose, but we needed a way to identify the coded dispatches from the routine ones."

"Then the rest of what Glasse said is true. . . . Morgan is spying for the Americans?"

"Morgan is doing what he can to even out the odds a little. He never did consider himself an Englishman. Father and his whole life-style was something foreign to Morgan from the very beginning. He is an American, Summer. He was born there, and I wager he'll die there, and he may not fly a naval pennant anymore, but the secretary of war depends on him as if he was still commanding from the bridge of an American warship."

"What if war comes? Will he fly the pennant then?"

"No," Roarke shook his head. "He's worn the uniform once and the experience left a bitter taste in his mouth. Besides, he knows he can accomplish far more without being shackled by rules and codes of conduct. He'll keep right on doing what he is doing now: running the blockades, stirring up a few distractions to keep the British noses pointed in the wrong directions, and, if he's lucky, taking a few Union Jacks along the way. He is a man who likes to make things happen, a man who hasn't the patience to wait around to be caught up in events instigated by someone else."

He glanced up at Summer. "It is the kind of man he is. He drives himself hard and expects nothing less from the people around him. I honestly do not think he could live any other way—he wouldn't know how to accept anything less out of life."

"I understand what you are trying to tell me," she said. "And no, I don't suppose he would. Frankly, that is what frightens me. I don't know if I can keep up with him."

The twinkle returned to Stuart Roarke's eye. "Well, if it helps you any to know, he's been absolute hell to live with this past year. When he fell, he fell hard, and now I can see why. I don't think you have anything to worry about."

Summer flushed warmly. "There is nothing special about me, Stuart."

"Then he has gone to a great deal of trouble for nothing

special. He has broken a lot of his own rules in bringing you along, not to mention the chance he took going to the gala with no one but the delightful Mrs. Teague for protection." He laughed. "And speaking of chances, I'll have you know my own neck was in danger when he received that note. Finding out you were Sir Lionel's daughter was hard enough on his vanity, but when I had to tell him about your marriage to Winfield"—he rolled his eyes skyward—"we had to practically strap him down to keep him from storming the house and making a widow out of you then and there. As it was, my Bett came close to losing a husband."

Summer was grateful she had a squirming bundle in her arms to afford her the excuse not to meet Roarke's eyes. "How are your wife and son?"

"Thriving," Roarke declared. "Alexander is just past his first birthday—by God, it's June 27—ten days ago today, and if I didn't know better, I'd say there was a little of Morgan in him. On the other hand, he has Bull Treloggan for a grandfather, so I shouldn't have expected an archangel."

Summer laughed. "Are you still having father-in-law problems?"

"Still? They'll be with me forever, I fear. Lately he's taken to staring at me for long periods of time, flexing his hands like so—" He demonstrated as if he had a throat to throttle. "It has taken all of Bett's charm and most of Morgan's considerable powers of persuasion to get the bastard to be even that congenial."

Summer was laughing so hard Roarke took advantage of the opportunity to transfer Sarah to his own knee.

"Ahh, you're a beauty," he crooned. "Just like your mama. I think I should act on my son's behalf and seal a marriage pact now before any other bucks lay an eye on you. What do you say, Princess? Shall we scratch a pledge in the mainmast?"

Sarah gave an expressive sigh, jammed her thumb in her mouth and snuggled her cheek against his chest.

"Well, now, isn't this a cozy scene," Morgan said from the forecastle. He was leaning casually against the bulkhead, his muscular arms crossed over his chest. "I leave you alone for half an hour, and you win my daughter over and have my woman laughing like a jaybird."

Roarke grinned. "Aye, and half an hour more and I'd have your ship and your crew as well."

Sarah's head lifted abruptly, and the suction was released from her thumb with a wet smile. She too had seen Wade.

Roarke crooked an eyebrow. "I do believe I am being tossed over for a prettier face. Come along then, Papa, hold your daughter if she's so determined. I've a course to plot."

Morgan straightened from the bulkhead as Stuart stood and handed Sarah into his huge hands. He was too stunned for a moment to do more than stare eye to eye with Sarah.

"Mind you don't drop her"—Roarke murmured dryly—"she might break."

"Hey—"

"Give her to me," Summer laughed, stretching out her arms. Morgan handed Sarah down gingerly, then stood at the rail admiring mother and child.

"Did you and Roarke have a pleasant chat? I warrant I have few secrets left."

"Your brother is a fine gentleman," she observed. "A fine friend, too. He doesn't deserve your sarcasm."

"He has only my respect," Wade said truthfully. He held Summer's gaze before looking out across the blue expanse of the sea. "I suppose he also told you we'll be making port by this evening. You'll be able to go ashore and buy what you need for yourself and the child."

"Tonight?"

"Aye. I've some business to attend to on Martinique. How long we stay depends on how soon my business is completed."

"Or on when the *Gyrfalcon* arrives?"

Wade frowned. "Roarke's tongue was extremely loose, I see."

"What will you do if the *Gyrfalcon* fails to arrive?"

"She'll arrive."

"How can you be so positive? The *Caledonia* could block the harbor indefinitely."

"Bull has his orders; he'll follow them. He's to let anyone on board who cares to go. He's to let them search bow to stern if they insist. When they find nothing and no one, they'll have no choice but to allow her to leave port."

"Bennett will be livid," she said, shuddering inwardly.

"Better a livid man than a dead one."

Summer averted her eyes. "What is to stop him or my father from ordering the ship impounded and the crew placed under arrest?"

"On what grounds? The *Gyrfalcon* has committed no infractions. All of her charts and logs carry her own imprint; her crew has been orderly and has broken no laws. It is no fault of hers or her captain if the naval incompetents on shore mistook her for another ship on appearances alone. Not even Farley Glasse could find justification to hold her."

"I don't think he needs justification for anything he does, Morgan. If he wants to impound the *Gyrfalcon,* he will."

"In which case, he'll be dealing with Bull Treloggan's temper. Something which even I avoid at all costs." He reached down and tucked a finger under Summer's chin, forcing her to raise her eyes to his. "The *Gyrfalcon* will come. She'll meet us at Fort-de-France, mark my words."

"You took an awful chance with the ship and crew."

"We all take chances. It keeps the blood flowing." He laughed suddenly and dropped his hand. "And besides, we'll see just how badly the British want us if they follow the *Gyrfalcon* into French waters."

"I don't understand."

"You mean Roarke left something out?" He laughed again. "I cannot say as I blame him. You see, my lady, while you may have become my prime concern, you were not the sole reason for the need of a decoy this trip."

Summer sighed. "I thought there might be more to it."

"Did you now," he grinned slowly.

"I am not entirely addle-brained. You had to have been in the islands already for Father to send the invitation and for Glasse—or whoever—to send the note. Dare I ask what you have in the hold at this very moment?"

"No." His grin lingered. "But by God, you should have

been a man. We could have run the English right out of the Caribbean."

"And why does my being a woman impose such a strain?" she demanded. "Women are capable of being just as cunning and underhanded as any man I know . . . and some even feel the need to have their blood set to flowing at times. Have you never heard of Anne Bonney or Mary Read? They operated one of the most successful pirating ventures in these waters."

"Aye, and they were also hung for their efforts. Is this your way of telling me you plan to take up the life of a buccaneer now? This from the same woman who protested so ardently to preserve her reputation."

"Well, you have seen nicely to that, sir. *You* made the choice, not I. Laugh at me if you like, but now that I am here, and now that I am to be a part of your life, Morgan Wade, it will not be the part that stays behind waving dutifully as you sail off toward the horizon. If that is what you expect of me, then you'd best let me off at the first opportunity."

"Or what?" he asked, folding his arms across his chest and regarding her without the least effort to conceal the amusement in his eyes. "There is a war brewing, madam, in case you have not heard the rumors. When it comes, these islands will be smack in the middle of it. What would you have me do? Let you stand braced at the bowsprit, a cutlass in each hand, a babe fastened to each breast, while you ward off boarders?"

A hot surge of color flooded Summer's cheeks as she stood up. "I would expect you to treat me as if I meant more to you than simply a convenience for your bed. If there is a war coming, I am just as much a part of it as you are. If I wanted to shirk all responsibility and hide my head in the sand to avoid the unpleasantness, I could have done so quite comfortably with Bennett."

She spun on her heel and in her haste to leave the deck ran headlong into Thorny. He steadied her and the baby and touched a finger to his grisled brow.

"I jest come ter tell ye, I cut a ripe fine crib owt'n an odd crate we 'ad lyin' about. The wee lass should fit in snuglike, better 'n a heap o' canvas on the floor—eh?" He stood gaping after Summer as she brushed past him, then glanced at the captain. "Did she jest say what I t'ought I 'eard 'er say?"

Morgan strode past him without a word, his expression as ominous as a thundercloud.

Summer went directly to the cabin. Her eyes were burning, but she refused to give in to the tears, knowing that if she did, it would only reinforce Morgan's view of her capabilities. Good heavens, she didn't want to go into battle with him, but neither did she want him to assume she would be content to trade one stale life for another. She saw the cradle Thorny had fashioned and blushed deeply at the thought of the expletive that had come so easily to her lips. It was proof, if nothing else, that she could adapt.

She was settling Sarah into the cradle when she heard the door open behind her. She turned, expecting to see Morgan, but it was Stuart Roarke.

"Oh. Sorry, Summer. I should have knocked. I thought you were still topside. I just, ah—" He indicated the desk with a clumsy gesture, his words trailing off when he saw her expression. "I'll only be a minute."

"Take as long as you like," she snapped. "Or just pretend I am not here at all. I gather from your captain I should familiarize myself with the feeling."

Roarke smiled warily and adjusted his spectacles. He crossed over to the desk and shuffled through the papers on top until he located the one he sought. Summer glared at him throughout, remembering that he had a wife and child as well. No doubt he had offered her the same conditions that Wade took for granted.

Roarke kept glancing at her as one might glance at a pane of glass about to shatter. A dull red crept up under his tan, darkening him to a ruddy hue by the time he was back at the door.

"I have a notion you and my father-in-law are going to get along just fine," he muttered and pulled the door shut behind him.

20

THE CHIMERA glided past several heavy cannon emplacements as she sailed into the French port of Fort-de-France an hour before midnight. Morgan Wade had an understanding with the French commandant: sanctuary if the need arose, in exchange for a share of whatever cargo he was running at the time. He did not often make use of their generosity. He considered the French boorish and greedy, their islands nothing more than penal colonies, their governing officials corrupt and not to be trusted.

Summer had remained in the cabin all afternoon and evening, emerging only when she heard the anchor splash into the water. Morgan had come below twice in all that time: once to scribble hasty notations in his log, once to change for going ashore.

"Are you expecting trouble?" she asked, seeing him tuck a long-snouted pistol into his belt.

"The French are fickle in handing out their favors," was the only grunted answer. He paused by the cradle and glanced down at the sleeping child before he strode to the door.

"Morgan?"

He stopped and half turned.

"Be careful," she whispered.

He said nothing, and she was left with the echo of his boots as he climbed to the deck. A general murmur of orders followed, then the creaking of oars being fitted into the oarlocks of a longboat.

Summer went up on deck and stood in the shadow of the bridge, tracking the progress of the boat by the slip and swish of the oars. It was a black night, and the stars were well hidden behind banks of cloud and low-lying mists. Droplets of moisture clung to the rigging, glittering like jewels in the faint glow of the riding lights. The *Chimera,* she was not surprised to see, was well out in the center of the bay with a clear sighting on both flanks to forestall any surprise visits from stealthy boats. Her gunports were closed, and the appearance was of an easy watch, but she had heard the scraping of movement below and guessed that Wade's gun crews were not far from their posts.

Moored within four hundred yards was a French frigate, her masts showing like skeletons, her own ports open and aimed squarely at the privateer.

Summer shivered and wondered what Roarke's orders were in the event he suspected trouble or if Wade failed to return within a specified time.

"Ye should stay b'low, lass," Thorny's voice rasped out from the darkness beside her. "'Tis a ripe foul night, an the dampness'll work a rot in yer lungs if'n ye don't 'ave a mind."

"How long will the Captain be gone?"

"Dunno. Depends on what the devil wants in trade."

"The devil?"

"Aye. Napoléon's pimp, ee is. Biggest t'ief in the Caribee, monsewer de Ville. Deals with bot' the Brits an us privateers, dependin' on who offers the best profits fer 'is troubles." He spat over the side to emphasize his contempt. "Ee 'as a ripe fine respect fer Cap'n Wade, though. Ain't 'ad the balls ter refuse 'im n'owt yet."

Summer turned back to the rail. Lights were sprinkled along the broad curve of the bay, brighter where the activity on the wharves would be at its peak. She gave up hope of catching a glimpse of the longboat and walked slowly back toward the stern.

"Summer?"

She looked up and saw Roarke leaning over the rail of the bridge.

"Still angry with me?"

"No, of course not," she sighed, accepting his hand as he helped her up the ladderway. "And I'm sorry. I should not have behaved so childishly."

"You had every reason to behave as you did. I doubt whether many women would have behaved as calmly as you have this far." He grinned and handed something to her. "Here. You want to have a look?"

It was a brass spyglass, almost three feet in length when fully extended.

"Just hold it to your eye and turn this ring at the bottom to sharpen the image."

Summer obeyed his instructions and was startled to see the shoreline come so close she felt as if she could reach out and touch it. She lowered the glass and the lights were just a distant twinkle again.

"He's about halfway across," Roarke said, pointing out where to aim the end of the spyglass. Summer raised it and slowly shifted it back and forth over the water until she located the shadow of the moving dinghy. She could see the reflection of the lights in the water dripping from the oars. The passengers' features were in shadow, but had it been daylight, she was sure she could have counted the hairs on their chins.

"This is rather a remarkable glass," she said, handing it back.

"Isn't it, though. Makes even a dot on the horizon take shape."

Summer saw the faint smile on his lips and shook her head in amazement. "Are there any limits to what you think you can get away with?"

"If there are, we haven't found them yet," he chuckled. "It certainly wasn't our fault the British were slipshod at guarding their prized panther when it was in port."

"You went on board the *Caledonia?*" she gasped.

"I had to amuse myself somehow while Morgan was at your father's party. Between watching him and watching the *Chimera* . . . or the *Gyrfalcon* . . . no one bothered to watch the *Caledonia.*" He lowered the glass. "We only intended to copy some of her documents, but this beauty just happened to be lying on the commodore's desk, and—"

"—and of course you could not resist," she concluded. "My God, I am beginning to believe everything I have heard about how easy it is to make fools out of Englishmen."

"Only some of them," Roarke said pointedly. "Others seem to be determined to bring it on themselves."

She met the dark eyes and was surprised to see, without the spectacles, a faint resemblance she had not been aware of before. Both brothers managed to say a great deal without having to move their lips.

"You obviously agree with him that a woman's place is at home by the hearth," she said bitterly.

"It isn't a case of whether I agree or not, or even if I want it that way or not. It's strictly a case of where a man's mind is in the crucial second before he makes a decision that could either save his life or lose it for him. Where do you think Morgan's mind is right now?"

"On his wretched meeting."

"You think so? Take another look. Go on, the boat should be in some light now—tell me what you see."

She took the telescope and peered through it, resentful of being treated like a child.

"Do you see the boat?"

"I see it."

"And Morgan?"

"No—yes, there he is . . . I think . . . yes, he's facing this way."

"Facing this way?" Roarke said evenly, taking the glass back. "A man rowing into hostile surroundings, not knowing what to expect on shore—and he's facing this way?"

Summer bit down on her lip. Stuart saw the confusion misting her eyes and smiled gently. "Don't worry, Mr. Monday will keep an eye on him."

"Oh, Stuart, it's all my fault. Most of the arguments we have are my fault. He says it's because I'm stubborn and obstinate and have a terrible temper. . . ."

"Which you are and you do. But then so does he. And don't forget, he's used to having had absolute control over his life for thirty-four years. It will take him a while to adjust."

"But what if we don't have a while?"

"I beg your pardon?" Her voice had been so soft, Stuart had to lean forward to hear.

"I said what if we don't have a while?" She was looking out over the water, and the tears in her eyes were reflecting the harbor lights. "Stuart, you've had him for nine years; I've only had him a handful of nights and days, half of which were spent plotting a way to stick a knife between his ribs. All of the months I carried his child I kept remembering a look or a touch or a gesture. . . . I could bear it, though. I could bear it because I *knew* I would never, ever be seeing him again.

"I know full well one of these days I really will lose him. It may not happen tonight or next month or next year—please, dear God, perhaps not for a dozen years. But it will happen. He has to pay for all of these risks and chances he takes. It is inevitable. And I can accept it, I *have* accepted it because he takes too great a part in shaping his own destiny for me to even think of trying to stop him or discourage him. At the same time, I don't think I could watch him sail away from me and survive to see him sail away again . . . not knowing if it was the last time or not. His way of life terrifies me, Stuart, but living without him now terrifies me even more."

Stuart Roarke regarded the slender, lithe wisp of a girl standing beside him, and his heart went out to her. He remembered the endless hours he had spent pacing the crests of Bounty Key waiting for an overdue ship, and he was surprised by his lack of insight. He thought of his own wife, wondering if she had this same, burning fear in her eyes at this very moment.

"I'm sorry, Summer. I honestly do not know what to say."

She faced him and the tears were glistening down the length of her throat. "Say you'll watch out for him. Say you'll keep him safe and make sure he comes back to me."

Stuart took her into his arms, holding her while the sobs racked her slender shoulders.

"He'll come back to you," he promised quietly. "You have my life on it."

Morgan returned to the *Chimera* three hours after his longboat had gone ashore. His mood was grim, and he was obviously displeased with the concessions he was expected to make. Summer was wakened out of a light sleep by the sound of voices in the cabin and turned a sleepy eye on

Morgan and Stuart Roarke conferring over a sheaf of papers at the desk. A quantity of rum was consumed while the two men debated in barely audible tones. Cigar butts were tossed one after another out the open gallery window, and finally, with the dawn streaking across the sky, Roarke pushed away from the desk and left Morgan alone, staring thoughtfully out the window.

Summer slipped out of the bed, gathering the folds of the oversized shirt she was using as a nightgown around her. She went and stood behind the chair, and it took five full minutes before he realized she was there.

"Sorry," he murmured, setting a partially smoked cigar in the tin cup. "Did we keep you awake?"

"Yes." She smiled and ran a hand through the shaggy black hair. "But I didn't mind. I rather like listening to you—to both of you. Do you know, the more I see you together, the more alike you seem. I'm amazed I did not see the resemblance before."

He welcomed her into his lap and wrapped his arms around her, burying his face and lips in the scattered silk of her hair. She sighed and rested her cheek on the hard curve of his shoulder, content simply to share his warmth.

"You sounded angry when you first came in," she said. "Do the French want too much from you?"

He sighed wearily. "They always want too much. This time the bastard thinks he has me over a barrel. He wants a third of my cargo—he says his protection is easily worth twice as much, but he is, after all, a reasonable man. Reasonable. I should line up my guns on his château and show him how reasonable I think he is."

Summer stroked her hand over the swell of his broad chest, letting her fingers steal beneath the loose cambric. She was astonished at how the mere scent of his skin made her body tingle.

"And then he had the gall to insist we join him for dinner tomorrow. If there is one thing I detest, it's eating pea soup and crow at the same meal."

"Will you go?" Summer ran her hand down to the hard, flat belly and started working the leather belt tab free of the buckle.

"I have no choice. Furthermore, I'll probably meet his

price; I have no choice in that, either. But not without making him squirm a little, you can be sure of that."

She kissed the underside of his chin. "Oh, I have no doubt at all, Captain Privateer. You're very good at making people squirm."

"I happen to know his superiors in la belle France are not too happy with monsieur le general's dealings with the British. They fail to see the humor in his making a fortune selling the English prisoners of war they send him instead of putting them to work in the government cane fields as intended. . . . What the hell are you doing, wench?"

"Squirming. But you just go right ahead and tell me all about Monsieur de Ville. I'm simply *yearning* to know everything."

Morgan's eyes narrowed. "Yearning, eh?"

His hand slid up beneath the shirt she was wearing. He filled his palm with the exquisite tautness of her breast, feeling her shiver and press closer to his shoulder.

"So you are," he murmured, and his arm scooped under her knees. He stood and carried her to the bed, his mouth moving hungrily over hers.

"Morgan—" She kept a tight grip on his neck so that he could not straighten from her for a moment. "—I'm sorry. I'm sorry about this morning, about what I said. It's just that, well, every time I turn around, I seem to be facing something I have never had to deal with before. I don't want to be a burden on you. I don't want to be the cause of you worrying or . . . or . . ." She stopped when she saw the amusement curving the corners of his mouth. She loosened her hands, and her eyes took on a greenish cast. "That is twice I have apologized to you, sir. It would do irreparable damage to my character were I forced to do it again."

Morgan laughed and kissed the tip of her nose. "You don't have to apologize to me, Governess. For anything. You just have to be patient with me. You're not the only one facing things you've never had to deal with before."

She looked up at him, and her eyes shone. "In that case," she whispered, "could you please first deal with my name? Summer . . . Winter, if you prefer . . . Spring . . . anything but"—she wrinkled her delicate nose—"*Governess.*

It was Michael's idea, and I did not think much of it at the time."

"Summer," he murmured, and his hands parted her shirt. He kissed each glorious breast; then his lips moved tauntingly up to the hollow of her throat. "Summer Wade. Aye, it has a certain ring to it, wouldn't you say."

"Summer . . . Wade? But—"

"No buts," he said against her mouth. "To my mind you have been my wife since that night on Bounty Key."

21

"MADAME WADE. How can one country declare the open sea her private domain? How can England dare to blockade the entire Atlantic? How can she dictate where ships may go, who they may trade with and where they may purchase their goods? *Non.* The English accuse our emperor of being a fanatic and a despot, while at the same time your king seeks to control the entire world trade!"

Summer glanced uncomfortably at Morgan Wade, seated across the wide oak table from her, and earned one of his maddeningly lazy smiles in return. She looked at the general, a lean, elegant man in his middle forties, and steeled herself against a rise in temper.

"Monsieur de Ville," she said carefully, "I might remind you that England is not the only country guilty of seizing the ships of other nations. The Americans should have just as much cause to complain against your policy of simply confiscating the cargo you desire and throwing the crews into French prisons. Your captains do not even have a valid excuse to do so."

"And British captains do?"

"It is a well-known fact that British deserters hide out on board American ships."

"So many deserters, madam, would surely leave your British Navy sorely undermanned. They use the excuse as a convenient reason to stop and search ships, nothing more. If there are no deserters on board, they invent them."

"That is an outrageous lie, sir. The Royal Navy would never stoop to such tactics."

General de Ville smiled wanly and turned to Morgan. "Captain Wade, we defer to your superior knowledge. You were on board the *Chesapeake,* were you not, in that infamous case of mistaken identities?"

"There was no mistake," Morgan said. "The British boarded her ten minutes out of Norfolk and demanded the arrest of four of our crewmen, claiming they were deserters."

"Claiming?" Summer asked, recalling the uproar only dimly.

"Three of the men were born and raised in America. The fourth had not seen England for over a decade. The British had false papers for their arrests and made sure they stopped the *Chesapeake* when she was unprepared to fight back . . . a bad habit they have not lost over the years."

"Why would they invent papers?" Summer demanded.

"The *Chesapeake* was a heavy frigate," Morgan said evenly. "They wanted to search her. They also wanted to demonstrate just how far they were prepared to go if our ships insisted on trading with whomever they pleased. England was attempting to put us in our place."

"Ahh, and you were serving in the capacity of lieutenant at the time, were you not?" The general leaned back in his chair, swirling the contents of his wineglass. "As I remember hearing it, the incident was the cause of your resigning from the navy?"

"There were several reasons why I resigned," Wade countered. "The court-martial of an innocent man only brought them to a head."

"Commodore Baron, yes, a true gentleman. Cited for taking an unready ship out to sea. The first American ship to strike her colors—to surrender—was she not?"

"The commodore had no choice. The decks were laden with cargo; the crew was not yet settled to its duties. The British fired three broadsides into us before we could even signal our intentions. Had the colors not been struck, there would have been a needless waste of human life."

"All the same, it was gallant of you to stand behind your commanding officer. A shame for the American Navy, though. You would have been a credit to them now, instead of a mere pawn to anger their enemies."

Morgan's expression did not change except for the slightest darkening of his eyes. De Ville looked disappointed that his bait was refused and glanced at Summer.

"Madame Wade, you are a refreshing change from most Englishwomen I have met. I am pleased to see the captain has the same luck in his women as he does in his business dealings. But surely all of this talk of war and politics must bore you? My own wife refuses to listen to any conversation that does not concern itself with scandals or gossip. She also flatly refuses to leave Paris for the heat of the tropics. Héloïse, *ma chère*"—de Ville smiled toward his mistress—"perhaps you and Madame Wade would care to freshen up before we adjourn to the game room? The captain and I have some business details to settle, and then we shall join you directly."

"Of course." The woman nodded and a servant instantly appeared behind her chair. Héloïse Marchant was tall and gracefully slim; every movement seemed calculated to give pleasure to the beholder.

The gentlemen stood while Summer and Héloïse took their leave. Immediately cigars were produced, the brandy was poured, and the conversation changed from light banter to the more weighty matters of finance.

"You have no doubt heard of the convoy sent out of Jamaica by the English not two weeks ago?" de Ville asked.

"The one hundred merchant ships?" Wade nodded. "Aye, we knew about it."

"And it did not pique your interest?"

"One hundred armed vessels and two first-rated ships of the line? I cannot say it made me want to rush out after them."

De Ville grinned. "A pity. Together we could have captured some of the profits from their fine sugarcane harvest this year. They were also transporting most of their illegal gains home to England, were they not? The prize cargoes belonging to our respective nations?"

"The Marlowe brothers tell me the warehouses on the islands have indeed been stripped to the timbers."

"Perhaps they are anticipating a warm summer?" de Ville suggested. "Their King George is feeling the sting of

Napoléon's victories. . . . Perhaps a quick victory of their own is planned to bolster their spirits."

"Against the United States? A war now would not be a quick one, General, and both sides know it."

"Then you have reason to doubt the rumors that your Congress is on the verge of declaring?"

"The war hawks have been eager to declare war for two years now. Each time the vote is put to Congress, it is either defeated or ridiculed off the floor."

"And of course you are hoping there are enough cool heads in Washington to keep it that way?"

Stuart Roarke cleared his throat and shifted uncomfortably on his seat. Morgan ignored him, however, and met de Ville's probing hazel eyes.

"It is no secret, General, that I would welcome the opportunity to buck heads against the British."

De Ville laughed suddenly, smoothly. "And to that end you play your dangerous games with Commodore Winfield? The man is unstable. You are the only quarry who continually eludes him . . . continually and flamboyantly, I might add. This latest taunt will undoubtably strip his superiors of whatever control they had over him. It could well provoke him into a fatal error in judgment."

"One can only hope, General," Wade murmured.

De Ville laughed again. "*Bon.* To business, then," he said and raised his brandy snifter in a toast.

"One-fifth was the amount I believe we agreed on," Wade said easily. "Mr. Roarke has brought the facts and figures with him if you would care to inspect."

"I would be most interested indeed," nodded de Ville, "and the amount agreed on was one-third."

"Mr. Roarke has advised me that one-third is impossible. A loss of that amount would make our profits negligible, and I am sure you understand profits, General. If I cannot turn a profit this trip, I cannot hope to meet"—Wade's teeth flashed in a quick smile—"certain other commitments I have made."

"Commitments, *monsieur?* What commitments could be more important to you than the protection of your two valuable ships?"

Wade's grin broadened. "Perhaps a shipment of iron,

already cast and assembled. Approximately eight hundred tons in all."

"Cannon?" de Ville was startled. "Did you say eight hundred tons?"

"I did. Five merchantmen in all. They are slated to arrive on the fifteenth of July."

"But eight hundred tons . . . that would be—"

"Three hundred cannon," Wade supplied dryly. "Of course, the numbers that come directly into my hands will depend on the numbers I can afford to purchase."

De Ville stroked his pencil-thin moustache. "You said merchantmen. Are they not intended for the naval base?"

"Originally they were, aye."

De Ville leaned back in his chair. It was a constant threat, being so close to British strongholds. One day he would waken to find his island ringed by British warships. So far the war on the European continent had commanded too much money and manpower to spare anything on a handful of islands four thousand miles away, yet the members of Napoléon's government expected de Ville and his fellow commandants to hold their own against increasing threats from the English and the Spanish. Three hundred cannon, or some percentage thereof, would ensure de Ville's health for some time.

"You understand that terms of credit are impossible," Wade said. "My . . . friends . . . are insisting on payment on delivery. In gold."

"*Mon Dieu*, yes, of course. And three hundred cannon at roughly—?"

"Enough," Roarke interjected, cutting off any mention of a price.

De Ville shot him a look of annoyance. "Already cast and assembled, you say?"

That too was a well-known safeguard. With piracy rampant and ships of all nations prowling the Atlantic and the Caribbean, cannon were often shipped to their destinations in parts. If a ship was captured carrying only breech caps and trunnions, the weapon would be useless to the captor. In the same way, if the ship was lost to a natural disaster, the cost of replacing only sections of the guns would be considerably less.

"Fine English cannon?" de Ville glanced up sharply.

"The best her foundries have turned out," Wade nodded. "They measure in at twenty calibers, and they'll fire a twelve-pound shot fifteen hundred yards accurately."

De Ville drew on his cigar, glancing from Wade to Stuart Roarke. "Such a weapon exists in quantity? And the Marlowe brothers are able to sell them to you?"

"The Marlowe brothers?" Wade's handsome face assumed a look of innocence. "Did I say the shipment was arranged through the Marlowe brothers?"

Roarke raised his brandy glass, lingering over the taste of the liquor to conceal his frown.

"If it was the Marlowe brothers," Wade continued blithely, "I would have less difficulty. But I am dealing cash, I am dealing quantity, and I am dealing on reputation alone—mine."

"On the other hand," Roarke murmured, straightening, "we can hardly allow such a sweet deal to slip through our fingers. Our American compatriots will pay handsomely to have something like this dropped at their doorstep. Even Lafitte has made us an admirable offer."

"The pirate?" de Ville's brows shot up. "You would form an alliance with a pirate rather than come to me out of respect for our past friendship? But I am crushed."

"Don't be," Wade said dryly. "Lafitte's offer was not to my liking."

"Offer?"

"We will naturally need protection shipping the guns after we have picked them up. Lafitte has offered us two ships."

"I have three at my disposal this instant," de Ville said hastily. "For a percentage of the merchandise, I could smooth the way for you gentlemen and assure you a safe passage as far as the Florida coastline."

"And your idea of a fair percentage?"

De Ville forced his excitement under control. It could be an elaborate bluff . . . or it could represent staggering profits. "One-third, gentlemen. Just the sum we have agreed upon today."

Wade looked away. "Impossible. Lafitte's offer was for a

fourth. And I hoped you would reconsider and allow us to wait for Captain Treloggan on sheer goodwill."

De Ville smiled. "One arrangement has nothing to do with the other, my friend. I shall match Lafitte's offer of one-fourth, however, and add that you may have the hospitality of my harbor on that occasion to store the guns if need be."

Wade's laughter rumbled from his chest. "Not likely, *monsieur*. My final offer is one-sixth of what we carry today and one-fifth of the cannon. That is the very best I can do, and at that, I am drawing heavily on past friendship."

De Ville's tapered fingers rapped lightly on the tabletop. He could sense from the discomfort showing on Stuart Roarke's face that Wade was trading a good deal more away than he had intended. At the same time, he could see that the captain was through with dickering. To push him any more would be to lose everything.

"*Vraiment*," de Ville smiled and raised his glass. "We have a deal. A pact you will not regret, gentlemen. Marcel—our best cognac! Ah . . . when might I expect to have my services called upon, Captain?"

"I am on my way now to dispose of my cargo and return with the required payment for the first shipment. Three weeks, more or less."

"*Bien, bien*. I shall alert my captains." He set his hands on the table and pushed to his feet. "That concludes our business then? *Oui, bon*. Let us rejoin the ladies before they grow weary of waiting. You and your lovely wife will of course remain for the night, Captain? The accommodations are quite modest, I am sorry to say, but she should find it a pleasant relief from a ship's berth."

Wade bowed slightly. "She will be delighted, I'm sure."

"And you, Monsieur Roarke? I could perhaps arrange for a suitable companion?"

"Thank you, no, General. I have work to do aboard the *Chimera*. If you tell me which of your men to see about the cargo, I will make all of the arrangements for the morning."

"All work and no entertainment," de Ville shrugged. "But it shall be as you wish. Gentlemen . . ."

Roarke hung back as they followed the Frenchman out of the dining hall.

"You barely came out of that one with your pants on," he muttered. "Cannon with twenty-inch caliber? Fifteen hundred yards? Where the hell did you come up with those figures?"

"He bought it, didn't he?"

"Aye, and he has you and Summer under his roof while he checks with his artillerymen to see just how he should render payment."

"What will they tell him?"

Roarke clamped his teeth down on his cigar. "That Napoléon has twenty-caliber cannon on the line right now making mincemeat out of the Russians."

Wade grinned. "There, you see? You worry too much."

"And if you don't mind, I'll just keep worrying until you and Summer are back on board the *Chimera* and we're away from this damned cesspool."

Wade's laugh rolled along the length of the cantilevered hallway. He gave Roarke some last-minute instructions, then followed de Ville through the door leading into the drawing room. He walked straight to Summer and leaned over, grazing her lips briefly with a kiss.

"The general has generously offered satin sheets and a feather mattress for the night. Shall I say we accept?"

"But Sarah . . ."

"She'll be all right. I've told Roarke to find a respectable girl from the village to take back on board with him tonight to see to the child."

"Oh, but—" Summer bit her lip and saw where the dark blue eyes had strayed. That afternoon Wade himself had purchased the gown she wore, and although his gaze told her repeatedly that the fit was perfect, her alarm at seeing the pink half-circles threatening to pop over the royal blue satin bodice kept a rosy flush high in her cheeks.

"Besides," he murmured, "I believe I would like you all to myself tonight." He straightened and smiled at de Ville. "As you predicted, *monsieur,* my wife would be delighted to accept the invitation."

"*Bon!* And now perhaps we can amuse ourselves with a round or two of cards. Shall we—?" He indicated a baize-covered oak table in one of the immense marble alcoves featured at intervals around the huge room. "*Le Chien?* Two thousand a set?"

"Fair," Wade agreed and held out his glass to be refilled.

"Two thousand what?" Summer whispered, following him to the card table.

"Seashells, my lovely. And by evening's end, we'll own the whole damn beach."

Summer gasped as the last button was freed and her breasts relaxed gratefully within the loosened folds of cloth. Morgan's hands slid around to claim each firm mound, earning a second gasp and an armful of swaying femininity. He laughed and released her to continue the task of removing her clothes.

"One would think," he said dryly, "a lesson would have been learned having gone through a similar experience once before. Spirits taken on an empty stomach . . ."

Summer swallowed hard and felt the room take a half-turn. "I had exactly two glasses of wine before dinner."

"And four brandies after."

"Four? I thought I only had one."

"One glass, perhaps, but it was filled three times."

"Oh."

"Yes, oh. How is this . . . better?"

"Yes, thank you. I'm sorry; I just couldn't seem to breathe all of a sudden."

"Don't worry about it. It probably did you good to ease up on your oh-so-proper conduct." He grinned and added, "And it isn't every day the general has a beautiful woman sing 'God Save the King' from his balcony."

Summer covered her mouth and swung around, staring up at Morgan in horror. "I didn't, did I?"

"At the top of your voice."

"Oh, no . . . why didn't you stop me?"

"And miss de Ville turning apoplectic? Not a chance. Around you go again; I'm almost finished."

Summer sighed and presented him with her back. He worked deftly and quickly on the bindings, letting each layer of silk and linen fall to the floor around her ankles.

Her hair had been dressed formally, and he took a great deal of pleasure in pulling the long pins out one at a time and uncoiling the thick blonde ringlets over her shoulders.

She hardly noticed.

"Sarah is probably miserable," she said.

"She'll be fast asleep by now."

"And hungry."

Wade smoothed his hands down her arms and planted a kiss low on the nape of her neck. "So am I," he murmured. "Get into bed."

She sighed expressively and stepped out of the puddle of her clothing. She stopped beside the enormous canopied bed and grimaced.

"What is it?"

She took a deep breath. "I have never seen black satin sheets in my entire life. I was not even aware such things existed."

Morgan unbuttoned his coat and loosened the ruffled jabot at his throat. "You'd be surprised at some of the trinkets de Ville keeps lying around."

"Trinkets?" she asked, turning too sharply and having to reach for support from the newel post. She fought off a length of filmy mosquito netting and frowned at Wade.

The dark blue eyes grew speculative for a moment; then he laughed softly. "No, my pet, you are far too innocent. Perhaps by the next trip I will have corrupted you enough to let you forget you are Governor Cambridge's daughter."

"I have forgotten already. Poor Father. I hope the shock has not been too great for him."

Morgan's jaw tensed. "And Winfield?"

"Bennett Winfield," she mused, fluffing out the netting. "He is only a name to me now. Why do you suppose I can say it without hating myself? Or without hating him? I don't, you know. I think I could pity him if I tried, but I cannot bring myself to hate him."

Morgan removed his brocaded burgundy waistcoat and finished stripping off his shirt, not wanting to think exactly how much he could hate Winfield without trying.

Summer dragged back the heavy quilted satin coverlet and crawled onto the bed. The sheets were wickedly cool against her flesh, and she purred in mild astonishment when her body sparked suddenly with a thousand delicious sensations. She closed her eyes and stretched luxuriously, aware of Morgan moving to stand at the foot of the bed.

The willowy, sensuous body stood out against the black sheets like an alabaster statue. Her hair was a shock of gold, her mouth a moist, seductive pout. Her breasts were firm and rounded, holding to their perfect shape instead of pillowing flat on her chest as she stretched. The cornsilk thatch of hair at the junction of her thighs caught the lamplight and glowed like a tiny flickering pool of flames.

Morgan's heartbeat thundered throughout his body, and he was loathe to move, loathe to shatter the moment too quickly. He saw her eyes open slowly, catlike, to fasten on him.

"Come and try the sheets, Captain Wade," she invited.

He dropped his shirt on the floor. "I'm of a mind to tell you first . . . you have never looked so lovely."

"Nor you so far away," she whispered. "Come here to me, Captain. *I'm* of a mind to make you a son this night. A tall, beautiful son with black hair and blue eyes."

The belt joined the shirt and waistcoat on the floor, then the buff-colored breeches were peeled down and flung aside.

"Oh, my, yes," she breathed, leaning up on one elbow. "A very fine son, I think."

He smiled and started to reach for the lamp to turn down the wick. Summer caught his hand and rerouted it, kissing the calloused palm and sighing as she directed it lower on her smooth body. She pulled him down beside her on the black satin sheets, shivering as his body strained hungrily for her. On impulse she urged him flat on the bed and rose above him, taking almost as much pleasure in seeing the surprise register on his face as she did in flaring her thighs and settling over him. She braced her hands on his chest, squeezed her eyes tightly shut and drew him slowly, repeatedly upward. She felt his hands on her waist guiding her, holding her as the first shocks of raw ecstasy shuddered through them both. He held her until she could scarcely breathe through the tremendous surges of energy, and then she collapsed in a weak, damp bundle on his chest, grateful for the arms that immediately wrapped around her. She felt a flush of embarrassment stain her cheeks and was thankful he could not see her face.

"I suppose that came from my calling you an innocent," he murmured, and she was startled upright by a gentle laugh.

"May I ask what is so amusing?"

"You," he said and gathered up two streaming fistfuls of her hair. "One day I'll explain to you why it is a damn fool thing to do to take a man off guard like that—" He rolled with her and gazed down for several long moments before the smile faded and his body grew hard and taut again. "But for now, we'll just make sure my son has a firm welcome."

Georges de Ville slid the wall panel into place noiselessly.

So. The daughter of the Governor of Barbados. The wife of Commodore Bennett Winfield. Wade's audacity was near epic proportions!

He should have remembered the reports Gaston related last summer. Summer? Yes, and how could one fail to recall the name itself? Summer Cambridge . . . Summer Winfield . . . Summer Wade. There could not be three in the world with such an unusual name.

De Ville walked quietly out of the darkened cubicle, closing the door carefully behind him. He was in what he affectionately thought of as his inspiration chamber. Comfortable cushions, thick fur rugs—the couch was seductively curved and plumped with pillows; the balcony afforded a spectacular vista overlooking the harbor and the night lights of Fort-de-France. A side door on the opposite wall opened to another viewing room identical to the one he had just left, a room where one could relax and enjoy without the need to participate.

He had many things to ponder as he left the suite and went along the hallway to his upper-floor study. Like all of the rooms in the villa, it was oversized and ornately decorated, a fact which obviously made his guest feel uncomfortable.

De Ville arranged his features into a semblance of an apology and went toward the hearth. "Forgive me for the delay. Business, you understand."

"Of course."

De Ville made himself comfortable and poured a brandy. "We were, I believe, discussing the reasons why I should allow you the use of my harbor for your nefarious activities?"

Farley Glasse smiled wanly. "Morgan Wade is as much of a threat to you as he is to us. He has not confined his activities to harassing British shipping, as you well know."

"Nor have the French privateers," de Ville said. "He captures our ships; we capture some of his countrymen; it is all quite fair and equitable."

Glasse tried another tack. "Over the years, my government has proven itself to be more than equitable. I believe the British Admiralty has paid you handsomely for the return of our prisoners of war."

"Indeed, quite handsomely. And as I recall, Admiral Stonekipper's son was among the first lot offered. *Non, monsieur,* the one exchange has nothing to do with the other. We are enemies. Our countries are at war. If anything, I should be helping the privateer against you."

"Ah, but then you would not have the *Chimera* and all she carries to dispose of as you will. I want only Morgan Wade. The ship, the cargo, her armaments—all are yours, General. As to the crew and officers—a word to the American War Office will provide you with a pleasant surprise. You will be paid extremely well for their release."

"And the woman?" De Ville asked. "She is of no interest to you?"

Glasse inhaled sharply. "None."

"Does Commodore Winfield share your sentiments?"

The ferret eyes showed mild surprise, but it passed quickly. "The man is a fool. He has allowed his jealousy to govern him rather than his hatred."

"I was not aware the two were so different."

"Hatred is cold and efficient if handled correctly. It allows one to look carefully for a man's weakness and exploit it regardless of the cost. Jealousy is often irrational and renders a man vulnerable to mistakes in judgment."

"We all make mistakes in judgment, Monsieur Glasse. Just as we are all governed by emotions. Love, hate—"

"Greed," said Glasse.

De Ville looked up from his brandy. "Indeed. Greed plays a prominent role in all of our lives. For instance, what is to stop me from simply taking the *Chimera* myself? Ransoming Wade to his compatriots in the War Department would bring as much as his ship and crew combined."

"It would also bring an end to the peaceful coexistence we have shared in these islands," Glasse said pointedly. "We have refrained from laying you under siege or bombarding your shores because of your continued cooperation. You provide a service we need, but you would be under British rule within weeks should our benevolence be placed in too much of a strain. You would not find the Americans rushing to your aid. Their contempt for Napoléon is almost as great as our own."

De Ville sipped slowly, allowing the brandy to burn the edge off his temper. He had taken a dislike to Farley Glasse the moment he had laid eyes on the man, and it was showing no sign of improving. He lacked finesse. He lacked the skill to be a diplomat or to deal in matters that required delicacy. He was a crude man, beneath contempt. And he had shown his trump card early on, a definite sign of ineptness.

Two British ships had been taken by the French a month earlier. The manifests showed that their cargoes had been forwarded to mother France along with the prize ships, as per Napoléon's directives . . . but with a few minor deletions. Deletions amounting to a tidy fortune once the goods were resold on the black market. Glasse was now hinting at the existence of duplicate manifests and at the possibility of their ending up in the hands of the government. The discrepancies would be noted, and no doubt the guillotine would be polished in anticipation of receiving one ex-commandant from the island of Martinique.

"If I agree to your terms," de Ville asked dourly, "how do you propose to take control of the *Chimera?* Wade's men are not fools, nor are they easily overwhelmed."

"He has agreed to your terms for sanctuary, has he not?"

"We arrived at a suitable figure, *oui*."

"And he will expect your men to do most of the work involved in the transfer of the cargo?"

"It has been so in the past," de Ville murmured, disliking the Englishman more.

"And no doubt he will want to return to oversee the work himself. I should think twenty of my men substituting for your laborers should raise no undue alarm."

"Twenty men? You would need a brigade to take Wade and his crew."

"Or one man who knows precisely where to strike for Wade's weakness and how to use it against him."

"And you do, *naturellement?*"

"Naturellement," Glasse laughed gratingly. "I can even tell you she has big blue eyes and auburn hair."

22

SUMMER WOKE to a pounding in the base of her skull that threatened to blow the top of her head off. She was alone in the bed: Morgan was standing at the window smoking one of his thin black cigars.

"Is it . . . oh . . . it cannot be morning already," she moaned, holding her temples.

Morgan turned from the window and grinned. "Unfortunately it is, and a fine one, too, if you had a head on you to see it."

"I can see perfectly well," she said, glaring at him. "Two of everything."

Wade snorted and tossed her the smock and underpinnings she had come ashore in. She noticed that her fancy evening gown was gone from the floor and in its stead, folded across the chair waiting, was the plain white muslin frock and green bolero jacket she had worn when she left Bridgetown.

"You'll have to dress quickly if you don't want to leave here in a sack over my shoulder," he said, leaning down to catch at her. He swung her legs over the side of the bed and pulled her upright, laughing at the wave of color that came into her face. "And if you haven't the stomach for it, go in there first."

Summer followed his finger to the dressing room. "I'm fine. If you just had the decency to wait until after dawn. . . ."

"It is eight A.M., and I am leaving this château in five minutes, with or without you."

Summer pushed her hair away from her face and

shoulders, shivering in the cool morning air. She reached for her smock and tugged it over her head, fastening it quickly, not wanting to test Morgan's patience. His frown was lazily interested as she wriggled into her pantalets and snatched the underpetticoat up to her waist, tying it to every other ribbon on the smock. The white sheath fluttered over her shoulders, followed by the short-sleeved green jacket and the dainty green satin slippers.

She scowled at him as she walked past into the dressing room. When she emerged, her face was scrubbed a soft pink, her breath smelled faintly of peppermint tooth soap, and her eyes had regained some of their sparkle.

"I'm ready," she announced and glanced around the room. Her gaze lingered a moment on the rumpled black satin sheets and she flushed, recalling her behavior of the night.

"If nothing else," he murmured, reading her thoughts, "we will have interesting tales to tell our children about where they were conceived."

He laughed at the look on her face and slung a bulging kit bag over his shoulders.

De Ville, they were informed politely, was still abed. Morgan declined the offer of breakfast and left a flustered group of servants in his wake as he strode down the front steps of the château and assisted Summer into the coach that seemed to appear at the gates from nowhere. The driver's window slid open, and a familiar black face filled the square of light.

"Cap-tan."

"Mr. Monday. Any sight yet of the *Gyrfalcon?*"

"None, Cap-tan. We post a double watch all night, but all we see is a Frenchman."

"Rating?"

"Merchant. Two masts, mebbe ten-gun."

"How long ago?"

"One hour. Her cap-tan come ashore quicklike, but he doan put up no flags."

Morgan did not care for the sound of that. "Let's get the hell away from here."

The trapdoor slid shut again.

"What does it mean, no flags?"

"It means this isn't the port of call. She isn't signaling the merchants she has a cargo for sale."

"Oh," Summer said and promptly lost interest. Wade regarded her quietly for a moment, then glanced out the window as the coach pulled away from the curb.

Georges de Ville dropped the curtain back into place as the coach rounded the curve in the road and rattled out of sight behind the trees. The harbor was visible through the sheer lace, and he directed his attention to the scattered vessels of all shapes and sizes moored within the bay. Further out he saw the harsh outline of the French warship *Condor* dwarfing the nearby fishing boats. Sixty-four guns were at his disposal on a signal to the captain, but what could he do . . . order the *Chimera* blown out of the water?

His gaze wandered to the sleek silhouette of the privateer standing against a brilliantly blue sky. The thought that it might soon be his did not please him. The thought of a scavenger like Glasse triumphing over an eagle like Wade did not please him. There too, what could he do?

"Georges?"

The voice was a soft purr behind him. De Ville turned, and his heart did a peculiar flip, the way it seemed to do each time he was met with the sight of Héloïse's magnificent body. She lay there unashamedly exposed to the bright daylight, showing off every curve and swell to perfection. His wife's body was pale and bloated with soft living; her disposition was as sour as her breath. How could he even contemplate returning to France, whether in favor or not?

"Are you coming back to bed?" she murmured sleepily.

"Soon, *ma vie*. Soon."

De Ville frowned at a sudden urgent tapping on the bedroom door. Héloïse stirred and nestled deeper into the pillows as he drew on a robe and answered the summons. It was a red-faced, out-of-breath aide holding out a crumpled dispatch.

"*Mon general* . . . the captain of the merchantman . . . he brings news and begs his apologies, but he insisted you be disturbed. . . ."

De Ville took the paper and unfolded it, scanning the cramped lines in annoyance. His eyes widened, and he stopped halfway down the page to return to the top and begin again.

"Where is he? Where is Captain"—he looked at the signature—"Prudhomme?"

"Below, sir, in the parlor. He said to bring the note first—"

"Yes, yes . . . Jacques—" He looked up sharply. "Call for my carriage at once. And send a man immediately to the harbor—*non!* Go yourself. At once! Find Captain Wade and tell him he *must not return to his ship until I have spoken to him!*"

"Oui, mon general."

"And send Captain Prudhomme up to me at once. I will speak with him as I am dressing."

"Oui, mon général."

"Allez! Vite!"

Stuart Roarke met the carriage at the dock. He reached out a hand to Summer and helped her disembark, answering the question in her eyes before she could ask it.

"Sarah is fine. The girl I hired from the village is clean and respectable and looks nearly as happy with the babe as you do."

"Does she have children of her own?"

Roarke shook his head. "Neither her husband nor her only child survived the trip across from France recently. She has been nursing a woman's son since then, but I gather she is not happy with the arrangement. You'll like her though," he added wryly. "She has a fine sense of what should and what should not be endured on a ship. She also has Mr. Phillips tripping over his own feet."

Summer looked thoughtfully out across the harbor to the *Chimera*. How many times would Sarah provide Morgan with the necessary excuse to forbid her going ashore with him or doing the countless other things she was determined to share? The pain in her breasts had diminished; the past four or five days had been too hectic. She knew her milk would come back if she wanted it to, and yet . . . if she hired a wet nurse . . .

"Morgan—?"

He sensed her question and forestalled it. "We'll discuss it later. Roarke—how do we stand?"

"De Ville's men arrived about an hour ago. Thorny and Phillips have everything well in control."

"Where did she come from?" Wade asked, indicating the French merchant brig with a nod of his head.

"I don't know, but she sure came in in a hurry. I was just thinking of moseying on over to ask."

Wade's eyes shifted to the flat-bottom barge pulled up alongside the *Chimera*. It was low and squat in the water and already stacked with crates. He heard a disturbance behind them and saw a horse and rider galloping down the road from the direction of de Ville's chateau. Both he and Roarke stepped protectively in front of Summer; both unsheathed the dirks they wore strapped to their belts.

The horse and rider skidded to a dusty halt only a few feet from the two men, scattering pedestrians and winning a volley of hurled oaths.

"Captain Wade!"

"Stop right there," Roarke said, holding out a warning hand, "and state your business."

"I come on the general's orders," the man gasped. "He begs that you wait and speak to him before you return to your ship."

"So where the blazes is he?" Wade demanded.

"Not ten minutes behind me, *monsieur.*"

Wade glared up the road, then along the wharf and out across the harbor. "Very well, I'll wait and see what the prince wants. Roarke, you might as well go on ahead and take Summer across. There is no need to come back. Monday and I will stay here until the barge is away from the ship. I might just mosey over myself while I'm waiting and find out what goes with the merchantman."

"Aye, Morgan, as you like."

"Run up a signal if you sight the *Gyrfalcon.*"

"Aye. Coming, Summer?"

She hesitated, torn between a desire to remain with Morgan and a longing to see her daughter. Wade solved the problem by turning her toward the waiting longboat and whacking her affectionately on the rump.

"You're needed more on the ship now. I might be here for a few hours. Go on. Go and hire yourself a nurse."

Summer's face lit up with a smile. She ran back two steps and kissed him fleetingly before she joined Roarke on the jetty. He climbed down into the longboat first and swung her carefully down, waiting until she was settled before he gave a sign to the two burly oarsmen.

Summer watched Morgan move away from the water's edge and walk along the wharf, his head bent slightly in conversation with Mr. Monday. She saw the negro break away and head for the crowded storefronts, and in those few seconds, she lost sight of Morgan behind an old shed.

She sighed and felt Roarke's eyes on her.

"How did the rest of the evening with de Ville go?"

"Fine. He's quite a dandy, isn't he? And Héloïse"—Summer tilted her head ruefully—"she made me want to keep straightening my skirts and sitting taller and checking to see that my hair was not hanging all about my shoulders. She is lovely."

"I suppose she is. I don't think you have much to worry about, though."

Summer sighed again and startled Roarke pleasantly by slipping her arm through his. "Oh, Stuart, it worries me sometimes that I feel so content. I have gone against every rule I have been raised to respect and obey. Heaven knows I tried to fight it, but I just seem to end up fighting myself."

"They have a word for it, you know," he smiled.

"Yes. Yes, I do love him. And I'm not really afraid of anything when I'm with him. . . . do you think that's wrong?"

"Not at all. Everyone should feel that way once in their life."

She lifted her eyes to his. "Do you? Do you and your wife . . . I mean . . ."

He nodded and smiled. "Yes. We do. I've been damned lucky in the past few years: to have found Morgan and become a friend to him, and to have a woman like my Bett to go home to."

"I'm very anxious to meet her," said Summer shyly.

"And I daresay she would agree, Stuart Roarke, that she is the one who is extremely lucky."

Roarke grinned. "Would you care to tell my father-in-law that when you see him? I need all the support I can get. And yes, I think you and Bett are going to become fast friends—which makes me three times lucky . . . four, when I finish carving out that betrothal agreement."

Summer laughed and followed his gaze over her shoulder to see how close they were coming to the *Chimera.*

"What is in those crates?" she asked, shielding her eyes from the bright sunlight reflecting off the water.

"Tea and silk," he replied blithely, then saw the look she threw him and laughed. "And gunpowder and copper."

"Copper?"

"Aye. Almost worth more than gold these days. Navies cannot build ships without copper to sheathe the hulls. England has none of her own; neither does America. Our buyers in Barbados found out about this shipment when Winfield seized a Spaniard trying to break past the blockade. The cargo was slated to be a part of the convoy that recently left Jamaica for England, but our people managed to substitute the crates and—*voilà.*"

"The convoy? You mean the hundred ships? You knew about it?"

"Not many secrets remain secret hereabout. We knew about the convoy for several weeks before it sailed, long enough to alert the right ears back home to have a reception committee waiting where the escort ships broke away at Bermuda. Morgan even toyed with the idea of following it and picking off the stragglers, but when he heard the *Caledonia* was one of the escorts, he thought he could better stir Winfield's ire by being in Bridgetown for the commodore's return."

"I see," she said softly.

Roarke squeezed her arm. "This was long before he knew anything about you and Winfield. The rivalry between the two of them goes back a long, long way."

"Yes, I know. To Tripoli and the war against the Barbary Coast pirates."

"They were there under different flags," he nodded, "and

I suppose you could say it began there. But did you also know that Bennett Winfield was on the *Leopard* when she opened fire on the *Chesapeake?*"

Summer's eyes widened. "No, I didn't."

"Well, he was. Winfield was one of the officers who went on board the *Chesapeake* after the bombardment to take possession of the four American sailors. He and Morgan came within spitting distance of one another."

Another small fragment of Morgan's life fell into place. Would she ever completely know him, Summer wondered?

"Good, we're here," said Roarke, and leaned out of the boat to assist one of the oarsmen in maneuvering the small craft closer to the barge. They made use of the loading ramp to secure the two vessels together, and Summer breathed an audible sigh when she had the solid deck of the *Chimera* beneath her feet. Roarke was a step or two behind her, and behind him, two of the men working on the barge brought up the rear.

Roarke felt a prickle at the back of his neck and slowed. Summer was laughing and saying something about the tribulations of being a sailor's wife; she was smoothing the wrinkles in her skirt and shaking out the dampness caused by the spray from the oars. Nothing looked wrong or out of place, but . . .

Thorny was not at the gangway. Some of de Ville's men were near the mainmast, several more were poised at the rails on either side of the main entryway. There did not seem to be any activity going on, and yet most of the faces were tense and shiny with sweat.

There was more. There were no men working in the rigging. No men lounging about watching the Frenchies work. There was a netful of crates sitting by the cargo bay, but the winch ropes were slack, as if the full load had been sitting there for some time—*waiting.* Roarke glanced along the quarterdeck and saw Jamie Phillips, white-faced and standing rigidly on the bridge. There was an ugly gash down the side of his cheek, and the blood was running in thin trickles down to the collar of his shirt. One of de Ville's men was standing beside him, something strictly against Roarke's and Wade's orders.

All of this Stuart noted in a matter of seconds. His eyes

flicked to Summer, now almost a dozen paces away from him. He heard himself shout and saw her startled reaction, but it was too late. Before he could reach her and push her back toward the gangway, he saw three of de Ville's men running forward to cut him off. His knife was in his hand and without conscious thought, he slashed out at the first man who came within range. The man screamed and staggered back, clutching at the split edges of his belly. Two more replaced him, closing in on Roarke with their own knives flashing in the sunlight. Something hot and sharp was driven into his back, into his ribs, into his shoulder. He was spun around by the force of the blows, and as he fell, his spectacles flew off and were lost to a glare of harsh light.

Roarke heard a high-pitched scream and saw the blur that was Summer, intercepted as she ran back toward him. He was on his hands and knees, but even that effort seemed too much all of a sudden, and he let his head hang from his shoulders, amazed at the clarity with which he saw the blood splattering on the polished wood of the deck. He groaned and the sound filled his brain, deafening him so that when he slumped forward onto the bloody planks, the silence of the encroaching blackness was a welcome relief.

Summer's scream died on her lips. She continued to struggle against the rough arms that circled her waist, but now her hands covered her mouth, and she could only stare in horror as Stuart Roarke's life ebbed out onto the deck.

"Release her," came a slick, cool voice from the companionway.

Summer ran to Stuart and fell heavily to her knees beside him. She brushed trembling fingers down the side of his face, smoothing away the brown hair that had fallen to cover his eyes. The sob caught in her throat when she saw how ashen his skin was. His shirt was soaking rapidly, and the blood was staining her skirt and hands as she searched desperately for a way to hold back the sluggish red rivulets.

"Someone, please"—she cried—"oh, please, help me! He's still alive . . . he's—"

She heard a commotion from the bridge. Angry shouts and a curse were silenced by the same silky voice at the companionway, and in moments Mr. Phillips was on his knees beside her.

"Dear God, I'm sorry," he choked on the words. "We couldn't do anything. We couldn't warn you off. We couldn't fight them. They knew where everything was—the armory, the powder magazine—"

"The blood," Summer screamed. *"Can't you do something to stop the blood!"*

Mr. Phillips tore at his shirt. He folded it into a wad and pressed it to the wound beneath Stuart's ribs, the one that was bleeding hardest. The cut on Mr. Phillips's cheek had sent blood flowing onto his shoulder, and it mingled now with his sweat to run in weblike paths down his chest. He shouted for two of the *Chimera*'s crewmen, who leaped forward without waiting for the approval of their guards.

"Ease him on to his back—carefully, dammit! Thorny! We need Thorny up here! Throw him in the water barrel if you have to, but roust him up here right away . . . with bandages and the medicine kit."

"Thorny?" Summer gasped. "What happened to Thorny?"

"De Ville's bastards knocked him out cold when he tried to break for the deck rail to shout a warning to Mr. Roarke."

"De Ville's men? But how—?"

Mr. Phillips looked up past Summer's shoulders. She saw the anger and hatred distorting his young face . . . and something else. She remembered the voice ordering her release, and she whirled to face the companionway.

Farley Glasse, dressed in workman's breeches and a rough cotton shirt, stood in the shadows, a smile curving the thin lips.

"Welcome aboard, Mrs. Winfield. I trust you enjoyed your evening ashore?"

"You!" she cried, and the tears froze on her lashes. "How did you get on board this ship?"

"It was . . . shall we say, *childishly* easy."

He saw a further jolt of horror register in the gray eyes.

"Where is Sarah?" she hissed. "What have you done with my baby?"

Glasse savored the flashing hatred a moment longer before he tilted his head in a command. A girl was pushed roughly into the sunlight, her arm pinched cruelly in the grip of a man dressed in the same manner as Glasse. The girl was no more than twenty, deathly pale, rigidly frightened, but holding Sarah protectively to her bosom as if there were not a gleaming metal gun barrel thrust against her temple.

Summer cried out and started to rise, but Mr. Phillips's hand stopped her.

"He won't allow anyone near them," he whispered urgently.

Summer looked at Sarah and the nurse, then at the gun.

"What do you want?" she asked Glasse.

"Come now, my dear Mrs. Winfield, you know the answer to that. What have I wanted all these long months?"

Morgan! Dear God, she thought, Morgan would be rowing out to the *Chimera* as blind to the situation on board his ship as she and Stuart had been. He would stand no better chance.

Stuart groaned in the depths of his pain. His body had a spasm and the movement sent a fresh torrent of blood gushing from his wounds. Summer was overwhelmed by a sudden sense of helplessness and did not care that her voice came out in a pleading whisper.

"Please . . . he has to have help. A doctor . . . could we send for a doctor?"

Glasse arched a brow. "And announce to the world and Morgan Wade that there is trouble on the *Chimera?* Really, Mrs. Winfield, you must indeed think me a fool."

"I think less of you than that," she retorted bitterly. "Will you at least allow him to be taken below out of the heat and sun?"

Glasse studied her face a moment, then nodded. "Take your Mr. Roarke wherever you like for the good it will do. He looks quite beyond salvation, if you ask me."

Mr. Phillips started to surge to his feet, and this time it

was Summer who restrained him. "No. It won't help to get yourself killed."

"Listen to her, young man, it is sound advice." Glasse pointed to the gun. "And I will not hesitate to order either the woman or the child shot if any other of these brave men take it upon themselves to play hero. I would truly hate to see it happen, but I assure you it will if I deem it necessary. Go ahead, Mrs. Winfield, move the man if you like. In fact, I suggest you all wait together in the captain's cabin."

Mr. Phillips nodded to the two crewmen, who gently eased Stuart onto a litter. He moved beside them slowly, keeping a steady pressure on the wounds.

Summer remained on her knees on the bloody deck. She saw something reflect the sunlight, and she leaned over, picking Stuart's spectacles up off the planking. Her hands trembled as she folded the wire arms neatly across the lenses. She wiped a smear of blood from the glass onto her skirt, swallowing back the revulsion as she saw the other glaring blotches of crimson marring the white muslin. Her hatred grew until it nearly choked her. She looked up at each of Glasse's men in turn, but none of them held her gaze longer than a few seconds. Only Glasse displayed neither shame nor discomfort at her wordless accusation.

Summer stood slowly and walked past him into the shadowy hatchway and down the short flight of steps. Thorny was bending over the captain's bed when she entered the cabin, muttering orders to himself and to Phillips. There was a badly discolored lump swelling on his neck just below his ear. His head and shoulders were dripping water down the front of his shirt; his old eyes were blinking repeatedly, desperate to clear away the residue of fog.

The cabin was a shambles. The drawers of the desk had been rifled and emptied, as had the shelves and cupboard. The lock on the cabinet behind the desk had been smashed, and the cabinet's contents scattered on the floor. Lying open on top of the desk was Morgan's logbook, his bundled letters of marque, and the small gold case that contained the Granville seal.

Glasse would be content that he had his proof now.

There would be nothing to stand between a mock trial and a swift hanging. Summer wondered what Glasse's reaction would be if he found out his efforts had centered around the wrong man all this time? If he was to discover he already had Edmund Granville in his possession, would it be enough? She did not think so.

Summer laid Stuart's spectacles carefully on Morgan's desk. She stared at her bloodstained hands briefly, then went to the corner and poured some water into the metal washbowl and carried it to the bedside. Thorny barely grunted an acknowledgment. She stared at the blood on her hands again and went back to the pitcher, washing first, then stripping off the frivolous green jacket and snatching at the hem of the spattered white dress. No one paid any attention as she flung it aside and took one of Morgan's shirts out of the cupboard, belting it overtop of her shimmy and petticoat with a length of twine.

She wanted to help, but she feared she would only be in the way. Instead, she moved quietly about the cabin tearing cotton into strips when she heard an order for bandages; she fetched water from the barrel in the corridor when it was needed and emptied the bowls of bloodied water out the gallery windows when the contents became sickeningly dark. Thorny called for a fire to be lit in the stove, and Summer had to look away and bite down hard on her lips to keep from screaming when a heated iron was applied to the wounds to cauterize them. Stuart remained blessedly unconscious through the ordeal, through the hours Thorny worked over him like a man possessed.

When there was nothing more to be done, the old sailor slumped brokenly into a chair, his shoulders drooping, his hands limp on his knees, his fingers still clutching the needle and thread he had used to stitch one of the lesser wounds.

"I don't know, lass," he muttered. "We stopped the bleedin', but ee's weak. Ripe weak ee is, an' I cain't say as I know 'ow ee's lasted this long. Must o' lost 'arf the blood in 'is body. Wish't I knew if'n there were sum'mit else a proper 'ealer would do. Sum'mit ter stop the p'isen, if'n there be any. Ee's like me own son, ee is. 'Im an' the cap'n both, like me own sons."

Summer's eyes filled, and she laid a hand on Thorny's bony shoulder.

"Very touching," Glasse drawled, watching from the leather chair. His boots were propped up on Wade's desk, and he was enjoying one of the thin black cigars. He had come below a half hour earlier, and his patience was obviously suffering with the failure of Morgan Wade to make an appearance in the harbor. It had become necessary to send the laden barge away from the *Chimera* to allay any suspicions that might arise on shore. The men had returned with the news that the privateer was nowhere on the waterfront; neither he nor the negro had been seen for hours, or if they had, no one was willing to say.

Summer had managed to keep the relief from showing on her face. The longer Morgan remained on shore, the more likely it was that Glasse would make a mistake. Already his hand shook as he knocked ash from the tip of the cigar onto the floor. The ferret eyes moved constantly—from the clock to the door, from the door to the gallery windows, from the windows to the ceiling to the clock to the door. He had expected the trap to spring swiftly shut, catching them all at once. Now he was forced to wait, and it was beginning to tell on his nerves.

One mistake, though, and Morgan would know something was wrong. Mr. Phillips was watching Glasse's every move and praying for an opportunity to strike. The two crewmen who carried the litter to the cabin had been ordered out, but Summer had seen the quick exchange between them and Phillips. There were one hundred and forty of Wade's men aboard and twenty of Glasse's. A word was all they needed, she was sure, but no one would or could do anything as long as Glasse controlled the gun at Sarah's head. She was Morgan's child, and no one on the *Chimera* would do anything to jeopardize her life in any way. For that, Summer was filled with pride and a fierce new loyalty, but it also sickened her at heart to see the humiliation she was causing them.

She poured water into the small metal bowl and rinsed out a square of linen torn from her petticoat. Stuart's face was beaded with sweat even though his body was ice-cold to the touch and frequently racked with shivers. Thorny had piled blankets on him to counter the shock, but he seemed to grow paler by the hour, to sink a little deeper into the void.

There was a knock on the cabin door, and Glasse was on his feet instantly. A boat was heading out for the *Chimera*, he was told. It was not Wade. It was the Frenchman, Georges de Ville.

Glasse's face mottled with a sudden rush of anger. "What does he want now? Why the hell is he coming out here? My God, if Wade is watching—" He stopped and flexed his fists. "If he thinks he can demand more money for his cooperation, he is sadly mistaken."

"His cooperation?" Summer asked. "He knew about this?"

Glasse glared at her. "Shocked, Mrs. Winfield? Allow me to shock you further then by telling you he not only cooperated, but he fully intends to collect the *Chimera* as his payment. He must have been told you were brought on board several hours ago and wants to be assured of receiving his property intact. Sit down, Mr. Phillips—" Glasse snarled at the young second mate. "You'll have plenty of opportunities to deal with Monsieur de Ville after we've finished here."

"You surprise me, Mr. Glasse," Summer said calmly, leaving the bedside. "You work for the British government. You say your loyalty borders on that of a zealot. You decry traitors and sympathizers, yet you form an alliance with a Frenchman—to catch one man whose alleged crimes in no way equal those of the enemy you are dealing with. Why?"

"Alleged crimes?" said Glasse hoarsely. "There is nothing alleged about the crimes Edmund Granville has committed. He will pay for what he has done."

"No court in the land," she countered evenly, "not even the king himself would condone the use of a three-month-old child as a means of capturing a man."

The rage and hatred had turned the two black eyes boring into her into glowing coals. "I will use any means at my command, Mrs. Winfield. I have spent the last thirteen years of my life searching for Sir Edmund Granville, and I do not intend to let him slip away from me again. I thought your husband would be the one to finally end it, but the fool let him get away. Now I will use Granville's ship, and I will use his crew. I will use you, and I will use his daughter without any qualms whatsoever. Oh, yes, Mrs. Winfield, *his* daughter. Your husband kindly confided his shame to me one night over a bottle of rum. The use of Edmund Granville's mistress and child is a greater irony than I could have hoped for."

He stopped and wiped at the sheen of moisture on his brow. He stared at the dampness on his hand and frowned, rubbing it distastefully on his trouser leg.

"Thirteen years ago," he continued in a low voice, "he killed my only daughter. He beat her to death in a sordid little hotel room and then ran away when his money and his title could not buy him an easier way out. I vowed I would find him one day and make him pay—if it took my last dying breath to do it. And I will, Mrs. Winfield. If I have to take you and your daughter with me—I will."

"But . . . he didn't do it." Summer cried. "He didn't kill her."

"And how would you know that?" Glasse demanded.

"H-he told me."

"He confessed to you?" Glasse took a step toward her. "Edmund Granville confessed his crimes to you?"

"He told me he did not do it! He told me that he was drugged the night it happened, that he was framed by the dead woman's husband, and—"

"Ronald?" Glasse's momentary shock changed swiftly back to rage. "And you believed the lies of a murderer? What would you expect him to say, Mrs. Winfield? Would you expect him to admit to kidnapping and murdering a young woman while he was in the process of repeating his crime by luring you away from your husband? Lies, Mrs. Winfield! He told you lies, and you believed him. Well"—he laughed maliciously—"all the lies in the world will not save him now. All the lies and all the pleading and all the bastard children he has sired will not save him now!"

Summer flinched from Glasse's hatred as if it were a living thing. She backed away, fighting to hold in the tears that were brimming in her eyes. When she was stopped by the hard edge of the bed, she turned and saw to her greater horror that Stuart Roarke's eyes were open and burning directly up into hers. His hand trembled, and his fingers clawed their way to her wrist and wrapped tightly around it. His jaw muscles worked frantically, and the bloodless lips curled back with the effort it took to form a single plea. There was no sound behind it, only a silent, despairing plea: *Tell him!*

The tears spilled over her lashes and ran in a shiny path to her chin. She covered his hand with her own and held it briefly before she pried the fingers loose. She reached for the dampened square of linen and resumed patting the moisture from his brow. The soft brown eyes were still pleading with hers, but she only smiled gently and dabbed at the tears that flowed down his temples.

Farley Glasse witnessed none of the exchange. He stood with his back to the cabin's occupants, striving to regain the composure of which he was so boastful. He had almost succeeded when a tap on the door announced Georges de Ville's arrival.

The French commandant was dressed impeccably in tight white breeches and a cutaway blue jacket, the gold braid and gold epaulets of his rank matching the tawny gold in the depths of his eyes. He took in the condition of the cabin, the grim expressions on the faces staring up at him, and ended the inspection with Summer Winfield.

"Madam. A pity we have to meet again under such adverse conditions." He bowed curtly and turned to Glasse. "But what is the meaning of this, *monsieur;* I do not see the captain."

"Because he is not here," Glasse replied.

"Not here?" de Ville frowned. "But where—?"

"I was hoping you could tell me. The men I sent ashore could learn nothing. The good citizens of your city are a closed-mouthed lot."

"Mmmm. To you Englishmen, perhaps. I shall make enquiries of my own. In the meantime . . . what is that dreadful smell?" De Ville took out a lace-edged handkerchief and pressed its scented folds to his nose.

Glasse smirked and sat on the corner of the desk. "Cooked meat, General. With all of your experience on

Napoléon's marches, I'm surprised you can forget the smell so quickly."

De Ville coughed disdainfully. "What happens now, *monsieur?* You have his crew safely under guard, I presume?"

"Naturally. They're all nicely gathered together in the hold sharing the space with the hogsheads of black powder they were so eager to smuggle. Any hint of an alarm and my men will open fire on the kegs and—pfit! It will be all over for Wade's men—for the whole damned ship, I'd wager."

"I see. And if the captain does not soon arrive? How long do you propose to sit here in my harbor?"

"He'll arrive. When you return to shore, General, you will deliver an ultimatum to the captain. His life in exchange for the woman and child."

De Ville took a deep breath. "And if I cannot locate him?"

"You just spread the word around; someone will find him. It is three P.M. now. He has until dusk. That's when the *Northgate* has orders to move into position. This ship and everyone on it will go up in flames at that time if Captain Ashton-Smythe does not hear differently from me. You spread the word, *monsieur*. You have as much at stake here as he does."

"This was not a part of our agreement," de Ville said quietly.

"Consider this a new agreement."

De Ville pursed his lips. "What of Commodore Winfield? Was he not supposed to follow the *Chimera* from Bridgetown?"

Glasse's eye twitched in a nervous spasm. "He was. But with or without his support, I will accomplish what I have set out to do."

"I'm sure you will, Monsieur Glasse. You have done remarkably well as it is." De Ville approached the bedside and kept his nose delicately covered as he peered down at Stuart Roarke. Summer did not move or avert her eyes. She summoned every last scrap of contempt in her body and directed it toward the refined Frenchman.

"Monsieur Roarke's condition . . . it is serious?"

"If he dies, it will rest squarely on your shoulders," Summer said evenly.

De Ville seemed to notice the puffiness around her eyes, the swollen residue of her tears.

"Such a lovely face," he mused. "It pains me to see it so distorted by grief."

"The grief also will be yours, *monsieur*, when Captain Wade hears of your treachery."

"In matters of business, madam, one cannot allow emotions to dictate rules. I regret seeing the brave captain in such an irretrievable position, but . . ." He shrugged.

"I had thought you were friends."

"Friends?" The handkerchief was raised again. "My dear, in times of war there can be no friends, only illusions of such. A friend one hour becomes an enemy the next. Harsh, perhaps, but the Captain understands this as I do."

"If you have finished wasting our time, de Ville," Glasse broke in irritably.

"Yes. Yes." The general looked back at Summer. He frowned and wiped at a dried spot of blood on her chin. "Hold fast to your illusions, *ma chère*. They will see you through."

He pressed the handkerchief into her hand and bowed, striding briskly back toward the door. "Monsieur Glasse? A word in private if I may?"

Glasse followed the Frenchman to the door, muttering gruffly to the guard holding Sarah's nurse. She was yanked to her feet and pushed out the door ahead of Glasse, the gun in plain view at her temple.

It was the first time the three in the cabin had been left completely alone.

As soon as the door shut, Phillips was on his feet.

"Thorny," he hissed and glanced at the door.

"Aye." The old sailor darted over and stood with his ear pressed against the wood listening for sounds in the corridor.

Mr. Phillips went to the far side of the cabin, to the bookcase beside the dining table and chairs, and reached up over the carved pediment to run his hand along the recessed surface. He took down two razor-sharp filleting knives and a short-snouted pistol. He tucked one of the knives into his belt at the small of his back and handed Thorny the other while he scanned the possible hiding places for the gun.

"Mr. Phillips?" Summer whispered, her face ashen.

He finished secreting the gun under the mattress of the bunk near where he would be sitting and frowned at Summer. He looked at her outstretched hand and saw the lace handkerchief and the note that had been concealed within its folds.

"It's from Morgan," she said, and her voice trembled. "It was meant for Stuart."

Phillips was by her side in a pace. The note was brief, cramped onto a two-inch square of paper. Phillips read it twice, and when he looked back up at Summer, his face was hard and decisive. His grin was almost eager as he showed the note to Thorny, then tore it to shreds and fed it into the belly of the stove.

"Danged Frenchies," Thorny grumbled. "Cain't trust a one o' them, can ye? Jest when I were comin' ter hate 'im ripe proper, too."

"Can Morgan do it?" Summer asked Mr. Phillips. "Can he find a way to get on board?"

"He'll surely try, ma'am. But we have to be ready to help him. First thing is to find some way to get the baby away from the guard. I doubt if the captain knows about her being held as the prime hostage."

"If'n ye distract that barstard Glasse two winks, I'll see ter the young 'un," Thorny declared, patting the knife in his pocket.

"It's the bastard with the gun we have to distract," Summer said, and flushed at her own boldness.

Mr. Phillips seemed not to notice. "And we have to do it without raising an alarm. De Ville nicely managed to warn us how conditions stand with the rest of the crew. He also gave us a time—one hour."

"How do you know that?" Summer asked.

"A friend one hour becomes an enemy the next," he quoted. "He also referred to an illusion. Chimera means illusion, and that could be his way of telling us the *Gyrfalcon* is somewhere within range."

"And the *Northgate?*"

"Yes," he nodded grimly, "that, too. But they must already know about her. It was the *Caledonia* de Ville was interested in."

"Or *warning* us about," Summer suggested. "He said it was supposed to follow the *Chimera* out of Bridgetown. If it followed the *Gyrfalcon* instead, it could be out there now and the reason we only have an hour."

"By God, you're right," he murmured, and Summer flushed with the look of admiration he gave her.

"Hst!" Thorny crabbed away from the door and went to stand by the berth. Phillips returned to his seat at the foot of the bed.

"Whatever happens," he murmured to Summer, "stay beside Mr. Roarke."

"But Sarah—"

The door swung open, and Glasse strode through, his black eyes warily searching the cabin as he checked on the whereabouts of Thorny and Mr. Phillips. Satisfied that nothing was amiss, he nodded to the guard to bring in the nurse and the baby. Glasse laid his gun down on top of the captain's desk and sat in the leather chair again, prudently keeping the desk between himself and Thorny. The guard pushed the girl toward the table and chairs, again keeping the full width of the cabin clear. There would be no excuse for either of Wade's men to go anywhere near the Englishmen.

23

MORGAN WADE'S mouth and nose broke the surface of the water long enough for him to clear his lungs and draw in fresh oxygen. He ducked back beneath the side of the fishing ketch, clinging to the rope that was slung under the keel. The ketch moved swiftly out from behind the French warship *Condor,* hugging the shoreline until it could unobtrusively join the slow-moving flotilla of fishermen rounding the point into the harbor. The *Chimera* was several hundred yards away. The pilot of the ketch would stay on the inner edge of the flotilla, hopefully bringing Wade and Mr. Monday close enough to swim to the frigate unseen. Fifty feet from the ship would be ideal. They would be able to dive deep enough to avoid detection in the dark, rich blue water.

Mr. Monday was naked but for a belt strapped to his waist holding an assortment of knives; Morgan was dressed in a black silk shirt and black breeches.

De Ville had reported the position of the guards, the conditions under which the crew was being kept locked in the hold and the situation with the hostages in the aftercabin. The entry ports and gangways were well guarded; there were men in the bow and men in the stern and one perched high on the mainmast sweeping the bay periodically with a spyglass. There was only one way to get on board. A small loading bay had been built into the stern just above the storeroom where the fresh drinking water was kept. Roarke had designed it for two purposes, for loading the fresh water and for acting as an escape hatch if men were trapped belowdecks during a battle. It was an unusual addition, and Wade was counting on the fact that Glasse would be ignorant of its existence.

Morgan's lungs signaled the need for more air. He stayed as flat to the hull of the ketch as he could, knowing the eyes on the *Chimera* would be probing the flotilla, searching for signs of deception. Their ketch was as innocent as the scores of others. It was loaded to the gunwales with nets and silvery fish; the two elderly occupants rowed lazily and smoked on hand-carved pipes.

Mr. Monday's bald head was beside Wade's this time, breathing slowly, deeply, before the mighty chest swelled and he slipped back down the rope. Wade remained on the surface a moment longer, risking a glimpse of the *Chimera*. They were within a hundred feet, and there were shouts from the deck of the frigate warning the ketches to steer well clear of it.

Wade sank beneath the hull, using the taut rope as a guide. Mr. Monday was curled against the spine of the keel like a huge black barnacle, his eyes wide open, and he gave a broad wink when he saw Wade join him.

Thank God for you, Mr. Monday, Morgan thought. De Ville's gloomy report on the *Chimera* had scarcely produced a frown on the black face. He had accepted Wade's plan with a nod of approval even though they both knew it was reckless and foolhardy.

Wade heard three watery taps on the hull of the ketch. They were as close as the fishermen dared to get to the *Chimera*. Wade and Mr. Monday rose to the surface for their last bearings and to prime their lungs for a final swallow of air.

Eighty feet.

Morgan refused to think about the distance and concentrated on filling his lungs. On a signal, a boat farther ahead began veering away from the pack to head straight for the frigate. By the time it was within ten yards of the hull, the guards on deck had been alerted and were crowded at the bow, aiming their muskets threateningly at the three jeering French fishermen.

To Wade and Mr. Monday, moving like black wraiths more than a fathom beneath the rippling surface of the water, the sounds were indistinguishable from countless other muted plops and hums. They ignored everything but the mottled green gleam of the copper-sheathed hull coming closer and closer with each powerful stroke of their arms.

Two-thirds of the way across, Wade's lungs began to burn, and he saw, with a pang of alarm, that he had risen closer to the surface than he should have been. He had no way of knowing if they had been spotted from the deck. He released a stream of tiny silver bubbles from his mouth and angled his stroke deeper, noting that Mr. Monday had pulled well ahead and seemed to be swimming evenly and effortlessly. Wade clenched his teeth and released another jet of air to relieve the pressure building in his chest. The blood started to pound in his ears, and his arms were numbing rapidly as he clawed and pushed the water behind him.

Twenty feet to go . . . fifteen . . .

His vision blurred, and he could no longer see Mr. Monday or the *Chimera*. He knew he was in the shadow of the frigate because of the inkiness of the water, but he no longer had a sense of direction or distance. Worse, he was beginning to feel cramps along his ribs and thighs.

The last of his air escaped on a groan just as a stray current washed by and somersaulted him out of control. He fought toward where he thought the surface should be, but the current played with him a second time and he was slammed painfully into the crust of barnacles hanging from the bottom of the ship. He groped for handfuls of the weed and shells, hoping to pull himself hand over hand up the rounded hull. Something tangled around his wrist, and he struggled against it furiously, but Mr. Monday kept a firm grip and hauled his captain quickly up to the oily-bright surface.

Wade's head surged free of the water, and he gasped desperately for the fresh air, pressing his forehead on the timbers as he agonized to bring the pain and panic under control.

"You all right, my Cap-tan?" Mr. Monday asked quietly.

"Fine," Wade gasped. "Fine. Lead the way; I'll be fine."

"Yas, Cap-tan." Monday took one of Wade's scraped

hands and placed it firmly on his shoulder. "But you hold me now."

There was no hint of smugness on the black face, no air of superiority, only a deep-rooted respect. He knew few men would have attempted such a swim, let alone completed it. Wade blinked his eyes clear and nodded.

They were amidships and had to swim half the length of the hull before they were beneath the outcurved section of the stern where the hatchway was. There were crosspieces attached to the timbers affording Mr. Monday hand and toeholds as he swung himself up and out of the water. He worked the iron bolt free of its ring to release the inside pulley and grinned down at Wade to indicate that the latch was free and not secured on the inside. That had been the one drawback to their plan, the only insurmountable flaw that both men adamantly refused to mention or even think about.

Now they both felt a resurgence of confidence. The portal opened down into a small platform, where Mr. Monday knelt and thrust a hand out to Wade. The opening was large enough for one man at a time to crawl through the three-foot-thick outer shell and into the dark musty storeroom that ran the width of the ship. It was stacked with barrels of water and, at the far end, rum.

Mr. Monday closed the hatch and tied it off. The two men moved stealthily along the familiar corridors between the storerooms until they arrived at the ladderway leading to the gun deck above. Wade saw the guard stationed at the top and flattened against the bulkhead. Without needing to communicate his intentions to Mr. Monday, he waited until the Englishman had turned his head, then crept noiselessly up the steps.

The guard felt rather than saw the danger but was too late to save himself. Wade's arm went around the man's throat and his hand snapped the neck quietly and efficiently before the guard's arm could be raised. Mr. Monday caught the musket as it slipped from the lifeless fingers, and together he and Wade lowered the body through the hatch to the darkened deck below.

They located a second and third guard on the gun deck pacing between the forward ladderway and the gallery. Mr. Monday and Wade moved simultaneously when the guards reached the ladderway, darting out from behind two cannon to silence the intruders without so much as a hiss of escaping air.

Wade crept to the door of the galley, startling Cook into dropping a full crock of salted beef on the floorboards.

"By all what's holy, Cap'n! Where'd ye come from?"

"Never mind that now. Where are the rest of the men?"

"Locked in the cargo bay," Cook said promptly. "The scurvy dogs have 'em sitting in with the kegs o' black powder, and they say they'll set the whole of it off if'n a one of 'em moves."

"Any word from the aftercabin?"

"No, sar. Last I 'eard, he were still alive."

Wade's dark eyes narrowed. "Who was still alive? Has someone been hurt?"

Cook glanced from Mr. Monday to the captain. "Mr. Roarke, sar. He's terrible hurt. The limey sods caught 'im when he brung the lady aboard. Fought like Satan, he did, but it weren't no use. Four of 'em went after Mr. Roarke with knives—would'a left him to bleed to death, too, if not for the lady."

"The others?" Mr. Monday asked.

"Mr. Phillips were cut some. T'orny bought a lump on the back of 'is noggin . . . but it were Mr. Roarke what took the worst of it."

Wade's face had turned to stone. Only his eyes were alive, searing into the beams overhead as if he could see through the barriers into the aftercabin.

"Cap-tan?" Mr. Monday touched his arm.

"We'll deal with the guards in the hold first," Morgan said in a brittle voice.

"Aye," Cook said. "But they have orders to set off the powder if'n they 'ear a sign."

"Then we'll just have to make sure they don't hear anything," Wade snarled and turned abruptly. He wiped the blood from the blade of his knife and added a length of iron bar to his arsenal. Mr. Monday and Cook were close on his heels, their expressions as grim but not nearly as terrifying.

Sarah was crying fretfully and Summer could see how the sound was aggravating Glasse. She had been crying off and on all afternoon and no wonder: Glasse had not permitted the nurse to see to any of the child's basic needs other than feeding. Her clothes were soiled and wet, the tops of her legs were chafed red from the irritation. Summer dropped the cloth she had been using to wipe Stuart's brow and patted her hands dry.

"I would like to bathe my daughter now," she said to Farley Glasse.

"You would, would you?" He peered at her through a cloud of cigar smoke. "How motherly of you."

"You can see how uncomfortable she is. At least allow me to clean her and change her into dry clothes. She'll only cry longer and harder if you don't. You can have your bully hold his gun on me all the time, if you like. I will not do anything other than see to my baby."

Glasse pondered his answer a moment before the crying turned into a miserable wail and finally snapped his patience. He waved a hand curtly to the guard.

Summer ignored the look of stupefaction on Mr. Phillips's face as she walked over to where the nurse was sitting and took Sarah into her arms. For a full minute she could do nothing but hold the child close. The crying stopped immediately, and the big blue eyes peered up at Summer's face as if to say *finally*.

Summer whispered endearments, kissed and petted her daughter as she returned to the bedside. The berth was wide, and Sarah took up little space at the corner below Stuart's feet. Summer could hear the guard's harsh breathing over her shoulder, and she could sense the pistol aimed ominously at the back of her neck.

She could also see the edge of the barrel of the gun Mr. Phillips had tucked beneath the mattress.

She made a fuss of smoothing the quilt before she settled Sarah on top. She moved away and felt the guard's gun dig sharply into her flesh.

"I am only fetching water and clean clothes," she said.

The guard questioned Glasse and received a second curt nod, but instead of staying beside Summer as she had hoped, he merely moved the pistol so that it was pointed at the baby. Sarah chuckled and playfully reached for the gleaming iron barrel. Summer's heart sank and her mouth went instantly dry. She saw Mr. Phillips stiffen and Thorny's eyes bulge from the webs of crow's-feet.

"I recommend you get what you need and be quick about it," Glasse drawled.

Summer hastened to the sea chest which was filled with the purchases she had made the previous day. She found clean linens and clothes and went back to the bedside with a fresh basin of warm water.

"Excuse me," she said bitterly and stepped between the guard and the child.

How much time had lapsed, she wondered? She knew she held Glasse's attention, and she knew the guard would be doubly watchful for any sudden moves from her or Phillips, but at least he was within reach now. Thorny had deduced what she was about and had sidled away from the bed, grumbling to himself about his own shortcomings as far as Stuart's injuries were concerned. It was up to him to distract the gun away from Sarah, but could he do it?

Summer's heart flew into her throat at the sound of a sharp urgent knock on the cabin door.

"Come," Glasse barked.

It was one of his men. "You said to tell you if there was any movement out in the 'arbor."

"Well?"

"Boats. Fishermen, by the look of it, comin' 'round the point."

Glasse consulted the clock. Fishermen? Of course, they would be returning with the day's catch. "Anything unusual?"

"Not what I can see. Nets 'r full, the crews ain't too interested in us. Couple came close a while ago, but we chased 'em away."

Glasse cursed. "Warn them to stay well clear."

"Aye." The slits that were the man's eyes turned to Summer, and she felt a chill of recognition, although she was fairly certain she had never seen him before. He grinned and revealed several missing front teeth.

"Beavis," Thorny muttered. "Ye ripe bluddy barstard. No wonder the limey sods knew where ter 'it us."

"Your captain should'a been nicer to his crew, mate," Beavis sneered. "Should'a shared the spoils equal."

Summer gasped as the voice struck a chord in her memory. The afternoon in the hold . . . the attempted rape . . . it had been this man.

He saw that Summer recognized him and the leer broadened. "Remember me now, do you, Governess? I ain't forgettin' neither that you owe me something. Maybe I'll just get 'round to collectin' it this time."

"Get back on deck," Glasse ordered. "And keep your eyes on those fishing boats. If any of them ignore your warning, open fire."

"Aye." Beavis grinned and blew a kiss at Summer before he left the cabin.

"An old acquaintance of yours, Mrs. Winfield?"

Summer's gaze was iced with loathing as she looked at Glasse. "His presence here appeals to me as much as yours does."

Glasse smiled and replaced the cigar between his teeth. "In that case, perhaps I should reconsider and allow him the pleasure of your company until Captain Wade deigns to join us?"

"Ye're jest low enough ter do sum'mit like that, ain't ye?" Thorny growled, and his hand fell to his hip pocket. The knife came up, gleaming and deadly, and his arm moved in a blur as he launched himself squarely at Glasse's chest.

The nurse jumped up from the chair and screamed, costing both Glasse and the guard a jarring loss of concentration. Mr. Phillips's reaction was delayed, but only by a split second as he saw the guard's head turn away from Summer. His leg shot straight up and he propelled himself off the bench, catching the guard's wrist with his foot and causing the fingers holding the heavy weapon to flex open. His hand came up in the same forward motion, driving the thin blade of the filleting knife hilt-deep into the Englishman's unprotected belly. Phillips jerked it once, then again in a killing stroke and lurched as the weight of the writhing guard slumped against him.

Summer had fallen forward to shield Sarah's body with her own as soon as she had seen Thorny move. The sudden violence of the action startled the baby into crying, but Summer only pressed closer and squeezed her eyes tightly shut, wishing she could block out the sounds as well as the sight of what was happening around her.

Stuart Roarke swam against the clouds of pain and blackness, hearing the muffled cries from the baby and the choked screams that came from the foot of the bed. He strained forward and managed to roll up on his elbow, then to reach down and with a massive effort pull Summer out of the way.

Glasse's reflexes were swifter than Thorny had anticipated, and he avoided the driving point of the knife by diving onto the floor behind the desk. His gun was on the desk top, but it was too far out of reach. He saw the guard slouched over Phillips and saw that the only chance he had to redeem the situation was to alert the men outside on the deck.

Thorny pulled his knife out of the leather padding of the chair and let it fly with a curse when he saw Glasse darting across the cabin. He was rewarded with a grunt of surprise from Glasse and the sight of the knife sinking into the man's shoulder as he plunged out into the companionway. Over the pounding of boot steps, Thorny heard Glasse shouting to his men. Mr. Phillips shoved the deadweight of the guard to one side, and both he and Thorny dashed out of the cabin in pursuit.

There was a sound of musketry, but the dreaded blast and rumble of gunpowder did not immediately follow. Instead, Phillips realized with a jolt, the muskets were being fired *from* the cargo hatch, not toward it.

Glasse had realized the same thing and veered toward the gangway, clutching a bloodied shoulder as he clambered one-handed down the ladder into the quarterboat moored to the side of the *Chimera*. He screamed for the men gathering at the entry port to follow him, and when the boat was crowded, he slashed at the mooring cables and pushed it away from the hull.

Morgan Wade smashed the iron bar repeatedly against the lock sealing the doorway to the hold. On the third attempt it gave, and he wrenched the door wide, shouting for his men and leading a stream of them along the gun deck to the armory. But by the time the crew was armed and at the deck rail, Glasse's dinghy had threaded its way into the fishing ketches and firing after him was impossible without risk to the innocent fishermen.

Wade saw Phillips and ordered the deck cleared and the anchor raised. He lashed out commands to get the *Chimera* ready to sail, then ran back along the quarterdeck toward the afterhatch and his cabin. Thorny was shouting curses over the side of the ship, and when he saw where the captain was headed, his voice trailed away and he ran after him.

Morgan burst into his cabin and stood at a dead halt in the doorway, his chest heaving, his eyes wild as he searched out Summer. She was standing at the side of the bed, the baby cradled in her arms, her hand holding tightly to Roarke's. There were tears on her cheeks. Her eyes were round with fear and her mouth slack as she whirled and faced the door. Morgan held his breath and his hand fell from the doorjamb.

Summer cried out and ran to him, flinging her arm around his neck, and felt herself and Sarah crushed into his embrace. She could not speak. She could only sob and say his name in snatches of breath, and in the end he half carried her as he walked over to the bed.

Roarke's eyes were open, but they seemed unable to focus on anything. The blanket had fallen back, and the bandages over his ribs were showing fresh bright red stains.

"Morgan? M-Morgan, is that you?"

"*Stuart* . . . aye, lad, it's me."

"Thank God," came the dry whisper. The brown eyes rolled and fluttered a moment before he was able to turn them and find Summer's face. "I told you . . . I promised you he would come back."

Summer bit down hard on her lip. "Yes, Stuart, you

promised. Now promise me you will lie quietly. You mustn't try to talk now."

"I may not have the chance later," he smiled weakly. "Morgan?"

"Aye, lad?" He took the cool, dry hand in his. Wade was shocked to feel how little strength was in it, how gray the normally lively face was, how dull and flat his eyes were.

"Glasse . . . where?"

"Over the side before I could break the hold open. He's bound for the *Northgate,* by my guess, but it won't save him. Not now."

"You're going after the *Northgate?* Morgan . . . you know you can't."

"Why? Because we'll start a war? You're too late, Roarke. The fighting has already begun, and Decatur himself was in the squadron that fired the first shots. The message from de Ville—the reason he tried to stop us—*we're at war!*"

"War?" Roarke whispered, and a spark of life came into his eyes.

"Aye, Roarke. Congress declared ten days ago. Commodore John Rodgers was turned loose with his squadron to go after the Jamaican convoy and ran into a British war sloop instead. The French merchantman brought the news to de Ville, along with an eyewitness account of the Americans opening fire on the Union Jack. The mighty British tucked tail and ran within a few hours."

"War . . ."

"I need you now, Stuart. Dammit, you can't die on me! *I need you!*"

The eyes fluttered open again. "I'll try, Morgan. I swear, I'll . . . Morgan?"

"Aye, Stuart?" he had to lean closer to hear.

"If . . . if something happens . . . take care of my Bett for me. Tell her . . . tell her I loved her and . . . and thank her for me. I never had a chance to thank her." Roarke swallowed dryly and for the briefest moment his hand tightened on Morgan's. "I never thanked you, either . . . for being a friend as well as a brother. I told Summer I was twice lucky . . . three times. . . ."

"*Stuart!*" Wade held his breath. He squeezed Roarke's

hand in his, afraid to let go, afraid that if he did so, the life he held would simply slip away.

Thorny leaned past his captain and touched a hand to Stuart's pulsebeat. "Ee's dropped off again, Cap'n. It's what ee needs now . . . sleep."

Wade nodded and tucked Roarke's hand gently down by his side.

"Work some of your magic for me, old friend," he whispered to Thorny. "Keep him alive."

"Aye, Cap'n. Ye'll 'ave me best."

"Morgan?"

He glanced at Summer and saw the reflection of his own fears in the depths of the gray eyes. He drew her into his arms and held her, unashamedly taking strength from the trust she had in him. "Are you all right?"

She nodded. "I am now. Are you honestly going after the *Northgate?*"

Wade's dark eyes flicked to the bed. "Aye. And when I've finished with her, I'm going hunting for a panther. Gather your things together quickly now; we haven't much time to get you ashore."

"Ashore?" she gasped and pushed out of his arms. "You're not sending me ashore!"

"A battle at sea is no place for a woman and child!"

"But I am *your* woman and Sarah is *your* child. Our place is here with you." Summer's gray eyes glistened. "You will need me, Morgan. You will need someone to tend the wounded. From what I know of the *Caledonia,* you will not be able to spare any able-bodied men from your guns. Send the baby, yes, and the nurse if you must . . . but no, Morgan, I will not leave you. Not again."

Wade searched her face for some sign of weakness—something he could use to fight her—but there was nothing.

"I prefer not to leave either, *m'sieu,*" came a soft-spoken yet determined voice beside them. The young girl who had been brought aboard the *Chimera* to do simple nursing duties with a baby for one night stood next to Summer and faced the tall, rugged sea captain unwaveringly. "You will need many hands to take care of the wounded, *non?*"

"Damn me for a fool," he murmured, looking from one defiant face to the other, "but I believe you both mean it."

The nurse moved closer, and Summer felt a cool hand slip into hers for courage.

Both girls nodded.

"Very well, but you'll do exactly what Thorny tells you to do, and you'll stay away from the gun decks when the fighting starts?"

They nodded again.

The dark blue eyes shifted once more to the bed. "If you need me—for anything—I'll be topside on the bridge."

He kissed Summer once, briefly, then left the cabin.

24

WITHIN FIFTEEN MINUTES the *Chimera* was under way and heading into the open water beyond the Baie de Fort-de-France. Farley Glasse's longboat had reached the wharf, and Mr. Phillips had been able to track his movements with the aid of the spyglass until the galloping horses had carried the warmonger and his surviving compatriots into the hills and out of sight. According to de Ville, the *Northgate* was waiting just past the elbow of land that shaped the northern tip of the bay. Glasse would be able to reach his ship with time to spare. It was only a question now of which frigate could pull away from the hampering drafts and currents created by the land mass and command the best position for the battle ahead.

The *Chimera*'s decks were cleared. The gunports were opened, the muzzle lashings were taken off and the breeching tackles attached, readying the big twenty-four-pounder guns for action. Buckets of sand and ash were scattered on the planking to ensure the men's footings; sponges, crowbars, and handspikes were laid alongside each cannon, and the trolleys were stacked high with solid cast-iron balls. Three small bundles were hoisted to the tops of the three masts, and a moment later, under a rousing cheer from the bare-chested, eager crew, the bindings were tugged loose and the Stars and Stripes snapped open in the brisk wind.

The *Northgate* was sighted as soon as the *Chimera* passed the tip of the peninsula. The two ships were barely a mile apart, sailing into the late afternoon sun on converging courses. The *Northgate* hoisted her battle flags and began to reduce sail, to take advantage of light and wind drift to unleash the first series of broadsides.

Morgan Wade, standing on the bridge, quietly passed an order to Mr. Phillips to turn the *Chimera* away from the *Northgate* and to ride with the wind long enough to increase their speed before her own sails were taken in. He saw sparks of orange flame and small plumes of smoke erupt from the *Northgate*'s starboard side as her captain tested for range, noting that the shots splashed harmlessly into the sea well short of the *Chimera*.

A second course change brought Wade's ship hard about, reducing the area she presented as a target but leaving her at a temporary disadvantage. She would be able to bring only her forward guns to bear if Morgan decided to open fire, while the British warship could and did begin discharging in earnest. The *Northgate*'s eighteen-pounder guns were loaded with double shot—two iron balls linked with chain—and aimed high in an attempt to destroy the *Chimera*'s rigging. She fired continually, backing away as she drifted out of position, only to pull up and set off more salvos as the privateer came closer and closer.

Wade could see plainly the frigate's deck and the officers moving up and down the lines to encourage their gunners. Their efforts were paying off, as two of the *Chimera*'s topsails collapsed, their canvas riddled with holes. A man was injured as rigging twanged apart and a spar swept wildly across the deck before it was gaffed and secured. Phillips, tight-lipped and anxious, looked to Morgan Wade three times for the order to turn the *Chimera*, and three times the response remained a cool, "Not yet, Mr. Phillips."

The *Chimera* thundered within one hundred yards, then fifty yards of the blazing warship without having fired a single shot. They were close enough to see the faces of the Royal Marine sharpshooters as they climbed up into the shrouds and prepared to rain down a hail of musket fire on the approaching ship. Wade, still scanning the enemy deck through the spyglass, lowered it suddenly with a grim smile of satisfaction.

"Now, Mr. Phillips. Bring her hard about. Mr. Monday—shall we give them a reply?"

The big negro grinned from his position on the quarterdeck. He threw his bald head back and let loose a bloodcurdling roar, one that had the veins on his neck rising into blue snakes and the gleaming muscles across his chest and arms cording into bands of sinew.

The gunlayers took up the cry, and at a distance of barely twenty yards, the *Chimera* presented her broadside to the *Northgate* and replied with everything she had. The volley was delivered almost as a single shot and given at such close range that not one of the heavy guns missed. The beams of the privateer had scarcely completed shuddering from the first tremendous recoil when a second roar from Mr. Monday unleashed a second volley, then a third, turning the entire side of the *Chimera* into an inferno of spark and flame. Wade's carronades—the smashers—hurled iron shots weighing forty-two pounds apiece into the hull of the British frigate, unseating its cannons, tearing out whole sections of timber, sending splinters of men and decking as high as the topsails. The long guns on the lower deck fed a murderous barrage into the *Northgate*'s belly, their superior weight and power driving the shot clear through the three- and four-foot-thick skin of the frigate.

The *Chimera* came up into the wind and crossed in front of the *Northgate*'s bow, so close that a man seated on the bowsprit could have reached out and touched the privateer. The dense acrid clouds of smoke were blown away long enough for Wade to seize the advantage and deliver several well-placed broadsides directly down the length of the *Northgate*. Her mainmast was blasted away, as were her steering sails and a good portion of her forecastle and bridge. Sail and rigging dropped down onto the ravaged deck, along with the scarlet-clad bodies of the sharpshooters who had had their footings shot out from under them.

Leaving the helm to Mr. Phillips, Wade joined his men as they shifted to the loaded portside cannon. He was stripped to the waist; his ebony hair was tied back from his brow under a bright blue bandanna. He prowled catlike along the quarterdeck, directing his men to fire at specific targets, calling repeatedly on the magnificent precision he had drilled into them to keep up the steady breakneck pace. The *Northgate*'s crew was dazed from the swiftness of the devastation, and Wade knew he could not afford to let them recover. He was outmanned, outgunned and outclassed by nearly twice the tonnage. He knew he had to smash their spirit as well as their armaments if he hoped to pull away intact.

Again and again the *Chimera*'s guns blazed, at times sending up such a steady flare of lightning from her cannon muzzles that she appeared to be on fire. The smoke clung to the crew's throats and nostrils, burning their eyes as unrelentingly as the incessant roar hammered at their ears. At every gust of wind Wade searched through the thick clouds for signs that the British had hauled down their colors. The *Northgate*'s mizzen and fore topmasts had been destroyed and hung crookedly over the sides, dragging the rigging behind. Not a single gun remained mounted on the quarterdeck, and she was beginning to wallow and heave under the amount of seawater slapping into the damaged hull. But the flag still showed determinedly from the broken mainmast. Ashton-Smythe's pennant and the array of battle flags had fallen, but they too reappeared stubbornly over the remnants of the forecastle.

By contrast, the *Chimera* was remarkably unscathed. She had not suffered any major damage, and the crew, still driven by the bitter memory of the past eight hours spent as prisoners aboard their own ship, poured round after round into the buckling ship, equally determined not to stop or lessen the punishment until the British frigate admitted defeat.

Forty minutes into the battle, Mr. Phillips appeared again at Morgan's side to ask if they might fall off and effect repairs to the torn sails. The *Chimera* was losing steerage, and he could not hold to the tight pattern Wade had ordered much longer.

"How much longer?" Wade demanded, his face and chest streaming sweat.

"Two passes, Captain, no more. Even then we'll be counting on the drift."

A shot from the *Northgate* blasted through the deck rail not four feet from where Wade and Phillips stood, unseating one of the cannons from its carriage and hurling it squarely onto one of its gunners, crushing him to pulp in a matter of seconds. Blood splattered in all directions, turning the deck slippery at their feet.

"One pass, Mr. Phillips," Wade shouted. "Give me one more slow pass and we'll have them!"

Phillips stared aghast at the bloody twisted hand that protruded from the base of the cannon, recognizing the scarred wrist as belonging to one of his closest friends.

Morgan grabbed him roughly and spun him away from the gruesome sight and for one irrational moment cursed the absence of Stuart Roarke's solid presence beside him. In the next instant he saw the horror in Mr. Phillips's eyes and recalled too well his own reaction to hearing of Roarke's injury.

"One pass, Jamie. Can you give me one more slow pass?"

Mr. Phillips focused with difficulty on Morgan's face. "Aye, sir." He swallowed hard and added in a grinding voice, "Aye, sir! I'll bring you so close you'll be able to smell the bastards!"

Ninety minutes after her first gun had been fired, the *Northgate*'s flags came down.

Captain Emory Ashton-Smythe sat erect, his eyes fixed on a point on the horizon as he felt the bump and skid of the longboat touching against the *Chimera*. His uniform was streaked with blood and grime. He wore a bandage around his thigh and another on a shattered hand and had to lean heavily on one of the oarsmen before he could rise to his feet. Minutes later he stood on the *Chimera*'s main deck, his face ashen as he offered his sword in a formal surrender to Captain Morgan Wade.

"The honor is yours this day, sir. My compliments to your men."

"The victory was not an easy one, Captain Smythe," Wade said, refusing the proffered sword in acknowledgment of the Briton's courage. "Your men should find no fault with their behavior."

Ashton-Smythe's hands tightened on the sword and he lowered it. Behind him, Farley Glasse was shrugging off the assistance of two of Wade's men as he climbed through the gangway. His appearance was glaringly out of keeping with the grime and stench of battle. He was freshly washed and suited in clean clothing. His injured arm was cradled in a spotlessly white linen sling.

Morgan took a steadying breath before he addressed Captain Ashton-Smythe again.

"As you are no doubt aware, Captain, your ship and crew have now become the prize of the United States."

Ashton-Smythe stiffened, and his eyes looked into Wade's for the first time. "You dare to justify this in the name of your country, sir?"

"My justifications are a damn sight better than your own at this moment. But personal amenities aside, you are obviously not aware that as of ten days ago, June eighteenth to be precise, our two countries were officially at war."

The British officer's stony countenance cracked. His eyes widened, and his lips parted slightly, and a brief hint of color crept into his cheeks.

"Don't worry, Captain," Wade said dryly. "You do not have the distinction of being the first British ship to bow to an American. A countryman of yours has already taken that honor."

That seemed to shake the officer even more. "Who. . . . ?"

"I'm afraid I am not familiar with your lists, but the ship was the *Belvidera.*"

Ashton-Smythe's eyes were still locked to Wade's. "I have no recourse but to accept your word on the matter. My ship—"

"Your ship is beyond salvage. I have neither the crew nor the patience to tow her to port. If you have not ordered it as yet, I suggest you have your crew abandon ship immediately. I intend to sink her before I take my leave of these waters."

"Sink her? For what reason?"

"The same one you would have used to sink the *Chimera* had the outcome been reversed."

Ashton-Smythe reddened and remained silent.

"We will, naturally, replenish our stores from your

armory first. And any of your crew who can prove to me that they are Americans—deserters, if you prefer—will be offered the choice of joining us. As to the rest, I'm afraid you will have to settle for Monsieur de Ville's generous hospitality. That shouldn't be too much of a hardship—General de Ville has a rather amiable working relationship with the British."

This last statement produced such a smug and haughty sneer on Farley Glasse's face that Wade smiled.

"All of you will be permitted to sample the general's hospitality, with the exception of Mr. Glasse, that is. He and I have some unfinished business to settle."

"Mr. Glasse is a representative of His Majesty's government," Ashton-Smythe said quickly. "As such, under the terms of war, it becomes your obligation to treat him with the same courtesy you would any of my men. I expect Mr. Glasse to be allowed to accompany us ashore in strict accordance with those terms."

"The only terms Mr. Glasse will be leaving this ship on are my own. I have a badly wounded man below whose injuries were sustained before any of us were informed that a state of war existed. I have two women and a child on board as well who will speak volumes on the courtesies Mr. Glasse extended them. To my way of thinking, he has himself voided any so-called immunity he may have been entitled to."

"Those same words apply to your own situation, Wade," Glasse said archly. "Or should I call you Sir Edmund? A traitor, a spy, a murderer—" He glanced around coldly at the silent, glowering crew who had gathered about them. "The taint your captain bears is his alone, as it stands now, but what do you think will happen if you so much as raise a finger against me? I am unarmed. I am a helpless prisoner of war. Murder me now and the infamy will spread and you will all be hunted down like animals."

Mr. Monday stepped forward, but Wade's hand reached out in time, halting the huge negro in his stride.

"He'll be yours soon enough, Mr. Monday," Wade said quietly. "Let him speak his piece."

"Oh, I intend to speak, all right, Captain," Glasse spat. "I will tell anyone who cares to listen how you raped and brutalized an innocent young woman . . . how you lured her into a miserable hotel room and forced her to degrade herself, and when you'd had your fill, you beat her . . . beat her until her own father could not recognize her. Speak my piece? I have been wanting to shout my outrage for the past thirteen years!"

Glasse was trembling now. There was not a sound on the deck aside from the creaking of the spars and the slap and gurgle of water curling off the frigate's hull. Ashton-Smythe was clearly stunned by the accusation.

"Have you any proof to support your charges, sir?" he asked Glasse.

The black eyes were leveled on the officer. "I don't need any further proof than what I see before me. Look at him! Do you hear the almighty, brave Morgan Wade denying any of it? Ask him! Ask him if it's true!"

Ashton-Smythe looked at Wade. "Well, sir?"

"Your Mr. Glasse has been chasing his tail for thirteen years," Morgan said quietly.

"A quaint way to avoid a direct question, Wade," Glasse sneered.

"Ask me a direct question, and I will answer it. Thirteen years ago I was in a dozen different places."

Glasse's eyes glittered. "Then I shall rephrase my question. Where were you on the night of May fourteenth, 1799? A night that has seared itself into my own memory like few others."

Ashton-Smythe saw the smile on Wade's face as the dark blue eyes turned to him. "Perhaps you would be so kind as to tell Mr. Glasse where I was, Captain Smythe. May fourteenth, 1799."

Ashton-Smythe frowned, then blanched. Glasse saw the two men acknowledging something silently between them, and his patience gave way. "Well? Where was he? What further trickery is this?"

"There is no trickery," Captain Ashton-Smythe said quietly. "And I do indeed know where Captain Wade was that night." He whirled to face Farley Glasse. "And had I known this to be the root of your actions these past twelve months—these past twelve *hours*, I would have killed you myself!"

"What are you saying! He's a murderer! He's a—"

"You bloody, pompous fool," Ashton-Smythe said, shaking his head. "Thirteen years ago, in May, Morgan Wade was serving as a deckhand on board the British frigate *Africa* . . . as he had been for the ten months prior to that after being impressed into His Majesty's service. He remained on board until July of that same year, at which time he and one of the commander's personal slaves"—the Englishman's eyes settled briefly on Mr. Monday—"jumped ship off Saint Christopher. There was quite a row at the time, especially when he resurfaced several months later, praised by the Americans as a hero for his reckless escape, and was taken on by Commodore Preble himself."

"The escape was not so reckless, Captain," said Wade. "As I recall, the man holding down the ghost watch that night was such a poor shot we could have moved an army out."

"You were lucky it was a dark night, Wade, and you were doubly lucky my knowledge of musketry was limited at the time. I would have shot you then with a clear conscience"—Ashton-Smythe turned to Glasse contemptuously—"whereas I would never presume to condemn a man without the benefit of giving him a fair trial first or, at the very least, checking all of the facts before I dared to go to such lengths to confront him."

Glasse blinked stupidly. "There was no mention of any Wade on any of the registries. I checked, I tell you, and there is no mention of a Wade anywhere, any time before the summer of '99. He is Granville, I swear it."

"Indeed he is, sir," Ashton-Smythe replied evenly. "And a single question would have told you he is *Matthew* Granville . . . and as I knew him, Matt Grange. He changed his name on board the *Africa* to avoid notoriety, yes, but not for the reasons you mentioned. He changed it again when he joined the American Navy."

"A man does not change his name so many times without having something to hide," Glasse insisted, groping desperately for straws.

"Nor does he necessarily keep the one he was given if he thinks it could cause discomfort to someone he has left behind."

Glasse's jaw sagged and he stared at Wade. "No. I don't believe it. You're lying!" He looked at Ashton-Smythe, and his face reddened. "You're both lying! You're lying to protect each other!"

The British captain sighed and gazed out at the hulk of the *Northgate*. He could see and hear the confusion as the survivors searched the wreckage for signs of life.

"Why should I do that, sir?" he murmured wearily. "I fear nothing could protect me from the scorn my men must be feeling toward me now."

"You have no idea of the scorn you will be feeling," Glasse spat. "I intend to see you placed before a court-martial and have your stripes torn from your shoulders!"

Ashton-Smythe grasped the oak of the deck rail with his good hand. "Perhaps it is no less than I deserve. My God . . . after the business I have done here today, perhaps it is better than I deserve. One hundred brave souls placed their trust in me, and I . . . I squandered them for the sake of one man's twisted hatred. One hundred dead, and the tally may yet rise." He compressed his lips into a bloodless line and turned to Wade. "Winfield will not rest until he sees you dead, Captain. He considers the taking of the *Chimera* to be his holy grail."

"Thank you for the warning. But he should pray that I do not find him first."

Captain Emory Ashton-Smythe stared long and hard into the piercing blue eyes before he finally nodded. His shoulders seemed to droop as if the weight he carried was suddenly too much to bear.

"You had best see to your crew, Captain Smythe," said Wade. "My men and I will do all we can to help you transfer your wounded ashore."

"What do you intend to do with Glasse?"

"Nothing less than he deserves."

"But . . . you cannot just murder the man. Good God, you would be as inhuman as he is."

"I did not say he would die from his punishment. Glasse will leave this ship alive—although I cannot swear he will want to be."

Ashton-Smythe swallowed several times, then nodded again.

"Where do you think you are going?" Glasse demanded when he saw the British captain turn toward the entry port. "You cannot leave this ship without me! You are honor-bound and duty-bound to protect me—*with your own life if need be!*"

"If I were honor-bound to do anything, sir, it would be to stand here and witness your punishment for the crimes you have committed. I'm afraid, however, I simply do not have the stomach for it right now. I have too many *brave* men who need me more."

Glasse lunged after the captain, but two of Wade's men stepped quickly in front of him.

"Smythe! *Smythe!* You can't just leave me! Smythe, you bastard! You can't leave me! I'll have you hung! I'll have you hunted down and scourged for the yellow-bellied coward that you are!"

"Seize him up, Mr. Powell," Wade ordered solemnly. "In the shrouds, if you please."

"No!" Glasse backed away and tried to dash for the freedom of the open gangway. Two burly seamen caught him easily, wrenching his wounded shoulder and dragging him, screaming and kicking, to the side of the ship. It took two more men to hold him while his wrists were bound to the rigging by hempen ropes and the clothing he wore was sliced from his body.

Mr. Monday stood on the break of the deck, his face expressionless as he slowly uncoiled a twelve-foot length of oiled leather.

"No! *No!* You can't do this! I am a subject of His Majesty King George! I am a prisoner of war! I am—"

"Slow and easy, Mr. Monday," said Wade. "One cut for every man on board this ship . . . and as many again for the discomfort he has caused Mr. Roarke."

Mr. Monday's teeth gleamed whitely across his face. He swung the whip over his head in an arc, bending his powerful body to give the stroke his full force. He brought the leather humming through the air and cracked it across the narrow shoulders and ribs.

"Aughhhh!" Glasse's whole body jerked from the agony, and he writhed against the ropes that secured him to the shrouds. He barely caught his breath before the lash

curled around him a second time, leaving a second thin weal of blood to mark its bite. The knife wound he had suffered at Thorny's hands began to weep fresh blood, but after a while, when the hum and crack of leather became rhythmic, one source of blood became indistinguishable from the rest.

25

SUMMER WAS EXHAUSTED. Any thoughts she might have had concerning the noble, valiant duty she had volunteered for had vanished five minutes into the battle preparations. Thorny had been instantly transformed into a demon, barking orders and cursing with a vengeance until both girls were more terrified of what he might do if they balked at an order than of the order itself. Every spare sheet of linen and cotton had been torn into strips for bandages. Half-a-dozen needles had been threaded in readiness, and a basin of rum was heated, into which Thorny had set his dreadful assortment of tools. Knives, pincers, scissors and even a carpenter's saw were brought from the stores and placed in the room he would be using as a surgery.

It had been necessary to move Stuart to a lower deck since the captain's cabin had, on more than one occasion, received the enemy's shot. Sarah had been bundled into her cradle and placed alongside Stuart's litter in the storeroom adjacent to the surgery, and Summer had been dispatched to remain with them, tearing bandages, until she was needed.

When the terrible pounding from the guns overhead commenced, she had sat frozen by Stuart's side, the baby pressed to her bosom, her head buried in the nest of quilts. At one point she had felt Roarke's hand resting on her shoulder to reassure her, but for the most part, Summer sat numb, deafened and blinded by the terror of the shelling.

There was no lull to gather her shattered nerves together and no easy way to learn how to cope with the horror of the wounds that trickled into the storeroom. The air smelled of lamp oil and blood, of raw gunpowder and the acrid bitterness of scorched flesh. She cleaned and wrapped burns. She splinted a broken arm and tied off the stump of a severed finger, managing to keep her stomach until the poor man had thanked her profusely and staggered back to his station.

Each man brought stories with him of what was happening on the gun decks. Each sound of footsteps in the corridor sent Summer's heart thudding into her throat. The excitement and pride she heard in the men's voices did nothing to ease the dreaded thought of seeing Morgan's crumpled, bleeding body carried in on a litter. Two such bodies were brought in, dead before Thorny had a chance to look at them. Several more were fed quantities of rum and laudanum when their wounds were deemed too severe to be helped. They lost seven crewmen in the opening stages of the battle, and the sights and sounds of misery and pain became as steady as the blasts from the guns.

When silence finally did rattle along the length and breadth of the ship, the three working in the surgery were too frantic to do much more than pass a brief glance at one another before bending to their gruesome tasks again. Neither Summer nor the nurse, Gabrielle, dared to ask if it was over; they simply braced themselves to watch for what Thorny referred to as the die'ards.

"When ye see the likes o' them comin' 'ere ter 'ave an 'and sewed tergether what's near fallin' off, ye'll know the main fightin's gone past."

The diehards failed to show, and the running footsteps, the sound of frantic activity and the rocky motion of the *Chimera* continued.

After what seemed like an eternity of welcomed silence, a particularly loud rumble from the deck overhead caused Gabrielle to gasp and drop the swab she was holding out to Thorny. It was not the sound of resumed gunfire; it was more like the rumble of an angry earthquake.

Thorny merely chuckled and sponged out the wound he was working on with a corner of his shirt. "That be the other sign, lass. Remember it, on account o' it bein' music ter the ears of a body stuck b'lowdecks."

"But what is it, *m'sieu?*" Gabrielle whispered.

"Trunnions," he announced. "Means the guns'r bein' 'auled in an' tied off. N'owt too tight, mind. Many a time a dead ship's come back ter life ripe unexpectedlike. An, less'n I'm mistook"—he cocked his head to one side—"they be only the port guns. Starboards'r stayin' owt ter finish the kill."

Both women looked up. "Finish the kill?"

"Means the cap'n ain't in a gen'rous mood," he said, screwing up his nose as he removed a hunk of iron from his patient's thigh. "Ee ain't pleasured ter give the Frenchies a prize, an' ee ain't of a mind ter drag 'er nowheres 'imself. Ee'll drill 'er till she sinks. . . . 'and me them swabs, girlie. What yer doin? Fallin' ter sleep on me?"

Gabrielle handed Thorny a wad of linen, but her eyes were fastened on the door of the storeroom. Mr. Phillips was standing there, his handsome young face hidden beneath layers of grime and sweat.

"W-a-all, now, if'n it ain't one o' the first die'ards. Didn't I tell ye? Where'r ye 'urt, lad?"

"No, no . . . I'm not hurt, Thorny." Mr. Phillips smiled at Gabrielle shyly. "Nothing aside from a few bumps and bruises, that is. Captain Wade sent me down to see how we stand with the wounded."

"Wounded, eh?" Thorny scowled from Phillips to Gabrielle to Summer to the panting, sweating man on the bench. "Ripe lot o' queries we been 'avin 'bout the wounded all afternoon. Bafflin', ain't it, 'ow we ain't got an 'eap more with nobody's mind stayin' on business."

Phillips reddened and smiled at Summer before he cleared his throat and addressed Thorny again. "How is Mr. Roarke?"

"'Angin' on. Ow's the Kameery?"

"Hanging on," Phillips grinned. "I still don't believe we did it, Thorny. We took the *Northgate!*"

"Cap'n fixin' ter scuttle 'er?"

"He hardly needs to. She's been hulled so many times

her sides are kindling. You can see clear through her in places."

"Hmph . . . ahh, got the barstard—" He flipped a second chunk of metal onto the floor and chuckled at the sailor. "All done, lad. Ye can leave go o' yer wind now if ye've a mind to. Eh? What's that ye say, Jamie lad?"

"The captain would like you topside when you're through here. He . . . ah, has one other man who needs tending."

"Tendin'? What kind o' tendin'? Why'n't ye bring 'im down 'ere?"

"Well, ah . . . I believe the captain prefers you to bring a dose of turpentine with you and treat the man on deck."

"Turps? Who 'ad call ter be lashed? N'owt one o' our boys, I 'ope?" He looked truly stricken at the thought.

"No, sir. One of theirs. An Englishman."

Thorny's face screwed up to ask the question, but Summer had already recognized the look on Mr. Phillips's face.

"Farley Glasse," she breathed.

"Yes, ma'am. I wasn't supposed to say so. . . . the captain didn't think you ladies needed any more upsetting. But yes, ma'am, the captain ordered Mr. Monday to give him two hundred and fifty of his finest."

Summer wiped her hands on the apron she was wearing and started to the door. Mr. Phillips moved quickly to block her path.

"It isn't a very pretty sight, ma'am."

"Neither was anything I saw this afternoon."

"No, ma'am, but the captain won't like you going on deck just the same."

Summer gazed up at him unwaveringly. "Please stand aside. I have no intention of wasting any sympathy on Mr. Glasse; I merely want to go up on deck a few moments. For the past several hours I have been hearing more than I care to about what the captain *said* or what the captain *did*. . . . I have yet to see the captain myself to know if he even said or did half the things he is purported to have done."

"Ma'am, I swear—" Phillips stopped. He saw Thorny's nod and moved reluctantly out of the way.

Summer climbed the two flights of ladderways to the main deck. Nearly every member of the crew she passed stopped what they were doing to touch their forelocks respectfully and murmur a startled greeting. Just as many stories had come up from the lower deck during the fighting as had gone down—about her gentle touch with the wounded, about the smile she gave every man along with the treatment. Thorny's skill was unquestioned, but his manners sent few away from the surgery with a flush in their cheeks and praise for their bravery ringing in their ears.

Summer stepped out of the hatchway and blinked with amazement at the eerie sight that stretched out before her. It was almost pitch-dark; only a thin band of hazy light hovered across the horizon. A mist was curling out from the land to cover the ship, cloaking the torn sails and rigging with cottony wisps of moisture. Bits of wreckage littered the deck, and somewhere up ahead, sailors were shouting to heave to as three cannon blown off their carriages were angled back into position.

Sections of missing rail were being hastily rewoven with thick cables, and topmen were busy overhead to repair and fit new spars and attach new canvas where the old had been destroyed. No one was idle. Many men she recognized as having passed through the surgery, their bandages soiled and stained brown from dried blood.

She wiped her hands again, more of a nervous gesture now, and walked out onto the deck. Lanterns were strung every few feet, attracting swarms of small insects and fat moths. The wind had died away, and the *Chimera* sat steadily on the smooth surface of the water, a hive of activity in contrast with the still night.

She heard a shout behind her and jumped as a bucket of water was splashed across the deck. As she turned, a distant glow of lights caught her eye off the starboard side, and she changed direction to stand at the rail and look out at what remained of the frigate *Northgate*.

It was less than fifty yards away, covered in lanterns which showed clearly the unbelievable extent of her damages. There was not a mast or beam or bulkhead that rose more than six feet above the gutted deck. Her masts lay, for the most part, at odd angles over the rails, their sails and lines drooping into the water. Smoke snaked out of countless holes in her hull and Summer guessed that anything salvageable had long since been removed and the fires simply left to burn.

Mr. Phillips had been correct. There was no need to put any more holes into her.

"Danged shame, that is," Thorny grumbled, joining her at the rail. "N'owt a very fit end fer a fine sailin' ship, is it, lass?"

"It could have happened to the *Chimera*," she reminded him.

"Aye. Could."

"What has become of the crew?"

"Shipped ashore, be my guess. Given ter the Frenchies ter get what they can fer 'em. Don't fret none, them limeys'll be traded off 'ome in no time."

Summer shook her head. "Whose side is de Ville on, Thorny?"

"De Ville's," he grunted and spat over the rail. "Onliest side ee's ever been on."

He muttered on his way past the heaps of broken spars and salvage to find the bridge. Summer stayed to view the *Northgate* a while longer, then she, too, pushed it out of her thoughts and wandered forward to the bow.

She saw Morgan when she was still partially hidden in the shadows thrown by the huge mainmast. He was standing on the bridge, his hands were gripping the rail, and a frown was creasing his brow as he stared down into the center of a group of men gathered on the forecastle. He was dripping wet as if he had just come out of the sea, and Summer could hear the sounds of other men in the water scrubbing the stink and sweat of battle from their skin.

Morgan looked so much like her memory of the very first time she had seen him that she could not move. His hair was again curled wetly against his cheeks and neck; his chest was bare and shining with the moisture trapped beneath the pelt of black hairs. His trousers clung like a second skin, outlining the power in every muscle and sinew.

One of his arms was marked where her pistol shot had

grazed it—had it only been three nights ago she had stormed aboard demanding her daughter back? There were cuts and scrapes and bruises that she had fully expected to see . . . and she felt suddenly foolish for her fears.

The dark blue eyes were on her in the next instant, and he pushed away from the rail and swung his broad frame down the ladder.

"What is it? Is something wrong—is it Stuart?"

"Oh, no. No, nothing is wrong, I—" She heard a choked scream from the group up ahead and her cheeks paled.

Morgan took her arm and guided her forcefully back the way she had come. "This is no time for you to be out for a casual stroll on the deck."

"I know, but I . . . I just wanted to see you, just for a minute."

His voice softened. "Haven't you been getting my messages?"

"Yes. And I know how busy you are, and I know you don't have time for anything but your ship right now, but . . . I just . . . wanted to *see* you. I wanted to know you were all right."

He raised a hand to cradle her chin. "And do you believe it now?"

She lowered her lashes. "Yes. I'm sorry. I was being foolish."

"But you couldn't help thinking someone was keeping some horrible truth from you?"

"Something like that," she murmured.

"Some pirate's wench you're going to make," he said, and the lazy smile was on his lips. "But I suppose I shall have to get used to someone worrying about me now whether I like it or not. I did bring it on myself, didn't I?"

"You did indeed," she sighed and pressed her cheek into his shoulder.

"A lucky thing you waited until now to come up. I've been on the *Northgate* for the past half hour or so, although I don't imagine anyone could have convinced you of that."

"You left the ship without telling me?"

"The plain truth of the matter is," he paused, and his

hand dropped from her chin, "I came down twice to see you before I went, and both times you were busy with the men."

She lifted her head. "You came to see me twice?"

"Aye." He added quietly, "You don't think I believe everything I'm told, do you?"

Summer did not know whether to laugh or cry. She straightened away from him and changed the subject before she did either.

"Mr. Phillips said you had Farley Glasse flogged."

"Mr. Phillips talks too much. But yes, I had him flogged. A punishment far too light for his crimes by my way of thinking. At any rate, as soon as Thorny seals off the cuts, Glasse will be on a quarterboat and bound for perdition. I haven't a care for what becomes of him after that."

"And the *Northgate?* Are you really going to sink her?"

"I believe I have already. At the speed she's taking on water, she won't ride out midnight. By then, hopefully, we'll be long gone. This blasted calm is the only thing keeping us here now, but we'll try towing her out past the windbreak. The *Gyrfalcon* has signaled a breeze out where she's sitting, so—"

"The *Gyrfalcon?* She's here?"

"Aye. Straight out"—Morgan pointed into the blackness and gave a deprecatory laugh when there was nothing to see—"past the fog, that is. She's sending in two of her longboats to help with the tow."

Summer was not looking out at the fog. She was trying to account for the sudden concern she saw in his eyes.

"It's the *Caledonia,* isn't it?" she asked. "Is that what really worries you?"

Morgan frowned. "This is war, my lovely. What worries me is that it will get a good deal worse before it gets any better. Had I known—" He hesitated, and the gray eyes widened.

"Had you known . . . what?"

"Had I known I was bringing you to this—" Still he could not finish the sentence.

"I am not afraid, Morgan," she whispered. "How can I be when I am with you? Please, don't ever regret taking me away from Bridgetown. You have given me more in the time we have been together than I would have had in a thousand years if we were apart. And please don't take all of the blame on yourself for my being here. Had I truly wanted to leave your ship in Speightstown, nothing on this earth could have stopped me."

He smiled, and the warmth of his arms wrapped around her. "And had I truly wanted you off my ship earlier today, none of your temper tantrums would have saved you. Selfish of me, wasn't it?" His lips brushed her forehead. "You could have been killed."

"It only makes me believe that you meant what you said."

"On which occasion, madam," he murmured dryly. "You seem to recall an uncanny number of things I have said."

"On the occasion when you promised me we would never be apart again."

"I said that?"

"You did."

He was debating an appropriate response when a shout from the topmast erased the smile from his face.

"That will be Treloggan," he said and turned abruptly away from Summer.

She followed him at a slower pace, keeping her distance, hoping not to be noticed too soon and ordered back down below.

John Bull Treloggan could have earned his name on appearances alone. He stood a full head taller than Morgan, easily commanded a hundredweight more on the scales and was the proud owner of such a fearsome countenance Summer almost turned and ran below voluntarily. The lower half of his face was bearded. Black and wiry, it hung to midchest, plaited in a score of braids and crusted with gold and silver beading. His eyes were coal black and sunk into dark hollows. The skin that showed between the beard and the red bandanna he wore was so badly scarred and pockmarked it could have been chiseled from lava rock.

Stuart Roarke, already settled firmly in Summer's mind as being a brave but cautious man, lost considerable ground in her estimation as she wondered at the sheer lunacy of anyone who would steal away in the middle of the night with this man's only daughter. Even harder to imagine was the possibility of Bull Treloggan siring anything that could have begun life as soft and pink as Sarah.

Bull was not the only cause of Summer's frozen stance in the shadows. Climbing through the gangway right behind Captain Treloggan, dwarfed to comic proportions and trying valiantly not to cry, was a scruffed and grimy figure who heard Summer's gasp and answered with a shriek of his own.

"Summer!"

"Michael! Michael, what on earth—!"

He flew across the deck and hurled himself into Summer's arms. She looked over the top of his head, shaking hers in bewilderment in answer to the scowl on Morgan's face.

"Stowed away, he did," Bull Treloggan grunted in a voice that sounded like slabs of marble grinding together. "Would've thrown him right off again when he poked his head up for air, but he sniveled and caterwauled and claimed to be kin to you, Wade. Thought I better bring him along in case you wanted the pleasure of seeing him dance from a yardarm yourself."

Morgan's smile was not entirely one of amusement. "I'll give it serious thought, by God. What the hell are you up to, lad? Why did you stow away aboard the *Gyrfalcon?*"

"I thought it was the *Chimera,* sir," Michael said, swallowing hard. "I . . . I wanted to be with S-Summer. I wanted to w-warn her."

"Warn her? About what?"

"About Commodore Winfield, sir." Michael's face was pale as he turned it up to his sister. "He was dreadfully angry when he found you gone. I . . . he thought you took Sarah and ran away. I tried to tell him what h-happened, but he wouldn't listen. He . . . he said I helped you."

"Take a look at his backside," Bull muttered.

Michael's arms tightened around Summer's waist and his whole body flinched as he buried his face against her.

"Michael?" she whispered. "What is it? What did he do to you?"

Morgan did not wait for explanations. He lifted the

boy's shirt and angled the trousers down. Welts the width of a finger rose in crisscross patterns across his buttocks. Michael pressed his face closer to Summer, and her eyes swam as she raised them to Morgan's.

"I never thought he'd hurt Michael. . . ."

"That were the other reason I fetched him along," Bull muttered.

"Can I stay with you?" Michael sobbed. "Oh p-please, Summer, I won't get in anyone's way. I'll work hard, and I w-won't eat much and . . . and I'll stay out of everyone's w-way, you'll see."

"Of course you can stay," Summer cried. "Hush now, of course you can stay. But where was Father throughout all of this? Why didn't he stop Bennett? How could he just stand there and let Bennett hurt you?"

"Oh, Summer—" his narrow shoulders quaked, his eyes and nose streamed wetly—"he didn't even try to stop him. Bennett said it was all Father's fault. He said it all happened because Father had let you do as you pleased for so long. He . . . he told Father that Sarah was a . . . that she was Captain Wade's baby and that if what you were doing was found out, it would ruin them all. Father got all red and started shouting back, and then—" Michael's mouth worked, but the words failed to come out.

"And then what, Michael?" she asked.

He glanced owl-eyed around the deck of the *Chimera*. "And then Admiral Reg burst into the study and told everyone that we were at war with America. He was laughing, and Father laughed, too, and Bennett . . . and then everyone went rushing out into the streets. Everyone except Bennett. He pushed me up against a wall and said that both you and I were traitors now and that if I thought to do anything more to warn you, he would be justified in having me shot. He still thought the *Chimera* was in the harbor, you see." Michael's eyes sought out Bull Treloggan and his voice faltered. "Only it wasn't the *Chimera*."

Bull took up the story from there. "Seems the lad bribed a boatman to bring him out. After we found out who the hell he was and why the hell he was on my ship, we listened to his story and figured it would be smart to put on sail and leave. We were kind of held up some, though, when an armed boarding party came out of nowhere and ordered us to strike the colors. Some fancy-dressed popinjay stood on my deck under a white flag and said he was claiming my ship in the king's ruddy name."

"What happened?" Morgan said, his brows knitting together.

"C-Captain Treloggan broke the lieutenant's musket in his bare hands," Michael whispered in awe. "He just took it and jolly well bent it in half."

"Bull—" Morgan had a feeling he knew what was coming.

"Eh? Oh, we scuffled about and ended up putting the lot of them in the drink to swim ashore. We ran up sail faster than a peppered dog and would've given 'em a warm round to remember us by, but the harbor was full of boats—celebrating the war, you know?—and the way to the *Caledonia* was fair blocked. It didn't stop Winfield though. He sounded his bells and had his guns run out before we were half-past."

The crew of the *Chimera* who had gathered around fell silent. They knew the *Caledonia* carried better than eighty guns, and being caught in such tight quarters as Bridgetown's harbor, without steerage or room to maneuver, the *Gyrfalcon* would have been as vulnerable as the *Northgate* had been.

Bull grinned suddenly. "And we would have been in a hell of a fix if someone hadn't snuck on board the night before and poured wax into the Brit's touchholes. Most of his guns were jammed tighter than a whore's—" He saw Morgan glance sharply in Summer's direction, and the word was chewed into a mumble. "Bah! Where is that bastard despoiler of a son-in-law of mine anyway? It isn't often Bull Treloggan has the mind or the reason to thank any man . . . *Roarke!*"

"Stuart's been injured," Morgan said quietly.

"Eh? Injured, you say? How badly?"

"Badly enough. And you haven't mentioned anything about your own damages."

The gnarled black brows crushed together. "We heard your thunder, Wade. My lads were itching to come in and lend a hand—would've come in the dog boats if I'd let them, but I thought we'd best stay put and keep a sharp eye on the horizon. Hell, I knew you wouldn't need us anyway."

"It wasn't a question of needing you or not. I didn't want to take the chance on both ships being damaged at once. A wasted precaution, I gather. Do I get an answer on the *Gyrfalcon?"*

Bull's black eyes glinted at him from their hollows. "You know I've never run from a fight in my life. The minute Winfield ran his guns out, my lads were there with an answer. On the whole we put on a damn fine showing against a ship of the line. A couple of my boys went down, including my chief gunner, Fortby, but they all gave three hearty cheers and near mutinied when I wouldn't bring them up alongside the *Caledonia."* The burly shoulders shrugged. "But I couldn't see the sense of taking on a Goliath alone. We took our tails and got out of there while we still had the windage to."

"You did the right thing," Morgan insisted. "And the only thing, under the circumstances. You're damned lucky you weren't pounded to splinters. Did Winfield give chase?"

Bull's scowl cleared, and he surprised the complement of crewmen by winking broadly at Michael. "Aye, Old Winifred tried. He called for sail as soon as he saw that most of his guns were frozen. Sheets were falling like clouds, they were. I reckon it took six, maybe eight hours just to replace the rigging Roarke's men sliced through and another twelve on top of that when he tried to steer the great bloody sow out of port and found out the cables were cut to his rudder."

Summer, standing quietly with Michael, recalled the smile on Stuart's face. . . . *They were so busy watching the* Chimera, *no one bothered to watch the* Caledonia. . . . Fools, she thought. They deserved to lose to men like these, who were willing to take nothing for granted and risk everything on an ideal. She looked up proudly as Bull spoke again.

"There ain't nothing out there but a cat's-paw moving over the water. We'll have to haul this fine lady some to find the breeze. Right now, though, I think I'll take a pint of your best down and share it with my son-in-law. Injured, you say? *Bah!* I'll put such a fear into his soul as to what I'll do to him if he tries to make a widow out of my Bett, he'll be on deck doing a jig for us by morn. You coming, Wade?"

"I'll be along," Morgan said, spying Thorny walking back from the forecastle. "I want to make sure all the rubbish is cleared from the decks."

"Aye, best I see him alone first at that." Bull guffawed loudly and strode to the stern, followed by a wake of crewmen.

Morgan watched him go; then the dark blue eyes probed the darkness and the fog as if willing it to lift so that he could see what lay beyond. Winfield was out there somewhere, he knew, tasting the same kind of rage that had driven them all against the *Northgate* this afternoon. Together the *Chimera* and the *Gyrfalcon* might be equal to the task of meeting the huge warship, but both of his ships were damaged. He would not know the extent of the *Gyrfalcon*'s wounds until he went on board and inspected for himself. He could only conclude the damage was worse than Bull was willing to admit or there would have been no keeping him out of the fight with the *Northgate*.

Both crews were short of men. The British had released six who claimed to be Americans, but Wade alone had lost ten. The *Chimera*'s crew would face the entire British fleet if it thought it was what he, Morgan Wade, wanted . . . but was it? Ashton-Smythe's words still rang clearly in his ears: It would indeed be a waste of brave lives.

His attention was drawn to a loud, plaintive wail that seemed to reach out to him from the listing hulk of the *Northgate*. The groan became louder and continuous, and as he watched, the battered hull lost its remaining strength and slid down into the water. All that was left behind was a frenzy of bubbles and churning white foam.

26

Bennett Winfield stood over Summer, his face expressionless, his pale blue eyes flat and impassive. His uniform was crisply white, a glaring affront in light of the terrible destruction surrounding them on the *Chimera*'s main deck. He was holding something behind his back, something Summer could not see in the shadows, but something she instinctively feared. She felt the scream rising in her throat and covered her mouth with her hands. Bennett only smiled and moved closer. He brought his hands forward into the light, and she saw what it was that he held.

"No! No, oh God . . . *no!*"

"Summer?"

"Noooo!"

"Summer!"

She opened her eyes and the echo of her scream was still ringing in her ears. Her brow was bathed in sweat, and her fingers were clutching the tangled cloak she was using as a blanket. Morgan stood over her, not Bennett. His face was taut and anxious, his grip on her shoulders was firm as he tried to calm her wild thrashings.

"Morgan?" she gasped. "Morgan, you're alive!"

"Of course I'm alive, why wouldn't I be?"

"But . . . I saw Bennett. . . . He was here!"

"No one was here," he said gently. "You were having a dream. A nightmare."

"A . . . dream?"

"That's all it was. Hush now—" He stroked her shoulders and smoothed the silky blonde hairs back from her face as she tumbled gratefully into his arms. "It's all over. You're safe."

Summer blinked away her tears and peeked past the crook of Morgan's shoulder. She saw the lamp on the desk and the charts, the familiar diamond-paned gallery windows and even the smoking stub of a thin black cigar thrown hastily into the tin cup.

"A dream?" she whispered. "But it was so real."

Morgan held her away from him a moment, and his thumbs brushed lightly over her cheeks to remove the residue of tears. "Nightmares usually are. Do you feel better now?"

She nodded and welcomed the solid comfort of his chest again as he held her close.

Summer could not remember when she had come to bed, and she had no idea of the time. It was dark; she could see that much from the windows. She could also feel the steady thrumming of water beneath the keel of the *Chimera,* telling her they were sailing fast and easy.

By contrast, the tow had taken long, laborious hours, and when they had arrived beside the *Gyrfalcon,* it was to discover that the calm had followed them out. There was no possibility of towing both ships for any length of time, so Morgan and Bull Treloggan had ordered their crews to work steadily on repairs. They kept the masts fully rigged and the canvas wetted down to make use of the faintest puffs of wind.

All night long the men had toiled. In the stillness both ships had rung with the sounds of hammer and nail, saws and shouted commands. Dawn had broken over the spine of Martinique, showing the island still capped in mists and giving no relief by way of winds or motion on the glassy surface of the water. Morgan had been plainly ill at ease at being becalmed so close to the French port, for although the land was just a purplish splash in the distance, it blocked out two-thirds of the horizon. There could be a dozen British warships laying off Cap Salomon and he would not know it until the wind appeared.

The work had continued in shifts throughout the day. Summer was kept as busy as any crewman. She and Gabrielle had tended the wounded while Thorny accompanied Morgan across to the *Gyrfalcon* to see if he could be of any assistance with their injured. Gabrielle had cared for Sarah's needs on top of her other duties, and Summer had found the girl's silent courage a much-needed inspiration.

The *Gyrfalcon*'s damages were worse than Bull had implied, but not as severe as Morgan had imagined. Aside from sail and rigging damage which was well under repair, its mainmast was cracked midway down and threatened to give under any kind of strain. Its port battery of guns was reduced by a fourth through direct hits from iron shot. Its casualties numbered fewer than Wade's, but there were more wounded to balance it out.

Both captains had to agree reluctantly that it would be wise to head north when the calm lifted and make for Bounty Key. That was the last thing Summer recalled—seeing Mr. Phillips in the doorway of the surgery announcing that Captain Wade was back, the wind was picking up, and the *Chimera* was going home.

"How long have I been asleep?" she asked.

"Not long enough," he said sternly. "It's been hardly an hour since I found you asleep in Stuart's arms and carried you up here. You're lucky I am not a jealous man."

"I should go back," she began and started to move out of his arms.

"You are not going anywhere," Morgan frowned.

"But Stuart—"

"Roarke is fine. Thorny is with him, and there isn't a thing you could do for him that Thorny can't. He has orders to call me if there is any change. Besides, Bull's talk must have truly put the fear into him; Thorny says he's gained a little strength back."

"Couldn't we bring him up here? It's so damp and cold down below—"

"We'd only have to move him again if there was any sign of trouble, and it would be harder on him for it. He's resting comfortably; I want you to do the same."

"Sarah?"

"Right here," he said and moved to one side so that Summer could see the cradle and the sleeping baby. "Gabrielle is asleep in the next cabin, and I believe I even managed to convince Mr. Phillips to close an eye."

Some of the tension left Summer's face. "Who is sailing your ship?"

"Mr. Monday never sleeps," Morgan said and added with a grin, "And there appears to be a new and mighty determined addition to my crew standing right up there alongside him."

Summer had forgotten all about him. "Michael?"

"He's requested to be formally added to the muster roll—and not just as a cabin boy. He claims to be both a sharpshooter and an expert swordsman."

"You didn't do it, did you?"

"I couldn't see the harm. He was so emphatic he won a smile from Mr. Monday and permission to share the watch on the bridge—a rare feat by any standard."

Wade turned his face toward the lantern light, and Summer was shocked to see the dark smudges of weariness underscoring his eyes. She bit her lip to hold back the tears and laid her cheek on his shoulder.

"You should be the one trying to sleep."

"Aye, so I've been told. I just thought I'd go over the charts one last time—"

Summer turned his head forcibly and silenced him with a kiss. She moved back toward the far side of the bed and held out her arms to him, hearing a sigh as he capitulated with a murmured "Only for a minute."

He wrapped his arms around her and rested his head between her breasts. Summer stroked the black waves lightly, lovingly, and was soon rewarded by the sound of his deep, even breathing.

Was it her fault, she wondered? Was she the cause of his troubles? He would never have gone to the Governor's Ball if he had not received the phony note and thought it a plea for help. He would not have sent the *Gyrfalcon* into Bridgetown's harbor if not for the need to distract Glasse's spies long enough to spirit her away.

She closed her eyes and tried not to relive each and every wound she had treated during the battle with the *Northgate*. She tried not to think of Stuart Roarke lying in his dark, dank berth below . . . but the images would not go away. Nor would the tears that began to flow hot and fast down her temples into her hair.

Her sobs were stifled as Morgan's hands moved in his sleep, up beneath the folds of her clothing, freeing them to the heat of his body. She held him and responded to his hunger. She welcomed the pain of his need and the swift, desperate release he sought.

She cried out and dug her hands into his massive shoulders, moving with him, moving for him, frantic for every last ounce of strength she could steal from him. She heard the groan that was her name, and she continued to spiral higher and higher, tearing into the man who was her love and now her life. A blackness that was no part of anything frightening or fearful claimed her, and she soared on its crest, knowing her destiny was locked to his forever and that no matter what the outcome of the next few days or weeks or years might be, she would forever belong to the raging sea and sun that was Morgan Wade.

Commodore Bennett Winfield leaned against the high-backed chair and took a deep swallow of brandy while he contemplated the pale features of Captain Emory Ashton-Smythe seated opposite him.

"The Admiralty will not take the loss of the *Northgate* lightly," he said at length, "nor will they view your conduct as being anything less than deplorable. You were entrusted with one of the finest ships and crews in the Caribbean—by my request, I might add—and you've thrown it all away."

Ashton-Smythe reddened, and his mouth pressed into a thin, bloodless line.

"You took a ship of the line that mounted fifty-two guns against a smuggler who carried women and children on board and you invited humiliation on yourself and on His Majesty's navy. Have you nothing to say?"

Ashton-Smythe's jaw worked as he fought for the appropriate words. "Wade's men had a better command of the available firepower, sir. He managed three rounds to every two of mine, and his tactics—"

"Yes," Bennett drawled interestedly, "tell me about his tactics. He enjoys fighting at close quarters, I'm told."

"Close?" The captain's eyes lifted from the snow white

table linen. "He came within hailing distance before he even presented his broadside . . . and far too fast for my gun captains to correctly adjust their aim. I for one have never seen anything like it. My men were certain he intended to ram us."

"And so they panicked?"

"No, sir. They continued at their posts. But the angle was such that only the guns amidships were effective. Whereas when he opened fire"—Ashton-Smythe paused and shuddered involuntarily at the memory—"every one of his guns scored a hit. Repeatedly, continually . . . my men were driven back from the sides, or else they were slaughtered where they stood."

"Yes, yes," Winfield prompted, "and then what?"

"Then his helmsman cut in front of our bow and . . ."

"And raked you straight down? I seem to recall hearing that he used that same ploy against the sultan's fleet out of Tripoli. But surely a shipload of Barbary pirates can hardly be compared to veteran sailors of the Royal Navy?"

"No, sir," Ashton-Smythe said. "But they bleed the same and they die the same. Once the main battery was destroyed, I could see no hope for the situation. And no choice but to take in the colors before the rest of my men went down with the ship."

"I see. And I suppose you had no choice but to accede to Wade's demands where Mr. Glasse was concerned?"

"Mr. Glasse's conduct was reprehensible. It was totally out of the bounds of reasonable behavior, and had I known his intentions or his motives earlier, I would never have permitted him to land at Fort-de-France."

"He was only attempting to obey a directive, Captain. To capture Morgan Wade and return him for trial."

"He placed the lives of your own wife and child in jeopardy along with innocent civilians—and I dare say he considered the entire crews of both ships expendable for the sake of his own twisted revenge."

"Had his plan succeeded, he would have captured Morgan Wade without firing a single shot."

"Yes, and he would have hung an innocent man in the process."

"So *you* say."

Ashton-Smythe pushed stiffly to his feet. "Are you questioning my loyalty as well as my ability?"

"If I was, Smythe, you would have even less flesh on your back than Glasse does. Now sit down and control your histrionics. I merely find it difficult to understand why you defend a man who is responsible for kidnapping my wife and baby daughter."

"I did not know they were on board at the time," the captain said tersely. "Mr. Glasse chose to keep that information to himself until we were well into the battle."

Bennett glanced away and gazed thoughtfully out of the windows of his cabin. His spacious quarters aboard the *Caledonia* were luxuriously furnished, boasting separate sleeping and working facilities, the former with a four-poster canopied bed, the latter including a dining suite in oak with seating for ten officers. His desk was carved from the finest teak, his service was china and sterling silver, and the brandy he enjoyed was the best commandeered from his past raids on French merchantmen.

"Did you happen to see my wife at all?" Bennett asked in a low voice.

"No, sir. Mrs. Winfield remained belowdecks."

"Then we must assume she is still being held against her will. Unfortunately Mr. Glasse's reports have been somewhat incoherent. In any case, we must also assume she is still very much alive and in need of a merciful return to the bosom of her family."

Ashton-Smythe met the cold, pale eyes of his commander. He knew Winfield would go after the *Chimera* whether he had a justifiable excuse or not. Just as he knew, suddenly, that Mrs. Winfield was no more a hostage than Morgan Wade was guilty of the murder thirteen years ago.

"I'm afraid I have no knowledge of the conditions on the *Chimera* after the confrontation," he said. "But the ship did not appear to suffer much damage to her hull, so—"

"So I may assume that wherever Wade is holding my wife and child, they are safe?"

"Yes, sir."

"Good. Let us hope they remain that way. I have a burning desire to see my wife alive again." Bennett flipped a thumbnail to the catch of his pocket watch. "You estimate he has four hours on us, give or take?"

"He wasted no time when the calm lifted."

"And damn my luck in approaching Martinique from the west. We could have had him a day sooner. As it is, he'll be heading north for Bounty Key. Two damaged ships shouldn't be too difficult to spot on the horizon." Bennett finished the last swallow of brandy and stood up. "You will naturally remain on board the *Caledonia* . . . in an advisory capacity."

"My men, sir?"

"De Ville has assured me they will be treated hospitably until such time as we return for them."

"Yes, sir."

"Now if you will excuse me, I'm told Glasse has been asking to see me again. Poor man. The doctor tells me he won't live out the night." Bennett paused at the door and looked back. "You should clean yourself up, Captain. Have that hand treated properly and see the ship's barber. I would as soon not have my men or my officers reminded of your recent debacle."

27

AN URGENT CLANGING of the ship's bell brought Morgan bolt upright in bed, instantly awake. Summer took a moment to rub the sleep from her eyes, and in that moment Wade had pulled on his breeches and stamped his feet into his boots and was out the cabin door. Summer dressed quickly and was not far behind, amazed at how easily her stomach churned with fresh panic.

The gunports were opened as she reached the deck, the lashings were off the cannon and the cork tompions were removed from the iron muzzles. The bright sunlight revealed the scars from the battle with the *Northgate,* and Summer could not help but wonder if the *Chimera* would ever regain her beauty and polished grace.

Summer ran along the quarterdeck toward the bridge, searching for signs of what had caused the alarm, but saw nothing beyond blue sky and dazzlingly clear water. Mr. Monday was talking to Morgan in a rapid undertone; Morgan in turn was staring along the brass spyglass, holding it steady on some point in the distance. From the look on his face, Summer knew it had to be the *Caledonia.* Mr. Monday fell silent beside him, and Mr. Phillips clenched his fists and leaned on the rail.

It was not until she heard the faint, muffled pounding that she whirled around quickly and understood the grimness on the men's faces.

"Michael . . . is it the *Gyrfalcon?*"

Her brother tore his eyes away from the two small sets of sails on the horizon. "She fell back during the night. Captain Bull kept lighting signals that he was all right, that the sea was clear behind him, and then . . . he just turned away suddenly and . . ."

Summer felt the deck tilt and realized, with a second jolt, that the *Chimera* was tacking sharply about. On Morgan's order Mr. Phillips shouted for more sail, and Summer was pressed back against the bulkhead as men clambered past her and swarmed up into the rigging. She was close enough to overhear what was being said on the half deck above her.

"It will take an hour, maybe more to reach her," Morgan cursed.

"Why didn't Captain Treloggan signal, sir?"

"I don't know, Mr. Phillips. But you can be sure I intend to find out. Can we work up any more speed?"

"We're fully rigged as it is, sir. We haven't an empty yard anywhere."

"Then we'll have to lighten her," Morgan decided. "Put some strong backs on the winch and off-load those bloody crates of copper. Get a pump in the stern and do the same with most of the drinking water. I want three more knots by the end of the hour."

"Aye, sir," Mr. Phillips said and vaulted down the ladder.

"Dammit, Monday, Jamie had a good question. I'll kill Bull myself when I lay my hands on him if he doesn't have a damn good explanation."

"Mebbe he t'ink he givin' us a chance to get away," Mr. Monday said. "Mebbe he know two ships woan make it."

Morgan's jaw tensed and he raised the glass, sweeping it across the horizon. "Where the devil are we, anyway?"

"Bird Islands over there," Monday grunted, pointing westward.

Morgan took a deep breath and cursed. Bird Island was a favorite rendezvous point for smugglers and privateers, and the chances of stumbling across a British revenue cutter were excellent.

Mr. Monday only grinned and shrugged.

Morgan lowered the glass and looked down, seeing Michael standing in the shadow of the bridge and beside him, Summer.

"You'd better go below," he ordered harshly. "Both of you."

"Sir?" Michael frowned and turned away from the deck rail. "You said I was part of the crew now."

"We're headed into a fight, boy. This is no time for games."

Michael's cheeks flushed angrily. "I know it's not a game, sir. But I recall you saying once that every man on board your ship had to pull his own weight; there could be no special treatment for anyone—including a governor's son. Well, sir, I am not the governor's son any longer. I am a full member of your crew. As such I . . . I demand to be treated the s-same way. I am not afraid to fight the *Caledonia*. You won't regret hiring me on."

Morgan's eyes had narrowed during the breathless speech, and now they widened in an expression intimating he was dangerously close to the edge of his patience. "*Hired* you?"

"Yes, sir. I should expect to share in the prize when we take her."

The dark blue eyes flicked to Summer. Instead of finding support, he was met by a proud smile and a similar calm defiance.

"Mr. Monday," he growled under his breath, "take your new powderboy down and explain what his duties will be."

Mr. Monday chuckled dryly and left the bridge.

"Thank you, sir," Michael cried. "You won't be sorry."

"Mr. Cambridge, we put men to death for even looking pale on board this ship. You may be sure *I'll* not be sorry about anything. Do we understand each other?"

Michael returned the penetrating gaze for a moment, then swallowed hard. "Aye, sir."

"As for you"—Morgan's attention shifted to Summer after Michael was led away by Mr. Monday—"I'll deal with your obstinacy once and for all when this is over."

"Yes, Captain. Is that a promise?"

"It is, by God."

"Then I look forward to it, sir," she said. "Eagerly."

The *Gyrfalcon* was reeling under the amount of shot raking across her hull. The upper deck was caught in a terrible deluge that rained iron and fragments of lead from exploding canisters of grapeshot. The dead and dying were strewn about the bloody planking, and its defenses had withdrawn to the shielded lower gun deck, where incredibly enough, the gunners were still maintaining a steady reply to the *Caledonia*'s onslaught. The battle was forty minutes old, already twice as long as Commodore Winfield had confidently predicted it would take to destroy the privateer.

Bull Treloggan refused to leave the bridge of his ship. He roared as many oaths across the span of ocean dividing the two ships as his cannon retorted with shot. Twice he had to drag bodies away from the wildly spinning wheel and guide the helm himself until a replacement appeared. Five, six, seven shots from the Royal Marine sharpshooters zinged close to his head, and three times his body staggered as eighteen pounds of iron gouged through the deck within arm's reach. He merely threw his head back and bellowed the louder for the insult; cursing the Britons' aim, cursing their training, cursing their lack of nerve to come too close to the *Gyrfalcon*. He was bare-chested, and his skin shone from the rivulets of blood where flying fragments had sliced into him. His face streamed sweat, his beard glittered; both hands were burned raw from loading and firing hot cannon.

He blessed Stuart Roarke each time he heard the deep-bellied explosions from the four sixty-four-pound carronades his son-in-law had mounted on the lower deck for him last year. They had already worn a dent in the *Caledonia*'s arrogant striped hull and had slashed its masts and rigging so that the panther's maneuverability had been vastly reduced. Like a feisty terrier, the *Gyrfalcon* made use of its lightness and greater speed to attack, fall back, attack, to circle around and attack again. Bull did not stay in position long enough for the *Caledonia*'s precision gunners to aim let alone unleash anything near to its capabilities. And their frustration was showing in the poor marksmanship, in the haste with which they attempted to reload and fire.

Unlike the decking Roarke had specially reinforced to withstand a pounding, the black panther was catching each heavy shell the *Gyrfalcon* spat at her and was suffering damage on all decks. Twice the shots landed so close to the outer skin that her ports were blown from the inside and the cannon tipped out and into the sea. It did nothing to impede the deadly eruptions from the three full decks of cannon, but it struck a proud chord in Bull's heart to see the mighty giant feeling more than just the annoying bite and scratch it had expected.

The *Chimera* came in fast before the wind and reduced to fighting sail as it sidled into position. Bull's crew cheered feverishly as it commenced heavy fire from all of its guns, even though it was beyond the range Wade preferred. But it earned the panther's attention, and the white-and-navy-clad officers on the *Caledonia*'s bridge could be seen redirecting the helmsmen to bring it about and line its guns on the new arrival, giving Bull's men a much-needed breather.

Wade's big twenty-fours were aimed and fired without a visible break in the clouds of smoke. The *Caledonia* responded vigorously with its thirty-two-pounders, heavier guns but not as accurate against a fast-moving target. The *Chimera* cut in swiftly, moving out again too quickly for the British gunlayers to compensate. Even so, it caught more than a fair share of direct hits, and Winfield praised his men as he saw Wade's foresails hanging in tatters. He pursued the privateer, hoping for an opportunity to cross Wade's bow and deliver a broadside similar to the one that had so unnerved the gunners of the *Northgate*. Wade saw what the commodore was about and pulled sharply up into the wind, ordering his headsails backed so that his ship glided to a dead halt in the water. Instead of ending up in front of the *Chimera* as planned, Winfield found his broader, slower ship head-on to Wade's port battery. The Yankee gunners blasted the length of the *Caledonia,* managing five scorching rounds in all before Winfield could correct his fatal miscalculation.

Both ships veered onto parallel courses, firing as fast as their guns could be swabbed, loaded and discharged. Wade sheered off again and crossed behind the panther's stern, this time ordering double shot up against the masts and rigging. The *Gyrfalcon,* meanwhile, had limped up beside the *Caledonia* and resumed pouring into it with the awesome carronades.

Two shots arced simultaneously at the British ship's stern gallery windows, shattering the carved trim and sending a spray of exploding glass out into the sea. Moments later yellow tongues of fire snaked from the gaping wound, along with billowing clouds of black smoke. The frigate was beginning to handle poorly, beginning to lumber and roll in the troughs created by its own recoils.

Wade and Treloggan managed to take the *Caledonia* in two more devastating cross fires, turning its decks into shambles and blowing away the braces that held its remaining foresails aloft. The yards holding the sails gave and fell like axed trees, dropping men and canvas into the ocean. One of its light carronades was blasted from the quarterdeck and flew across the breadth of the ship, carrying the bloody pieces of three crewmen with it.

The *Chimera* tacked away to give the crew a chance to clear the smoke and debris from underfoot. The *Gyrfalcon* followed Wade's lead, peeling away from the *Caledonia*'s wake and ploughing drunkenly back across its own wash. The British ship, unable to mount any fresh canvas, maintained a steady crawl forward while its officers screamed for makeshift repairs.

In the sudden lull of battle, all that could be heard were the hiss and snap of fires and the cries and groans of the wounded.

Commodore Winfield walked the length of the main deck, kicking and berating his gunners, shrieking at the men lying dazed against the rails, barking hoarse curses at his midshipmen and ordering them to whip the crew into fighting form again.

Some of the men, already discouraged, went below to the storerooms and broke into the kegs of rum. Even the lowest gun deck had been penetrated by the American shot, and the British seamen—poorly fed and liberally treated to the lash—were in no mood to pull together for the sake of Commodore Winfield's reputation.

As for the officers, they were appalled by the staggering losses they had sustained so far. Eighty of its four-hundred-and-nine-man crew were wounded or dead. They had expected to blow apart a pair of crippled privateers and instead were hard-pressed to hold their own against two brilliantly commanded fighting machines.

The *Gyrfalcon,* sorely damaged itself, looked as unready to haul down its colors as it had when it first thundered in on the attack.

The *Chimera,* the sleek and graceful twin, could already be seen hoisting new sail and preparing to bring the battle home again.

For the first time the *Caledonia*'s crew believed the story of the *Northgate*'s demise. They believed the privateer took it single-handed, and worse, they began to believe their own black panther could be next.

Bennett Winfield's jaw was set. His face was shiny with sweat, and his eyes were alive with an unnatural gleam as he presided over a hasty council of war on the afterdeck.

"Sir, the wounded—"

"The wounded will be seen to in due time. Another hour, no more, and they'll have a brace of prize ships in their possession to take the sting of their cuts away."

Bennett's artillery officer stepped forward. "Sir, the crews on my eighteens are being decimated. Another cross fire like the last one and you'll have no upper battery to speak of. There is simply no protection; they're too exposed. The rails are gone; most of the carriages are either dangerously loose or knocked clean away."

"Sir, the rigging lines are hopelessly snarled."

"We carry replacements, don't we?" Winfield hissed.

"Yes, sir, but with the steering sails gone—"

"I need steerage, Mr. Turner, and I need it now! Without it we might as well sit here and invite their shells aboard!"

"The men are splicing sir, but I need time."

"How much time?"

"Sir, the fires—"

Winfield balled his fists and turned to the new interruption. "What about the fires, Mr. Halpern? Are you going to tell me we have run short of water or buckets?"

The young midshipman stammered as he looked around the circle of gritty faces. "N-no, sir. But the aftercabins are all ablaze. I need more men to keep the fires from spreading. The last round they put to us carried some incendiary."

"Have we nothing to respond with?" Winfield demanded of his quartermasters.

"We have explosive shot, yes, sir, but the mortars are gone."

"All of them?" Bennett gasped, disbelieving the condition of his fine panther.

The gunnery officer broke in again. "Whoever is directing their fire knows the layout of our decks and the placements of our weapons. He's firing on us by divisions and aiming for our close-range weapons. He hits and runs, sir. He moves too fast for our thirty-twos to be of much use. There is no question that we are damaging them in return, but it still remains that both privateers are managing five rounds to every two or three of ours."

"Excuses!" Winfield screamed. "Do you hear what you are giving me—*nothing but excuses!* I want us in close. I want us to take the battle to him now."

Captain Emory Ashton-Smythe saw the horror of the *Northgate*'s last half hour replaying itself before his eyes. "Wade cannot afford to let you take the battle to him, and he knows it. He'll keep you tight, he'll keep you sailing in circles, and as long as you keep trying to use his own tactics against him, he'll be able to anticipate and cut you down."

Bennett whirled on him. "Explain that remark, sir. I am in command of this ship. The tactics I have called for are my own!"

Ashton-Smythe pushed himself painfully to his feet. "Your panther is on fire, Commodore. Half of your guns are useless; your wounded are drunk and pleading for quarter. To continue the battle will mean risking another third of your crew—are you sure it is worth it? Neither of Wade's ships is in condition to give chase. Perhaps we would be wiser to—"

"To what?" Bennett demanded. "To run away? To concede another victory to that . . . that . . ." Winfield's face mottled angrily, and his voice was laced with contempt. "By God, Glasse was right. You are a coward. A gutless, spineless coward and a disgrace to the uniform you wear."

Ashton-Smythe looked down at his scruffy uniform, at the filthy bandages on his hand and thigh, then at the bloody shambles of the deck stretched out before them. "Call it cowardice if you like, Commodore. I simply consider the lives I save worth far more than a gold stripe and an admiral's berth."

Winfield's eyes flashed their hatred as he watched the slumped shoulders of Ashton-Smythe pass him and head for the ladderway. He reached down suddenly, grabbing at the hilt of his saber, and withdrew it from the sheath. He lunged forward, but one of the junior officers jumped out and pushed Smythe clear as the point of the sword was driven deeply into the wood of the bulkhead. Two more officers leaped forward, wrestling the sword from Winfield's hands, while still others placed themselves protectively between the commodore and the stunned captain.

"Let go of me," Winfield said, his face livid with fury. "Let go of me at once, or I'll have you all stripped of rank before the day is done!"

His officers stared at one another aghast, none of them certain of what to do next. To disobey was to mutiny, to release him was inviting a possible murder. They all shared a deep respect for Captain Ashton-Smythe; he was a fine officer and a fine gentleman. But they also shared a deep-rooted fear of the naval judicial system. Mutiny in wartime could only result in death—regardless of the provocations.

Ashton-Smythe observed each earnest face in turn, sensing what was going on behind the rapid exchange of glances. "I have already made one decision, gentlemen, and am content to live with it. This one is up to Commodore Winfield."

"But you said yourself, the lives of the men—"

"The navy does not concern itself with lives, Lieutenant Cornish, only numbers. You have the numbers to continue the battle; that is what the record will show."

"My God, sir—look!"

The *Chimera* and the *Gyrfalcon* were gathering headway, coming in fast behind the British ship and drawing apart so that the *Caledonia* would be trapped between them.

One by one the anxious faces reverted to Bennett Winfield. The two men pinning his arms in restraint loosened their grips and stepped aside. Lieutenant Cornish, the artillery officer, stood ramrod-straight as he faced his commandant.

"Your orders . . . sir?"

Bennett tugged the wrinkles on his uniform smooth and glared a promise at each of the six ashen faces. He delayed his answer long enough that the first salvos were unleashed from the approaching privateers and tore into the hull of the *Caledonia.* He barely flinched as a shower of splinters shot past him.

"Mr. Turner—" he said through clenched teeth, "how long will you need to give me steerage?"

Turner moistened his lips. "An hour, sir. I can give you tops and fores in an hour."

"Get your crews on it *now.* Scavenge if you must, but *give me steerage!* Mr. Cornish, since you are so eager to test the generosity of your enemy, you may have the privilege of lowering the colors to half-mast. We'll see exactly how warm the water is."

Mr. Monday was set to roar for the gunners to fire a third volley, when he saw the Union Jack flutter halfway down the mainmast. He spun on his heel and cupped his hands around a shout to Morgan Wade, who had replaced a fallen gunner at one of the barrel-shaped carronades. Wade fed the hefty forty-two-pound shot into the smoking muzzle of the cannon, tamped it down flush against the wadding and gave the powderman the thumbs-up signal before he moved away from the gun and went to stand by Mr. Monday.

"What do you suppose he's up to?"

Monday wiped impatiently at a gash on his forehead that was sheeting blood down his temple onto his neck. His hands were burned and scraped, as were Wade's, and one of the gleaming white teeth that created his fearsome grin had been broken level with the purplish gums. He grinned anyway and shook his head.

"Doan know, Cap-tan. Mebbe he have enough?"

"Aye, and maybe it will snow in the islands next week."

Mr. Monday frowned and pointed to where the *Gyrfalcon* was drawing up behind the *Caledonia*. Its cracked mainmast had been shot away, and it was moving sporadically under the windage of two partially rigged masts. Bull had also seen the flag run down and was having difficulty holding position as he waited for a sign from Wade. He would have to either fire or fall away and circle around for another pass.

It could be precisely what Winfield was hoping for.

"Stand the gunners down, Mr. Monday. Mr. Cambridge!"

"Aye, sir?" Michael stepped forward, his face and hands sooty with gunpowder, the white of his shirt liberally coated with grease and ash.

"Relay an order to the helm. Tell Mr. Phillips to signal Captain Treloggan to hold as long as he can."

"Aye, sir!" he cried and scampered away.

Ten minutes later there was still no sign of movement on the decks of the *Caledonia*. The *Gyrfalcon* had gone too far ahead and had to turn away; Morgan estimated that during the next hour or more he would be without support. His gunners crouched by the cannon, waiting. His topmen perched on the shrouds, ready to manipulate the yards on a moment's notice.

Colored flags burst out suddenly on the bows of the *Caledonia*. It was a request for safe passage for a gig to approach the *Chimera*. A reply was run up in the *Chimera*'s rigging, and minutes later a small dinghy rowed out from behind the warship carrying four oarsmen and three uniformed officers.

Morgan Wade was on the bridge, his hands on his hips, his blue eyes tracking the longboat alternately with the *Gyrfalcon*. Bull was making good use of the time to jury-rig more sail to his two remaining masts, buying back—hopefully—the ability to maneuver faster. But Winfield's men were also working frantically to lower damaged sails and spars and lash fresh canvas aloft.

Whatever Winfield's ploy was, Wade decided, he had missed a glaring opportunity.

Mr. Phillips appeared at the foot of the ladderway. "Commodore Winfield is requesting permission to come aboard. He has two of his officers with him."

"Invite them aboard, Jamie," Wade nodded and shrugged into the clean shirt Michael had fetched from his cabin.

Bennett Winfield stood inside the main entry port, the plumes of his bicorne rifling smartly in the breeze. His face was without expression; his hands were held at ease behind his back. One booted foot was poised slightly ahead of the other, hinting broadly of impatience and disdain. The pale blue eyes raked the length and breadth of the *Chimera*, settling on the faces of the sweaty gunners, noting damages, types of shot, formation of crews—then lifting to examine the condition of the sail and lines, skimming over the men braced high in the yards holding muskets at the ready. Lastly he noted the *Chimera*'s captain striding across the quarterdeck, as battered and bruised as his ship, yet seemingly as impervious to defeat.

"You have done a remarkable job of holding together," Winfield murmured when Morgan stopped in front of him. "Two battles in as many days . . . Decatur will be overjoyed."

"My personal dealings have nothing to do with Captain Decatur . . . however, he has been known on occasion to smile for less."

Bennett looked away. "I understand my wife is still on board. I should like to see her—alone, if you don't mind."

"That will depend a great deal on whether she wishes to see you or not," Morgan said, crossing his arms over his chest, "and it definitely will not be alone."

"The penalty for kidnapping is severe, Wade."

Morgan's smile was deceiving. "I hardly think you are in a position to cite my crimes . . . Winfield."

"Nevertheless, I should like to see her. To assure myself she is still alive and well and to offer her the opportunity of returning to the *Caledonia*."

Wade's eyes narrowed. "What makes you think she would want to go?"

"What makes you believe she would choose to die on board this ship?"

Morgan studied the arrogant upper-crust veneer for a moment, then called quietly over his shoulder, "Mr. Cambridge?"

Michael, who had been keeping himself behind Morgan so as not to draw attention to his presence on the *Chimera,* stiffened at the sound of his name and moved forward. "Aye, sir?"

"Would you see if your sister would care to join us in my cabin? Tell her Commodore Winfield 'requests' it."

Michael looked up at Wade and whispered, "Does she have to?"

The captain noticed the spark of anger in Winfield's eyes, and his smile returned. "Not if she doesn't want to, lad. Gentlemen—shall we conduct our business in more comfort? Mr. Monday, will you join us. . . . Mr. Phillips, I'll want to know if anything on that ship moves."

"Aye, sir!"

Once inside the brightly lit aftercabin, Wade indicated seats for the Englishmen while he crossed over to his desk and settled into the leather chair. He took a cigar from the humidor and handed the tin to Mr. Monday to pass to the officers. The cigars were lit, brandy was offered and accepted, and Wade leaned back wondering at the air of complacency of the commodore.

Without further preamble, Bennett Winfield spoke. "I believe it has become apparent, Wade, that we have the destruction of your ships within our grasp."

Morgan's teeth appeared in a white slash and clamped down on the cigar. "I was under the impression it was the other way around."

Winfield looked amused. "Come now, Wade. You really don't think you or your ships are in any shape to continue the battle, do you? I've seen the condition of your deck. I've come aboard in good faith to offer amiable terms of surrender. End it now while you still have a crew able to take advantage of His Majesty's generosity."

"I sampled your Majesty's generosity once before, and it didn't leave the sweetest taste in my mouth. As to my crew, I imagine they are in about the same condition as yours. My gunners estimate at least a third of your cannon are exhausted—so much for your fancy improvements—and you've barely enough sail aloft to hold her steady."

"We'll be steady enough to finish you, Wade, and your pirate friend."

Wade exhaled a thin stream of smoke. "There is another alternative, you know."

"I'm listening."

"It's a little old-fashioned, but we'd save a hell of a lot of innocent lives. Just the two of us, Winfield. Any method you choose."

The commodore's gaze locked with Wade's. He, Bennett, was an expert swordsman, and his reputation as a marksman had earned the respect of his peers. He'd participated in four duels in the past, all to his credit. It would indeed be a pleasure to feel the blade of his sword pierce into Wade's flesh, to kill him slowly so that he might savor the memory for years to come . . . but then Wade would not have forwarded the suggestion if he was not accomplished in his own right, and to lose now, when the *Caledonia* was all but assured of victory . . . "Oh, I think not, Captain. I should not want to rob my men of the pleasure."

The door to the cabin opened suddenly, and Summer stood there, her pale face surrounded by the wisps of hair that had worked loose from the long shiny braid. She was dressed in trousers and a shirt, having found a skirt to be a nuisance and impractical. Her hands had been scrubbed hastily clean, but there was blood on her clothing and spatters on the incongruously dainty green satin slippers.

Bennett's officers stood instantly. The commodore rose leisurely and let his gaze move slowly down her body. "Summer. Thank God you are safe."

"Bennett," she murmured. "Gentlemen . . . please sit down." She glanced nervously toward Morgan. "You wanted to see me?"

Wade propped his boots on the corner of his desk and watched the play of expressions on the commodore's face. "Your husband made the request. He seems to think you are being held here against your will."

Bennett turned angrily to his two officers. "Wait on deck for me."

The men looked surprised, but they complied with a

hasty shuffle of chairs and boots and indirect glances at Summer and Morgan Wade. She stood to one side of the door as they exited, then obeyed Wade's command to shut it behind them.

"Madam," Bennett said, "I have come to take you back to the *Caledonia*. The child also, and your brother if he has a desire to come with us."

Summer resisted the temptation to run to Morgan. Instead she walked slowly to a chair, quite proud of herself that she could do it without her knees buckling.

"No, thank you, Bennett. We are happy where we are."

"Happy? You call this"—he indicated the state of her clothing with a smirk—"cause to celebrate?"

"I am content, Bennett," she repeated quietly. "Possibly for the first time in my life."

His mouth turned down. "I recall a woman seated in an English garden who once told me much the same thing with much the same degree of conviction. Then, of course, it was parties and jewels and happy flirtations that contented her, and she did not want to leave it all behind for what she referred to as some humid little island. If this is another whim of yours, Summer, I guarantee the novelty will be a brief one."

Summer held her anger in check. "I am not the same woman you met in England, Bennett. I have grown up a great deal since then."

"And you have accepted a great many more responsibilities as an adult—including the vows you took on your wedding day. No one forced you into accepting them at the time. No one forced you to become my wife."

"I was never your wife, Bennett. I was a convenience. You said yourself it was a marriage of greed and ambition."

"I also told you I had true feelings of affection for you, madam," he said tautly. "Affections you chose not to return, despite my efforts."

Summer's gray eyes narrowed. "Efforts? Are you referring to the threats or the blackmail or the disgusting—" She bit off the words and clenched her hands tightly on her lap. "I'm sorry, Bennett. I prefer better things for myself and my baby."

"And you think you can find them on a doomed ship in the middle of the Caribbean?"

This time she did look at Morgan. "I already have."

A flush crept up beneath the commodore's tan. "Your wish to see me humiliated is excusable to a certain degree, but do you mean to stand by and see your father's career and reputation destroyed? They will be, you know. As soon as word reaches his enemies in political circles that his daughter has become a traitor and has run away with her Yankee lover."

"My father has been governor for twelve years. In all that time he never once placed anyone else's concerns above his own. His choice to come to these islands was made so quickly and so selfishly that he could not delay the move from England one month so that my mother could be safely delivered of the child she was carrying. My marriage was arranged with his career in mind, and no doubt Michael's future was slated to aggrandize it as well. Fortunately I have come to my senses in time to realize that someone else's choices do not necessarily have to rule my own. Father is a survivor, he always has been. He will find a way to survive this, I'm sure."

"Whereas you will die on board this ship," Bennett said harshly.

"But by my decision, no one else's."

"And the child? And your brother? Aren't you playing God a little yourself?"

Summer's temper flared. "If *I* have nothing to go home to, Michael has even less, thanks to you and Father. You have managed to cheat him of his birthright. You have beaten him and berated him, and I do not believe for a moment you would treat any of us any differently if we did return with you. Your only reason for making this profound gesture is, as far as I can guess, to save appearances. You're not worried about my life or Sarah's life or Michael's future . . . and certainly not Father's career! You're worried about your own!"

Bennett stared at her for a long moment before he sat back in the chair and laughed unexpectedly. It was a smooth, calculated laugh, and she was familiar enough with the sound of it to feel the hairs prickle upright along the back of her neck.

"Indeed I am, madam. Furthermore, I intend to do everything in my power to see that you and your lover add to it immensely today. I have extended my offers to you both. I strongly recommend you reconsider your answers before I return to the *Caledonia*. I will allow you your lives, the shell of one ship, and an escort back to Bridgetown as my prisoners."

Morgan Wade removed the cigar from between his teeth and flicked the ash unhurriedly from the tip. "And if I tell you you can take your offers and go straight to hell with them?"

"You will gain a moment's verbal gratification and nothing more," Winfield said evenly.

"I'll settle for that."

The commodore rose and tucked his bicorne under his arm. "You have heard my final offer. There will be no others forthcoming."

"And you are hearing my final warning: Get off my ship while you are still able to."

The pale blue eyes were like chips of ice as Bennett gave Summer and Morgan each a parting glance. He pushed the chair out of his way and strode to the door, yanking it wide as he went out into the companionway. Wade crooked his head to Mr. Monday to follow, then lowered his boots from the corner of his desk and crushed out the cigar before he went to Summer.

He grasped her shoulders gently, and it did not require much urging to have her lean gratefully against him.

"You are quite a woman, you know. If I had the time . . ."

"You don't," she said, forcing a timid smile. "But keep that thought warm, sir. Perhaps it will speed you about your business."

He grinned, kissing her hard and fast before he left the cabin. Summer remained standing alone in the middle of the room, needing several minutes to steady her knees enough to carry her back to her work below.

28

WHILE COMMODORE WINFIELD was aboard the *Chimera,* his men had repaired or replaced his damaged sails and spliced the necessary rigging to give the *Caledonia* back its steerage. The *Chimera* and the *Gyrfalcon,* therefore, were both caught off guard when the British frigate turned with the wind and started streaking away from them. Within minutes Bull Treloggan gave the order to crowd on more sail and was in hot pursuit, ignoring the caution Wade immediately signaled. Seeing the *Gyrfalcon* pull further and further away, Wade barked orders for Mr. Phillips to add speed, but a sudden gust of wind tore loose a mainsail and the *Chimera* floundered.

When more than a mile separated the two ships from Morgan Wade, the *Caledonia* veered sharply and cut a wide swath around behind the *Gyrfalcon.* Winfield then poured three tremendous broadsides into the *Gyrfalcon,* probing the entire length of the startled ship. The two remaining masts were blown apart, and the frigate was easy prey for Winfield's guns. Cannon were dismounted, the forecastle became a smoking crater of crushed timbers, and Bull Treloggan's roar was silenced as a solid ball of iron smashed through his chest. His body was hurled through the air, landing in a broken heap against one of his beloved carronades.

While the Yankee frigate drifted helplessly, the *Caledonia* pulled around to its starboard side, firing into the almost-stationary target with the deadly thirty-two-pounders. The lower gunports were silenced one by one as a hail of shot exploded through the reinforced timbers, driving the men back to safety.

Once more the *Caledonia* wheeled about, keeping the *Gyrfalcon* between itself and the frantic efforts of the *Chimera* to move in to assist. Wade ordered his guns double shotted and aimed high, but even the threat of losing its sails again did not deter the *Caledonia* from the kill. By now it was so close to the *Gyrfalcon* that some of Wade's shot showered the deck of the privateer. But it did not matter. There was no one left alive on the upper decks, and those huddled below were too stunned to care.

As the *Gyrfalcon*'s guns fell mute, the British warship sidled within ten yards, and on a signal from the bridge, fired a ferocious round simultaneously from all three decks, hitting the crippled privateer with such force the remaining timbers in its hull crumpled. Water poured into the gaping wounds and began to fill the lower decks. The bleeding, hunched figure of a man emerged from the rubble and stumbled up to what was left of the bridge and desperately waved a white flag of surrender.

Winfield raised his arm again. His gunners were momentarily shocked, but they reacted quickly to his shouted order and touched the smoldering wicks to the powder, blasting another round into the dying Yankee frigate.

Morgan Wade's hands would have crushed the oak of the rail where he held it had his hatred been transformed into physical strength. He shouted for more sail and dangerously overtaxed his straining ship, caroming in before the wind as he saw Winfield give the order for yet another devastating volley.

The *Chimera*'s guns fired point-blank, obliterating the *Caledonia*'s foremast, causing the huge ship to rise up in its bows. It was caught in the turbulence and flung sideways, slashing a deep gouge into the stern of the *Gyrfalcon* and dragging the smaller ship with it as it reeled around. The sound of oak tearing into oak screeched out across the surface of the ocean, and when the smoke cleared, it revealed a twenty-foot length of the *Caledonia*'s bowsprit and stem wedged fast to the *Gyrfalcon*. Bull's men trapped below streamed up onto the deck and, having nowhere else to go, reached for grappling hooks and boarding pikes and began clawing up the side of the *Caledonia.*

Wade's ship struck the panther from the other side, lashing into it with hooks and ropes and using its own forward momentum to jar the Englishmen from their footings a second time. The *Chimera* shuddered with the impact, but its timbers held, and Morgan Wade, cutlass in hand, was first over the rails, slashing and hacking his way across a boarding plank onto the deck of the warship. He was followed by every able-bodied man the *Chimera* boasted. Sweat and blood gleamed as brilliantly as the steel blades of the dirks and swords; the air rang with the stinging shrill of steel on steel. The crew from the *Gyrfalcon,* no longer faced with the prospect of dying with their backs pressed to the deck rails, cheered and surged forward to join forces with their comrades.

The Britons reeled under the frenzied assault, falling back in droves as the privateers cut a great bloody path across the breadth of the *Caledonia.* They slid on gory planking and screamed for orders that did not come. Pockets of scarlet-clad marines threw their muskets down, while ordinary seamen ran below and sought refuge in the deepest, darkest recesses of the ship. The companionways and storerooms became clogged with the wounded and with those no longer wanting to prolong the battle.

Morgan fought his way along the length of the quarterdeck to the bridge, a broadsword in each hand, leading a spearhead of his men toward the shouting, fighting circle of dazzling blue and white uniforms that were the *Caledonia*'s officers. Mr. Monday fought on his right, sending Englishmen cringing back in waves at each mighty whack of his cutlass. Mr. Phillips took a musket ball high in his shoulder, and the impact sent him headlong onto his knees, but he pushed himself up again and resolutely plunged back into the fray. Two of the *Chimera*'s crewmen peered up into the maze of twisted yards and rigging to locate the source of the gunfire and saw a lone marine frantically working to reload and fire his musket. Both men set their dirks between their teeth and swarmed up either side of the shrouds, so terrifying the soldier that he lost his grip on the musket, then on the spar, and fell thirty feet into the churning mass of humanity on the deck.

Wade slashed his way to the foot of the ladderway leading up to the bridge. There were at least a dozen men between himself and Bennett Winfield, but there was no holding him back now that he could see and hear his enemy. Winfield was braced on the deck, wielding his sword as if he were on an open field with a fencing master. His white breeches were grimy and splashed with blood; his neatly clubbed blond hair had shaken from its velvet ribbon and clung with sweat and filth to his neck. The pale blue eyes glowed like embers, and as they searched the area around the bridge, they found and clashed with Morgan Wade's.

Winfield backed up several steps, his face rigid with hatred. His gaze went to the side of his ship, to where the *Chimera* pulled and tugged against the grappling lines, and when he looked back at Wade, there was a slow, terrible smile on his lips. He sheathed his sword and vaulted up over the fife rail, landing on the deck below. In a few strides he balanced his way across a boarding plank and jumped onto the deck of the *Chimera*.

Morgan's lips pulled back from his teeth in a snarl, and he slashed at the man blocking his path. He raced after Winfield, leaped onto the rail and hacked at a length of rigging to use to swing his weight across the narrow gap separating the two ships. He saw Winfield glance over his shoulder before he vanished through the main hatchway leading down below. Morgan whirled and descended through the forehatch, hoping to cut the commodore off before he could follow the trail of wounded to the storeroom surgery.

The residue of smoke and powder hung thick in the air of the gun deck. There were wounded and dead scattered among the warm cannon; some were propped listlessly against the guns nursing dreadful wounds and burns; some lay facedown in pools of their own blood.

Morgan picked his way cautiously along the row of crouching cannon, conscious of the sounds of men fighting and men dying overhead. He passed the gangway where

Michael and Summer had tried to escape at the Sirens so long ago and paused, seeing a reflection of sunlight glint off something up ahead. It proved to be a musket barrel propped against one of the wooden trunnions, trapped in a stray beam of light that filtered in through a ventilation shaft.

Having more than half the length of the ship to go and countless obstacles in between, Morgan shrugged aside his caution and ran along the deck, passing the ladder Winfield had used to descend, and barely hesitated before he plunged down the hatchway leading to the lower deck. He missed a second glint of light that should not have been there. He misread the hiss and punch of steel striking out from the shadows until it was too late and the blade of the sword was already buried deeply in his flesh.

Summer and Gabrielle worked alone in the surgery. Thorny had been called away to answer a plea from a man who could not be moved because there were no spare hands to carry the litters. Summer had hoped she would be better prepared this time to handle the horror, but she was not. Her stomach—emptied violently long ago—was tied in knots, her mouth was dry, her hands trembled so badly at times that she had to stop what she was doing and squeeze them together. Gabrielle was whiter than the apron she wore. When she spoke, it was more often than not in shocked, whispery French.

There was a hopeful moment when the cannon stopped firing that Gabrielle and Summer had looked to Thorny for the same wink and cackled assurances as before. But he had merely paused over the shattered limb he was amputating to shake his head, before he bent back to his task. When he followed the sailor who had come to fetch him, his only comment was "Drop the bar down over the door be'ind me an don't lift 'er fer no one, understand?"

"But the wounded—"

"Wounded'll wait. Ye keep the door locked, d'ye 'ear me?"

Summer had nodded wordlessly. Behind her, Stuart Roarke forced himself into a sitting position, and although his face streamed sweat and his breath came in tortured gasps, he painstakingly loaded and readied two heavy pistols.

Thorny's absence stretched from ten minutes to fifteen, then twenty, and the corridor outside the surgery echoed with cries for help. Summer could not tolerate it any longer and was lifting the bar from the door, when she was jarred off her feet by the impact of the *Chimera* grinding against the *Caledonia*. She fell heavily against a wooden bench and rolled sideways, saved from an ugly meeting with a spiked pole by Roarke's quick hands. Still, she was dazed. Sarah was screaming from fright, and Gabrielle had shrunk back into a corner, weeping silently.

"Are you hurt?" Stuart asked hoarsely. "Summer! Are you hurt?"

"N-no . . . no, I don't think so."

She pushed to her knees, swaying uncertainly against a blinding wave of pain. Her fingers probed the back of her skull and came away sticky with blood.

"You are hurt, let me see."

"No, it's nothing. I just bumped my head. . . . oh God, my poor baby."

Summer reached into the cradle and lifted Sarah out, holding her tight and rocking her until the terrified wailing stopped. There wasn't time to do more. Summer settled the tearful baby back into the nest of blankets and crawled past Stuart to check on the wounded man who had been thrown from the bench in the turmoil. He was alive but unconscious, and she struggled with the deadweight fruitlessly for what seemed like eternity before Gabrielle roused out of her shock enough to help.

That done, Summer looked back at the door. The bar had fallen back into place and was rattling furiously as someone on the outside strove to get in. Her hand was still on the latch when the door was flung inward and the body of a dead crewman tumbled through and onto the floor. Summer started to bend over him, when a flash of white caught her eye. She looked out into the companionway and gasped when she saw the bloodied tip of a sword pointed unwaveringly at her throat.

"On your feet," Bennett Winfield hissed. "Slowly, though, I wouldn't want my hand to slip and sever that lovely neck of yours."

Summer could not move. She continued to stare at him, to refuse to believe what her eyes were telling her . . . until the sword moved and the cold blade depressed her skin.

"I said on your feet," Bennett snarled. He bent forward, and his free hand grasped her roughly around a wrist, yanking on it until she was standing in front of him. He twisted her arm sharply, pinning her hand and wrist up between her shoulders.

"Now then, you're going to come with me. We're going to back out slowly, we're going to climb up to the top deck, and then we are going to go back to my ship." The pale eyes circled the cramped storeroom. "If anyone moves or tries to stop us, she's dead. You"—he looked at Gabrielle—"relieve your friend of his pistols and bring them over here."

Gabrielle moved haltingly to where Stuart was sitting and took the two heavy pistols from him. Winfield lowered the sword long enough to tuck one of the guns beneath his gaping tunic and to dump the second into a nearby barrel of water. He pressed the edge of the blade into Summer's throat again and tightened his grip around her wrist, forcing her to lean hard against him. He backed up slowly, dragging her with him into the corridor.

"You see, my dear, how easy it was to make this decision?"

"Morgan will kill you," she whispered.

"Your lover is dead, Mrs. Winfield," he snarled. "His ship and crew are mine."

"Dead?" she gasped.

"Very much so. I told him, I told you both there would be no more offers forthcoming. He chose to ignore me and so paid the price. You will pay my price as well, Summer dearest. Every single day for the rest of your life . . . however long that may be."

He kept her arm twisted high, but Summer was too numbed by shock to feel the pain of it or to care where he was taking her. Morgan was dead. Morgan was dead. . . .

Bennett pushed her toward the stern, past the wreckage strewn about, to the ladder leading up to the gun deck. She stumbled up the first flight of steps, then the second, and emerged on the quarterdeck just as a burst of wild cheering erupted from the bridge of the *Caledonia*.

Bennett's eyes were glazed with triumph as he raised them to the deck of his ship. His jaw hardened, and his face drained of color. His fingers dug into the flesh of Summer's wrist as he saw the Union Jack hauled down from the foremast and waved aloft by a half-dozen of Wade's crew.

"No . . ."

"Let her go, Winfield. It's over."

Summer cried out softly and turned as much as the blade of the cutlass would allow, searching through her tears for the source of the deep baritone.

Morgan stepped out from behind the trunk of the mizzenmast. The breeze blew his ebony hair forward over the bright blue bandanna; his shirt was torn and bloody, and even though he clutched his ribs to control the flow of blood, one side of his trousers was soaked crimson.

He raised his sword toward Winfield and held it steady. "Let her go, Commodore. This is between you and me; it always has been. Finish it here and now . . . if you're man enough to face me without the help of a squadron of guns behind you."

Bennett had not moved so much as a muscle. The men on the *Caledonia* slowly fell silent, and both the American and the British crews focused on their commanders.

Bennett's fingers loosened from Summer's wrist. She heard the hard metallic clang of his sword hitting the deck as he threw it aside, but her relief was short-lived. She was shoved roughly out of the way as Bennett reached beneath his tunic jacket and withdrew the pistol he had taken from the storeroom. He seemed to move in slow-motion, taking the perfect dueling stance, cocking the gun as he turned and aimed for a point dead center of the wide brow opposite him. The silence of the deck was ripped apart in the ensuing explosion of gunpowder and shot.

Summer screamed and started running toward Morgan. Terror froze the last of her tears on her lashes so that she could see both men clearly and she could see the enormous, growing red blotch marring the white shirtfront.

Bennett's look of triumph faded and was replaced by disbelief. He stared at the pistol in his hand, then at the spreading stain on his chest. He had only a fraction of a second to focus on the dark hatchway before his eyes dimmed.

Stuart Roarke lowered the smoking pistol and leaned heavily on the support of Gabrielle's narrow shoulders. Sweat had soaked the front of his shirt, and his skin was a sickening shade of gray.

Morgan threw aside his sword and reached his brother's side in time to catch him as he fell forward out of Gabrielle's grasp. Together he and Summer guided Stuart to one of the flat-topped capstans and eased him to a seat.

"You were supposed to be dead," Stuart gasped. "I heard him say you were dead."

"So I would have been if you hadn't come along," Morgan said, slumping down beside him on the capstan. He cursed and pressed a hand to his ribs again. "And don't sound so disappointed. There's still time."

"A fine pair we make," Stuart grinned. "Are you certain we've won?"

Morgan raised his dark blue eyes to the deck of the *Caledonia*. Mr. Monday was there, his fist clenched around the captured Union Jack. By his side, grinning with equal abandon, was Michael Cambridge. Further on, Jamie Phillips vaulted down to the *Chimera*'s deck and caught Gabrielle as she ran into his arms.

Morgan looked across at Bennett Winfield's sprawled body, then at Summer's golden beauty. His arm tightened around her shoulders, drawing her close to him as he buried his lips in the silk of her hair.

"Aye, Roarke, aye. We've won."

29

Morgan Wade stood on the bridge of the *Chimera,* his hands braced on the deck rail, his face carved from granite as he watched the last of the salvage brought aboard from the *Gyrfalcon.* The frigate was still wedged to the bow of the *Caledonia,* although it was showing evidence of breaking away as the weight of the water in its belly dragged it down. Bull Treloggan's body had been found and sewn reverently into a burial shroud and committed to his watery grave along with the bodies of the forty-three other dead comrades. The British saw to their own casualties—a horrendous one hundred and twenty in all.

There were shouts and groans from the *Caledonia*'s wounded as they were lowered into the longboats to be ferried to the small crusty knoll of Bird Island. Now and then a body turned up among the living, and it was slipped unceremoniously over the side with a hasty sign of the cross and a muttered prayer. Morgan intended to keep only a skeleton crew of British on board to supplement his own men; the rest would await rescue from a passing ship. Part of him wanted to sink the *Caledonia* where it stood, but the practical side of him knew the value in terms of morale of towing such a prize to an American port. It would prove that the invincible British Navy was not so invincible after all.

Bennett Winfield's body had been set into a litter and covered by his country's flag. The surviving officers had insisted that it be allowed to accompany them to Bird Island for eventual burial on British soil. Captain Ashton-

Smythe had been the one selected to put the request before Captain Wade.

"You can do whatever you like with him, Captain," Wade said, wincing as he stood away from the rail. His wound had been cauterized and bound in linen strips, but he steadfastly refused to go below until the last of the wounded were seen to and the transfer of prisoners was completed. The Briton marveled at the man's strength even as he suffered the nauseating aches and weak flushes from his own days-old wounds.

"I would as soon set him to rest here," Ashton-Smythe remarked, looking away from the American, "but we must have our pomp and ceremony to whitewash the disgrace."

"There was no disgrace in the loss," Wade said carefully.

"Firing on a surrendered ship?" Ashton-Smythe shook his head slowly. "I still cannot believe he ordered it. Worse, I cannot believe the men obeyed. It seems as if I am always apologizing to you for our conduct, Captain Wade. You are always the victim of our worst moments, yet always the gracious victor."

"Our countries are at war, Captain. Suppose we save our apologies until the end of it."

"If it was that simple, I could. But we both know this had nothing to do with politics. I believe Winfield was quite insane in the end. Not that it gives us an excuse for this day's behavior. We had an opportunity to stop him, and we didn't. . . . That makes us all a little mad, doesn't it?"

With difficulty, Ashton-Smythe withdrew his saber from his scabbard and held it out to Morgan. "You would do me an honor by accepting it this time. They're bound to strip it from me when we reach Bridgetown anyway."

"This was none of your doing."

The captain smiled wearily. "Can you honestly see them crucifying a dead hero? No, not if what you said about the *Belvidera* is true. My God, three ships in under a week? We'll be lucky if we come out of this war with any self-respect at all. We've sadly underestimated you Yankees . . . again. I repeat, sir, the honor would be mine."

Wade accepted the burnished sword and the formal salute from Captain Ashton-Smythe.

"Ten of Winfield's crew carry papers proving them to be Americans. Another dozen or so have no papers but are vehement about their birth *not* being on British soil. I have left the names and documents with one of your men."

"Thank you," Wade said and watched the officer turn to leave the bridge. "Emory . . . ?"

Smythe halted and half turned.

"You're welcome to join us. We need good men in command."

The Briton looked startled, then smiled sadly and shook his head. "But thank you. You need someone on the other side to give you a little trouble."

"Like that night on board the *Africa?* Were you really that poor a shot?"

Ashton-Smythe looked into the dark blue eyes and his own sparked suddenly in their depths. "I believe at the time I held both the silver and the gold crosses for regimental sharpshooting. Of course, we all have our bad days."

"Of course." Wade stretched out his hand. Captain Smythe took it and held firmly for a moment before he turned and left the bridge.

Summer waited until the tall officer had limped away from the ladderway before she joined Morgan.

"You British never cease to surprise me," he murmured, placing the saber carefully to one side.

"I thought you were beyond surprises."

He snorted. "Madam, if I ever say that again in your company, you have my permission to take another shot at me."

"I think I shall hold you to that."

He arched a brow. "I believe you would. How is Stuart?"

"Resting. Finally. As you should be." Morgan waved away the comment impatiently. "He insisted on having his own cabin, however. He said he wouldn't have as far to climb the next time he was needed."

Morgan grinned. "And the child?"

"Hungry. I don't think she will forgive me too soon for

ignoring her all day. But then, I'm afraid I'm not much use to her anymore. . . . I'm not much use to anyone right now. Thorny hasn't spoken to me since he found out I unlocked the door; Gabrielle is taking care of Sarah. . . ."

He saw the shine on the edge of her lashes and pulled her into the circle of his arm. "Never mind. You'll have my son to look after one of these days. If he's anything like his father, he'll be hungry twenty-four hours a day, and he'll not be content to settle for second-best."

Summer smiled up through her tears. Morgan felt himself drowning again in the huge gray eyes and wondered that she could ever consider herself useless. She had worked as hard as any of his men today—harder. She hadn't complained once since leaving Fort-de-France and hadn't shown any sign of weakening or faltering even though he knew she must have died a thousand times over the past two days.

He glimpsed a slender figure moving across the deck below them.

"Mr. Cambridge!"

Michael skidded to a halt and mounted the steps to the bridge.

"Aye, sir?"

"Captain Ashton-Smythe has just left the deck. See if you can find him and ask him to join us briefly before he leaves the *Chimera*. I have a small favor to ask of him."

"Aye, sir. Has it to do with the *Caledonia?*"

Morgan frowned. "No, Mr. Cambridge, it does not. If it was your business to know—*which it isn't*—I might tell you it has to do with making an honest woman out of your sister."

Michael's mouth popped wide. "Aye, sir!"

He started away but halted after only a few paces. "Does this mean I can expect a promotion, sir? To midshipman perhaps? I mean, you can't very well keep your brother-in-law a powder monkey forever, can you?"

Wade's eyes screwed into slits, and his chest swelled with a deep breath. "By God—"

"Yes, sir!" Michael said quickly. "On my way, sir!"

He flashed an impish smile at Summer and ran off. She tried very hard not to smile, but it was hopeless.

"You find his brass amusing, do you?" Wade demanded.

"I think he will fit in perfectly with the company, yes. As for you making an honest woman out of me, I don't recall being asked. I call it extremely brassy to assume I would want to leap into another marriage when I have just managed my freedom from the first. I rather like the idea of retaining some independence."

Morgan regarded her several long moments before a half-smile came to his lips. His arm tightened around her, lifting her inches off the deck as he kissed her full on the mouth. Some of the crew stopped what they were doing to cheer and hoot. Many more copied the startled look on Ashton-Smythe's face as he and Michael paused by the deck rail.

Summer was flushed and breathless when he finally released her. Her heart was pounding in her breast, and her limbs were wobbly as he slowly set her back down.

"Now, what was that about keeping your independence?"

"Nothing," she whispered. "Nothing at all."